WAITING FOR THE LAST TRAIN

Great-aunt Caroline received Campion in her little sitting-room, as usual, and listened to his request in amused silence.

"You want me to leave my house?" she said at last, when he had finished. "Certainly not. My dear young man, at my age physical danger, that is to say the danger of death, is ever present wherever I am. In fact," she went on unexpectedly, "my position now is that of someone waiting on a platform for a train already overdue. No, I am afraid that whatever you tell me I shall remain where I am."

Campion took his defeat calmly. "If I were only sure," he said, "it would be different. There is an explanation of this affair which frightens me. If it is the truth, no one in this house is safe."

"No one in this house is safe," she repeated. "Almost my exact words to you, young man. But I shall not stir, and you may do as you please about the others. And you yourself, Mr. Campion—what a curious name that is; I wonder why you chose it?—what do you propose to do?"

Campion looked hurt. "I remain here where I am, if I may."

Agatha Christie

Death on the Nile
A Holiday for Murder
The Mousetrap and Other Plays
The Mysterious Affair at Styles
Poirot Investigates
Postern of Fate
The Secret Adversary
The Seven Dials Mystery
Sleeping Murder

Dorothy Simpson

Last Seen Alive
The Night She Died
Puppet for a Corpse
Six Feet Under
Close Her Eyes
Element of Doubt
Dead on Arrival

Elizabeth George

A Great Deliverance
A Payment in Blood

Colin Dexter

Last Bus to Woodstock
The Riddle of the Third Mile
The Silent World of Nicholas Quinn
Service of All the Dead
The Dead of Jericho
The Secret of Annexe 3
Last Seen Wearing

Michael Dibdin

Ratking

John Greenwood

The Mind of Mr. Mosley
The Missing Mr. Mosley
Mosley by Moonlight
Murder, Mr. Mosley
Mists Over Mosley
What, Me, Mr. Mosley?

Ruth Rendell

A Dark-Adapted Eye
  (writing as Barbara Vine)
A Fatal Inversion
  (writing as Barbara Vine)

Marian Babson

Death in Fashion
Reel Murder
Murder, Murder Little Star
Murder on a Mystery Tour
Murder Sails at Midnight

Dorothy Cannell

The Widows Club
Down the Garden Path
coming soon: Mum's the Word

Antonia Fraser

Your Royal Hostage
Oxford Blood
A Splash of Red
coming soon:
Cool Repentance
Jemima Shore's First Case
Quiet As A Nun

Margery Allingham

Death of a Ghost
Police at the Funeral

POLICE AT THE FUNERAL

Margery
Allingham

BANTAM BOOKS
NEW YORK · TORONTO · LONDON · SYDNEY · AUCKLAND

*This story, the characters in it, and the
bridge in Grantchester Meadows, are
figments of the author's imagination,
and have no reference to real incident,
living people, or topographical facts*

POLICE AT THE FUNERAL

*A Bantam Book / published by arrangement with
the author's estate*

PRINTING HISTORY
Originally published October 1931
Bantam edition / November 1989

ISBN 0-553-28506-8

Bantam Books are published by Bantam Books, a division of Bantam Doubleday
Dell Publishing Group, Inc. Its trademark, consisting of the words "Bantam
Books" and the portrayal of a rooster, is Registered in U.S. Patent and Trademark
Office and in other countries. Marca Registrada. Bantam Books, 666 Fifth
Avenue, New York, New York 10103.

PRINTED IN THE UNITED STATES OF AMERICA

O   0 9 8 7 6 5 4 3 2 1

To

MY SEVEN PATERNAL UNCLES

CONTENTS

1

"Here Lies a Benefactor"

When one man is following another, however discreet may be the pursuer or the pursued, the act does not often pass unnoticed in the streets of London.

There were at least four people who realised that Inspector Stanislaus Oates, only lately promoted to the Big Five, was being followed down High Holborn by the short, squat, shabby man who yet bore the elusive air of a forgotten culture about him.

The Inspector walked with his hands in the pockets of his raincoat, his collar turned up until it almost met the brim of his battered trilby. His shoulders were hunched, his feet were wet, and his very gait announced the dejection which he felt.

There was very little to show the casual passer-by that the square man, who might have been a bookmaker's tout, was following the Inspector. He himself would have been astounded to know that anyone had guessed that he was aware of the policeman's existence, but old Mrs. Carter, who sells flowers outside the Provincial Bank, recognised Mr. Oates and observed his trailer, and wondered what he was up to, aloud, to her daughter who was waiting for the "late extra" *Evening Standard* van, and getting her high-heeled shoes full of water from the stream which was sweeping down the gutter.

The Commissionaire standing on the steps of the big Anglo-American hotel saw the two men also, and congratulated himself that nothing much escaped him. Old Todd, last cabby in the rank before Staple Inn, also made a note of the spectacle as he sat staring listlessly over his steel-rimmed glasses waiting for the evening rush, wondering if his one remaining brake would hold in this blasted rain.

And lastly, the Inspector himself was aware of the circumstance. One is not a policeman for twenty-five years without becoming peculiarly sensitive to the fact that one is not alone in one's promenading, and the silent companion at the discreet distance becomes as real as if he were at one's side.

To-day the Inspector was aware of it and took no notice of it. There were many people who might have considered that they had sufficient grievance against him to meditate an attack on Mr. Oates, but no one, so far as he knew, who would risk making such an attempt in broad daylight in the heart of the city. He squelched on, therefore, through the rain, lost in his own private depression. That lank, good-tempered man running to fat only at the stomach was oppressed by nothing more than a mild attack of dyspepsia coupled with the uncomfortable premonition that his luck was out and that something unpleasant was going to happen. His was not an imaginative nature, but a premonition is a premonition, and he had just joined the Big Five, so that his responsibilities, should anything difficult turn up, would be by no means decreased. Moreover, there was the rain, the dyspepsia which had sent him for the walk, and again the rain.

In the centre of the blinding storm which blew across the Viaduct he paused and upbraided himself. The vague presence behind him was his least irritant. Hang it! this rain was soaking him. He was out of the district of hotels, and thanks to the care of a grandmotherly government no public-house would be open for another hour and a half. His trouser legs were flapping clammily against his ankles, and in jerking up his raincoat collar he had spilt a small waterfall from his hat-brim down the back of his neck.

There were a thousand and one things he might have done. He could have taken a taxi back to the Yard or to some restaurant or hotel where he could have dried at leisure, but his mood was perverse, and he looked about him aggressively. The rawest constable on this beat, he reflected, must know of some shelter, some haven in this wilderness of offices where a man might dry, warm himself, and perhaps smoke a forbidden pipe in pleasant if dusty privacy.

London, like all great cities which have been built and rebuilt for upwards of a thousand years, has all sorts of odd corners, little forgotten patches of valuable land which still belong to the public, hidden though they are amid great stone masses of private property. Standing on the Viaduct, Stanislaus Oates cast his mind back over twenty years to the time when he himself had been a constable in London, raw from the provinces. Surely he had walked this dreary street on his way home from a Holborn beat; surely there had been some retreat where he had polished up the answers for the terrifying oral examination in the spring, or pencilled an absurdly glorified account of his doings to the trusting and lovely Marion still down in Dorset.

The buildings around him changed, but the lie of the land was the same. Memory returned to him, patchily at first like a landscape seen through leaves, but suddenly he recollected a musty smell of warm sacks and hot waterpipes. And then it all came back to him—the dark passageway with the shaft of light at the end, the red door in the wall with the bucket outside and the statue facing it.

Immediately his spirits rose considerably, and he set off, penetrating farther into the city until a sudden turning brought him face to face with a narrow archway squeezed in between two palatial wholesalers' doorways. The paving stones within the passage were worn narrow strips set crazily together, and on the whitewashed wall was a small battered notice half obliterated by dust and further obscured by the shadow, which stated simply: "*To the Tomb.*"

Down this alley Inspector Stanislaus Oates plunged without hesitation.

After some fifteen yards of tunnel he emerged into a little yard, the face of which had not altered since he had first known it, nor, for that matter, for the last hundred years. Here brown-black buildings rose steep on all four sides, framing a small patch of grey unfriendly sky. The reason for this peculiar airshaft in the very centre of an ancient block of buildings took up by far the larger half of the yard and consisted of a rectangle of sparse yellow grass surrounded by railings, in the midst of which reposed the stone effigy of a man in doublet and hose. A tablet at the figure's feet announced to the curious:

> *Sir Thomas Lillyput*
> *He bought this land*
> *His bones wherein to lie*
> *Disturb him not lest ye be stirred*

When ye shall come to die
Lord Mayor of London, 1537,

and underneath, in more modern script:

Here lies a benefactor
Let no one move his bones.

The pious or perhaps superstitious magnates of a later London had so far respected Sir Thomas and his property that they had built their businesses around him and not directly above or beneath him.

The builder of the block above the passage, however, had utilised the yard as an entrance for coal since the strictly legal right-of-way was too narrow to admit of its use as a goods entrance, and the red door which the Inspector remembered on the right of the effigy led into the somewhat archaic heating arrangements of the ancient firm who occupied the east block.

The door was propped open by a bucket as it always had been. To the Inspector's livening eyes it appeared to be the same bucket, and he wondered if Old Foxie—the name came back to him with delightful familiarity—was still stoking. His depression was lifting at every step, and he advanced jauntily, restraining an absurd inclination to kick the pail as he passed into the semi-darkness of the furnace room.

"And this, if I mistake not, Watson, is our client," said a voice out of the gloom. "Good Heavens! The Force!"

After his first start of surprise the Inspector swung round to find himself facing a young man perched insecurely on a pile of débris in the warm murky shelter of the stove. A shaft of light from the furnace lit up the figure, throwing him into sharp relief.

The Inspector had a vision of a lank immaculate form surmounted by a pale face half obliterated by enormous horn-rimmed spectacles. The final note of incongruity was struck by an old-fashioned deerstalker cap set jauntily upon the top of the young man's head.

Chief Detective-Inspector Stanislaus Oates began to laugh. Ten minutes before he had felt that spontaneous mirth was permanently beyond him.

"Campion!" he said. "Who's after you now?"

The young man struggled down from his throne and held out his hand.

"I'm waiting for a client," he explained airily. "I've been here half an hour already. What are you looking for?"

"Warmth and a little quiet," said the other querulously. "This weather upsets my liver."

He took off his raincoat, shook it peremptorily and spread it over Mr. Campion's late resting place. This performance he repeated with his hat, and edged as near to the boiler as he could without burning himself. His companion regarded him with a faintly amused expression on his slightly vacuous face.

"Quite the little cop, still, I see," he said. "What's the idea? 'Old Bobby revisits the scene of his first arrest'? 'The sentimental journey of a Big Fifth'? I hate to seem inquisitive, Stainislaus, but I'm expecting a client, as I said before. In fact, when I heard your footsteps I thought you were the mysterious she, and I don't mind telling you my heart sank."

The Inspector turned from the furnace and looked at his friend attentively. "Why the fancy dress?" he inquired.

Mr. Campion removed the monstrous tweed erection from his head and looked at it lovingly.

"I called in at Belloc's on my way down here," he observed, "and I caught sight of it. They tell me they make one a year for a rural dean, who wears it for a local ratting gala. I had to have it. Just the thing in which to interview a romantic client, don't you think?"

The Inspector grinned. The warmth was beginning to percolate into his bones and his *bonhomie* was fast returning.

"What an extraordinary chap you are, Campion," he said. "I'm never surprised when you turn up in the most amazing places. I shouldn't have said there was half a dozen men in London who knew of this little hideout. Yet the first time I call here in twenty years I find you sitting here in fancy dress. How do you do it?"

Campion unbuttoned the flaps of the deerstalker meditatively. "The amiable Lugg put me up to it," he said. "He's still with me, you know—bull pup and *femme-de-chambre* combined. I was looking for some suitable spot to interview a young lady who has been so grossly misinformed that she believes I'm a private detective."

The Inspector knocked out his pipe against the boiler.

"Funny how these ideas get about," he said. "What do you call yourself these days?"

Campion looked at him reprovingly. "Deputy Adventurer,"

he said. "I thought of that the other day. I think it sums me up perfectly."

The Inspector shook his head gravely. "No more Chalices?" he said. "You put the wind up me last time. You'll get into trouble one of these days."

The young man beamed. "Your idea of trouble must be very advanced," he murmured.

The Inspector did not smile. "That's what I mean by trouble," he remarked, pointing through the open doorway to the railed-in patch of grass. "There'll probably be no one to write 'Here Lies a Benefactor' at your feet, though. What is it this time? A scandal in High Life? Or are you out to crush the spy system?"

"Neither," said Mr. Campion regretfully. "You find me here, Stanislaus, indulging in a silly childish desire to impress. And, incidentally, to get my own back. I'm meeting a lady here—I've told you that about six times. You needn't go. I don't know her. In fact, I think you might add to the tone of the interview. I say, couldn't you go out and borrow a helmet from one of your boys on point duty? Then she'll know I'm telling the truth when I introduce you."

Mr. Oates became alarmed. "If you've got some silly woman coming here, don't you tell her who I am," he said warningly. "What's the idea, anyhow?"

Mr. Campion produced a sheet of thick grey notepaper from his inside pocket.

"Here's a lawyer's letter," he said. "I like to think it cost him personally six-and-eightpence. Go on—read it. I'll help you with the long words."

The Inspector took the paper and read the letter to himself, forming each word separately with his lips and emitting an intermittent rumble as he half spoke the phrases.

> 2, *Soul's Court*, *Queen's Rd.*,
> *Cambridge*.

My Dear Campion,
I have always imagined it more likely that you would eventually come to consult me in a professional capacity than I you. However, the Gods of Chance were always capricious as a woman—and of course it is a woman for whose sweet silly (in the Saxon sense) sake here I am craving your services.

You wrote me such an amusing piece of trivia when I announced my engagement that I feel sure you have forgotten the incident completely. Still, it is for my fiancée, Joyce Blount, that I now write you.

As perhaps I told you, she is at present—poor child— employing herself as a species of professional daughter-cum-companion in the house of her great-aunt, a prodigious old Hecuba, widow of the late lamented Doctor Faraday, of "Gnats" (circa 1880). They are an elderly family of quite ridiculous proportions and hers is an invidious task.

This, then, is the thesis. At the moment Joyce is quite absurdly worried by the disappearance of her uncle, Andrew Seeley, one of the household, who has been absent for about a week. I know the man, a veritable type, and a sponger, as are most of the family, I am afraid. It seems to me to be most probable that he won a few pounds on a horse (this somewhat second-hand sport was a favourite of his, I know) and has taken the week off from his Aunt Faraday's iron discipline.

However, Joyce is as obstinate as she is delectable, and since she has determined to come to Town to-morrow (Thursday, the tenth), to consult some suitable specialist in the matter, I felt the least I could do would be to give her your name and address and then write to warn you.

She has a very romantic nature, I am afraid, and hers is a dull life. If you could give her at least the thrill of seeing the sleuth himself, perhaps even sleuthing, you would be rendering your eternal debtor he who begs always to remain, my dear fellow,

Your devoted,
Marcus Featherstone.

P.S.—Were I only in London—εἴθε γενοίμην—I should be absurdly tempted to spy upon the interview.

P.P.S.—Gordon, whom you may remember, has at last gone to uphold the British Raj in India, as, of course, he will. Henderson writes me that he has "gone into drains," whatever that may mean. It sounds typical.

The Inspector folded the letter carefully and returned it to Campion.

"I don't think I should cotton to that chap myself," he observed. "Nice enough, I have no doubt," he went on hastily. "But if you're set up in a witness box with a chap like that chivvying you he makes you look a fool without getting the case on any further. He thinks he knows everything, and so he does pretty nearly—about books and dead languages—but has he the faintest idea of the mental process which resulted in the accused marrying the plaintiff in 1927 in Chiswick, when he had already married the first witness in 1903? Not on your life."

Mr. Campion nodded. "I think you're right," he said. "Although Marcus is a very good solicitor. But cases in Cambridge are usually very *refeened*, I believe. I wish that girl would turn up if she's coming. I gave Lugg explicit instructions to send her here the moment she arrived at Bottle Street. I thought this would provide a peep at the underworld which would be at once clean, safe and edifying. The kind of girl Marcus can have persuaded to marry him must be mentally stunted. Besides, her trouble seems to be absurd. She's lost a very unpleasant uncle—why worry to look for him? My idea is to sit up on this convenient structure, array myself in my little ratting cap, and make a few straightforward comments on Uncle Andrew. The young woman, deeply impressed, will return to Marcus, repeating faithfully all that she has seen and heard—that sort always does. Marcus will deduce that I am rapidly proceeding binwards, and he will scratch my name out of his address book and leave me in peace. How's business?"

The Inspector shrugged. "Mustn't grumble," he said. "Promotion has always meant trouble, though, as far back as I can remember."

"Look out," said Campion suddenly. "She comes!"

The two men stood listening. Wavering footsteps echoed in the alleyway. They advanced almost to the yard and then retreated a little way.

"A lame man wearing number nine boots, smoking a cheroot and probably a chandler's mate by profession," Campion murmured, putting on his tweed cap. "Sounds like 'good sensible' shoes anyhow," he went on more seriously. "I hope Marcus hasn't picked a thundering English rose."

Mr. Oates glanced through the slit between the half-open door and the post. "Oh," he said casually, "it's that bloke."

Mr. Campion raised an enquiring eyebrow.

The Inspector explained. "I was followed from the Yard

to-day," he said. "I forgot all about the man in the rainstorm, to tell you the truth. I suppose he's been hanging about outside the entrance here ever since I came in. Probably somebody with a grievance, or some lunatic with an invention to offer me for detecting the criminally-minded on sight. You'd be surprised what a lot of that sort of thing I get, Campion. I suppose I'd better see him."

The rain had stopped for the time being, although the sky was still cold and overcast. Stanislaus Oates stepped out into the court, walked to the mouth of the passage, glanced down at it and then stepped back again into the shelter of the yard. Campion stood in the doorway of the boiler-room to watch the comedy, lank and immaculate, the ridiculous tweed cap perched on the top of his head.

The footsteps sounded again, and a moment later the square man with the hint of lost respectability about him emerged.

At close quarters he presented a more complex appearance than had shown at a distance. His reddish face was puffy, and coarse skin and deep lines almost obscured the natural regularity of his features. The suit, which he wore with an air, was grease-spotted and disreputable, a condition not improved by the fact that at the moment it was practically soaked. Despite his furtive glance round there was an air of truculence about him, and he fixed the Inspector firmly with his slightly bloodshot eyes.

"Mr. Oates," he said, "I should like to speak to you. I have a piece of information which may save you and your friends a lot of trouble."

The Inspector did not reply, but stood waiting for further developments. The man had revealed a remarkably deep voice and an unexpectedly educated accent. Interested, Mr. Campion advanced incautiously out of his hiding-place, and the intruder, catching sight of his somewhat unconventional appearance, broke off abruptly, his jaw dropping.

"I didn't know you had a companion," he said sullenly.

"Or a witness?" suggested the Inspector dryly.

Mr. Campion removed his hat and stepped out into the yard. "I'll go if you like, Inspector," he said, and paused abruptly.

All three men stood silent. Down the alleyway echoed the sound of high-heeled shoes clicking sharply on the stones. Mr. Campion's visitor had arrived.

She came into the yard the next moment, the very antithesis

of his expectations. A tall, slender young woman, smartly dressed in the best country-town tradition. She was also young, much younger than Campion had supposed. She looked, as the Inspector remarked afterwards, like some nice person's kid sister. She was not beautiful. Her mouth was a little too large, her brown eyes too deeply set, but she was definitely attractive in her own rather unusual way. Mr. Campion was glad that he had removed his ratting "cap." Subconsciously his opinion of his friend Marcus improved. He stepped forward to meet her, holding out his hand.

"Miss Blount?" he said. "My name's Campion. I say, I'm awfully sorry I bothered you to come all this way."

He got no further. The girl, whose glance had travelled past him to the two other men, now caught sight of the squat stranger who had something of such interest to tell the Inspector. An expression of terrified recognition crept into her face, and the young man was alarmed to see a wave of pallor rise slowly up her neck and spread. The next moment she had taken an uncertain step backward, and he caught her arm to steady her. The Inspector sprang towards them.

"Look out," he said. "Bend her head down. She'll be all right in a minute."

He was fishing for his flask when the girl straightened herself.

"I'm sorry," she said. "I'm all right. Where is he?"

The two men turned, but of their square acquaintance there was no sign. Rapidly retreating footsteps down the passage told of his escape. Oates started after him, but when he reached the end of the alley and looked up and down the street the evening rush was well under way. The pavements were crowded, and of the mysterious stranger, the sight of whom had so startled Mr. Featherstone's fiancée, there was no trace.

2

The Luck of Uncle Andrew

It was in the taxicab as they were speeding over the slippery road towards 17A, Bottle Street, Mr. Campion's Piccadilly address, that Miss Joyce Blount eyed the young man who sat beside her and the Inspector, who sat opposite, with the engaging smile of youth, and lied.

"That man who was with you in the yard?" she said in reply to a tentative question from the Inspector. "Oh, no, I have never seen him before in my life." She looked at them straightly, the colour deepening a little in her cheeks.

Mr. Campion was puzzled, and his pleasant vacuous face wrinkled into a travesty of deep thought.

"But when you saw him," he ventured, "I thought you were going to faint. And when you—er—recovered you said, 'Where is he?'"

The red in the girl's cheeks deepened, but she still smiled at them innocently, engagingly.

"Oh, no," she repeated in her clear, slightly childlike voice, "you must have made a mistake. Why, I hardly saw him. He conveyed nothing to me. How could he?" There was a distinct air of finality in her tone, and there was silence for some moments after she had spoken. The Inspector glanced at Campion, but that young man's eyes were expressionless behind his enormous spectacles.

The girl seemed to be considering the situation, for after a while she turned again to Campion.

"Look here," she said, "I'm afraid I've made a horrible fool of myself. I've been dreadfully worried, and I haven't had any food to-day. I dashed out without any breakfast this morning,

11

and there wasn't time for lunch, and—well, what with one thing and another I got a bit giddy, I suppose." She paused, conscious that her explanations did not sound very convincing.

Mr. Campion, however, appeared to be quite satisfied. "It's very dangerous not to eat," he said gravely. "Lugg will minister to you the moment we get in. I knew a man once," he continued with great solemnity, "who omitted to eat for a considerable time through worry and mental strain and all that sort of thing. So that he quite got out of the way of it, and when he found himself at a stiff dinner party he was absolutely flummoxed. Imagine it—soup here, entrée there, and oyster shells in every pocket of his dinner jacket. It was a fiasco."

The Inspector gazed absently at his friend with an introspective eye, but the girl, who had no experience of Mr. Campion's vagaries, shot him a quick dubious glance from under her lashes.

"You are the Mr. Campion, Marcus's friend, aren't you?" she said involuntarily.

Campion nodded. "Marcus and I met in our wild youth," he said.

The girl laughed, a nervous explosive giggle. "Not Marcus," she said. "Or else he's changed." She seemed to regret the remark immediately, for at once she plunged into the one important subject on her mind. "I came to ask you to help us," she said slowly. "Of course Marcus wrote to you, didn't he? I'm afraid he may have given you an awfully wrong impression. He doesn't take it seriously. But it is serious." Her voice developed a note of frank sincerity which startled her hearers a little. "Mr. Campion, you are a sort of private detective, aren't you? I mean—I'd heard of you before Marcus told me. I know some people in Suffolk—Giles and Isobel Page. They're friends of yours, aren't they?"

Mr. Campion's habitual expression of contented idiocy vanished. "They are," he said. "Two of the most delightful people in the world. Look here, I'd better make a clean breast of it. In the first place, I'm not a detective. If you want a detective here's Inspector Oates, one of the Big Five. I'm a professional adventurer—in the best sense of the word. I'll do anything I can for you. What's the trouble?"

The Inspector, who had been alarmed by Campion's frank introduction of his official status, had his fears allayed by the girl's next announcement. She smiled at him disarmingly.

"It—it isn't a matter for the police," she said. "You don't mind, do you?"

He laughed. "I'm glad to hear it," he said. "I'm just an old friend of Campion's. It sounds to me as if he's the kind of man you want. Here we are. I'll leave you with your client, Albert."

Mr. Campion waved his hand airily. "All right," he said. "If I get into serious trouble I'll let you know and you can lock me up until I'm out of danger."

The Inspector departed, and as Campion paid the cabby the girl looked about her. They were in a little cul-de-sac off Piccadilly, standing outside a Police Station, but it was the doorway at the side through which wooden stairs were visible, which bore the number 17A.

"When I was here this afternoon," she said, "I was afraid I was coming to the police station. I was greatly relieved to find that your address was the flat above it." She hesitated. "I—I had a conversation with someone who told me where to find you. A rather odd person."

Mr. Campion looked contrite. "He was wearing his old uniform, wasn't he?" he said. "He only puts that on when we're trying to impress people."

The girl looked at him squarely. "Marcus told you I was a kid with a bee in my bonnet, didn't he?" she said. "And you were trying to entertain me for the day?"

"Don't mock at a great man when he makes a mistake," said Mr. Campion, escorting her upstairs. "Even the Prophet Jonah made one awkward slip, remember. I'm perfectly serious now."

After two flights the stairs became carpeted and the walls panelled. They paused at last before a heavy oak door on the third floor. Mr. Campion produced a key, and the girl found herself ushered across a little hall into a small, comfortably furnished room vaguely reminiscent of one of the more attractive specimens of college chambers, although the trophies on the walls were of a variety more sensational than even the most hopeful undergraduate could aspire to collect.

The girl seated herself in a deep arm-chair before the fire. Mr. Campion pressed a bell.

"We'll have some food," he said. "Lugg has a theory that high tea is the real meal which makes life worth living."

The girl was about to protest, but at that moment Mr. Campion's factotum appeared. He was a large lugubrious individual, whose pale waste of a face was relieved by an immense pair of black moustaches. He was in shirtsleeves, a fact which seemed to dismay him when he perceived the girl.

"Lumme, I thought you was alone," he remarked. He turned to the visitor with a ghost of a smile. "You'll excuse me, miss, being in negligée, as it were."

"Nonsense," said Mr. Campion, "you've got your moustache. That's quite a recent acquisition," he added, turning to Joyce. "It does us credit, don't you think?"

Mr. Lugg's expression became even more melancholy than before in his attempt to hide a childlike gratification.

"It's lovely," the girl murmured, not knowing quite what was expected of her.

Mr. Lugg almost blushed. "It's not so dusty," he admitted modestly.

"High tea?" said Campion inquiringly. "This lady's had no food all day. See what you can do, Lugg."

The lugubrious man's pale face became almost animated. "Leave it to me," he said. "I'll serve you up a treat."

An expression of alarm flickered for an instant behind Mr. Campion's enormous spectacles.

"No herrings," he said.

"All right. Don't spoil it." Mr. Lugg retreated as he grumbled. In the doorway he paused and regarded the visitor wistfully. "I suppose *you* wouldn't care for a tinned 'erring and tomato sauce?" he ventured, but seeing her involuntary expression he did not wait for an answer, but shuffled out, closing the door behind him.

Joyce caught Mr. Campion's eye and they both laughed.

"What a delightful person," she said.

"Absolutely charming when you get to know him," he agreed. "He used to be a burglar, you know. It's the old story—lost his figure. As he says himself, it cramps your style when your only means of exit are the double doors in the front hall. He's been with me for years now."

Once again the girl subjected him to a long penetrating glance. "Look here," she said, "do you really mean what you said about helping? I'm afraid something serious has happened—or is going to happen. Can you help me? Are you—well, I mean—"

Mr. Campion nodded. "Am I a serious practitioner or someone playing the fool? I know that feeling. But I assure you I'm a first-class professional person."

For an instant the pale eyes behind the enormous spectacles were as grave as her own.

"I'm deadly serious," he continued. "My amiable idiocy is mainly natural, but it's also my stock-in-trade. I'm honest, tidy, dark as next year's Derby winner, and I'll do all I can. Hadn't you better let me hear all about it?"

He pulled out the letter from Marcus and glanced at it.

"An uncle of yours has disappeared, hasn't he? And you're worried? That's the main trouble, isn't it?"

She nodded. "It sounds quite ordinary, I know, and uncle's old enough to take care of himself, but it's all very queer really and I've got a sort of hunch that there's something terribly wrong. It was because I was so afraid that I insisted on Marcus giving me your address. You see, I feel we ought to have someone about who is at least friendly towards the family, and yet who isn't biased by Cambridge ideas and overawed by great-aunt."

Campion settled himself opposite her. "You'll have to explain to me about the family," he said. "They are fairly distant relations of yours, aren't they?"

She bent forward, her brown eyes strained with the intensity of her desire to make herself clear.

"You won't be able to remember everyone now, but I'll try to give you some idea of us as we are at the moment. First of all there's Great-aunt Caroline Faraday. I can't possibly describe her, but fifty years ago she was a great lady, wife of Great-uncle Doctor Faraday, Master of Ignatius. She's been a great lady ever since. She was eighty-four last year, but is still quite the most live person in the household and she still runs the show rather grandly, like Queen Elizabeth and the Pope rolled into one. What Great-aunt Faraday says, goes.

"Then there's Uncle William, her son. He's sixty odd, and he lost all his money in a big company swindle years ago and had to come back and live under aunt's wing. She treats him as though he were about seventeen and it doesn't agree with him.

"Then there's Aunt Julia, his sister, Great-aunt's daughter. She never married and never really left home. You know how they didn't in those days."

Mr. Campion began to make hieroglyphics on the back of an envelope he had taken from his pocket.

"She's in the fifties, I suppose?" he inquired.

The girl looked vague. "I don't know," she said. "Some-

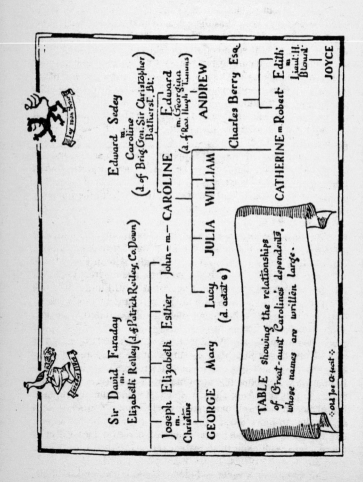

TABLE showing the relationships of Great-aunt Caroline's dependents, whose names are written large.

times I think her older than Great-aunt Faraday. She's—well, she's 'spinster of this parish.' "

Mr. Campion's eyes were kindly behind his spectacles. "On the difficult side?"

Joyce nodded. "Just a bit. Then there's Aunt Kitty, Aunt Julia's younger sister. She got married, but when her husband died there wasn't any money left. So she had to come back home, too. That's how I come in. My mother was her husband's sister. My people died young and Aunt Kitty looked after me. When the crash came I got a job, but Great-aunt Faraday sent for me and I've been a sort of companion to them all for the last eighteen months. I pay the bills and do the flowers and see about the linen and read to the family and all that sort of thing. I play Uncle William at chess, too, sometimes."

"All the jolly fun, in fact," murmured Mr. Campion.

She laughed. "I don't mind," she said.

He consulted the letter again. "Hold on, where does Uncle Andrew come in? I see his name is Seeley."

"I was coming to him. You see, he's hardly a proper uncle at all. He's a son of Mrs. Faraday's younger brother. He lost his money in the same swindle as Uncle William, and he came to live at home at about the same time. That must be about twenty years ago."

"Twenty years?" Mr. Campion looked startled. "Haven't they done anything at all since then? I say, I beg your pardon, you took me off my balance."

Joyce hesitated. "They were never much good at working," she said. "I don't think so, anyway. I think great-uncle realised it: that's why he left most of his money to his wife, although she had a large fortune of her own. There's just one thing I ought to explain before I come to the important part. When I say great-aunt manages the show, I mean it literally. The mode of living of the house hasn't altered since she first set it down about eighteen-seventy. The house is run like clockwork. Everything is just on time. Everyone has to go to church on Sunday mornings. Most of us go by car—it's a nineteen hundred and thirteen Daimler—but we take it in turns to go with great-aunt, who drives in a victoria in the summer and a broughham in the winter. Old Christmas, the coachman, is nearly as old as she is. But of course everyone knows them and the traffic is held up, so they're all right."

Enlightenment spread over Mr. Campion's ignoble face.

"Oho! I've seen them," he said. "I was up at Cambridge with Marcus, you know. I saw the turn-out then. Heavens, that's years ago!"

"If it was a grey horse," said Joyce, "it's the same one. Pecker. Pecker, the unsurpassable. Well, wait a minute. Where have I got to? Oh, yes. Well, we all live in Great-uncle Faraday's house in Trumpington Road, a little way out of the town. It's that big L-shaped house that stands back on the corner of Orpheus Lane. There's a high wall all round it. Great-aunt is thinking of having it heightened, because when people come past it nowadays on buses they can see over."

"Socrates Close," said Mr. Campion.

She nodded. "How did you know?"

"One of the sights," said Mr. Campion simply. "Or it was in my young days. Yes, that's all fairly clear in my mind. Now we come to Uncle Andrew."

The girl took a deep breath. "It really happened last Saturday week, at dinner," she said. "This is rather awkward to say, but I think you'll understand. Great-aunt treats the others as dependent children, and naturally, as they're all rather old and very human, they're inclined to quarrel in a sulky, old sort of way. That is, all except dear old Aunt Kitty. She's just sweet and silly and rather helpless. But Aunt Julia bosses her terribly. She also tries to boss the two men and they seem to hate her, and they don't like each other at all either, and sometimes they sulk horribly for days on end. There'd been one of these quarrels about nothing in the air for about a week, and I think there would have been an absolute row if it hadn't been for great-aunt, who doesn't allow rows any more than she allows early morning tea, or the gramophone on Sundays.

"Well, when we were having dinner—eight courses and all stiff and solemn, you know—suddenly, just when the atmosphere had become unbearable, and I thought when Uncle William was going to forget himself and bang Uncle Andrew over the head with a tablespoon—great-aunt or no great-aunt; and Aunt Julia was on the verge of hysterics, and Aunt Kitty was crying unobtrusively all over her salad, there was the most colossal crash, apparently right in the middle of the room, you ever heard in all your life. Aunt Kitty screamed, like a very small train, and jumped up. Uncle William forgot himself and said 'hell' or 'damn' or something—I've forgotten now. Aunt Julia was just about to settle down into her hysterics, and Uncle Andrew dropped his fork, when great-aunt sat up very stiff in her high-backed chair and rapped on the table with her fingers. She's got hard bony hands, as though she were wearing tiny ivory thimbles. She said, 'Sit down, Kitty,' very quietly. Then she turned to Uncle William and said, 'Really! You've lived in my house long enough to know that I will not have obscene words uttered at my table. Anyhow, all of you ought to know that that clock weight falls down once every fifteen years.' Uncle William said, 'Yes, mother,' and no one spoke at all for the rest of the meal."

"After dinner you opened the door of the grandfather clock," said Mr. Campion, "and you found the clock weight had fallen down. That's how all we great sleuths sleuth—quickly."

She nodded. "There was quite a dent in the wood at the bottom of the clock. I asked Alice—she's the housemaid, she's been there thirty-five years—and she said great-aunt was quite right, it was fifteen years since it fell, and she was the last person who saw the weight before it disappeared. I know this doesn't sound very important," she hurried on, "but I must tell things in their right order or I shall get us both muddled."

She was interrupted at this moment by the arrival of Lugg, now resplendent in a grey woollen cardigan. He wheeled a tea-wagon on which was a miscellaneous collection of his own favourite delicacies.

"There you are," he said with pardonable pride. "Potted shrimp, gentleman's relish, eggs, and a nice bit of 'am. I made tea. I like cocoa meself, but I made tea. 'Ope you enjoy it."

Campion waved him out of the room and he departed, muttering audibly about ingratitude.

"I see from your description of Socrates Close that Lugg must be kept out of this," observed Mr. Campion.

Joyce regarded him gravely. "It would be as well," she admitted. Over the meal she continued her story. Her face was animated, but her anxiety freed her from any suspicion of sensation-mongering.

"Uncle Andrew disappeared on Sunday," she said. "If you knew our household you'd realise that that was extraordinary in itself. Sunday is the day when Great-aunt Caroline has us under her eye practically the whole time, and if anyone wanted to slip away unnoticed, Sunday would be hardly the time to choose. It was my turn to drive in the four-wheeler. Great-aunt doesn't change to the victoria until the end of May. Of course we have to start twenty minutes before the others, and they usually go for a drive round afterwards, so that we get home before them. On that Sunday Aunt Julia and Aunt Kitty were home already when we arrived back," she went on. "Great-aunt Caroline was rather annoyed at that, because she thinks the drive does them good. She asked after the others, and Aunt Julia said that Uncle William and Uncle Andrew were walking home. That was rather curious in itself, because the two old dears had been at daggers drawn for over a week. Great-aunt was very interested. She said she hoped the exercise would do them good, and that they would learn to live together like gentlemen and not a pair of militia officers. She was rather annoyed at lunch time when they hadn't arrived back, although Aunt Kitty and I had made it as late as we could.

"We were half-way through the meal before Uncle William came in. He was very angry and hot from hurrying, and he seemed very surprised that Uncle Andrew hadn't got back before him. As far as we could make out from his story Uncle Andrew had insisted on walking home from church when William didn't want to, had tried to take a ridiculous roundabout road—I think Uncle William said through Sheep's Meadows. Finally they quarrelled about the route."

She paused and glanced at the young man apologetically.

"You know what stupid things people do quarrel about if they don't like one another."

He nodded comprehendingly, and she went on.

"Uncle William was naturally rather reticent about what was said, because a quarrel of that sort always does sound so stupid when you retail it afterwards. But apparently it was all Uncle Andrew's fault—or so Uncle William said. Uncle Andrew wanted to come home via Grantchester, which is of course an incredibly long way round. Uncle William was cold and rather hungry, and so, after walking along for a bit quarrelling violently, Uncle William said—or says he said"—she corrected herself hastily—"——'you go your own damned way, Andrew, and hang it! I'll go mine.' So they parted, and Uncle William came back and Uncle Andrew didn't. And he hasn't come back yet. He's simply vanished—there's no sign of him. He can't have gone off, because he hadn't any money. I know that, because he borrowed half a crown for the collection plate from Aunt Kitty, and great-aunt never lets him have much money anyway, because as soon as he gets it it goes to the bookmakers."

"You can't go by that," said Mr. Campion helpfully. "He may have won something. People do sometimes."

"Oh, but he hadn't—not then!" The girl spoke vehemently. "You see, that isn't quite all the story. Great-aunt thinks that backing horses is not only wicked, but rather vulgar, which is slightly more important. So to save most furious rows all round we used to do all we could to keep Uncle Andrew's little investments as quiet as possible; otherwise there was a dreadful scene. He used to lose his temper with great-aunt and sit snapping out mingy little digs at her until she got really riled and ordered him to his room as if he'd been a schoolboy. Then he had to go. It's all rather shocking to you, I suppose," she added apologetically.

"Not at all," said Mr. Campion politely. "Carry on."

"Well, I usually go round the bedrooms every evening to see that Alice has turned down the beds properly. Of course she always has, but great-aunt likes me to go. When I went into Uncle Andrew's room on Sunday night there were two or three letters on his table, ready stamped waiting to be posted, and one half-written one that he had been at work on, I suppose, when the bell for church rang. So you see he couldn't have meant to go off. You don't go away and leave half your letters unposted and another unfinished. Anyhow, I posted the letters that were sealed, and shut the blotting-pad over the other one. One of them was to his bookmaker. I didn't notice the others. When he didn't come back on Monday morning great-aunt was very stern and tight about the mouth. 'Bad blood, Joyce,' she said to me. 'No sense of personal discipline. Tell your Uncle Andrew to come to the drawing-room to see me the moment he arrives.' Aunt Julia and Aunt Kitty preserved a sedate silence most of the time. I believe Aunt Kitty did say something about 'Poor wayward Andrew,' but Aunt Julia was down on her like a ton of bricks. Uncle William was consciously virtuous. I think he rather enjoys Uncle Andrew being away. He can be as pompous as he likes without getting a dig from Uncle Andrew to make him crumple up and look foolish. By the end of the week, of course, we were all rather alarmed, and on Sunday, Aunt Julia said something about going to the police and having an S O S or something broadcast if that could be arranged. But great-aunt was horrified, and Uncle William backed her up. She said that Uncle Andrew couldn't possibly have lost his memory, because no one even faintly connected with the Faradays ever had done such a thing. Aunt said she never had had the police in her house and never would, but that if Aunt Julia was really alarmed she could write round to all the other relatives and tactfully inquire if they'd seen Andrew. Aunt Kitty caused a mild sensation by saying she had already done that, on the Tuesday after Uncle Andrew had disappeared, and that no one appeared to have heard of him. So the matter was dropped for the time being.

"Then on Monday . . ."—the girl was speaking faster now and her cheeks were very bright—". . . two queer things happened. First of all there was a telegram for Uncle Andrew. Alice brought it straight to me because that was an arrangement Uncle Andrew had with us so that great-aunt shouldn't know about the bookmaker. Any telegram that came when he was out used to be taken straight to me. I opened it, and it said: 'Turkey Carpet won 75-1. Congratulations. Cheque following. Syd.'

"As it was from the bookmaker it didn't seem to help much, so I put it in the drawer of the writing-table in his room. The next morning I had to look out for the letter."

She paused and looked at Mr. Campion with unflinching youthful eyes. "It wasn't just curiosity," she said, "and I didn't steam it or anything—I just opened it. You see, I thought that if the cheque was for a small amount uncle might be careless about it and not trouble to come back to collect it if it meant a row with great-aunt. But if it was a large amount I thought he would have been watching the papers, would realise how much he'd won and would risk any row that might be coming to him. The cheque gave me a shock. It was for nearly seven hundred and fifty pounds. I put it in the drawer with the telegram and I felt much happier, because I knew—I felt certain—that uncle would come back during the day. But in the afternoon an idiotic thing happened that terrified me somehow, I don't know why. A man came to see to the grandfather clock. There'd been some delay over it. And the weight had gone."

She looked at the young man dubiously. "I suppose that sounds awfully trivial?"

Mr. Campion, leaning back in his chair, regarded her solemnly through his spectacles.

"No," he said. "No, I quite agree with you. That's rather a beastly thing to happen. You searched for it, of course? Asked everybody?"

"Oh, yes, of course. We hunted everywhere. But there's no trace of it, and, you know, they're difficult things to lose."

Campion nodded. "This is very interesting," he said. "When did you decide to call in outside help of some sort?"

"Yesterday," she said. "I waited all Monday night, and all Tuesday, and all yesterday morning, and I got more and more frightened. I went to great-aunt, but she was still very adamant about the police. In the end I persuaded her to let me put the whole thing in Marcus's hands. He was horribly superior about it, of course, but in the end he put me on to you and here I am."

"Ah, Marcus," said Mr. Campion. "How does he come into it exactly? He's rather immature to be the family lawyer, isn't he?"

The girl smiled. "I suppose he is," she agreed, "but you mustn't tell him that. As a matter of fact it's his father, old Hugh Featherstone, who is great-aunt's real solicitor, but he's very old and so naturally Marcus does most of the work."

"I see," said Mr. Campion. "Why exactly do you want to find Uncle Andrew?"

The suddenness of his question startled her a little, and she answered after a moment or two of hesitation.

"I don't, frankly," she said at last. "That is, not personally, if you see what I mean. Uncle Andrew isn't a lovable character. But then nor are any of them really, except perhaps poor Aunt Kitty, or great-aunt herself in a terrifying way. The house is quieter without Andrew. But I want to find him because I'm frightened. I want to know that he's all right, that something terrible hasn't happened."

"I see," said Mr. Campion slowly. "I suppose you've taken some steps—you've made enquiries yourself? You've looked for him? I mean he hasn't sprained his ankle in a ditch or he isn't staying at the 'Boar'?"

She looked at him reproachfully. "Oh, of course, I've done that," she said. "But I tell you there's absolutely no trace of him. I haven't gone round making a fuss, you know, because naturally—well, gossip gets round fast enough in a place like Cambridge without one helping it. I'm afraid you'll think it rather cheek of me coming to you with so little to tell you. But—oh—I don't know—I'm afraid——"

Mr. Campion nodded. "You're afraid that something more serious than an ordinary accident has happened to him," he said, and added with disarming frankness, "and, besides, you've something else on your mind, haven't you? Now that the Inspector isn't here, won't you tell me—who was the man in the yard who gave you such a shock?"

The girl started and turned to him, the colour very bright in her cheeks.

"You're right," she said. "I was lying to you before. I did recognise him. But he's nothing to do with this. Please forget all about him."

Mr. Campion did not answer for some moments, but remained staring in front of him, a completely vacant expression on his face. Then he glanced up at her.

"You may be right," he said. "But I think we ought to start square. I loathe going into things with my eyes shut."

She took a deep breath. "He had nothing to do with it," she said. "*Please* forget him. Are you going to help me or not?"

Mr. Campion rose to his feet. She feared that he was debating how to make a polite refusal without sounding sulky, when Lugg appeared in the doorway.

"Telegram," he said. "The kid's waiting. Any answer?"

Mr. Campion tore open the orange envelope and spread out the flimsy sheet of paper within.

"Hullo," he said, "this is from Marcus. A real Cambridge telegram. Must have cost a fortune. Listen. '*Can you come back with Joyce at once? Rather terrifying developments here. Would appreciate your professional assistance in the matter. I am having your room prepared for you in anticipation. See evening papers. The* Comet, *if I know them. Marcus.*'"

Joyce sprang to her feet and looked over his shoulder.

"Terrifying developments?" she said huskily. "Oh, what's happened? What's happened?"

Campion turned to Lugg, who was watching the scene from the doorway with a certain professional interest.

"No reply," he said. "By the way, you might drop out and get a *Comet.*"

"The late special is in the kitchen," said Mr. Lugg majestically. "And I think I know what you're lookin' for. 'Arf a tick."

Two minutes later he returned. "'Ere you are," he observed, pointing to a paragraph at the top of a front page column. Joyce and Campion read the headlines together.

FAMOUS SCHOLAR'S NEPHEW FOUND
SHOT DEAD IN RIVER

MISSING FOR TEN DAYS

CAMBRIDGE, THURSDAY.
(From our Special Correspondent.)

The body of a man, bound hand and foot with cord and with a bullet wound in the head, which was taken from the River Granta this morning near the University bathing pool, has now been identified as that of Mr. Andrew Seeley, nephew of the late Doctor Faraday, of St. Ignatius College. Mr. Seeley had been missing from his residence on the Trumpington Road for the last ten days. The Cambridgeshire Police have not yet decided whether to appeal to Scotland Yard in clearing up what may prove to be one of the most sensational mysteries of the year.

The discovery, as reported exclusively in our earlier editions, was made by two Indian students of the University.

3

"Something Rather Terrifying . . ."

"If you don't mind pulling up here I'll get out. This is the house, you see."

The words were murmured apologetically into Mr. Campion's ear as the elderly Bentley sped down the London Road towards the towers and spires of a deserted Cambridge out of term. He slowed down obediently and glanced with curiosity at a great dark house on the opposite side of the road. From where they sat a large portion of the building was visible through the decorated iron-work of the drive gates.

Mr. Campion's pale face wore an enquiring expression. "It hasn't altered outside," he said.

"Or inside," said Joyce. "Does it occur to you," she added,

lowering her voice a little, "that there's something rather—rather awful about it?"

Somewhat to her relief the extraordinary young man at her side took her remark quite seriously, or at any rate he appeared to do so, for he turned again to the house and sat staring at it thoughtfully for some moments.

It was in darkness save for the half-circle of light above the front door, but nevertheless, in spite of the misty twilight of the late evening, its shape and general details were clearly discernible. Built some time in the beginning of the last century, it was spacious, L-shaped and gabled. The windows were small, however, and the creeper-covered walls looked gloomy. The cedars on the lawn in the angle of the building made fantastic shapes against the night sky. There was nothing definitely unpleasant about the house, but it had some of the grim dignity and aloofness of an institution and the sightless expression of a house in which all the blinds have been drawn.

Mr. Campion returned to the girl. "Are you sure that you want to go in at once?" he said. "Why not come down to see Marcus first?"

She shook her head. "I don't think I will, if you don't mind. They're all a little helpless. They may need me rather badly, if it's only to get them all hot-water-bottles. Good-bye. Thank you for coming."

She slipped out of the car before he could stop her, and he watched her hurry across the road, through the iron gates and down the drive. He waited until the dark hall-door opened, and the sudden rectangle of light appeared and swallowed her up. Then he let in the clutch and proceeded down the gentle slope into the town.

A thick mist from the fens had settled over the whole valley. Campion's big car wound its way carefully through the narrow streets, now ghostly and deserted, save for a few townsfolk hurrying to their homes to escape the dank vaporous air. As he drove he was conscious of a vague sense of disappointment: this was not the Cambridge of term time, the Cambridge he had known, but a chill mediæval city, whose carved stone porticos encircled only closed doors.

As he turned off Queen's Road and entered Soul's Court he found the precise tidy little square in darkness also, although every house was occupied. Here was one of those remaining fortresses in England where the modern code of familiarity with one's neighbours had not yet penetrated. Here shutters were closed, and silence was preserved, not so much in order to hide one's affairs as from a polite desire not to embarrass one's acquaintances by obtruding any aspect of one's private life upon them.

As he pulled up outside Number Two, Soul's Court, the gracious Queen Anne front was dark as the others. No flicker of light escaped the old-fashioned wooden shutters across the big lozenge-shaped windows.

He dismounted and pulled the iron bell. Heavy footsteps on the tiles within brought him to attention and the next moment, as the door swung open, he was met by that strange individual odour of a well-ordered, lived-in house, a pleasant mixture of furniture-polish, warmth and tobacco. The maid who admitted him was a gaunt Cambridgeshire woman well past middle age, the severity of whose uniform had not been modified by the recent emancipation of her sex. To modern eyes her starched embroidered cap had some of the glamour of an archaic head-dress. She allowed herself a single withered smile in the young man's direction.

"Mr. Campion," she said. "Mr. Marcus is in the dining-room. Cook has set something cold for you."

Campion, somewhat startled by the discovery that a decade had made no change in the Featherstone household, or indeed in the good woman's appearance, smiled affably and parted with his hat and coat.

"How's the rheumatism?" he said, not daring to risk a guess at her name, but backing on the ailment.

He was rewarded by a half-hearted flush of pleasure, and a "still hangs about me, thank you, sir." Then she set off down the panelled corridor, her white apron crackling and her heavy shoes clattering on the coloured tiles. A moment later Campion found himself confronting his old friend.

Marcus Featherstone rose from a high-backed chair by the fire-place and advanced to meet him. He was a man of about twenty-eight and of a type peculiar to his age and upbringing. His big figure was clothed with a species of pre-arranged carelessness; so that his suit, although well-cut, was definitely on the loose side, and his curling reddish-brown hair was uncontrolled and a little too long for the fashion. He was not unhandsome in a dry ascetic way, although it was evident from his manner that he endeavoured to look older than he was. But at the moment, in spite of his air of faint conscious superiority, he was frankly in a state of panic. He came across the room and shook Campion by the hand.

"Hallo, Campion, I'm so glad you came," he said. "I'm afraid my molehill has turned out to be a mountain after all. Have some food, won't you?" He waved vaguely to the dining table. He spoke jerkily, creating an odd impression of shyness which was flatly contradicted by his casual manner.

In the bright light from the enormous crystal chandelier over the table Mr. Campion looked even more vacant and foolish than usual, and when he spoke his voice was vague and inconclusive.

"I read the papers before I came down," he said. "Quite a bad business."

Marcus glanced at him sharply, but there was no sign of anything but the utmost gravity in the other's face. He went on, still speaking with that faint inconsequential air which irritated so many of his acquaintances.

"I left Miss Blunt at Socrates Close. A charming girl. Congratulations, Marcus."

The over-bright lights, the polished walnut and gleaming silver, combined with the slightly low temperature of the room, contrived to foster the extraordinary formality which distinguished this odd reunion. Campion became more and more vague, and Marcus's natural frigidity nearly succeeded in silencing him altogether.

Mr. Campion partook of some cold ham with ritualistic solemnity, Marcus attending to his wants with grave politeness, clinging resolutely to the hard and fast law of etiquette, which demands that a newly-arrived guest must be instantly fed, preferably upon something cold.

As for Mr. Campion, he seemed completely unaware of anything out of the ordinary in the situation. To be summoned to a catastrophe and met with cold ham might have been the most usual of his experiences. It was only after he had finished his meal and accepted reverentially the proffered cigarette that he glanced up at the other, a polite smile upon his lips, and remarked in a slightly high-pitched conversational tone: "Many murders for the time of year?"

Marcus stared at him and slowly reddened disarmingly.

"Still the same damn fool, Campion," he said explosively. "I've had a feeling you were laughing at me all the time you've been eating."

"Not at all," said Mr. Campion. "I was remembering. You got your blue for deportment, didn't you?"

Marcus permitted himself a smile which humanised him instantly. The next moment, however, he was his grave and anxious self again.

"Look here," he said, "I don't want you to think I've got you down here under false pretences, but the fact is I'm in a hole"—he hesitated.

Mr. Campion waved his hand. "My dear fellow," he said deprecatingly. "Of course I'll do anything I can."

Marcus looked relieved and, since the rheumatic maid had returned to clear the table, suggested that they should retire to the privacy of his study. As they went up the narrow polished oak staircase he turned to Campion, once more apologetic.

"I expect you're rather accustomed to this sort of thing?" he murmured. "But I may as well admit that I've got the wind-up."

"I seldom get more than one body a quarter," murmured Mr. Campion modestly.

The room they entered was a typical Cambridge study, æsthetically impeccable, austere, and, save for the two deep arm-chairs before the fire, slightly uncomfortable. As they entered, a wire-haired fox terrier of irreproachable breeding, rose from the hearthrug and came to meet them with leisurely dignity. Marcus effected an introduction hastily.

"Foon," he said. "Written 'Featherstonehaugh.' "

Somewhat to his host's embarrassment Mr. Campion shook hands with the dog, who seemed to appreciate the courtesy, for he followed them back to the hearthrug, waiting for them to be seated before he took up his position on the rug again, where he sat during the rest of the proceedings with the same air of conscious breeding which characterised his master.

Marcus Featherstone presented the unhappy spectacle of a man who has reduced at least the trivialities of life to a thought-saving if somewhat rigid code, suddenly confronted by a situation for which even the best people have no set form of behaviour.

"You see, Campion," he said suddenly, as they sat down. "Joyce is in the thick of it. That's the real snag as far as I'm concerned."

Campion nodded. "I quite understand," he said. "Fire ahead with the story. Mr. Seeley was a friend of yours, I suppose?"

The other looked up in surprise. "Hardly," he said. "Didn't

Joyce explain? Seeley was a very difficult customer. I don't think he had many friends. In fact, I can't think of anyone who liked him. That's what makes it so excessively awkward." He frowned and paused, but after a moment's hesitation pulled himself together and continued. "I first heard about the trouble this afternoon. Old Mrs. Faraday sent for my father, but the governor's away, thank heaven. Cambridge doesn't suit him in the winter. I went down myself and found the whole house in an uproar. That is, in a sort of suppressed ferment."

He leant forward as he spoke, his eyes on the other man's face.

"Mrs. Faraday was taking charge herself, of course. There is an amazing old woman for you, Campion. There were a couple of detective-inspectors of the Cambridgeshire C.I.D. in the drawing-room when I arrived, and they were as nervous as a knife-boy at a servants' ball. Roughly, the facts are these, Campion. The 'Varsity doesn't come up until next Wednesday, as you know, but there are always one or two Indian students about out of term time. Two of these men, bug-hunting along the river bank, found the body in the river in Grantchester Meadows, some way above the bathing pool. It was caught up in some willow roots and may have been there for days. That stream is deserted this time of year, and the weather's been beastly anyhow. They gave the alarm. The police came along, put the body in the mortuary, and discovered a visiting card that was still legible in the wallet, also a presentation watch with the name engraved. That sent him doubling up to Socrates Close of course, and William Faraday went down to identify the body."

He paused and smiled grimly. "It's a most amazing thing," he went on, "but Mrs. Faraday insisted on driving with him. She sat in the car outside and waited. Think of it! She's eighty-four, and an autocrat. I'm frightened of her myself. Then William went on to the police station, where he made a statement. It was not until we were up at the house that they told us about the shooting. Until then we thought he had been drowned."

Campion sat forward in his chair, his pale eyes vague behind his spectacles, his tone still inconsequential.

"About the shooting," he said. "What happened exactly?"

The other man's expression changed and he grimaced reminiscently. "He was shot through the head," he said. "I saw the body afterwards. Shot through the head at very close range. There might have been a simple explanation for that, of course, but unfortunately he was bound hand and foot and they can't find the gun. I saw the Chief Constable of the county to-day; he's a friend of father's, a delightful old boy, Anglo-Indian family, a 'wallah of the old school, don't you know.' Our chat was completely unofficial, of course, but in confidence he gave me to understand that there's no doubt about it—it's murder. In fact what he said was: 'It's murder, my boy, and damned unpleasant murder at that.' "

A ghost of a smile appeared upon Mr. Campion's lips and he lit another cigarette.

"Look here, Featherstone," he said. "I must warn you. I'm no detective, but of course I'm open to help. What d'you think I can do for you exactly?"

His host hesitated before replying. "I'm afraid it's rather a delicate matter to explain," he said at length, in his curiously dry voice. "When I first asked you to come down I had some vague idea that you might assist me to prevent a particularly unpleasant scandal. You see," he went on, smiling sourly, "this is one of the few places left in the world where it's not only considered unfortunate, but atrocious bad form, to have one of your relations—or clients—mysteriously murdered. Of course, it's quite beyond the bounds of scandal now," he hurried on, "but I feel, if I may say so without being offensive, that it would be very useful for me to have someone I knew who was not bound by the edicts or—well—scruples of convention to assist the police on our side. Someone who would hold an intelligent watching brief, someone utterly trustworthy, and, if you will forgive me, my dear Campion, for using a revolting term, someone who is a gentleman. In other words," he added, unbending slightly and becoming almost ingenuous, "the governor is almost eighty himself and not really capable of the job, and I've got the wind up."

Campion laughed. "I see," he said. "I'm to play my speciality rôle—the handy man about the trouble. I say, I hope the police like me. This isn't the sort of idea they cotton to as a rule. I'm afraid it's practically impossible to go gaily in 'assisting.' However, I've got friends, as Lugg said to the beak. I'll do anything I can for you, but I must know the full strength. Things look rather hot for Uncle William, I suppose?"

The other did not reply, and he went on:

"Tell me the worst. I'm a ferret for information. And after

all, you don't want me turning up with the family skeleton in my beak, wagging my tail and shouting miaow, as it were."

Marcus took up the poker and jabbed meditatively at a particularly solid piece of coal. The stiffness had faded out of his manner, leaving him an oddly defenceless person without his affectations. "If I didn't know you, Campion," he began—"and why you insist on calling yourself that I can't imagine—I should never dream of putting this to you at all. But the thing that's frightening me is the family."

His tone gave the two words an ominous significance.

"There's rank evil there," he went on unexpectedly, fixing his bright eyes on the other's face and speaking with an intense sincerity which finally removed any trace of his former frigidity. "There they are, a family forty years out of date, all vigorous energetic people by temperament, all, save for the old lady, without their fair share of brains, and herded together in that great mausoleum of a house, tyrannised over by one of the most astounding personalities I've ever encountered. Imagine it, Campion, there are stricter rules in that house than you or I were ever forced to keep at our schools. And there is no escape."

"You see," he went on earnestly, "there's no vent to the suppressed hatreds, petty jealousies, desires and impulses of any living soul under that roof. The old lady holds the purse strings and is the first and final court of appeal. Not one of her dependents can get away without having to face starvation, since not one of them is remotely qualified to earn a sixpence.

"Now in that atmosphere, although I don't like to think it, I can't help imagining that anything might happen."

"You are certain, in fact," said Mr. Campion, "that it's one of the family."

Marcus did not reply directly. He passed his hand over his hair and sighed. "It's terrible," he said. "Andrew was not even robbed. If only someone had stolen his wallet I should feel more helpful. Or if he'd fallen in the river trying to take a short cut home to score off his cousin it wouldn't matter much. However, that is all ruled out. I saw the body. Someone tied him up and then practically blew his head off. The police hadn't found the gun half an hour before you came. I'm afraid there's no doubt about it. As the Chief said this afternoon, it's 'a perfectly obvious case of murder.'"

"Why?" said Mr. Campion.

The other stared at him. "Well, you can't get away from the evidence," he said.

"Oh, no, I didn't mean that. I mean, why should anyone murder him? As far as I can gather he seems to have been a perfectly normal old nuisance—just like anyone else's uncle, in fact. And he had no money. That in itself should have insured him a long life."

Marcus nodded. "That's the trouble," he said. "Of course there is this bookmaker's cheque, but the police doctor is convinced that the body had been in the water at least a week. So that's no good. Over and above that, he seems to have had nothing but petty debts. That's the whole point of it: none of the family have any money at all, except the old lady, who is definitely wealthy. No, there's no motive that I can see."

"Save of course," said Mr. Campion, "the fewer men the greater share of the plunder in the end, so to speak."

Marcus jabbed again gloomily at the fire.

"Even that's no good," he said. "Strictly in confidence, of course, though I fancy the whole family know this, old Mrs. Faraday altered her will some little time ago. Under the new provisions, Andrew Seeley, her nephew by marriage, was to receive nothing at all. When she died, therefore, he must either starve or depend upon the problematic charity of his cousins. It was his own fault. *De mortuis nil nisi bonum,* you know, but he wasn't a pleasant customer. A petty cantankerous little person, a strain of the bounder in him. I often felt like kicking him myself. But then, they're not charming, any of them. The old lady has an element of grandeur about her, and Catherine is quite a kindly soul, although of course I do hate stupidity in a woman. What really frightens me is that I can easily imagine myself feeling like murder if I lived in that house."

"Julia," said Mr. Campion, who had listened with astonishment to this recital from the prosaic Marcus. "How about Julia? She's an unknown quantity at the moment. I understand from Joyce that she's a spinster and difficult."

Marcus considered the matter. "I've never been able to understand whether Julia is unfriendly and deep, or merely unfriendly," he said. "But to tie a man up, and shoot him, and chuck him in the river when she was known to have been driving home from church—why, my dear fellow, don't be ridiculous."

"I suppose it did happen then?" said Mr. Campion dubiously.

Marcus shrugged his shoulders. "Who can tell?" he said. "Certainly William was the last person who saw him alive. I fancy that if the police found the weapon William would be under lock and key by now." He looked up abruptly. Heavy footsteps sounded in the passage outside, and were followed by a discreet tap on the door. The elderly maid reappeared carrying a silver tray with a card on it, disapproval manifest on every line of her face. She presented the tray to Marcus without a word. The young man took the missive in some surprise, and after glancing at it handed it to Campion.

MR. WILLIAM R. FARADAY.
Socrates Close,
Trumpington Rd., Cambridge.

The proximity of the man they had been discussing was brought home to them startlingly by the primly engraved name. Campion turned the card over to discover a few words scrawled in a flamboyant hand cramped to fit the space.

"Shall be greatly obliged if you can spare me a few moments. W.F."

Marcus raised his eyebrows as he saw it, and pocketed the card absently. "Show him up, Harriet," he said.

4

"The Four-Flusher"

"This is the point to be considered, then," murmured Mr. Campion. "Is this 'Enter a Murderer,' or 'Innocence appears disguised as Mars'?"

There was no time for comment. Marcus rose to his feet as the door opened to admit Uncle William.

He came bustling in, a direct contradiction to any of

Campion's preconceived ideas. Mr. William Faraday was a shortish, tubby individual in a dinner-jacket of the "old gentleman" variety, a man of about fifty-five, with a pink face, bright greedy little blue eyes, yellowish-white hair, and a moustache worn very much in the military fashion, without quite achieving the effect so obviously intended. His hands were pudgy, and his feet, in their square-toed glacé shoes, somehow enhanced the smug personality of their owner.

He strode briskly across the room, shook hands with Marcus, and turned to survey Campion, who had also risen. There was a gleam of welcome in the little blue eyes which changed ludicrously to frank astonishment as he saw the young man. Involuntarily he put on a pair of pince-nez which he wore suspended from a broad black ribbon.

Marcus effected the introduction and the old man's surprise increased.

"Campion?" he said. "Campion? Not the—ah—Campion?"

"One of the family, no doubt," said that young man idiotically.

Mr. Faraday coughed with unnecessary violence. "How do you do?" he said conciliatingly, and held out his hand. He then turned to Marcus. "That dear girl of yours, Joyce, came in just now," he observed gustily. "I—er—gathered from her, don't you know, that you might be in this evening, and that's why I—er—ventured to call. Thank you, my boy." He sank into the chair which Marcus set for him and shouted to Campion, who was moving politely towards the door: "No, no—don't go, you, sir. Nothing to conceal. I've come to have a chat with Marcus about this disgusting scandal."

The truculence in his tone would have been comic in any other situation, but his little blue eyes were frightened behind the bluster, and he appeared a slightly pathetic, overheated old person, blowing and fuming like the proverbial frog.

"This is a bad business, Marcus, my boy," he continued as the others resumed their seats, Marcus taking a high chair in the centre of the group, with Foon at his feet. "A very bad business. We shall need good brains to get us out of it without making ourselves the gossip of the whole county. Extraordinary typical of Andrew," he added, with a sudden startling increase of volume in his tone, "that he couldn't even leave this world without making a lot of bother for us all. They kept me up at the police station talking for about an hour this afternoon."

He cast an enquiring glance at Mr. Campion, and his dubiousness concerning that young man's possible use in such an emergency was as apparent as though he had spoken it. He returned to Marcus.

"Well, my boy," he said, "since your father hasn't come back yet—and, after all, he's getting on a bit now, isn't he?—what are we going to do about it? I told the police all I knew, which was damned little, between ourselves. They didn't seem at all satisfied, to tell you the truth, and if I hadn't known such a thing was impossible I should have suspected them of questioning my story, such as it was. Just like Andrew," he repeated. "I can see that fellow looking up from Hades, or wherever he is, and laughing at the precious uncomfortable situation he's got us all into."

Marcus, scandalised by this frank admission of the dislike which had existed between the two men, coughed warningly. But Uncle William was not to be detracted from the story he had set himself to tell.

"I don't know if you've told Mr.—er—Mr. Campion here what I told you up at the house this afternoon about Andrew's idiotic decision to walk home from church. I was held up behind, talking to an acquaintance in the porch—Miss Berry—very pretty girl—and when I came out he'd sent the car on. Otherwise I should have insisted on driving home, and then this whole trouble would have been averted, I suppose. Although why the police think it happened then I don't know; there doesn't seem to be any evidence on that point. Still, as I say, you know all that, don't you, about the words I had with the fool? I told the police that, of course. Most extraordinary! They seemed to think that it was odd that two men of our age should worry themselves about which was the shorter way home. But, hang it, as I said to the man—some fearful bounder in uniform—a fellow doesn't like to be flatly contradicted, whatever his age is. Besides, *my* legs were going to suffer. Andrew didn't carry the weight I do. Bit of a weakling, Andrew. Still, I suppose we must be respectful to the dead."

He paused, and sat looking balefully at the two young men before him. Marcus evidently felt no comment was possible. As for Mr. Campion, he remained grave and inconceivably vacant, his pale face blank and his long thin hands folded on his knee.

Uncle William trumpeted his next remark. The time had come, he felt, to get to the point.

"I came down here this evening for three reasons, Marcus," he said. "In the first place there's that dear girl of ours—and yours. I don't think that at the present time the Close is the place for her. Of course I have no authority with young people, but I think if you could put your foot down, my boy, we could get her to go and stay with that pretty little American friend of hers in the town."

Marcus was suddenly taken aback by this implication that he had somehow neglected his duty as a fiancé, and Uncle William, feeling that he had the advantage, continued:

"When I was a young man I wouldn't see the lady whom I had honoured by asking to become my wife mixed up with a filthy affair like this. See about it to-morrow. Well, that's one thing. The next is a point I forgot to tell the police, or rather I started to tell 'em, but they changed the conversation, don't you know. About the time Andrew was supposed to have met his end—that seems to me an important point, doesn't it to you?"

He turned a truculent pink face to Mr. Campion. That young man smiled at him affably.

"Quite," said Mr. Campion. "By all means."

"Well"—Uncle William grunted—"they've got it into their heads that Andrew died, or, at any rate, was put in the water, at ten minutes past one, presumably on the Sunday. They think that because the fellow's watch stopped at ten minutes past one. Now I told them, or at least I should have told them if they'd been interested, that the fellow's watch was always at ten-past one—or some other time. The fact was that it was broken, and always had been. It wasn't a good watch. I don't know why he had it on him. He hadn't worn it for years. I know, because I used to twit him about it at one time."

"You're sure the watch found on him was this particular watch?" said Marcus suddenly.

"Oh, yes. I identified it at the mortuary. Besides, it had his name on it. Presentation watch. When old Andrew lost his money in a swindling company twenty years ago the company gave him this watch, and a pack of compliments besides, and that's all he got for his money. A damned dear watch, I used to tell him. That used to annoy him." He smiled for a moment reflectively. "There. Well, that settles that, doesn't it?" he added.

"Then the third thing is rather more serious." He coughed and looked about him. It was evident that he felt he had some important revelation to make. "If you ask me, it's the most damned obvious thing I ever saw in my life who did this," he said.

If he expected to make a sensation by this announcement he was certainly successful as far as Marcus was concerned. The young man sat bolt upright, his face white and apprehensive. Uncle William leaned back in his chair.

"Cousin George," he said, with a certain amount of satisfaction. "I haven't mentioned it before to a soul. A fellow doesn't like to incriminate a relative—however distant, thank God—and besides that, there's my mother to consider. She can't bear the fellow. Won't have his name mentioned. I can quite understand it. He's a blackguard. By the way, I shall have to ask you both to use your discretion when this matter comes out, and not let the old lady know I put you on to the track. My mother's a very strong-minded woman, and even at my age I shouldn't like to cross her."

The others still waited expectantly, and he repeated the name.

"Cousin George. George Makepeace Faraday. Son of a dissolute brother of my father's, and a constant source of embarrassment and a trial to the family ever since the Governor—God bless him—died."

Marcus glanced at Campion in bewilderment. "I've never heard of him," he said.

"You wouldn't have." Uncle William laughed. "We old families, we have our secrets, you know, skeletons like everybody else. I expect your father knows. Don't know who from, though. My mother wouldn't soil her lips by mentioning the fellow's name. Blackmailing four-flusher, if ever I saw one."

"You'll have to tell us more about this, sir." Marcus spoke with some asperity.

Uncle William cleared his throat. "Very little to tell, my boy, except that it's obvious. There was some scandal connected with this fellow. I'd never heard it. Andrew didn't know either. Of course I very seldom speak to Catherine or Julia, but I'm sure Catherine's too harebrained and Julia's too ill-natured to hold any unpleasant information back for two minutes together. But mother knows, and I expect it's her secret. I had never heard of the fellow until I came to live at home after my—er—sad reverse when that damned scoundrel Andrew got me to invest my little all in one of his infernal companies." He blew his nose loudly and resumed:

"Then I discovered the fellow had a habit of descending upon the family, usually more than half-seas over. I don't know what happened at these visits, but he used to spend half an hour or so shut up with mother and come out looking as pleased as a couple of fighting cocks. I can only suppose he blackmails her, or begs damned ingeniously. Whatever it is, I wouldn't like to try it. I don't know how the fellow gets away with it." There was a distinctive note of wistful regret in Uncle William's querulous tone.

Marcus interposed. "This is all very interesting, sir," he ventured, "but even supposing George Faraday is—er—not a trustworthy person, what makes you think that he might possibly be the murderer of Mr. Seeley?"

"Because," said Uncle William triumphantly, "he called at the house the day before the Sunday that Andrew got himself killed. I remember it well, because the clock weight fell down at dinner. Very disturbing. George walked in almost immediately afterwards, and he had a long private interview with my mother in the drawing-room before he went off. But he was still in Cambridge on Sunday, because I saw him from the car on our way to church. Tight as an owl at eleven o'clock in the morning. I hope all this won't have to come out. It's a crime here to have any relatives who aren't actually in the services or the 'Varsity, much less a barrel-shaped, unshaven object in a shiny blue suit and a bowler hat who parades the town in the company of a tramp of the most obvious kind."

Mr. Campion sat up, a glimmer of interest behind his spectacles. Something in Uncle William's description of his disreputable cousin had recalled a half-forgotten impression to his memory.

"Mr. Faraday," he said, "not to put too fine a point upon it, would you say that this cousin of yours drinks heavily?"

"Like a sponge," said Uncle William emphatically. "I've known men like that before, in South Africa. Stop at nothing, and always come to a bad end. Invariably wore an Ignatius tie, too, the bounder."

Mr. Campion's expression became almost intelligent. "Has he got a puffy red face, bright blue eyes, a faint air of respectability about him, and a very deep cultured voice? Height about five feet four, inclined to squareness?" he said.

Uncle William stared at the young man with frank admiration.

" 'Pon my soul, that's marvellous," he said. "I've heard of you detective people—you know, about being able to tell whether a man a mile off is a plumber, or a market-gardener, without so much as a pair of field-glasses. Yes, that's George Faraday to a tee, and especially that bit about a 'faint air of respectability'; but that's misleading—very misleading. There isn't a white spot in that blackguard's soul. Ah well," he added complacently, "every family has its black sheep."

Mr. Campion glanced slyly at Marcus. That young man looked so startled that Campion had not the heart to explain this apparent fear of clairvoyance. Instead, he smiled with beatific satisfaction, and it was evident that Mr. Albert Campion, practitioner in adventure, had gone up in the company's estimation. In fact, Uncle William became definitely alarmed.

"Nothing much escapes you, sir," he said, almost apprehensively.

"Spies everywhere." The words leapt to Mr. Campion's lips, but he restrained them. "Has this George Faraday been seen in Cambridge since that day?" he inquired.

Uncle William leaned forward in his chair and made what he apparently thought was a dramatic announcement.

"No," he said. "Not a sign of the blackguard! Of course," he went on dubiously, "I don't see any motive. I don't see why he should kill Andrew any more than any of us. Come to that, I don't see why exactly anyone should kill old Andrew, unless they couldn't stand the sight of him. And if that's the motive anybody might have done it. No one could stand the sight of him. Damned unpleasant, cantankerous fellow, Andrew, I was up at Ignatius with him thirty-five years ago. He muffed his little-go twice, muffed his finals twice, took up medicine, muffed that, and had a shot at the Army, but his physique wasn't good enough. Then, of course, there was nothing left but the church, but he wouldn't think of it—no consideration for others, or he might be in a comfortable country living to-day instead of where he is, lying in the mortuary and making all this fuss."

He paused and glanced round him truculently.

"Sorry if I sound hard, but I have no patience with that kind of fellow. Damned dabbler in everything. When he came into his money he lost it, and mine too, in some infernal company promoting scheme. Muffed that so badly that he came out of it with nothing but a presentation watch, and even that seems to be going to cause more bother than it was ever worth." He rose to his feet. "Well, I've said my say, Marcus, and if you see fit to hand on this information about George to the police I wish you'd do it, because I don't want to upset the old lady by blabbing about the family. I expect you'll come up to the house to-morrow, and you, sir."

He turned to Campion. As he shook hands he attempted in the clumsy, slightly rude manner of the over-bred to placate the young stranger, whose truly miraculous powers he had just witnessed, for any lack of attention he might have shown him.

"D'you know, when I first came in, I was rather startled. I didn't realise that you were—er—er—in a sort of disguise, and it wasn't until you gave me that exhibition of really remarkable reasoning that I understood what scientists you fellows are."

Marcus escorted him to the door, and just before he went he buttonholed the young man to mutter breathily: "I may come up and see you some time, my boy. Little matter I want you to do for me. It'll keep—it'll keep."

When Marcus returned to the study he found Campion and Foon regarding the fire, each with the same degree of idle speculation.

"Well," he said, taking up his place in the group, "thank God for Cousin George. That was rather a lucky guess of yours, Campion. How did you manage it?"

"Astronomy, mostly," said Mr. Campion placidly. "Judicious advertising can make *you* famous. Why go on looking half-witted? Let me be your father. I saw the fellow once. He has a strong family likeness to William; that's why I connected him with the old boy's description."

Marcus looked up enquiringly, but Campion did not make any reference to the incident in the London courtyard of that afternoon. Instead he put a question.

"Had you heard of Cousin George before?"

Marcus hesitated. "I knew there was someone," he said inconclusively. "I heard it from Joyce, as a matter of fact."

Mr. Campion eyed him thoughtfully. He was on delicate ground.

"Any reason why Joyce should want to keep this fellow out of it, by the way?" he said casually.

Marcus looked surprised. "I don't think so," he said. "Why? I shouldn't think she'd exchanged half a dozen words with him in her life." He sighed with relief. "I feel thankful for small mercies," he said. "There was no love lost between William and Seeley, as you see, but of course this bad hat turning up like this rather lets William out, doesn't it? After all, if nobody had any motive the bad hat stands out as the most likely, doesn't he?"

"Working on the theory that it's habit that counts, I suppose," said Mr. Campion, shaking hands suddenly with Foon, who appeared to experience an urgent desire to do so. "Well, it may be so."

But in the back of his mind there remained three definite and unanswerable questions: Why, if George Faraday had murdered his second cousin for reasons best known to himself, had he taken the trouble to follow Inspector Oates to the Lillyput tomb, and what could he have possibly been going to say to him there? More extraordinary still, why had he fled at the sight of Joyce Blount? And why, most extraordinary of all, should she have denied all knowledge of him? Marcus's vivid description of the possible horrors of repression and depression in Socrates Close returned to his mind. He wondered, too, why an assassin should tie a man up before shooting him at such very close quarters. He moved uneasily in his chair. Mr. Campion was not a man who enjoyed horrors.

And then, of course, the next morning came the appalling news of the second of the Socrates Close murders.

5

Aunt Kitty's Secret Vice

Mr. Campion was not a naturally early riser, and when he descended the stairs the next morning he found that not only had Marcus preceded him, but that he was already entertaining a caller in the breakfast room. Campion, who was fully aware that this was a most unusual proceeding at

Soul's Court, was somewhat startled to see a bright-eyed, red-haired little squirrel of a young woman regarding him quizzically over a cup of coffee. Marcus, less formal than he had ever known him, was comparatively vivacious. He looked up as Campion came in and introduced the stranger.

"This is Miss Ann Held, Campion," he said. "Ann, this is the man we're relying on to get us out of all our troubles."

"For Heaven's sake!" said Miss Ann Held politely. "How d'you do?"

She was little more than twenty-five, and pretty in animation, if her features were more unusual than conventionally beautiful. She was so completely at ease and so startlingly American that Mr. Campion understood the total absence of any stiffness which might have been occasioned by the unconventional calling hour. As he sat down Miss Held explained her appearance with ingenuous friendliness.

"I saw the papers this morning," she said, "so I came right round to ask Marcus if there was anything I could do for Joyce. She's one of my best friends here. You see, there's no 'phone at that house, and I can't very well call. They won't want strangers about the place with this terrible business upon them."

Marcus chimed in. "I've been explaining to Ann that I'd be awfully grateful if she'd ask Joyce to stay with her until this thing is over," he said. "It wasn't a bad idea of William Faraday's."

Mr. Campion made no comment. Uncle William's solicitude for Joyce's comfort had struck him as remarkable in such a blatantly selfish man.

"I've been telling Marcus," Miss Held continued, her bright brown eyes flickering at Campion, "I'll certainly ask her, but I don't think for a minute that she'll come. Unless maybe Marcus puts his foot down." She glanced at the other man and smiled mischievously. "And I doubt if even such a product of England's finest educational system would dare do a thing like that nowadays, with us women getting so wild."

"Oh, I don't know," said Mr. Campion mildly. "Marcus has had his moments. Who supplied the statue of Henry the Eighth in Ignatius Square with one of the most useful products of a new domestic civilisation? A feat, moreover, which had not been attempted since the time when my venerable uncle, the Bishop of Devizes, did it in a fog, disguised as Mrs. Bloomer, then visiting the country. The lad has stamina."

Marcus looked at Campion in scandalised reproach. "If we're going into reminiscences," he said warningly, "as I sincerely hope we're not, I could unfold a tale or so."

Mr. Campion looked blandly innocent and Miss Held laughed.

"I just take that as another evidence of Marcus's mania for doing the right thing," she said. "It's more than an instinct with you, Marcus—it's a passion. Well, we'll leave it that you're to tell Joyce that I'm dying to see her, which is perfectly true. Of course, I don't want to butt in, but you know if there's ever anything I can do, the line's just got to be indicated and I'll be off down it like a rabbit."

She spoke with perfect sincerity, and Mr. Campion beamed upon her approvingly. As far as he could see, really attractive characters in this affair were going to be scarce, and it was delightful to find one at the breakfast table so unexpectedly on the first morning of his arrival.

It was at this point that the door of the room was opened with scant ceremony, and instead of the gaunt and rheumatic Harriet it was Joyce herself who appeared on the threshold.

At the first sight of her the three young people rose to meet her. She was incredibly pale and seemed to be on the verge of collapse.

"Why, child, whatever is the matter?" Ann Held put her arm round the girl's waist and drew her into a chair.

Joyce took a deep breath. "I'm all right," she said. "It's—it's Aunt Julia."

Marcus paused in the act of pouring out a cup of coffee for her. "Julia?" he demanded. "What's the matter with her?"

"She's dead," said Joyce explosively, and began to cry.

There was silence in the room for a moment while the other three assimilated the shock. The practical-minded Ann Held came to the most natural conclusion.

"Poor dear," she said. "I suppose all this business affected her heart."

Joyce blew her nose violently. "No," she said, shaking her head. "She's been poisoned, I think. Great-aunt Caroline sent me down to tell you."

Her voice died away in the room, which seemed suddenly to have become very cold. The horror of this bald announcement, coming in the very midst of the drama of Andrew Seeley's death, had, temporarily at any rate, a numbing effect. This was a development that neither Campion nor Marcus had considered.

Campion, who had never seen Julia, and was therefore only impersonally moved by Joyce's announcement, took command of the situation.

"I say," he said soothingly, "do you think you could tell us about it?"

Joyce pulled herself together before his quiet matter-of-fact tone and wiped her eyes.

"I don't know when it happened," she said. "Last night, I suppose, or early this morning. When Alice went to call her at seven o'clock this morning she was sleeping so soundly that she couldn't wake her. Thinking she was probably overtired, she let her sleep on. She didn't come down to breakfast at eight, and afterwards—about half-past—I took her some food on a tray. As soon as I entered the room I saw she was ill. She was breathing horribly, making the most dreadful noise, and the whites of her eyes were showing. I took the food away again and sent young Christmas—that's old Christmas's son, the one who drives the car—down to fetch Doctor Lavrock. He was rather late coming. They got the message muddled or something, and the doctor stayed to see another patient on the way. When he did arrive it was about half-past nine, I suppose. She must have died practically the moment he came into the room. Aunt Kitty and I were with her."

She paused breathlessly and they waited patiently for her to continue.

Joyce went on, eager to get the story out. "She never spoke and never seemed to wake up. The breathing just stopped, that was all. The dreadful part was that great-aunt didn't even know she was ill. You see, she never gets up until eleven o'clock, and we hadn't thought it was serious enough to disturb her before."

"What makes you say it was poisoning?" demanded Marcus suddenly.

"Dr. Lavrock," said Joyce. "He didn't say so in so many words, but it was quite obvious what he thought from the first moment he came in. You know him, don't you, Marcus? This isn't old Lavrock, the 'veteran doctor of Cambridge.' This is his second son, the one with the beard. He's known the family ever since he was a child; nowadays old Lavrock only comes to see great-aunt, and this one—Henry—looks after the rest of the family. He took one look at Julia this morning, examined her eyes, and promptly turned Aunt Kitty, who was practically in hysterics anyhow and in flood of tears, out of the room.

"Then he turned on me and said angrily: 'When did you find this out?' I told him—exactly what I told you. Then he asked me if she'd been depressed at all lately, and if Uncle Andrew's death had upset her and—well, I had to tell him that it had simply made no difference to her at all, and that if anything she was rather acidly glad about it." She shuddered. "It was horrible, with her lying there dead. He asked me a lot of other questions. If she'd had any breakfast. I told him no. I'd carried some up to her, and it was then that I'd found her so ill, and therefore I'd taken it down with me again.

"Then he started asking the most obvious things. Had anyone received a note from her? And we looked round the room together to see if there was a note. While we were doing this Alice came in with a message from Great-aunt Caroline, asking us both to go to her room immediately. The doctor posted Alice outside Aunt Julia's door with instructions to let no one go in, and when we got there we found that she'd been talking to Kitty, and knew practically as much about it as we did. The doctor was very straightforward, although, of course, he couldn't be snappy with Great-aunt. She took it amazingly calmly, sitting up in her great canopy bed, in a big lace cap. It was when the doctor said he'd have to report the matter at once to the coroner's office that she sent me down here for your father, Marcus, and if he wasn't back I was to fetch you. She also said that if Mr. Campion was here she'd be very pleased to see him. I suppose Uncle William must have talked about you to her when he came in last night."

She glanced at the other girl.

"You'd better keep away from us, Ann. This is going to be a terrible scandal. I'm as sure as I'm here that Aunt Julia never committed suicide. She wasn't that sort. Besides, the last thing she said to me last night was that I was to see that Ellen—that's the cook—'didn't let her hysteria over affairs that didn't concern her interfere with the culinary arrangements, and would I see that the bread sauce was better made to-morrow than it was this evening.' Whatever you do, you mustn't get mixed up in this."

Ann snorted. "Don't talk any more nonsense like that," she said. "If you expect anyone to go high-hat over a misfortune like this, you're on the wrong track where I'm concerned. I know it's no good asking you to come and stay with me now, but if at any time of the night or day you want to get away from it, come right round. I'll never forgive you if there's anything I can do and you don't ask me."

While the girls were talking Campion and Marcus prepared for departure. In the hall the young lawyer caught his friend's eye.

"Joyce thinks it's murder," he said dryly.

Mr. Campion made no comment. In a few moments the girls joined them and they all piled into the huge old-fashioned car. They dropped Ann in King's Parade and hurried on. The shock seemed to have silenced Joyce after her first outburst, for she sat huddled up beside Marcus, who was driving, and said nothing until they were safely in the drive leading up to Socrates Close.

In the morning sun the old house looked much less forbidding than it had done the night before. The virginia creeper and ivy had softened the severity of the actual building and it was spruce and well-kept in the Victorian manner, a rarity in these days of expensive labour.

The doctor's runabout stood before the door, and they pulled up short to avoid it. A plump middle-aged woman in a cap and apron admitted them. She was a little dishevelled and had evidently been crying. She greeted Joyce with a watery smile.

"Mrs. Faraday isn't down yet, miss," she said in a whisper. "She said would the gentleman wait for her in the morning room. But Mr. William and his sister are there."

"That'll be all right, Alice," Joyce spoke wearily.

The hall they had entered was large and gloomy. Nevertheless, the house exuded a solid Victorian welcome, a welcome of Turkey carpets and mediocre oil-paintings in ample gilt frames, of red damask wallpapers and the sober magnificence of heavy brass ornaments. But to two of the young people at least all this was subdued into a feeling of oppression: they knew the history of its inmates, and for them this great comfortable dwelling was a place of unknown horrors, of strange lumber from the lives of the family which had lived there ever since it had been built. To them it was a hot-bed, a breeding ground of those dark offshoots of the civilised mind which the scientists tell us are the natural outcome of repressions and inhibitions. To them the old house was undergoing an upheaval, a volcano of long fermented trouble, and they were afraid of what they were about to find.

They were taking off their things when the door opposite them opened and Uncle William's puffy red face appeared in the opening. He came forward with slightly exaggerated affability.

"I'm glad to see you—both of you," he said. "I suppose you've heard our terrible news? Julia now. Come in, will you? I believe my mother'll be down in a moment or two. She's upstairs just now talking to Doctor Lavrock. I suppose the man knows his business."

He escorted them into a room that would have been sunlit had it not been for the light holland blinds drawn down over the two windows which faced the drive. This, it was evident, was the main family sitting-room. Originally intended for a breakfast-room, it naturally retained a great deal of its original furniture. The mahogany breakfast table and sideboard shone as only well-cared-for mahogany can shine. The glazed chintz was slightly faded with much washing, and there were dents in the green leather arm-chairs by the immense marble fire-place which suggested long use, each by its own particular owner. Here were water-colours, old-fashioned too, whose naïve charm was bringing them rapidly back into fashion.

Uncle William, in carpet slippers, seemed a shabbier, less bounding figure in the morning light, and his military air had almost entirely vanished.

"Here's Kitty," he said, adding in a bellowed whisper: "I've been trying to comfort her, poor creature."

Aunt Kitty, quite as much flustered by the thought of meeting strangers red-eyed as by her tragic experience of the morning, rose from a low chair by the fire. She was a pathetic little woman, much older than her years, which were less than sixty. She was a fussy little person, fussily clothed in a black frock with tiny ruffles at the neck and sleeves. She was, too, the only woman Campion had ever seen in his life who wore a large gold watch attached by a bow-shaped gold brooch to her hollow bosom. Her eyes were red, as also was the tip of her nose, the only part of her face which was not wrinkled. She exuded an air of down-trodden virtue, an example of one who has carried gentleness to excess.

She shook hands with Campion without looking at him, and turned to Marcus, her handkerchief much in evidence.

"My dear boy, this is terrible," she said. "Poor Julia, last night so full of strength and vigour, so dominant, such a tower of strength to us all, and to-day lying on her bed upstairs——" She swallowed noisily and the little lace handkerchief went to her eyes again.

The situation, although an awkward one, could have been

handled perfectly by Marcus had it not been for the untimely attitude adopted by Uncle William.

"Come, come, Kitty," he said, planting himself squarely in front of the fire and resuming some of his erstwhile bluster. "We all know that Julia's death has been a bit of a shock, but we don't want to be hypocritical. I won't say I'm not shaken, and I'm sorry, too. Damn it all, she was my sister. Julia had too much of a dominant personality not to be missed. But she was an infernally bad-tempered old woman. Let's face the facts."

Aunt Kitty took her handkerchief from her eyes and turned upon her brother. She looked distressingly like a rabbit at bay. Her pale cheeks were faintly flushed with pink, and her red-rimmed blue eyes gleamed with righteous indignation as she dragged up the last ounce of spirit in her composition to meet this outrage upon the decencies.

"Willie!" she said. "Your own sister! Lying dead on her bed upstairs, and you speaking of her as you never would have dared to have spoken of her had she been alive to hear you!"

Uncle William had the grace to look discomforted, but his was not the temperament to accept these reproaches with dignity or even politeness. He blew out his cheeks, therefore, raised himself once or twice on his toes, and blared at Kitty, who was already more than a little astonished at her own temerity.

"I'd say anything to Julia's face," he said. "Always have done. She was a damned bad-tempered old harpy! And so was Andrew—they were a pair. This house will be a sight quieter without the two of 'em. Answer that if you can. And don't call me 'Willie.'"

Marcus, who was acutely embarrassed by this display of nerves and that offensive lack of consideration for others which one so often finds in family emergencies, turned away and contemplated the faded water-colour of the old gateway at Ignatius, but Mr. Campion remained looking at the brother and sister with his usual expression of friendly stupidity.

Aunt Kitty wavered, but having defied her brother once, she seemed unable to stop.

"Julia was a *good* woman," she said. "Better than you'll ever be, William. And I won't listen to you befouling her dear memory. It isn't as though she'd been buried. What you'll come to, *Willie*, with no religion to help you, I don't like to think."

Uncle William exploded. He was liverish, his nerves were on

edge, and like so many men of his type he regarded his immortal soul as something physical and indecent.

"Call me what you like, Kitty," he blared, "but I won't stand hypocrisy. You can't deny the sort of life Julia led you. You can't deny that she went out of her way to annoy Andrew and myself with a venomous tongue and darned greedy habits. Who used to have *The Times* sent straight up to her room and kept it there until three o'clock in the afternoon? She never shut a door after her in her life, and if there was any kind of offensive muck-raking to be done, she did it."

Aunt Kitty summoned all her frail forces for one last retort.

"Well," she said, her little body shaking with wrath at this outrage to all her instincts, "at least she never got secretly—*inebriated.*"

Uncle William stood petrified. There was a hunted expression in his little blue eyes as they glared at her balefully from his flaming face. When his complete suffocation appeared to be no longer probable, he recovered his voice on a note clearly louder and higher than he had intended.

"That's a damned lie!" he said. "A damned ill-natured lie! A prejudiced lie. You've got a poisoned mind, my girl. Haven't we got enough trouble as it is without trying to saddle me with a trumped-up charge——" His voice cracked and was silent.

Before this tirade Aunt Kitty suddenly crumpled. Sitting down abruptly in one of the high-backed chairs by the table, her eyes turned up and her mouth opening, she emitted the horrible pain-filled laugh of hysteria and sat there rocking to and fro, the tears streaming down her face, while Uncle William, forgetting himself entirely, shouted at her in a lunatic attempt to silence her.

It was Mr. Campion who stepped forward, and seizing one of the old lady's hands, smacked it hard; at the same time admonishing her in a tone utterly unlike his usual inconsequential murmur.

Marcus advanced upon Uncle William with no very clear plan in his mind, while Joyce assisted Mr. Campion.

It was at this psychological moment when the noise was at its height that the door swept open and Great-aunt Faraday appeared upon the threshold.

One cannot have an imperious personality for over eighty years without developing at least traces of the grand manner.

Mrs. Caroline Faraday, widow of Dr. John Faraday, Master of Ignatius, had the grand manner itself.

She was an old woman of striking appearance without any of the ugliness which great age so often brings to a masterful countenance.

It is worthy of note that two seconds after her appearance the room was in complete silence. She was very small, but surprisingly upright. It seemed to Mr. Campion's fascinated gaze that the major portion of her body was composed of some sort of complicated structure of whalebone beneath her stiff black silk gown. Around her tiny shoulders she wore a cape of cream rose point, and the soft web was caught at her throat by a large cornelian brooch. Her serene old face, in which black eyes gleamed as brightly as ever they had done, was surrounded by a short scarf of the same lace worn coif-fashion and held in place by a broad black velvet ribbon.

This display of lace was perhaps her only weakness. She possessed a vast collection and wore examples from it perpetually. During the whole of the terrible time which was to follow, Mr. Campion, who had an eye for such things, never saw her wear the same piece twice.

At the moment she held a thin black walking-stick in one hand and a large blue cup and saucer in the other.

She looked like a small eagle as she stood in the doorway glancing from one to the other of them standing before her like the naughty children she considered them.

"Good morning," she said in a voice which Campion found surprisingly youthful. "Tell me, is it necessary to make so much noise defending yourself, William? I heard you as I came downstairs. Must I remind you that there is death in the house?"

After an uncomfortable pause Marcus stepped forward. To his relief Mrs. Faraday smiled at him.

"I'm glad you came," she said. "Your father is still away, I suppose? Did you bring Mr. Campion?"

There was no wavering. Here was a woman completely in possession of her faculties.

Marcus ushered Mr. Campion forward and the introduction was made. Since Mrs. Faraday had her stick in one hand and the cup and saucer in the other, she made no attempt to shake hands, but bowed graciously, granting the young man one of her rare smiles.

"In a minute," she said, "I want you both to come into my

writing-room. But before that there is just this matter of the tea-cup. We are all here, so perhaps it were better if it were made clear now. I have already spoken to the servants. Will you shut the door, Marcus?"

She advanced into the room, a frail but completely commanding figure.

"Joyce," she said, "give me one of the little mats, will you?"

The girl opened a drawer in the sideboard and took out a small circle of embroidered canvas. When this had been placed over the polished surface of the table, Great-aunt Caroline put the cup and saucer down upon it.

"That," she said quietly, but with a distinct touch of reproof in her tone, "I found myself in Julia's room. It was just under the bed valance. I found it with my cane and Alice picked it up. It appears to have contained tea."

They were all still upon their feet, and from his position on the old lady's right, Mr. Campion was able to see a few dregs and tea-leaves in the bottom of the cup. The inquisitorial atmosphere rather surprised him, and he did not at first understand the air of domestic friction, the hint of a breach in the household routine. Still less was he prepared for the immediate results of Mrs. Faraday's enquiry.

Aunt Kitty, who until now had remained quietly sniffing into her handkerchief, suddenly burst into piteous and embarrassing tears. She came forward and stood fidgeting before her mother.

"I did it," she said tragically. "I made the tea."

Great-aunt Caroline remained silent, no third person in the room would have dared to have spoken, and Aunt Kitty continued humbly.

"Julia liked her cup of tea in the morning," she said pathetically. "And so do I. I got used to it when my poor Robert was alive. He liked it, too. Julia suggested—no, well, perhaps it wasn't she—but one of us thought that although morning tea isn't served here we shouldn't be doing any harm if I bought a little kettle and a small spirit stove from Boots', and made the tea in my room every morning before Alice brought in the hot water. We've done this for two years now. Every morning I made the tea and took a cup into Julia in my dressing-gown and bedroom slippers. I took it to Julia this morning. She—she was quite well then. Oh, mamma! if she put anything in her tea and drank it up I never shall forgive myself, I never shall."

At the end of this remarkable revelation there was another

outburst of sobbing, in which Joyce vainly tried to comfort her. Great-aunt Caroline regarded her daughter with a mixture of disapproval, astonishment and scorn. At last she turned to Joyce.

"My dear," she said quietly, "take your aunt up to her room, and if Dr. Lavrock is still in the house, ask him to give her a sedative."

But Aunt Kitty had not plumbed the depths of her self-abasement yet. Like many down-trodden people she had a strong, if somewhat misguided, sense of the dramatic.

"Mother," she said, "forgive me. You must say you forgive me. I shan't be myself again until I know that."

If old Mrs. Faraday had been physically capable of blushing, doubtless she would have done so. As it was, her finely crumpled skin took on a deeper shade of ivory and her bright black eyes were embarrassed.

"Catherine, my dear," she said, "you are evidently not at all well. Surreptitious early morning tea is not the matter which is worrying Dr. Lavrock or myself at the moment." She turned away. "Marcus, I want you to carry that cup very carefully for me. Mr. Campion, your arm, if you please. William, you will oblige me by remaining here until I send for you."

6

The Grand Manner

The strange procession wended slowly down the short corridor which led off the hall to the tiny sun-trap on the south side of the building which was Mrs. Faraday's own private apartment.

Mr. Campion seemed fully conscious of the honour which was being conferred upon him by the old lady, whose yellow-white fingers rested so lightly upon his arm. Marcus stalked behind them with the tea-cup. Mrs. Faraday raised her stick.

"In here," she said.

Campion opened the door and stood aside to let her pass. The

room they entered was a perfect Queen Anne sitting-room,
totally unexpected in this Victorian stronghold. The walls were
white panelled and hung with delicate mezzotints. The old rose
of the Chinese carpet was echoed in the brocaded hangings
which framed the gentle bow of the window. The old walnut
furniture reflected softly the bright fire in the grate. The
candlesticks were silver and the upholstery covered with needle-
work. A beautiful room expressing a taste in direct opposition to
the ostentatious solidity of the rest of the house.

Great-aunt Caroline in her laces seemed the natural owner of
such a period gem. She sat down at the open bureau and turned
to face them, one small ivory hand resting on the fine Italian
blotter within.

"I'll have that cup on my desk, Marcus," she said, "if you
don't mind. Thank you. Put it here on this piece of notepaper. It
takes three years of polishing to remove a damp ring from
walnut. You may sit down, gentlemen."

They took up their places obediently on wide Sheraton chairs
designed for a more ample generation.

"And now," she continued, turning to Campion, "let me
look at you, Rudolph. You're not much like your dear grandmother, but I can see the first family in you."

Mr. Campion flushed. The thrust had gone home and there
was a faint air of amusement in the old lady's face when next she
spoke.

"My dear boy," she murmured, "very old ladies only gossip
among themselves. I shall not expose you. I may say I quite
agree with your people in theory, but, after all, as long as that
impossible brother of yours is alive the family responsibilities
are being shouldered, and I see no reason why you shouldn't call
yourself what you like. Emily, the dowager, and I have corre-
sponded regularly—why, for the last forty-five years—so I have
heard all about you from her."

Mr. Campion faced the discovery of his more intimate affairs
with remarkable equanimity.

"My grandmother and I," he said, "are partners in crime, in
the eyes of the family at least. According to my mother, she aids
and abets me."

Great-aunt Caroline nodded. "I had gathered that," she said
primly. "Now to this terrible business. I understand from what I
can make of Joyce's story that Marcus has invited you to assist
him in this case. I should like you to act for me directly, if you

will. The spare room will be prepared for you and the firm of Featherstone will be instructed to pay you one hundred guineas if you remain in my employ for less than one month. Be quiet," she added sharply as Campion opened his mouth to speak. "You can refuse afterwards if you wish."

"I am eighty-four years old. You will understand, therefore, that in an emergency of this sort I am compelled to use my brain and other people's energies to protect myself and my household. I must also guard myself against such emotions as anger, grief or excitement which I have not now the strength to support."

She paused and regarded them with a grave placidity, which made her somehow inhuman. Mr. Campion realised that here was a woman of no ordinary strength of character, and her remoteness might have jarred upon him had it not been for the sudden illumination of her next remark.

"You see," she said quietly, "it is very necessary that someone in this household should consider things from an intelligent point of view. My poor children have not been blessed with brains, and that is why I have to conserve what strength I have in this way. You may think my attitude towards Julia's terrible death this morning is unnecessarily stoical," she went on. "However, I am past the age when it is proper for one to preserve the decencies by deceiving oneself. Whether it is because Julia has lived with me longer than any of my other children, or whether it is because she resembled my husband's mother, who was an irritatingly foolish woman in a generation when foolishness was fashionable, I do not know; but Julia has always struck me as possessing more than her fair share of stupidity and uncharitableness. So that although I am surprised and shocked by her death, I am not deeply grieved. At my age death loses much of its horrifying quality. Have I made all this quite clear?"

"Yes," said Mr. Campion, who had removed his spectacles, and with them most of his air of fatuity. "I understand. You want me to act as a kind of buffer between you and the shocks which we can only reasonably suppose are in store for us all."

Mrs. Faraday shot a swift glance at him. "Emily is right," she said. "You seem to be a very intelligent young man. I take it we have settled this first point, then. Now I want you to understand that I have nothing to conceal—that is, from the police. I want to give them every assistance I possibly can. In my experience nothing is ever gained by vigorous efforts to hush up trouble. Also, the quicker a thing is over the sooner it is forgotten. There is this matter of the newspapers, though. Reporters are beginning to besiege the house already. The servants have instructions, of course, to say nothing, but I do not consider it good policy to refuse all information to the newspapers. This, in my experience, antagonises them and they are apt to invent far more suggestive information than any they could possibly glean from oneself."

Once again she shot that bird-like enquiring glance at her audience, and appeared satisfied when they nodded their comprehension.

"I don't intend to see these people myself, you know," she went on, smiling a little at such an eventuality. "And of course William certainly must not see them. I hope you will arrange all that for me, 'Mr. Campion.' You will also attempt to find out who is responsible for these outrages, although I am not insulting you by suggesting that you behave like a policeman. However, what I particularly want of you is information as it arrives, so that I may not be overwhelmed by the results of it unprepared. And, incidentally, of course," she went on in her precise slender voice, "I need the presence of an intelligent person in the house from whom we may expect a certain amount of protection. Because," she continued, "it seems to be quite obvious that if these two murders emanate from the family, as I believe they do, then there is only one of us who is safe. In fact, unless some solution is arrived at it is only a question of time who is to be murdered next."

Her small voice died away and the two young men sat staring at this remarkable impersonal old lady as she sat in her gracious little room making these extraordinary statements.

It is so often that the emotions and the affections outlive the intellect in the very old that the effect of encountering an exact inversion of this process is apt to appear startling.

Great-aunt Caroline next turned her attention to Marcus. "I am not waiting until your father comes to make my arrangements," she said, "because I was calculating your age this morning. You must be nearly thirty, and I see no reason why you should not be even more useful than he, who, to my mind, has never really understood the art of growing old. Besides," she added, with a touch of grimness in her tone, "if a man is not worthy of responsibilities at thirty there is very little likelihood of his ever attaining to that state. William and Andrew are distressing examples of this. I remember putting this maxim to Mr. Gladstone in this very room many, many years ago. He said: 'Madam: if I admitted that I should never have become a politician.' But after dinner, in the drawing-room, he told me that I was quite right."

Just for a moment as she spoke there was a trace of the Caroline Faraday of the 'eighties, the brilliant hostess who had made her husband, that bad-tempered but erudite old scholar, the remarkable figure he had been. It was only for a moment, however; the next instant she was the little black eagle again, shrewd and impersonal.

"First of all," she said, "I must tell you, I suppose in confidence, that yesterday I had a short talk with my old friend's son, the Chief Constable of this county, and he promised me that everything should be done to clear up the mystery of Andrew's death. So that I fancy that Scotland Yard will have been asked to assist this morning. That is the first thing. But the important question at the moment is, of course, poor Julia."

She was silent for a moment, and they sat waiting.

"Doctor Lavrock," she said at last, "who has nothing but longevity in his family to make him in any way extraordinary, is convinced that it is suicide. I have no doubt," she went on placidly, "that he has a theory that poor Julia, after having been responsible for Andrew's death, was overtaken by remorse, and committed suicide. Of course, no one but an unimaginative fool who knew neither of the two people concerned would credit such an idea for a moment. However," she added, eyeing the young men judicially, "should nothing more occur and the police come to that conclusion, I see no reason why we should force an alternative upon them, at least in so far as the question of suicide is concerned."

Mr. Campion leant forward in his chair. "Mrs. Faraday," he said diffidently, "why are you so sure yourself that suicide is not the true explanation of Miss Julia's death?"

Great-aunt Caroline sighed. "Julia and Andrew disliked one another bitterly," she said, "and if Andrew had murdered Julia and then committed suicide, I do not think I should have been so astonished. But that Julia should kill herself is unthinkable. She clung to life as though she had ever got anything out of it, poor creature, and she certainly had not the physique, nor the opportunity, nor even the strength of character to tie Andrew up and then shoot him and drop him into the river. She was a year older than Catherine, remember, and a heavy cumbersome person who was terrified if she so much as got her feet wet. As to the actual facts, theorising apart, Doctor Lavrock has diagnosed acute conium poisoning, and the remains of the dose which Julia took are probably in that cup. You can see for yourselves that there is a sediment there."

She indicated the large blue tea-cup with a small bony hand.

"Doctor Lavrock wanted to take it away with him," she said, "but I told him quite firmly that he could leave it safely in my care, and I would hand it over to the police immediately they arrived, which should be at any moment."

The grim smile which flickered across her lips testified to a battle won. They did not attempt to speak, and she went on, still speaking quietly and in the same impersonal tone.

"My enquiries," she continued, "some of which you heard, have revealed one reasonable explanation and one rather curious fact, which may or may not be interesting. Catherine has confessed, however theatrically, to the making of early morning tea every morning for the last two years, a cup of which it was her habit to carry in to Julia, who has the next room to hers. Alice, the housemaid, it appears, knew of this custom. I was talking to her upstairs before I came down to find poor William making that disgraceful scene. Alice, it seems, used to collect the cups from under the two beds, wash them in the bathroom, and return them to the little cupboard where Catherine kept her paraphernalia."

There was a distinct touch of contempt in the old lady's voice on the last few words and she answered a criticism which she felt might be passing through their minds.

"Tea-drinking in the early morning has always appeared to me as an indulgence for which there is nothing but spinelessness as an excuse," she said. "I have never had it served in my house and I never shall." Having made herself quite clear upon this point, Aunt Caroline returned to the more important matter on hand. "The second fact I have discovered is strange," she said. "Alice, a most reliable and intelligent woman for her class, tells me she has noticed a sediment in Julia's cup every morning for the past six months. Therefore, until the dregs in this cup on my desk are properly analysed by the police, there must remain some element of doubt as to whether Julia was poisoned in her early morning tea or not. Also I must assure you that Julia was not in the habit of taking drugs. That is the sort of secret which no one could keep in a household like this. Well," she paused, and her quick black eyes rested on Mr. Campion's face, "may I expect you this evening? We dine at eight."

Campion rose to his feet. "I shall be delighted to do all I can, Mrs. Faraday," he said earnestly. "But if I am not to be a source of embarrassment to you I must know at least of the existence of the pitfalls into which I may stumble. Besides your immediate household, was there anyone else visiting this house round about the time of Mr. Seeley's disappearance?"

Great-aunt Caroline hesitated and her lips moved ruminatively. Finally she shrugged her shoulders.

"You have heard already of George Faraday," she said. "I was afraid this would have to come out. Yes, he was in this house the night before Andrew disappeared. I also saw him in the town when I drove to church the next morning."

An unusual sternness had come into the old face.

"I do not wish to have his name mentioned in this case if it can be avoided," she said. "I do not think for a moment that he could have had any possible interest in Andrew's death. Certainly he could expect no material benefit from it. The only death which could possibly assist him in any way is my own. Under my will he receives a small annuity, subject to his emigrating to Australia and payable only while he stays there. On the Saturday night before Andrew died he came to borrow money from me and actually obtained ten pounds. That is all I wish to say about him, save that he has no permanent address of which I know."

It was quite clear to both men that any further questioning upon this point could have only one result, and Mr. Campion at least appeared satisfied. His next question, however, was also of a delicate nature.

"Mr. William Faraday . . ." he began, and hesitated.

Once more Great-aunt Caroline came to his rescue. "William drinks a little," she said, "and so did Andrew." She spoke quite calmly and they suddenly realised that she had reviewed the situation in all its aspects and was taking them into her confidence as aides and allies, because she felt that in this way only could she muster enough strength to meet the storm which had broken over her.

"Neither of them was aware that I had any knowledge of this," she said. "William, I fancy, is the worse of the two. There is also the possibility"—she lowered her voice and spoke with great deliberation—"that William, who is both physically and mentally incapable of murder, may know something about Andrew's death, although I am certain he was not a party to it. But he was about twenty minutes later for luncheon on the Sunday either than he realised or than he cares to admit, and he has not yet been able to give me a satisfactory explanation for this. I shall look forward to seeing your father when he does arrive, Marcus, and you, Mr. Campion, I shall expect to see at my dinner-table this evening."

This was patently a dismissal, and the young men rose to make their departure. In the corridor outside Marcus shot a sidelong glance at Campion.

"What do you make of it?" he murmured.

A faint smile spread over Mr. Campion's pale face. "I hope I suit," he whispered.

In the hall they caught a glimpse of a tall, gloomy individual being shown into the library by the startled Alice, while two of his minions remained stolidly in the passage. Campion's face lighted up.

"Ah, the Boys in Blue," he said. "And Stanislaus Oates at the head of the inquisition. That's the first piece of luck we've had yet."

7

The Conjuror

Mr. Featherstone, senior, allowed a decent pause to elapse after his son's narrative came to an end and then, arising from his chair, walked slowly across his big private office. When he turned, his extraordinarily handsome face wore an expression of deepest regret. Both Campion and Marcus, the only other occupants of the room, were startled by his quiet observation.

"So it's come," he said. "I wondered when the bad blood in that family was going to show. Forty-seven years have I been in practice and it had to happen at the end of the time. Well, I'll go down and see Mrs. Faraday this afternoon. You say she is taking complete control? An amazing woman—always has been. She is as shrewd and quick as ever she was, but I don't think there's a spark of feeling in her body, unless it's for that little girl of yours, Marcus. It's a disgraceful business—disgraceful."

He paused before one of the long windows and looked down upon Regent Street below. The light falling upon his face revealed still more clearly his peculiar nobility of countenance. Mr. Featherstone senior's good looks, a secret vanity of his, were largely responsible for his many years of successful practice, and now, at the age of seventy, he loomed a tall and prophetic-looking personage. His white hair and beard were true silver. His eyes were grey like his sons, inclined to coldness, and he missed a good deal of what passed before him by steadfastly refusing to wear spectacles. He turned suddenly upon the two young men.

"You don't remember old Faraday, of course," he said. "He would be—let me see now—a hundred odd if he were still alive. He was the eldest of a large family, and the only one of them who was any good at all. The others ran right off the rails. John was a learned man. All the goodness in him seemed to run to that. Quite the opposite of his wife. She has intelligence, a different matter—never confuse the two." He paused and went on slowly: "I don't think she actually disliked him. She had a very great respect for him and made a fetish of his importance in a way. Even nowadays when I go there I'm always afraid I shall sit down by mistake in that yellow chair in the library."

Campion looked up enquiringly and Marcus explained.

"I ought to have warned you," he said. "In the library at Socrates Close there's a big yellow brocade-covered chair. Avoid it like the plague. It was old Faraday's own chair, you see, and as far as I know no one has ever sat in it since he died, certainly not in Mrs. Faraday's presence. Of course it's a pitfall for the unwary. It ought to be labelled. But, fortunately, they don't use that room except on state occasions."

"I will make a note of the yellow peril," said Mr. Campion.

Old Mr. Featherstone turned to look dubiously at the young man who had just spoken.

"You, Campion," he said. "I don't know what good Mrs. Faraday thinks you are going to be to her. I don't know what you think you're going to do. In my experience, and in everyone else's for that matter, the only way of making an appalling affair like this even bearable is to deal with it in a routine manner. No amateur jiggery-pokery ever has done anybody any good."

Mr. Campion accepted this gratuitous insult as if it had been a compliment of the highest order. He smiled affably.

"I'm to be a buffer. Not an old buffer, you know, but a kind of pad—a mechanical apparatus for deadening the force of a concussion, as in railway carriages. In other words, a sort of private secretary, I suppose."

Old Featherstone turned a cold and near-sighted eye in his direction.

"Don't behave as though you came from Oxford, my boy," he said. "Both the 'Varsities engender fools, but thank heaven we endeavour to breed our own special type."

Marcus glanced apprehensively at Campion. "I'm afraid my father is forgetting your reputation," he murmured apologetically.

But Featherstone, senior, had no use for any reputation that was under fifty years old.

"I warn everybody," he said testily, "this affair is pitch. And in my experience, if you touch pitch you get your hands dirty. I am only concerned in that affair at Socrates Close in an official capacity. There are times when the best of us must be selfish. Marcus, you're in it even more deeply. I suppose you can't get Joyce away? She's not exactly a relative, you know."

For the first time since Campion had known him a gleam of genuine anger came into Marcus's eyes.

"Joyce will do what she thinks and I shall abide by her decision," he said uncompromisingly.

The old man shrugged his shoulders. "There's no fool like a young one," he observed, "whatever they say."

Mr. Campion, who was becoming used to family friction by this time, was prepared for further skirmishes, but the proceedings were cut short by the entrance of an elderly clerk with the announcement that the car was waiting. A short period of bustle followed, while the old man was safely arrayed in his coat and hat and a largish woollen muffler and escorted safely downstairs into his chariot. Marcus came up the stairs looking relieved.

"Look here, Campion," he said, "d'you mind coming into my room? It's more comfortable than this one. Father will be gone for hours. By the way, when do you think this policeman is liable to turn up?"

"Quite soon now," said Mr. Campion, getting up and

walking across the passage with his friend. "He should have got the note I left almost immediately, and when he's finished his preliminary investigations he'll come toddling over here, if I know him. You'll like him. He's one of the best. I've known him for years. By the way, do you put all those famous names on the boxes in there to impress the unwary visitor?"

Marcus did not smile. "That's the only advertising they let us do," he said. "Here we are."

The room they entered was the smallest of the three which composed the offices of Featherstone & Featherstone. The house, a converted Georgian residence, was owned by the firm, and the other businesses in the building were of an order and propriety to make them suitable neighbours to such an eminently reputable concern.

It was a square comfortable room, light and airy, lined with panelled bookcases of polished mahogany and furnished with the same appropriate wood. Marcus sat down at his desk and Campion took up a position in the leather armchair before the fire.

"We shan't be disturbed in here," Marcus promised. "Important visitors are taken into the old boy's office. It's more impressive. Joyce and Ann are meeting here at about half-past four. I said I'd give them a cup of tea." He passed his hand nervously over his hair. "This business has upset everything," he said. "It makes you see life from an entirely different angle somehow, doesn't it?"

"Life in the newspaper sense," observed Mr. Campion, "is always seen from this point of view. Uncle William must be regarding himself as 'to-day's human story' by this time."

"Muckrakers!" said Marcus savagely. "I always read the murder cases myself, but when it comes to seeing people you know in print, it's rather different."

Campion nodded absently. "I'd like to know just how that woman came to poison herself," he said slowly.

The other man stared at him. "You think it was suicide?" he said. "I thought——?"

Campion shook his head. "Oh, no," he said. "That's the last thing I should say, on the face of it. But it's evident that Miss Faraday took quite passively a large dose of poison, and this could hardly have been done by mistake in the ordinary sense of the word. The sort of poisons that are kept in large quantities in a household are always of the corrosive kind—spirits of salt,

ammonia, carbolic—things quite definitely 'not to be taken.'
Besides, I've never heard of a suicide in which the door of the
room was not locked. People like to be alone when they kill
themselves. It's a purely personal affair, anyway."

"Quite," said Marcus, and was silent.

It was during this pause in the proceedings that the elderly
clerk appeared, to announce that a Mr. Oates was enquiring for
a Mr. Campion.

The two young men sprang to their feet as the Inspector came
in. That lank, slightly melancholy figure looked even more
dejected than usual as he hesitated just inside the door. Campion
grinned at him.

"Come for the body?"

The Inspector's slow childlike smile, which altered his entire
personality, dispelled the discomfort of what might otherwise
have been a solemn introduction.

"I got your note, Campion," he said. "I'm glad to see you,
Mr. Featherstone." He took off his raincoat and sat down in the
chair Marcus indicated, leaning back gratefully. As he looked at
Campion his smile broadened. "And I'm glad to see you, too, all
things considered," he said affably. "I suppose you're on the
right side of the law?"

"I'm not murdering this week, if that's what you suggest,"
said Mr. Campion with dignity.

Marcus looked a little shocked by this conversation, and the
Inspector made haste to explain. "I'm always running into this
man in business," he said, "and his position is generally so
delicate that I never know whether I dare admit to his acquaintance or not." He turned to Campion. "I hear from Mrs.
Faraday," he said, "that you are her personal representative,
whatever that may mean. Is this true?"

Campion nodded. The Inspector paused, and Marcus, realising that whatever the Inspector had to say he had no intention of
saying it before him, tactfully withdrew to his father's office. As
the door closed behind him Stanislaus Oates heaved a sigh of
relief and took out his pipe.

"This being the old lady's representative," he began cautiously, "does that mean you have some secrets to keep?"

"No," said Mr. Campion. "Apparently I am all out to
'apprehend the perpetrator of this dastardly outrage and bring
him to the punishment he so justly deserves.'"

The Inspector grunted. "On the level?" he demanded.

"Sure. You're O.K. by me, as they say in the States," said Mr. Campion idiotically. "What do you make of it? Dogged anything up yet?"

The Inspector rubbed his chin unhappily. "Damn all," he said. "I knew my luck was going to be out. I've been expecting trouble for days. Then there's that coincidence, me knocking into you with this girl Joyce Blount yesterday. A genuine coincidence always means bad luck for me; it's my only superstition."

Campion sat back in his chair, eyeing his friend owlishly. Now, he felt, was hardly the time to acquaint the Inspector with the even more important side of the coincidence in question. Stanislaus Oates went on grumbling.

"Just because I speak twelve different varieties of Yiddish and can carry on a conversation with a tight Swedish sailor, all of which are invaluable in the East End, I get promoted and promptly sent down on a case like this," he began. "I tell you, Campion, I can handle an East Lane harridan with Czech and Chinese blood in her veins, but that Mrs. Faraday is beyond me, you know. She speaks another new language I've got to learn. I didn't do so badly at first. In fact, when she came into that great library I thought I was going to like her. But as soon as we sat down and got started she froze solid——"

"And you sat there in a yellow brocade chair, looking uncomfortable, no doubt," said Mr. Campion.

"Yes," admitted the Inspector absently, and sat up a moment later, his eyes narrowing. "Here! No monkey tricks, Campion," he said. "How d'you know it was a yellow brocade chair? It looked imposing. That's why I chose it."

"Big policeman makes fatal error," said Mr. Campion, laughing, and went on to explain.

"Well, I'm hanged," said the Inspector ruefully. "But who's to know a thing like that? It's as bad as a caste system. Oh well, that accounts for that. How about you? Have you got any line on this yet? This death this morning, you know, that's murder whatever this doctor fellow says. Natural inference points to the other sister, the little snivelling one, Catherine Berry. That doesn't look as though it's going to lead us anywhere." He paused and shook his head like a puzzled dog. "As for the other case," he continued, "it's only reasonable to look toward the household for a motive. There's William, the pompous pink-faced party, there's the old lady herself, there's Joyce Blount.

Does any of these look to you like a murderer? Or any of the servants, for that matter? The whole thing doesn't make sense. I ask you, who's going to tie a man up and then shoot him, or shoot a man and then tie him up? It's ridiculous. I had a look round this morning and took the ordinary depositions. There are one or two interesting things in the house, but not much in the people." He frowned, and as Campion did not speak went on. "I think I see how that thing this morning was done, but I won't commit myself until I have proof. Well, this is the first time you and I have been on a case together, Campion, since nineteen twenty-six. I don't mind telling you I'm glad to see you."

"Nicely said," said Mr. Campion. "What is at the back of your mind? What are you hoping I'll say?"

The Inspector took out a notebook. "My shorthand man took down the verbatim statement," he said, "but this is just my own personal stuff."

"Filled with comic faces, mostly, I see," said Mr. Campion, glancing over his shoulder.

Stanislaus grunted. "About this cousin," he said. "Cousin George Makepeace Faraday. I heard about him from William. He was in the vicinity when the first chap died."

Mr. Campion resumed his chair and leant back. He knew from experience that it was no use trying to suppress anything of which Stanislaus had got wind.

"I say," he said, "I have no actual proof of this, so I suppose it isn't much good to the trained mind, but do you remember that fellow who tackled you yesterday, the fellow who bunked when he saw Miss Blount? I think that was Cousin George. Didn't you notice how extraordinarily like William he was?"

The policeman looked at him incredulously. "That would just make it impossible," he said. "It'd strengthen that coincidence, too, and that always means trouble. We can verify it, though. There's always the girl. What's she hiding, anyway? I say, you don't think that she . . . ?"

"My dear man, why should she? She stands to get most of the money in any case," said Mr. Campion hastily. "No, there's nothing in that. We're getting on too fast. There's the scandal connected with this Cousin George, remember, and a scandal in this crowd is very important, let me tell you. It may be something that would strike the ordinary man as comparatively slight. Cousin George may have had rickets as a child, or T.B., or been divorced. You're looking him up, I suppose?"

"Bowditch is on the job now. He's the bright specimen they've given me to keep me company." The Inspector stirred restlessly in his chair. "Oh, I know this is going to be a stalemate of a case and these are just the sort of people who have influence."

"And that means the workhouse," said Mr. Campion. "The girl-wife in the gutter and my godson having to forego his university career. Sounds like a film."

At the mention of his son the Inspector's good temper miraculously returned.

"Four years old," he said proudly. "Sings like anything." His smile faded and he returned gloomily to the matter in hand. "They're a rum lot up there, Campion," he said. "Something very queer in that house. We're up against a lunatic, of course, one of those 'sane' lunatics you can't spot. I had one down in Stepney last year. Philanthropic doctor chap. It took me six weeks to spot him, and we should never have fixed it on him if he hadn't gone right off his head and come across with the whole story under a little pressure. But the thing I don't like about this case down here is what I call the conjuring trick element." He was leaning forward in his chair, his heavy lids drawn down over his grey eyes, and Mr. Campion, who knew him and liked him, listened attentively. "When you see a conjuring trick performed," the Inspector continued, "a genuine conjuring trick— you know the sort of thing I mean, a fellow cutting a woman in two upon the stage or fastening a nigger in a basket and driving swords through the wickerwork—you are being offered circumstantial evidence of murder of the most damning kind, and yet no one is surprised when the lady walks on to the stage or the nigger climbs out of the basket. Now," he went on triumphantly, "the circumstantial evidence in this case is rather like that, only we know that the unfortunate man Seeley won't come trotting home from the river, nor will Miss Julia Faraday drive up to this office this afternoon. Mrs. Catherine Berry carried a cup of tea to her sister this morning. That sister promptly died from the homely conium poison, traces of which I have no doubt will be found in the cup. William Faraday went for a walk with his cousin Andrew Seeley; Andrew Seeley never came back. That's quite strong circumstantial evidence; not conclusive, but definitely strong. They quarrelled, too, of course. Now, neither Mrs. Berry nor the man William appeals to me as a probable murderer, but then only about four per cent of murderers hanged are of the killer type. Cousin George looked more probable, although I don't see how he could have done it."

He sighed and regarded Campion thoughtfully.

"You know," he said, "where I'm out of my depth again is that I don't see how these people's minds work. Frankly, we're not used to this sort of witness in a case. How many murders do we get in this class in England in a year? It's navvies, whizz-boys, car thieves, small tradespeople who run off the rails and commit murder, and I can talk to them. These people are more difficult. I don't see how their minds work. Even the words they use don't mean the same. For instance, half that old lady said to-day when I was sitting in her yellow chair didn't convey anything to me, yet she's no fool, I can tell that. D'you know who she reminds me of, Campion? Ever seen Justice Adams on the bench? Why, she might be him, especially with that lace thing over her head."

Campion grinned, and the Inspector took a carefully folded piece of paper out of his wallet and handed it to Campion.

"Here is something you can give me a line on, perhaps," he said. "What does this mean to you? I found it in Andrew Seeley's room, folded in the blotter in the top drawer of the writing-desk. Miss Blount told me she put it there when Seeley failed to return home on the Sunday night. Is there anything in it that I may have missed, or does it mean exactly what it says it means?"

Campion unfolded the paper. It was a half-finished letter written in a small tight hand that yet had in it a great many unnecessary flourishes. The address, "Socrates Close," was emblazoned at the top of the sheet in old English print. It was dated Sunday, 30th March, and ran:

My dear dear Nettie,

It is so long since I have heard from you that I feel almost ashamed to intrude myself upon you now. Life here is very difficult. I fancy we all get a little more trying as we grow older. Aunt's vigour is extraordinary; you would see very little difference in her.

W. rather alarms me. His health, for I suppose we must call it that in all kindness, is getting worse. I am afraid to irritate him. No one is so annoying as the man we do not quite see round.

When I think of you in your beautiful garden, with Fred

smoking his pipe on the terrace, I can hardly restrain the
impulse to pack my things and run down to see you both
for a week-end.

Now I must be off to church to hear the Reverend P.
rasping through the lesson—Genesis 4, Joseph and his
Brethren—very appropriate, if you remember. I shall
finish this when I return. It is not my week to drive with
aunt, thank heaven.

Au revoir.

Campion refolded the letter and handed it back to the
Inspector, who did not replace it in his wallet, but sat looking at
it, his forehead puckered.

"Well, it isn't the letter of a suicide," he said, "is it? And it
isn't the letter of a man who thought he might be murdered. Do
you see anything else in it?"

"In what way?" enquired Mr. Campion cautiously. "You are
not referring to 'your character from your handwriting,' by any
chance? As far as the actual matter contained is concerned, it
looks as though he was trying to cadge a free week-end. From
the handwriting I should say that he was in a hurry, had an
excitable nature, was conceited, secretive, energetic and probably a drinker. For further information, read my little pink book
entitled 'Character from Characters, or How to tell your Lover
by his Note.' But I don't suppose that really helps you?"

The Inspector answered absently. He was still staring at the
half-finished letter in his hand.

"It's not evidence," he said, "if that's what you mean. That
chap Seeley must have been a funny bloke. No one seems to
have been able to stand the sight of him. You have a look at his
room, too, if you get the chance. I don't mind you going in. I'm
not an imaginative man, but I didn't cotton to the personality of
that room. I wasn't attracted to Miss Julia's either. But his was
more extraordinary. There's a rum taste about that house
altogether. Oh, by the way, there's one other funny thing about
this letter. No one seems to know who it was written to." He
shook his head. "Extraordinary family. They don't seem to know
anything about each other."

"Did you ask Mrs. Faraday?" Campion enquired.

Stanislaus Oates nodded. "I asked her first, because she's
mentioned in the letter, but she couldn't or wouldn't help me. As
a matter of fact she said she had lived for eighty-four years and

had met a great many ladies in her time and could hardly be expected to remember all their Christian names. A remark like that shuts you up, you know. Still," he added, slipping the letter back into his wallet, "we've only just begun. The inquest on Seeley is fixed for to-morrow. That only means formal evidence of identification. We shall ask for an adjournment. That'll give us a day or two anyway. I understand the authorities want to get the whole business over quickly, because the 'Varsity is coming up the week after next. Funny people they are here! Deputy Coroner in charge and the coroner's court being distempered, so we've got to hold the inquest in an assembly room. I don't see why they can't have their schools or colleges or whatever they are somewhere out in the country."

Campion began to laugh, and Stanislaus joined him. "We all get fed up now and again," he said. "I wish I could find out how that conium got into the teacup this morning. I've gone over the room as well as I could, but they were taking the body away for the P.M. and that doctor and the sorrowing relations had tramped all over the room anyhow. They didn't like me, but I'm never a popular figure in the picture. However, as I say, I did my best and I couldn't find anything. There wasn't even a scrap of paper lying around. Of course, I may find something yet," he went on hopefully. "It's one of those cluttered-up rooms—even the bed wears petticoats. Still, at the moment it certainly looks as though the poison was brought into the room in the teacup, in which case it passes my understanding." He rose to his feet. "I'll have to go. Oh, by the way, that Cousin George. I asked for a photograph of him up at the house, but they hadn't got one. I must see that girl."

"She's probably here now," Campion remarked. "We're expecting her, and I think I heard the sound of feminine chattage outside some minutes ago. Wait a moment." He rose from his chair and disappeared through the doorway, to return some little time later with Joyce. She was still pale, but more self-possessed than she had been in the morning. She greeted the Inspector with a frigid nod, an expression of candid dislike in her quiet eyes. The Inspector plunged in manfully.

"Miss Blount," he said, "I first had the pleasure of meeting you yesterday in Tomb Yard, E.C. While we were there a man entered, caught sight of you, and left hastily. You were a little taken aback by the sight of him. Do you recall the incident?"

Joyce glanced at Campion, but that young man's expression

was blank and unhelpful. The Inspector was still waiting, and she nodded.

"Yes, I do," she said.

Stanislaus Oates cleared his throat. "Now, Miss Blount," he said, "think carefully, was or was not that man George Makepeace Faraday, referred to at Socrates Close as Cousin George?"

Joyce bit off the little exclamation which had risen to her lips. She turned appealingly to Campion.

"Must I answer him?" she said.

He smiled at her affably. "I'm afraid you must," he said, and added as the quick colour came into her face, "Mrs. Faraday is convinced that the police must know all they want to know. Was it Cousin George in the City yesterday? I'm afraid I'm to blame for the idea. He was so extraordinarily like William that I couldn't help pretending to be a real detective last night when I was showing off before Marcus. I described him and Uncle William recognised him. We want you to give us proof."

The girl turned to the Inspector. "Yes," she said breathlessly. "It was Cousin George. But you mustn't look for him, you mustn't find him. It would kill Aunt Caroline. Besides, I'm sure he's got nothing to do with it. Work it out yourselves, how can he?"

8

The Observations of Mr. Cheetoo

Even the ineffable "sacred rite" atmosphere which distinguishes any afternoon tea in Cambridge failed to make the little gathering any but a gloomy and dispirited affair on this occasion. After the Inspector's departure the company had assembled in Marcus's office and tea was brewed and sipped in silence. Two murders in the family have a sobering effect upon the most light-hearted, and even the irrepressible Miss Held was thoughtful and subdued. However, it was she who introduced the subject of Mr. Cheetoo.

"Mr. Campion," she said, "I don't want to put up any idea that isn't useful, and if I'm making a monkey of myself you mention it. But concerning that Indian student who discovered the body; he has told his story to the police, of course, but it occurred to me that if you would like to hear it yourself in an unofficial capacity I could fix that up for you almost right away."

Mr. Campion regarded her with interest. As she sat on the edge of her chair, a cream bun in her hand, she reminded him irresistibly of a little red squirrel holding a nut.

"I should like it immensely," he said. "By the way, I thought there were two of them."

"That is so," she agreed. "But one went for the police and the other remained with the body. It was in the paper this morning, as a matter of fact. That's the way I know about it. I noticed the name Cheetoo particularly, because during the vac. I've taken over the pups of a friend of mine, a Britisher taking the same subject as myself. I've got two years' research work, you know, that's why I'm here."

Campion nodded with comparative intelligence, and she went on.

"Well, just before I came in here this afternoon I looked up in my notebook to see how long I had free and I discovered that Mr. Cheetoo has an appointment for half-past five. Now you've never heard a man talk so much in all your life as this boy. He's so full of himself he can't keep his mind on his work for a split second, and I'm morally certain I shall have a verbatim account of that discovery of his, so if you care to come along and hear it I shall be delighted."

Marcus glanced across the room questioningly. "That would be an idea, Campion," he said. "Look here, Joyce and I will wait for you at Soul's Court. Then you can collect your things and I'll drive you both down to Socrates Close."

Thus it came about that Mr. Campion found himself walking across Parker's Piece with Miss Ann Held, in search of the man who found the body. Ann had rooms in a house in Cheshire Street, the home of two elderly schoolmistresses, and as they entered the large square hall the cold academic atmosphere rose up to meet them.

"Notice the odour of emancipation," murmured Miss Held.

"Come on out of this ice-box." She opened the door facing them on the right of the stairs and Mr. Campion followed her into the most charming feminine study he had ever seen. Here were two framed postcards of Florence, no monochromes of the Winged Victory and the Perseus, nor did a coloured reproduction of Ruskin's study as he left it, nor even the Doge, look down upon him from a severely distempered inglenook. Miss Held had followed her own taste. Modern American etchings, including two Rosenbergs, hung on the walls of an airy yellow-papered room. The furniture was good, sparse, and comfortable. Books lined all one wall, and the drapery was bright without being noisy. A friendly and unusual room in which to find a research student.

It was twenty-five minutes past five when they arrived, and Campion was barely seated before the fire when the maid shared by the scholastic ladies entered to announce the man he had come to meet.

At first sight Mr. Cheetoo was not an attractive person. He seemed to have embraced European culture with a somewhat indiscriminate zeal. The ordinary grey flannel trousers of the undergraduate were surmounted by a tightly-fitting tweed coat of a delicate pea-green, a garment which could have emanated only from Paris. He set his books down upon the table and bowed stiffly to Ann. She introduced Campion and Mr. Cheetoo repeated his formal gesture.

They had no difficulty in persuading him to talk. He was full of his own importance and broached the subject himself before he had been in the room two minutes.

"You have read the papers?" he enquired, looking quickly from one to the other, a gleam of childlike pride in his eyes, which he did not attempt to conceal. "I was the first on the scene. It was I who found the body."

Ann sat down at the table and he took his place opposite her. But it was evident that he had no intention of working, and he appeared delighted when she connived at this arrangement.

"Mr. Campion," she explained, "is a friend of the family of the dead man, and he is very anxious to hear all he can about the shocking affair. I knew you wouldn't mind telling him about your—er—discovery."

Mr. Cheetoo flashed an annihilating grin in Mr. Campion's direction.

"I should be glad," he said. "I am observant. I am also

scientific. I formed many conclusions. The police did not value them. To my mind they were not anxious to make clear."

Mr. Campion nodded affably and his pale eyes flickered behind his big spectacles. This was a type of witness that he recognised, and his heart leapt.

"You were not alone, Mr. Cheetoo," he said, "when you made your discovery?"

"No," the observant student admitted with some regret. "But it was I who remained by the body while my friend went for the police. I am to appear at the inquest tomorrow. But I have been told that my observations will not be of interest to the coroner."

"Too bad," said Miss Held helpfully.

Mr. Cheetoo nodded and turned to Campion. "You will be interested," he said firmly. "You will appreciate my observations. My friend and I were walking along the river bank searching for plants. My friend is a botanical student. As we approached the willow clump immediately beyond the bridge in the meadows I perceived a blackness beneath the water. There was also" —he turned apologetically to Ann—"an odour."

"Quite," said Mr. Campion hastily.

Mr. Cheetoo lived up to his reputation for observation. "I will omit those details which can be assumed," he said. "My friend would not touch the body. But I," he continued with pride, "am occidental. I am broad-minded. I pulled the body half out of the water. At first my friend recoiled; he is not courageous. His imagination is stronger than his observation. He is also more strict." He paused.

Mr. Campion looked at Ann and was relieved to see that she was not unduly apprehensive of the unpleasant details which must certainly be coming. Mr. Cheetoo continued.

"I sent my friend for the police and when he had gone I made my observations. I have the enquiring mind of the investigator. My first observation was that the man was a tramp. That was my error. The beard, I now find, grows after the decease has taken place. It was not a pleasant sight. The top part of the head had been opened and in some places was not in existence any longer. I particularly observed if there were powder burns, having read of same in light fiction. But the action of the water . . ."

Mr. Campion cleared his throat. "I understand the body was tied up," he said.

"I remarked upon that," replied Mr. Cheetoo, unperturbed by the interruption. "The legs were securely bound about the ankles with a length of thin rope. The hands had been tied behind the back, but the cord had rotted and they were now apart. There was a knot of rope, with a ragged edge around the right wrist and another about the left. From this I deduced that the body had been in the water for some time and had been buffeted by the stream. The loose rope had caught around the willow roots and had prevented the body from drifting farther. You must understand that this was not a pleasant sight. The corpse had swollen in the water. The rope was sodden and was already beginning to rot."

Metaphorically, Mr. Campion clung to the rope.

"This cord," he said, "what sort of stuff was it? New, save for the action of the water?"

Mr. Cheetoo considered. It was evident that he liked considering.

"Your question is curious," he said. "It is what I asked myself. I touched the rope. It broke easily. This, I said to myself, has been in use before it was put to this disagreeable purpose. It was of the nature of a clothes line."

Campion glanced apologetically at Ann. "I say," he said, "I wonder if you'd mind if I asked Mr. Cheetoo, purely in the interests of abstract science, of course, if he would be so awfully kind as to demonstrate on me exactly how this tying was done?"

"Why, certainly not." Ann looked startled, but not ruffled.

Mr. Cheetoo, on the other hand, was frankly delighted. He rose instantly in preparation. Ann pulled open a drawer in the table, from which she produced a ball of string.

"I haven't any clothes line," she said, "but I guess you'll be able to do something with this."

Mr. Cheetoo took the string, which he unwound with an air of sacrificial solemnity, which would have been comic in any other circumstances and very nearly succeeded in being so as it was.

"I measured ocularly the amount of rope on the body," he said, eyeing Campion sternly. "There was in my estimation five yards and possibly one-half. The shorter half of the cord was bound about the feet, thus."

He dived for Mr. Campion's legs and had the string round them in an instant.

"There," he said, standing back. "I demonstrated to my friend in exactly the same way afterwards. You will observe the two feet are held together tightly, knot in front. The hands were then fastened thus."

Mr. Campion's hands were pinioned and he stood on Ann Held's hearthrug inconsequential, smiling, and trussed like a chicken. Mr. Cheetoo stood back in triumph.

"Consider the completeness," he said.

Ann Held's bright eyes were dancing. "It's certainly effective," she said.

"Yes," said Mr. Cheetoo swiftly. "But not professional. The knots are ordinary. They were not sailor's knots."

Mr. Campion tried his bonds. "But when the body was found," he said, "the hands had become free."

"That is so," agreed Mr. Cheetoo. He darted behind Mr. Campion and severed the string which held his hands.

"Thus," he said triumphantly. "The cord, already rotten no doubt, gave way under the weight of the dead man's arms. And when I made my discovery he was bound like this." He pointed to Campion's two wrists, one of which wore a single noose held by a slip knot. The left wrist was more securely bound, with three strands wound about it.

Mr. Campion appeared fascinated by this information. "Allow me to congratulate you on your powers, Mr. Cheetoo," he said. "You have the true investigator's gift. Did you notice anything else about the man you found?"

Mr. Cheetoo considered once again. "There was the matter of the coat," he said. "The victim wore a heavy blue overcoat buttoned up to his throat. As if indeed," he added with portentous solemnity, "he had been aware of the storm that was to come upon him and had buttoned himself up against the elements."

Campion paused in the process of untying himself. "His coat was buttoned?" he said. "Are you sure?"

For a moment it seemed that Mr. Cheetoo was about to consider himself mortally offended.

"I am the observer," he said. "I have the eye. I noticed the coat was buttoned up to the neck."

Campion rolled the string neatly into a ball and set it down upon the table before he replied.

"How very odd," he said at last. "And his hat, was that anywhere near? He had a hat when he left church—a bowler, I believe."

"Of the hat," said Mr. Cheetoo firmly, "there was absolutely no sign. I observed in this morning's paper that it had not yet been discovered."

These two small points seemed to interest Mr. Campion more than any of Mr. Cheetoo's foregoing story. He remained standing on the hearthrug staring in front of him, his natural expression intensified.

Mr. Cheetoo was also thoughtful. "From my deductions made upon the spot," he said suddenly, "it occurred to me that this unfortunate did not drift very far down the stream."

Once again Mr. Campion turned to him. "Oh?" he said. "Why?"

"Because," said Mr. Cheetoo, "of the little footbridge. The water is high at this time of year. This little bridge creates an eddy which would have held the body close to it had the unfortunate entered the water at a point above the bridge. You can see for yourself. I was down there this morning making further observations. In my opinion, the body was thrown into the water somewhere between the bridge and the willow clump. There is no sign of a struggle on the bank, but it is probably ten days since the crime was committed and we have had much rain. There is also, nearly always at this time of year, a mist over the low ground near the river. This is my complete opinion. You are enlightened?"

"Absolutely," said Mr. Campion. "I could hardly have seen more had I discovered the body myself."

"Exactly," said Mr. Cheetoo, and Campion, feeling that he had interrupted the higher education of his informant long enough, expressed his thanks all round and gracefully made his departure.

Ann saw him to the door. "Well, I hope you're in a complete blaze of understanding," she murmured.

Campion grinned. "All seems to have been discovered," he said. "He ought to enjoy himself at the inquest. It certainly is an ill wind . . ."

But as he walked across the Piece a dozen disturbing thoughts wrestled in his mind. There were Uncle William's twenty-five unaccounted-for minutes to consider. Was it just possible that the old man had not parted with Andrew Seeley, but that he had accompanied him as far as the river and under cover of a ground mist had tied him up, shot him, hurled him into the stream and doubled back to Sunday luncheon? Immediately the circumstances which must have conspired to make such a procedure possible presented themselves to the young man in all their array of absurdity. If this supposition were correct, Uncle William must have sat for one hour and a half in church with fifteen feet of clothes line concealed upon him, to say nothing of a revolver. And before tying up the unfortunate Andrew, Uncle William had presumably buttoned up his victim's overcoat and purloined his hat.

Mr. Campion was discomforted. The Inspector's conjuror was distressingly in evidence.

9

Dirty Linen

At nine o'clock that evening Mr. Campion felt that beside the classical ordeals by fire and by water there should now be numbered the ordeal by dinner at Socrates Close. He could quite understand that no ordinary catastrophe could prevent its solemn ritual taking place, but he realised that its awe-inspiring progress was not lightened by the tragedy hanging over the house.

It was a devastating meal.

The dining-room was a large square apartment with crimson damask wallpaper and red plush curtains. Dark paint and a Turkey carpet did not tend to brighten the scheme of decoration, and, as Joyce remarked later, one felt overfed upon entering the room.

The large oval table was a veritable skating rink of Irish damask, and upon it there was set out every night a magnificent array of plate, the cleaning of which occupied the entire life of an unfortunate small boy in the servants' quarters. It was here that for the first and last time in his life Mr. Campion made the acquaintance of those silver-plated cornucopias which, in Victorian times, were supplied to the diner filled with hot water, so that he might warm his spoon before partaking of that greasy delicacy called thick soup.

On this particular occasion the great room seemed very empty and Campion realised that the two spaces at the table were made all the more conspicuous by the fact that the others had not altered what had evidently been their usual places for many years. Thus, Great-aunt Faraday sat at the head of the table in a high-backed arm-chair. Her black taffeta gown was cut with elbow sleeves, although her tiny forearms were covered by the frill of cream Honiton, which matched her fichu and the cap she wore.

William sat at the foot of the table, some considerable distance away from his mother and separated from her by an immense baroque silver fruit stand, which miraculously changed into a flower vase at its upper extremity.

Aunt Kitty sat next to William on his right, while Joyce was immediately upon Great-aunt Caroline's left. Mr. Campion himself had the place of honour upon his hostess's right, and the rest of the table was distressingly and pointedly empty.

Aunt Kitty's black evening gown, cut square and unfashionably low in the manner of 1909 or so, presented an appearance that was positively funereal, and even Joyce in her simple black dinner frock, emphasised the solemnity of the occasion.

Mr. Campion began to regard his own dinner-jacket as a garment of sorrow and William's bright pink face as a touch of unwarrantable levity in the sombre colour scheme.

The long meal, Mrs. Beeton's complete Friday menu for April in non-Roman Catholic households, was depressing rather than fortifying, and Great-aunt Caroline's hard and fast rules of general conversation almost defeated Mr. Campion's effervescent spirit. In the long silences he had plenty of time for observation.

There were several minor peculiarities in the setting of this unnerving ceremony, one of which was the fact that each diner had his own complete set of condiments, a circumstance which somehow increased the aloofness of the participants.

Another oddity was of a more cheerful variety.

Directly facing Mr. Campion, hung unsuitably beneath a large steel engraving of Ely Cathedral, was a red plush frame, in which reposed a coloured enlargement of a photograph of a bewhiskered gentleman in the regalia of some obscure and patently plebian order or society. Mr. Campion noticed with delight that this gentleman's hand rested upon a large pewter mug from the top of which there emerged much painted foam. It was not at all the trophy which one would have associated with Great-aunt Caroline or her household, and he wondered how it had come here.

When at last the meal came to an end the company trooped into the great drawing-room, the famous drawing-room of Socrates Close of the 'eighties. Although its styles of decoration had not been altered since that time it was still a beautiful room. Faded brocades and fussy ornaments abounded. The furniture was hard, misshapen and uncomfortable. But like everything that is perfectly in period, it had a charm of its own.

Aunt Caroline sat down beside an occasional table and turned to Aunt Kitty.

"I think we will play chess as usual, my dear," she said.

Aunt Kitty sat down obediently while William advanced solemnly towards a bureau whose panels displayed two bouquets painted, Mr. Campion felt, rather by a botanist than a garden lover. From this cupboard William produced a chess board and a box of carved ivory men.

Mr. Campion realised that he was looking upon a nightly ritual, and waited, not without apprehension, to see where he himself fitted into this ceremony.

Uncle William was showing signs of anxiety. He did not sit down, but stood watching his mother as her tiny white fingers set the red chessmen into line. At last he spoke.

"I thought Campion and I might smoke a cigar in the library, mother?" he said enquiringly.

Great-aunt Faraday raised her little black eyes to her son's face.

"Certainly, William," she said. "Mr. Campion, if I should have retired by the time you return, the rising gong rings at a quarter to eight. Have you everything in your room that you require?"

Mr. Campion, who had risen to his feet the moment that she addressed him, bowed instinctively.

"Everything is most charming," he said.

Mrs. Faraday seemed to consider that he had made the right reply, for she smiled at him and nodded to William, who, grateful at the release, which seemed to be unexpected, hustled Campion out of the room.

"The morning room's more comfortable," he said in a rumbling whisper. "Library always reminds me of the governor, God bless him. Never saw him at his best in the library."

They crossed the hall, therefore, and entered the morning room, in which a bright fire still burned.

"Sorry I can't offer you a drink," said Uncle William, blowing a little in his embarrassment. "The key of the tantalus has been removed again, I see. When people get old, you know, they get ideas in their heads. I'm no drinker myself, but—well, anyway, have a cigar."

He produced a box from the sideboard, and when the little ceremony of lighting up had been completed he sat down again in one of the green leather arm-chairs and looked across at Campion with hunted little blue eyes, incongruous in such a large pink face.

"Andrew used to sit in that chair you've got," he remarked suddenly. "I suppose the funeral will take place on Monday? Not a lot of flowers about at this time of year." He checked his meandering wits sharply and took refuge in a suitable sentiment. "Poor Andrew," he said, and coughed.

Mr. Campion remained silent, looking more vague than ever in a blue haze of cigar smoke. Uncle William's thoughts were racing to-night, however, leading him a fantastic dance from one subject to another, and presently he spoke again.

"Damn bad-tempered, evil-minded fellow, all the same," he said angrily. "No insanity in the family, thank God, or might have suspected a touch of lunacy—kindest thought." He paused and added with a grotesque droop of a baggy eyelid, "Drank like a sponge, under the rose."

There was no cosiness in the breakfast-room. The lights were not shaded, but sprouted unadorned from a brass water-lily floating upside-down in the white expanse of ceiling, and their cold blaze presented an atmosphere of hygienic chill which even the bright fire could not dispel.

Mr. Campion began to understand Marcus's remark of the previous evening: "If I lived in that house I might easily feel like murder myself." That atmosphere of restraint which is so racking in adolescence was here applied to age, and Campion experienced a fear of stumbling upon some weak spot where, beneath the rigid bond of repression, human nature had begun to ferment, to decay, to become vile. There was no telling what manner of secret lay hidden in the great house rising up over his head, yet he was acutely conscious of its existence.

He was brought down to earth again by the entrance of the stalwart Alice, who bore a silver tray with glasses and a decanter and syphon. She set it down on the table without a word, and he noticed that she did not glance at either of them, but hurried out again as noiselessly as she had entered. Then he caught sight of the other man's face and humour was restored.

Uncle William evidently regarded the intrusion as some sort of apparition. His astonishment was only equalled by his delight, and he rose to do the honours with an almost childlike satisfaction.

"The old lady doesn't forget when we've got guests in the house, thank the Lord," he said, sitting down again with his glass. "Hang it all! when a fellow's gone through what we've gone through to-day he needs a drink. I'm going out for a walk in a moment. You'll be all right, I suppose?"

He looked at Campion hopefully, and appeared relieved at the other's hearty reassurance. He swallowed a large whisky and soda and was about to make some final remark when Joyce reappeared.

"Hullo," she said in surprise, "going out?"

Uncle William coughed. "Thought I'd just have a constitutional," he said. "Haven't had any exercise to-day. That damned policeman kept me in all this morning chatting."

Joyce looked astounded, but she said nothing, and when the old man went out she took his seat, and Campion noticed that she held a cigarette-case. He took out his own hastily.

"I say, is this allowed?" he said, as he gave her a light. "Permit me to cure you of the tobacco habit in five days. Taken in curry, no one can tell my secret preparation from garlic."

Joyce laughed politely. "This is an indulgence," she said. "I'm allowed to smoke occasionally by a special dispensation. Authority winks its eye. As a matter of fact, it's rather sweet. Every evening after dinner Great-aunt Caroline tells me I may go upstairs to write my letters. I didn't understand it at first, but she told me that she had heard that young people nowadays enjoyed a suitably scented cigarette. It's quite respectable, you see. Even the Queen smokes sometimes, they say. But she thought I ought to have my cigarette in private, so as not to set a bad example to the aunts." She paused and shot a quick level glance at him. "It's rather beastly, isn't it?" she said.

"It's queer," he said guardedly. "I suppose this is the last household in England of its kind?"

The girl shuddered. "I hope so," she said. "Dinner was

pretty dreadful, wasn't it? It's like that every night, only usually, of course, the—the others are there, too."

"I enjoyed my dinner," said Mr. Campion valiantly. "But my etiquette book rather let me down. It says that light conversation may be effectively introduced while passing the cruet. In this, of course, I was frustrated, as we all had our own cruets. Otherwise, no doubt, I should have been the life and soul of the party."

Joyce reddened. "Yes, those salt cellars are an awful admission of uncharitableness, aren't they?" she said. "They were Andrew's fault. Some time ago, just after I first came, in fact, there was a disgraceful scene one night when Andrew refused to pass Julia the pepper; pretended not to hear her. Finally, when she insisted, he sulked like a child and said she had quite enough in her composition, without adding any more. Julia appealed to Aunt Caroline and there was a sort of nursery row. The next day everybody had their own condiments, and it's been like that ever since. It's one of those silly stupid petty little things that are a constant source of irritation to the flesh."

Mr. Campion was more shocked than he cared to admit by this slightly comic revelation, and he took refuge behind a barrier of cigar smoke. The girl went on holding her cigarette limply in her fingers as she stared into the fire.

"I suppose you noticed that photograph of Uncle Robert, too?"

"Who?" said Mr. Campion, appalled at the possibility of yet another implicated relative.

A faint smile passed over the girl's face. "Oh, you needn't be alarmed," she said. "He's safely dead, poor darling. He was Aunt Kitty's husband. And my mother's brother," she interpolated a little defiantly. "That photograph was taken when he was a young man. It was probably considered funny then. He was president of some early frothblowers' association, or something." She paused and eyed Mr. Campion squarely. "The family always considered that Aunt Kitty married beneath her. She didn't, though, as a matter of fact; not in my opinion, anyhow. Uncle Robert was a doctor with a poor practice. Well, Aunt Kitty kept that photograph and had it enlarged. Uncle Robert was rather proud of it, I believe, and it used to hang in his den. And when he died Aunt Kitty brought it here with her. Nothing would ever have happened about it if Uncle Andrew hadn't found it. He was like that, you know; always poking about into other people's things. He saw it on her dressing-table one day and insisted that it should be hung in the dining-room. He was so clever about it that Aunt Kitty was rather flattered. It was the first time that anyone had ever shown any enthusiasm for Uncle Robert and she was pitifully fond of him, poor darling." She sighed. "Everyone else saw, of course, just what Andrew meant them to see, another evidence of Uncle Robert's vulgarity. Uncle Andrew used to call it 'the mortification' when Aunt Kitty wasn't in earshot."

"And no one took it down?" said Mr. Campion.

"Well, no. You see, Uncle Andrew had made Aunt Kitty rather proud by hanging it there. You can see what a silly old dear she is. She doesn't see half that's going on around her. Great-aunt Caroline never seemed to notice the photograph, but Andrew enjoyed the annoyance it gave to everyone else. I know it's wrong to talk about him like this now he's dead, but you can see the sort of man he was."

"Not a beautiful soul,." murmured Mr. Campion.

"He was a beast," said the girl with unexpected vehemence. "Fortunately the others combined sometimes to keep him quiet. He had a devil, if you know what I mean," she went on, speaking earnestly. "If he had been allowed to have his own way he would have driven everyone off their heads. As it was, he moved even the meekest of us to a sort of frenzy of loathing at times."

She was silent for some moments and her mouth twitched nervously. It was evident that she was making up her mind to a confession of some sort. Suddenly it came.

"I say," she said, "I'm terribly frightened. After all, when a thing like this happens, ordinary family loyalty and restraint and things like that don't count much, do they? I'm afraid one of us here has gone mad. I don't know who it is. It might be a servant, it might be—anybody. But I think they're made in the—well, you know, the modern secret way, and they've killed Andrew because they couldn't stand him any longer."

"Aunt Julia?" enquired Mr. Campion gently.

She lowered her voice. "That's it," she said. "That's what's terrifying me. If it was just Andrew, somehow I don't think I should care awfully, not that I know what's happened to him. But now that Aunt Julia's—been killed, it shows that the thing I've been afraid of all along has started. If a lunatic starts killing he goes on, doesn't he? Don't you see, it may be anyone's turn next?"

Campion glanced at her sharply. This was the second person in the family who had put forward this suggestion.

"Look here," he said, "you'd better go and stay with Ann Held."

She stared at him, and he wondered whether she was going to laugh or be angry and was relieved to see her smile.

"Oh, no," she said. "I'm not afraid for myself. I don't know why it is," she went on calmly, "but I feel that it's all nothing to do with me. This is the older generation's affair; I just don't count. I feel that I'm just looking on at something that is working itself out. Oh, I can't explain!"

Mr. Campion threw the stub of his cigar into the fire. "I say," he said, "I ought to have a look at those two bedrooms to-night. Uncle Andrew's and Aunt Julia's. Do you think you could fix it?"

Joyce glanced at him sharply, a hint of alarm in her eyes. "We could sneak up now," she said. "There's a good hour before great-aunt goes up to bed. Hullo, though, I forgot. The police locked the doors."

The pale young man before her grinned. "If you could find me a hairpin," he said, "I don't think we need let that worry us. Don't be alarmed. I've got permission from my celebrated detective friend, the Arch Hawk-Eye himself."

Joyce looked at him in astonishment. "You don't really mean that, do you?"

"A hairpin or any nice piece of wire would do," said Mr. Campion. "This house is probably full of hairpins. Aunt Kitty's crowbar variety would do nicely. Your own are a bit flimsy, I should think."

Joyce rose to her feet. "Come on then," she said. "I know it sounds silly, but you'd better creep upstairs, because the servants are rather alarmed already. There are one or two plain-clothes men still hanging about the garden, you know, and, anyway, the staff has been put through a minor inquisition this evening."

"Too bad," he sympathised. "That's the worst of the police. You can't keep 'em out of the kitchen. It comes of keeping comic papers in the waiting-room at the Yard, I've no doubt."

The light in the upper hall was subdued. The plan of the rooms on the first floor was much the same as below. Thus,

Great-aunt Caroline's bedroom was directly above the drawing-
room, with Joyce's room beside it over the morning room. There
was a bathroom directly above the Queen Anne sitting-room,
and Kitty and Julia had rooms side by side over the library. In the
other branch of the L, William's room, Andrew's room and the
spare room, which had been allotted to Campion, ran side by
side over the dining-room and kitchen, with the service staircase
beyond. All these rooms gave on to a corridor whose windows
overlooked the drive. The servants' rooms and attics were on the
second floor.

As they reached the upper hall the girl laid her hand on
Campion's arm.

"Wait a minute," she said. "I'll get you the hairpin. Aunt
Kitty won't mind me borrowing one of hers."

Left alone in the softly lighted, thick carpeted hall, with its
dark paint and carved oak furniture, Campion, who was by no
means a nervous man, was seized by a sudden revulsion of
feeling which he could not explain. It was not so much a terror
of the unknown as a sense of oppression brooding over the
house, a suffocated feeling as if he were set down inside a huge
tea-cosy with something unclean.

It was evident that the girl experienced much the same
feeling, for she was very pale and inclined to be jumpy when she
came out to him a moment later, a coarse black hairpin in her
hand.

"Where first?" she whispered.

"Andrew's room," murmured Campion. "Are you coming
with me?"

She hesitated. "Shall I be any use? I don't want to be in the
way."

"You won't be in the way, if you don't mind coming."

"All right."

They moved silently down the corridor and the girl paused
before the centre door of the three which led off it.

"Here we are," she said. "That's your room on the left and
Uncle William's on the right. This is Andrew's."

Mr. Campion took the hairpin and squatted down before the
keyhole.

"This parlour trick of mine must not be taken as representative," he said. "Some people laugh when they see it and some
people kick me out of the house. I don't often do it."

All the time he was talking his fingers were moving rapidly, and suddenly a sharp click rewarded his labours and he stood up and regarded her shamefacedly.

"Don't tell Marcus," he whispered. "He's one who wouldn't laugh."

She smiled at him. "I know," she said. "Who's going in first?"

Mr. Campion opened the door slowly and they crept in, closing it silently behind them. The girl switched on the light and they stood looking about them. The room had the cold, slightly stale atmosphere of a closed bedroom in an old-fashioned house. At first sight Campion was startled. It was so different from what he had expected. Apart from a wall of bookshelves in the midst of which there was a small writing-desk, the room might have belonged to a modern hermit. It was large and inexpressibly bare, with white walls and no carpet, save for a small jute bath-mat set beside the bed. This was of the truckle variety, and it looked hard and thinly covered. A simple wooden stand with a small mirror above it served as a dressing-table and supported some half-dozen photographs. The simplicity and poverty of the room compared with the solid comfort of the rest of the house, was startling to the point of theatricality. A cupboard built into the wall was the only sign of clothes room, and a huge iron damper covered the fireplace.

The girl caught a glimpse of Campion's face. "I know what you're thinking," she said. "You feel like everyone else. Andrew liked to play at being the poor relation. This room is one of his elaborate insults to the rest of the family. Yet he liked comfort quite as much as anybody, and for years, I believe, this room was one of the most luxurious bedrooms in the house. Then, about a year ago, Andrew took it into his head to have it all changed. The carpet had to be taken up, the walls stripped and this stage setting of a prison arranged. D'you know," she went on angrily, "he used to bring visitors up here to show them how badly he was treated. Of course, the rest of the family was livid, but he was cleverer than they are. He used to make it look as though they were forcing him to live uncomfortably, which, of course, was absolute rubbish. He certainly had a most exasperating way."

Campion crossed to the bookcase and peered in. The volumes were standing on shelves on which leather dust frills had been nailed. The titles surprised him. It was quite a large library and appeared to be devoted to the best-known works of a

certain character. Uncle Andrew's taste in literature appeared to
have leant towards classical eroticism, although the more modern psychologists were also well represented. Mr. Campion,
picking up an early treatise on *Sex and the Mind*, found that it
had been the property of a medical library in Edinburgh,
purloined, apparently about thirty years before. He replaced the
book on the shelf and turned back into the room.

As he did so he caught sight of one of the few objets d'art it
contained. This was a relief of the *Laocoön*, evidently an ancient
rendering of the famous group in the Vatican. But the carver had
put something of his own into the work: in place of the noble
unreality of the original, here was an imaginative study in horror
which, in spite of its small size, seemed to dominate the
apartment. Joyce shuddered.

"I hate that thing," she said. "Aunt Kitty used to say it made
her dream, and Andrew wanted to make her hang it in her
room—until she got used to it, he said. He told her a long
rigmarole about conquering fear by willpower, and almost
persuaded her to take the thing. Probably he would have done so
if Julia hadn't sailed in to the rescue and put her foot down. That
was the kind of thing she liked doing. Oh, they're all so petty!
Aunt Caroline's strict, but she's strict in a big way."

Meanwhile Mr. Campion continued to wander round the
room. He peered into the clothes cupboard, opened the desk, and
finally came to a full stop before the dressing-table. An
exclamation escaped him, and he picked up a photograph of a
clerical personage, a white-haired and benevolent figure. It was
inscribed: *"To my old friend Andrew Seeley, in memory of our
holiday in Prague. Wilfred."*

Joyce looked over Campion's shoulder. "He's a bishop," she
said. "Andrew was secretly very proud of knowing him so well,
I think. He used to hint that they had the wildest holiday
together. Why are you staring at it? Do you know him?"

"I did," said Mr. Campion. "He's dead, poor old boy. That's
my sainted uncle, the Bishop of Devizes. He wasn't the sort of
old bird to go gay on a holiday in Prague, although he knew
more about dry-fly fishing than any man alive, I believe. But
that isn't the really extraordinary thing about this photograph.
The odd thing is that this isn't his handwriting. It isn't quite his
signature. In fact, it's a fake."

The girl stared at him round-eyed. "But Andrew said——"

she began, and stopped short, a contemptuous expression spreading over her face. "That's just like Andrew."

Mr. Campion set the photograph down. "I don't think there's much more to be seen here," he said, "and we haven't any too much time. Let's go on, shall we?"

She nodded and they tiptoed out. The relocking ceremony took some minutes, but Julia's door yielded almost immediately.

Seen directly after the late Uncle Andrew's den, Miss Julia Faraday's bedroom was an overbearingly cluttered apartment. It was crammed full of furniture of every possible description, and achieved fussiness without femininity. The two large windows had three sets of curtains each; Nottingham lace gave way to frilled muslin and frilled muslin to yellow damask looped up with great knots of silk cable which looked as though it would have held a liner. The keynote of the whole scheme of decoration was drapery.

The fireplace was surrounded with loops of the same yellow damask, and the bed, the focusing point, the rococo pièce-de-resistance of the whole room, was befrilled and befurbelowed until its original shape was lost altogether.

The bed interested Mr. Campion from the beginning, and he stood looking at it with respectful astonishment.

"They call that an Italian brass bed, for some reason or other," Joyce volunteered. "I think it's because of those wing bits with the curtains on. You see, they move backwards and forwards and keep the draught out. Not that there ever is a draught in this house."

The young man advanced towards the monstrosity and stood with a hand resting on one of the huge brass knobs which surmounted each post. For some moments he stood staring in front of him at the tapestry-hung brass railings beyond the expanse of eiderdown, and he turned and surveyed the rest of the room.

It was evident to a practised eye that a very thorough search had been made already. Glancing at the pantechnicon of a wardrobe with its quadruple doors, he realised that the police must have leapt upon this as a possible source of discovery, and he knew better than anyone that to search after a Yard man is so much waste of time. Yet somewhere in this room there was, he felt sure, some trace of the poison which had killed Aunt Julia. Joyce broke in upon his meditations.

"You never knew her, did you?" she said. "All these are

photographs of her." She pointed to an array of ornamental frames above the mantel-shelf. They were all of them portraits of the same woman in various stages of maturity, beginning with a heavy-featured girl laced uncomfortably into unbecoming garments and progressing gradually into corpulent middle age. The final portrait showed a grey-haired, stern-faced woman, whose lines of bad temper from her nose to her mouth were so deep that even the photographer had been unable to conceal them.

"She'd got much thinner lately," said Joyce. "And I think her temper had got worse, too. She may have been ill. Perhaps—perhaps it was suicide after all."

"Perhaps," agreed Mr. Campion. "That's what we've got to find out before we go outside this room. In fact, at this point a little elementary brain-work is indicated. After all, deduction is only adding two and two together. Look here, how does this sound to you? Aunt Julia was not the sort of person to take her own life. As far as we know she was poisoned by conium, which is one of the oldest, simplest forms known to man, and is simply another name for hemlock. It is also practically tasteless in tea." He paused and regarded the girl steadily. "Now Aunt Julia seems to have been in the habit of putting something in her tea every morning," he said. "We know that, because Alice had noticed a sediment in the bottom of her cup every day for the last six months. Therefore it's quite reasonable to suppose that Aunt Julia put the poison which killed her into her tea this morning under the impression that it was her usual dose of something or other. Now, what we have to find out sooner or later is whether she made a mistake off her own bat or whether someone intended her to make a mistake."

Joyce nodded. "I see," she said.

"Personally," said Mr. Campion, taking off his glasses, "I don't see how it could have been a genuine mistake if the poison was conium. It's simple enough to get hold of, but it's got to be prepared. However, the first step is to find out what it was that Aunt Julia put in her tea every morning. Some sort of patent medicine, obviously. That's Inspector Oates's idea, I believe. But what it was and where it is is still a mystery. You see, there's no trace of it. Neither Aunt Kitty nor Alice had ever heard of her taking anything regularly. Had you?"

Joyce shook her head. "No. As a matter of fact, great-aunt does the dispensing for the whole family. There's a medicine chest in her room, and the only other thing is a first-aid box in the upper hall. What sort of patent medicine were you thinking of?"

Campion considered. "Well, some sort of health salts, I suppose. You know—'Take as much as you dare and leap over the next gate grinning dangerously'—vide press. The only thing against that theory is that there aren't any health salts about, no empty tins or packets or anything. The Inspector has been over this room, and that means that there is no place large enough to contain a tin, say as large as a fifty Gold Flake, that has not been explored. They'll probably start on the rest of the house to-morrow if we don't spot it to-night."

The girl looked round helplessly. "It seems such a hopeless job," she said. "We don't even know what we're looking for." She eyed Campion curiously. Without his spectacles his appearance had gained at least fifty per cent, in intelligence.

He met her gaze. "You don't think," he said slowly, "that Alice could have brought anything into the room, do you? After all, she was the only other person about on this floor at that time of the morning."

Joyce shook her head vigorously. "Oh, no. She's such a good soul. She's the last person in the world to do anything like that. She's been here thirty years."

"Alice knows something," said Mr. Campion. "She just reeks of a secret. But I don't suppose it's anything to do with this."

"It isn't." The girl spoke involuntarily and then flushed scarlet, realising that she had betrayed herself.

Just for a moment Mr. Campion's pale eyes rested upon her face. Then he returned to his deductions.

"This patent medicine we're looking for," he said. "Since no one has ever seen it, it must have been hidden by Aunt Julia herself. That gives us a line. Let us put ourselves in her place. Suppose I am a heavy, lazy woman lying in bed. A cup of hot tea is brought to me. I wish to take something from its hiding-place, put it in my tea and return the packet to concealment in the shortest possible space of time and with the maximum of comfort. That leads us directly to the bed."

He sat down on the bedside chair. "Reconstruction of crime in the French manner," he murmured. "This stuff might be anywhere. Not in the pillows, not in the mattress; these things are moved every day. If it were small enough it might be sewn into the hem of the valance."

He bent down to examine the frill round the bedstead, but shook his head regretfully.

"No good," he said. "No hem at all worth speaking of." He caught hold of the thick brass bedpost to pull himself up, and as his fingers closed round the unusually thick rod an exclamation escaped him. "Of course!" he said. "The hiding-place of my childhood. The squirrel's hole of my earliest years."

He pointed dramatically to the big brass knobs at the foot of the bed. A short hysterical laugh escaped the girl.

"Of course," she said. "I had four little ones on my cot. They're hollow, and they unscrew, don't they? I used to hide bits of slate pencil in mine."

Mr. Campion was already unscrewing one of the immense ornaments.

"This is most likely the one," he said. "The bed-table side, you see."

The great ball was almost as large as a coconut, and screwed on to a threaded iron support as thick as a man's two fingers. It turned easily in his hand. Two or three twists brought it off, and they bent over it eagerly.

"Shake!" The girl hardly recognised her own voice. "If there's anything there it'll rattle."

He obeyed her, and a hollow knocking rewarded him. "I don't see how we get it out," he began, "unless—oh, I see." He put in his finger and caught the end of a red thread of chemist's string just as it was about to disappear into the ball. The next moment he had drawn out a wooden cylinder about three inches long. A little hole had been bored in the screw lid, the string threaded through and a coloured bead knotted on each side to prevent it from slipping. He set the brass knob back on its post, holding his find by the string.

"Look out," he said. "Don't touch it. This may be police property now. They're awfully touchy about people meddling with their exhibits." He carried the cylinder under the light on the dressing-table. The blue wrapper on the box was covered with small print, and they strained their eyes to read it. Aunt Julia's secret lay revealed.

"*Thyro-Tissue Reducer. A Pellet a Day Keeps the Scales at Bay. One Thyro-Tissue Reducer pellet taken every morning in tea will effectively reduce superfluous flesh. Guaranteed convenient and harmless. Thousands of testimonials.*"

* * *

Campion and the girl exchanged glances. "You were right," she said. "Was it a mistake?"

"I don't think it was suicide," said Mr. Campion. "Look here, I think we may as well open this." He took out a handkerchief and protected the cylinder with it as he unscrewed the lid. The inside of the cylinder proved enlightening. It held a tube of grease-proof paper folded in zig-zag creases, each fold of which had contained a white pellet. About half of these were empty.

Campion stood looking at the remaining pellets through the transparent paper. Finally he replaced them carefully in the box and screwed on the lid.

"This is it," he said. "It'll have to go to an analyst, though I don't suppose there's the remotest chance of the rest of these being anything but as convenient and harmless as they're supposed to be. Yet this morning's dose must have been impregnated by the conium or whatever it was."

The girl looked at him with horror and fear in her eyes. "Then we've made our discovery?" she said. "It was murder?"

Mr. Campion replaced his spectacles, and, wrapping the box carefully in his handkerchief, thrust it in his pocket.

"I'm afraid so," he said. "And murder by someone who knew what no one in the house has confessed to knowing—that Aunt Julia was trying to get her weight down."

10

Uncle William's Guilty Conscience

After a fifteen-minute audience with Great-aunt Caroline alone in the drawing-room, Mr. Campion returned to Joyce, who was waiting for him curled up in an arm-chair before the morning-room fire. She glanced up as he came in, and he noticed how pale and scared she was. He offered her a cigarette and lit one himself.

"Do you think that by the time I'm eighty-four I'll be like Mrs. Faraday!" he enquired. "No, don't say it. She is the most remarkable person I've ever met. I felt my allegiance to the firm required me to report our discovery to her before I told Oates. She took it marvellously. A very grand old bird. Stanislaus is right. She's exactly like a High Court judge. I say," he continued, turning on the girl suddenly, "I hope I haven't scared you unduly. But I thought you'd rather be in it, so to speak. After all, an explanation, however unpleasant, is better than a mystery."

She nodded vigorously. "That's how I feel. No, I'm awfully grateful, honestly I am. I was afraid you were going to be one of those clever people one reads about who know everything from the beginning and bring the whole explanation out of their sleeve when they've completed a chain of evidence, like a conjuror at a children's party."

Mr. Campion shook his head gravely. "I'm not the conjuror at this party," he said, and sat down before the fire. "Look here," he went on suddenly, "as a brother sleuth, what about this secret of Alice's? I don't want to force anything out of you. I'm only a mother's help in this business. But at least tell me this. Is Alice's little mystery anything of real importance, in your own opinion, or is it one of those dark and awful private worries that really have very little to do with the case?"

For some moments the girl did not answer, but stared fixedly before her, her brows wrinkled, her eyes troubled.

"I don't know," she said frankly. "Maybe you'd better hear it. It's a silly little thing, really, and may mean nothing at all. Alice told me this morning, as a matter of fact, when she brought in my hot water, and I know she hasn't mentioned it to the police. It's only this. The cord which was used to open and shut the skylight window in the old nursery upstairs has gone, or at least a great part of it has. One staple has been pulled out and a large chunk of rope cut off. Alice noticed it the other day when she went in to see if the room wanted airing. Naturally she didn't think anything of it then, but when Andrew was found tied up with clothes line or something like it she couldn't help remembering the window cord. She didn't want me to tell the police because she felt it would just be bringing the suspicion back to the house. That's all it is."

Mr. Campion was very grave. "You say there's quite a large bit of rope left?" he said. "That's important. I mean the two pieces can be compared if need be. Look here, since there's no telephone in the house, I think I'd better go and interview one of those plain-clothes men in the garden. He probably knows of a police call-box, somewhere about, and I'd like to have a chat with Stanislaus. It's only about half-past ten now."

The girl rose to her feet. "All right," she said. "Alice won't get into trouble, will she, for not telling?"

"Rather not. I give you my solemn promise about that."

The girl smiled at him. "I'm glad you came," she said. "I don't know what we should have done without you. I've got to go up now. Aunt usually goes to bed about half-past ten, and it's one of my jobs to put away her laces and lay out the different ones for to-morrow. I'll say good night to you."

"Good night," said Mr. Campion. "Don't be afraid."

She paused half-way across the room and looked back at him. "How do you guess what people are thinking?" she demanded.

Mr. Campion adjusted his glasses. "I was in the Income Tax Department for years," he murmured. "More passages from my sordid past next week."

A grudging smile spread over her face. "Forgive me," she said, "but don't you find your manner a—well, a detriment in your business?"

He looked hurt. "Can a leopard change his spots?" he protested. "I am as I am."

Joyce laughed. "Good night, Spotty," she said, and went out.

Campion waited until he heard the drawing-room door close and Great-aunt Caroline and her niece go safely up the stairs. Then he stepped gently out into the hall to make his way to the garden.

He had just reached the front door when it opened, and Marcus, followed by Uncle William, whose face was no longer pink, but a delicate shade of heliotrope, came into the hall. Both men stopped abruptly when they caught sight of Campion, and Marcus turned meaningfully to his companion. Beneath the cold, slightly unfriendly stare of the younger man Uncle William pulled himself together.

"Oh—yes, Campion," he said. "I'm very glad to see you. Is my mother in bed, do you know?" It was very much apparent that something had occurred. The atmosphere was strained between the two new-comers. Campion's curiosity was aroused. It looked as though Marcus was forcing the older man to take the initiative, and equally obvious that Uncle William did so unwillingly.

"Mrs. Faraday has only just gone upstairs," said Campion. "Do you want to see her?"

"Oh, good Lord, no!" Uncle William spoke vehemently and shut his mouth with a snap, glancing at his escort with furtive blue eyes.

Marcus turned to Campion, betraying that he had given up the idea of persuading Uncle William to open the proceedings.

"Look here," he said. "We want to see you alone for some minutes. Is there anyone in the breakfast-room?" He was taking off his overcoat as he spoke, and Uncle William imitated him, although somewhat grudgingly. Campion led the way back to the morning-room and Uncle William followed him, blinking a little in the bright light.

When Marcus came in he closed the door behind him. His face was unusually grave, and with sudden misgiving Campion realised that he looked like a man who had had a shock. Uncle William had also undergone a deep and subtle change. His bluster had deserted him almost entirely. He looked older, flabbier, and although there was still a faint truculence about him, it was the truculence of one who has been found out rather than one who fears he is about to be.

Marcus cleared his throat nervously. "Campion," he said, "as a solicitor, I have advised Mr. Faraday to bring his story to you. I have explained to him that I cannot do what he has asked me, but that I feel that you, in your position as Mrs. Faraday's professional adviser in this business, could probably help him more than anyone else."

"I like that," grumbled Uncle William. "You pretty well forced me to come here, you know that."

Marcus turned to him in exasperation, but he spoke patiently as though to a child.

"As I reminded you before, Mr. Faraday," he said, "Campion is not a member of the police, and as a professional man any secret of yours will be safe with him."

Uncle William spread out his fat hands. "All right," he said. "But I don't want to run my head into a noose. I don't know when I've been in such an awkward position in my whole life.

After all, you don't seem to see that whatever I've done I'm morally as innocent as a new-born babe. It's my affliction—like a fellow having a gammy leg. Hang it all, you've only got to do what I ask you, and there's no bother about it."

Marcus shook his head. "You don't realise," he said, "if you'll forgive me saying so. You don't see the legal aspect of this at all. Whatever your personal views of—er—crime and punishment are, the law is very definite on the subject. I must repeat my request to you. You're in a very serious position, Mr. Faraday."

"All right," said Uncle William, still a little sulkily. "Go on. You tell him. It seems a pity that a fellow's afflictions should be bandied about from mouth to mouth. Still, I suppose you know best. Go on," he repeated, his little eyes betraying his anxiety. "Let me hear how you see it. Strikes me as being one of the most natural things in the world."

The young man took a folded paper from his breast pocket and eyed Campion steadily.

"Mr. Faraday has just brought me this statement which he wishes to sign on oath," he said. "I will read it to you: *'I, William Robert Faraday, hereby declare that I have had something wrong with my nerves for the past eighteen months. I am liable to lose my memory completely and utterly for short spaces of time, never exceeding the half-hour, as far as I know. During these attacks I have no recollection of where I am or who I am and do not consider myself responsible for any action that I may at these times inadvertently commit.'*

Uncle William looked up. "I don't like that word," he said. "Say '*do*.'"

"'*Do*,'" said Marcus, and made a pencilled alteration. "This isn't in legal form, anyhow."

"'*I swear the foregoing is the truth, and nothing but the truth. Signed. William R. Faraday.'*"

"Well then, there you are," said Uncle William triumphantly. "That's clear, isn't it? All you've got to do is to witness that, Marcus, and date it as I told you. There's nothing dishonest about it. I've been meaning to come to you about this for months. You date it February; it'll be all right."

Marcus flushed. "But, Mr. Faraday," he said helplessly,

"you must realise the desperate importance of a move like this at such a time. I don't mind telling you that if you were anyone else who had come to me with a request like this I should consider it my duty to throw you out of my office, and it is only because you have convinced me that these facts are mainly true that I am down here with you to-night."

Campion, who had remained throughout the interview standing silent by one of the high-backed chairs, his inconsequential air more strongly marked than ever, now sat down and leant back, folding his arms.

"Could you describe these attacks of yours, Mr. Faraday?" he said.

Uncle William looked at him belligerently. "Of course I could," he said. "There's nothing much to describe. I just forget, and then, after a bit, I remember. An attack usually lasts about five to ten minutes, I believe. There's a name for it. It's called 'amnesia,' or something. If I get tired or over-exert myself it's liable to come on."

Mr. Campion seemed perfectly convinced. "I see," he said. "And very awkward, too. Have you had many of these attacks?"

"No, not a lot," said Uncle William guardedly. "Not many. But I'm getting worse. The first time it happened was last June. By the way, Marcus, you'd better alter that statement. It's not eighteen months, is it?"

"No," said Marcus acidly. "It's nine."

"Oh, well"—Uncle William waved his hands—"you lawyer fellows are so exact. Well, last June I was walking down Petty Cury on a damned hot day. My mind went blank, and the next thing I knew I was standing outside the Roman Catholic church with a glass in my hand. I felt an absolute fool and, naturally, rather alarmed. I didn't know what to do with the thing. I noticed one or two people looking at me curiously. The glass didn't tell me anything; ordinary tumbler, the sort of thing you'd get in a bar. I put it in my pocket finally and threw it into a field as I came out of the town. Most unpleasant experience."

"Most," said Campion gravely. "And has it happened since then?"

"Twice," Uncle William admitted cautiously after some hesitation. "Once last Christmas, just when I thought there was nothing in it after all. We had a dinner party here one night, and when everyone had gone home I remember walking down to the gate with Andrew to get a breath of fresh air. I remembered nothing more until I found myself shivering in a cold bath. It might have killed me. I don't take a cold tub now. When a man gets to my age he has to look after himself. Penalty of being an old athlete."

Marcus, who knew that the sum of Uncle William's athletic prowess was represented by the silver mug gained at a preparatory school in 1881, frowned on this unwarrantable assertion, but the older man rattled on.

"I asked Andrew afterwards—cautiously, you know—if he'd noticed anything odd. He asked me what I meant. He was as drunk as a bargee at the time, so I don't suppose he did notice anything."

"And the third time," said Mr. Campion curiously.

"And the third time," said Uncle William grudgingly, "was more unfortunate still. The third time was on the Sunday that Andrew disappeared—in fact, actually at the time that he did disappear. That's what makes it so awkward."

Marcus started violently. "Mr. Faraday!" he protested. "You didn't tell me this."

"I'm not a man who talks about my ailments," said Uncle William, betraying a slight thickness of speech which had been vaguely noticeable throughout the interview. "Well, there you are. Now you've got it. I remember standing in the road leading to the Grantchester meadows arguing with Andrew about the right way to go home—idiotical subject—quite obvious which was the right way. I remember parting with him. I was very rattled, don't you know, very upset, to think that a man could be such a fool. And that's when I lost my memory. When I came to I was just walking in the front gate, and lunch was practically over."

"That was twenty-five minutes later than you said in your statement to the police," remarked Mr. Campion unexpectedly.

Uncle William's cheeks inflated. "Perhaps so," he muttered. "All this insistence on time is very confusing. Well, there you are. Now you know all about it."

Marcus tried vainly to catch Mr. Campion's eye, but that young man remained polite and inconsequential, his eyes hidden behind his spectacles.

"I hope you won't think me unduly inquisitive, Mr. Faraday," he said, "but why didn't you tell one of the family of your illness? You were running a great risk. You might have got run over, for example."

Uncle William, hunched up in his chair, refused to look at either of them.

"I don't like talking about family secrets in front of strangers," he murmured, "but, as a matter of fact, my mother is getting old." He paused, and taking out a huge pocket handkerchief, blew his nose violently. "She gets ideas into her head," he went on. "For some time lately she has suffered from a delusion that—well, not to put too fine a point upon it, that I drink. Of course," he continued, his voice rising gustily, "I'm not a teetotaller, and in my time—well, there was a period not so very long ago when I used to get so infuriated living with a pack of ill-natured fools that I used to drown my sorrows now and again." Uncle William managed to convey the impression that he regarded himself as a man confessing to a past peccadillo with a good grace. "Well," he went on, his confidence restored, "it came home to me, don't you know, that if I told the family that I had been stricken with this affliction, having no medical knowledge at all, they might put it down to my having had a glass or two. Now you see how awkward it was."

Mr. Campion nodded, but it was Marcus who spoke.

"But, my dear sir," he protested helplessly, "don't you see the danger you put yourself in? Haven't you told anyone? Is there no one who can bear out this story?"

Uncle William rose to his feet. "Young man," he said sternly, "are you doubting my word?"

Marcus seemed about to point out that he was only human after all when Mr. Campion came to the rescue.

"The state of your health must have alarmed you, Mr. Faraday?" he said. "Didn't you feel like taking medical advice?"

Uncle William turned to him. His racing, muddled thoughts were reflected in his narrowed eyes.

"Naturally," he said cautiously. "But I didn't want to go to old Lavrock, telling him all my business. I don't say anything against Lavrock's discretion. He's a good fellow, I have no doubt. But I didn't want to go to the family doctor."

"It's a great pity you didn't go to someone," said Marcus, whose precise orderly mind was revolted by Uncle William's astounding display of untidy thinking.

"Oh, but I did," said the older man petulantly. "I did."

Both young men stiffened. "Who?"

But Uncle William seemed loath to speak.

"For God's sake, man!" Marcus's tone was urgent. "Don't you see the importance of this?"

Uncle William shrugged his shoulders. "Very well, then," he said. "It makes it more awkward than ever, but if you insist—Sir Gordon Woodthorpe, the Harley Street nerve man."

Marcus sighed, an expression in which incredulity and relief fought with one another.

"That makes it feasible, at any rate," he said. "When did you go to see him?"

"End of June," said Uncle William, still grudgingly. "We won't go into what he said. I never believed those fellows know as much as they're supposed to. Well, that's the truth, but I don't see how it's going to make any difference. I can't ask him to confirm my visit."

"Why not?" Marcus's suspicions returned.

"Because," said Uncle William, with great dignity, picking his words with elaborate care, "I thought it prudent to change my name for the occasion. I haven't been able to pay him either—if you must hear all my private affairs. Oh, I dare say he'd remember my case," he went on as the other opened his mouth to speak. "But if you think I'm going to allow you to expose me to a lot of threatening lawyer's letters or whatever these fellows take refuge behind, you're wrong. I've said all I'm going to say." He shut his mouth obstinately and turned away from them.

"But, Mr. Faraday, this is murder." Marcus planted himself before the old man and repeated the word savagely. "Murder. Don't you understand! There's nothing worse than murder. If you persist in carrying on like this, sir," he went on, with growing severity, "you're liable to be arrested."

"You sign that paper," said Uncle William. "It'll be all right then. I've been in several tight corners in my life, and always got out of them. And I shall do the same now. There isn't a man alive who can call William Faraday a coward."

"Not to say a fool," muttered Marcus under his breath.

Uncle William glanced up at him. "Don't mutter at me, sir," he said. "Speak out like a man."

Marcus appealed to Campion. "Can you explain to Mr. Faraday the gravity of his situation?" he said. "I can't."

"Hang it! I know it's grave," bellowed Uncle William, with unexpected violence. "Haven't I lost a cousin, and a sister? You two seem to forget this family's bereavements and come here worrying me about doctors. Let me tell you I've got to give evidence of identification at the inquest to-morrow, and that's going to be a very painful, trying and tragic experience. I'm not the man to be worried about petty doctor's bills."

"Inspector Oates will follow up any evidence, Marcus," said Mr. Campion unpardonably.

Uncle William looked from one to the other of the two young men, opened his mouth to speak, but thought better of it. He sat staring at them, grunting softly to himself like a simmering kettle. Quite suddenly he gave in.

"I took my old friend Harrison Gregory's name. Gave the club address, and called on the 27th of June," he said. "Now, you know, and I hope that satisfies you. It makes me look a fool, but then mother keeps us so short. She doesn't seem to realise that a man of my age must have a pound or two."

Marcus was scribbling the name on the back of an envelope. "Levett's Club, isn't it, sir?" he said.

Uncle William grunted. "Brook Street," he murmured. "Country member. Old Gregory'll be touchy with me. He must have been hearing from that fellow." He shook his head regretfully. "It seemed the best thing to do at the time."

Marcus shot a horrified glance at Campion, who seemed to be quite unmoved by this recital.

"I'll do what I can, sir." Marcus put the envelope back into his pocket. "I should destroy this statement, if I were you," he added, tapping the sheet of paper upon the table. "In the circumstances, I think it might be misleading. Campion, I shall come up to see you in the morning if I may. Until we can confirm this interview with Sir Gordon Woodthorpe perhaps this story should be kept from the police, although I realise that it will have to come out sooner or later. I think Mr. Faraday realises that, too," he added, glancing in Uncle William's direction.

Uncle William vouchsafed no reply, neither did he respond to Marcus's "Good night," but sat sulking in his chair until Mr. Campion returned from the hall whither he had accompanied his friend. Then he rose to his feet and picked up the statement which Marcus had left upon the table.

"Damned unobliging young pup," he observed. "I thought his father might be an uncivil old fool, but I didn't think the boy would be so difficult. Oh, well, I suppose I shall have to let him ferret out all this silly business with the doctor fellow. I don't particularly mind, of course, I only thought this was the easiest way." He dropped the paper into the flames and turned abruptly to Campion. "That policeman, Inspector Oates, came back here this evening," he said. "It was his harping on the exact time of the lunch on Sunday that made me realise that I'd better get this thing done if I was going to do it at all. That's what made me go to see Marcus this evening. How was I to know he would put up such a show of obstinacy?"

He paused, and Mr. Campion made no comment. Suddenly Uncle William sank back wearily into his chair. There was something almost pathetic in the glance he shot at the other man.

"Do *you* think I'm in a devil of a mess?" he said.

Mr. Campion's heart was touched. "You're in a mess," he said slowly, "but I don't think it's as bad as it looks. I don't know yet. Forgive me for saying so, but I suppose this story about Sir Gordon Woodthorpe is—well *bona fide*?"

"Oh, yes, that's the truth, unfortunately," said Uncle William, who seemed to be incapable of grasping the importance of such a helpful witness. "Of course," he continued, with devastating frankness, "I couldn't have done it, you know. I couldn't have killed Andrew. I didn't take a chunk of rope to church with me, I know that."

His little blue eyes blinked reflectively. "Figure not being what it was, I wear a very tight overcoat. Very smart. Why, I can't put a prayer book in my pocket without it looking like a hip flask. But a great chunk of rope! Someone would have noticed it. I should have, too. I may be forgetful, but I'm not feeble-minded, you know."

It was evident that a great deal of what Uncle William said was pertinent.

"Of course," said Mr. Campion absently, "there's very little to prove that your cousin was killed on the Sunday."

"Oh, well, then," said Uncle William with satisfaction, "that lets me out altogether. I know what I've been doing ever since then. I haven't had an attack since that day, thank God, and, besides, the weather's been so damned bad that I haven't been outside the house half a dozen times. Between ourselves, it's been so peaceful without Andrew that I haven't felt much inclination to leave the fireside."

"The other thing," said Mr. Campion slowly, "is the revolver. Ever had a revolver?"

The old man considered. "Had one in the Service, in the war, of course," he said. "I was stationed at Montreuil-sur-Mer—not

that it's on the sea. Inaccurate people, these foreigners. I—
er—had a staff job."

He looked at Campion fiercely, as though warning him not to
ask for further particulars.

"Yes, I had one then. I haven't seen it since. Hang it all, it's
not a thing you want in private life."

"Quite," answered Mr. Campion. "What happened to the
one you had?"

"With my kit, I suppose. I seem to remember that I put the
whole lot in a trunk in the old nursery. Yes, that's where it would
be."

"Let's go and have a look," said Mr. Campion, to whom the
word "nursery" had brought back the recollection of Joyce's
story of half an hour before.

"What, now?" Uncle William seemed loath to stir. "I told
the Inspector there wasn't a gun in the house," he said, "and
never had been. I resent this police catechising."

But Mr. Campion was not to be denied. "They're bound to
find it sooner or later," he said. "I think we'd better go and look.
I'm afraid they'll be searching the house to-morrow."

"Searching the house?" said Uncle William aghast. "They
can't do a thing like that. Or has this Labour Government made
that possible? I remember saying to Andrew: 'If these black-
guards come into power a gentleman's home won't be his
own.'"

"Once you call the police into the house—and you have to
call them in in a serious case like this—I think you'll find their
powers are very great. In the nursery, did you say?"

Still grumbling, Uncle William got up. "All right," he said.
"But we shall have to be quiet. The women are asleep, or ought
to be. I don't see why we shouldn't wait till the morning. It's
darned cold at the top of the house. No fires in the bedrooms
here unless it's a case of illness. That's the Spartan régime of the
old school." He paused hopefully, but finding Mr. Campion
adamant, he helped himself to the last of the whisky and soda
from the sideboard and, tossing it off, led the way upstairs.

Campion followed his globular panting figure up the staircase into the darkness of the upper hall. All was silent and a trifle
stuffy. Uncle William turned the corner and climbed the next
flight.

The second floor of the house was smaller than the others, a
place of narrow corridors and slanting ceilings.

"Servants sleep that side," whispered Uncle William, pointing towards that part of the house that was above Mrs. Faraday's room and the front hall. "The old nursery is down there. It's really only an attic." He switched on a light, which revealed a passage like the one below, three windows on one side and three doors on the other. Here the carpets were worn, the paint was scratched and unpolished, and it occurred to Campion that it probably looked much the same as it had done in the days when the young William and Julia had chased one another down it towards a little wicket gate which barred the exit at the top of the back stairs.

Uncle William opened the first of the three doors. "Here we are," he said. "These two rooms have been knocked into one. There was a night nursery, now used as a lumber room, at the end."

As he turned on the light a big dusty room leapt into sight. It was still furnished with the grim relics of a Victorian nursery. A worn red carpet covered the floor and brown painted cupboards and a chest of drawers stood stiffly against the atrocious blue and green wallpaper. There was a big wire guard over the fire-place and large steel engravings of a sternly religious character were interspersed by coloured texts on the walls. It was a depressing room. The iron bars of the windows, while useful, were hardly ornamental. Instinctively Campion glanced at the skylight. All was as Joyce had described. A piece of cord hung down forlornly from the dusty window, and it was quite clear that a staple to which the other end had been attached had been jerked out of its position. The section of rope which remained was not unlike clothes-line, being thicker and coarser than the usual window cord.

William did not appear to notice this defect. He stood looking about him.

"There's the trunk," he said, pointing to an ancient leather contraption which stood crazily in one corner beneath a standard globe and a pile of books. He led the way across the room, treading silently with elaborate care. Campion followed him, and between them they removed the obstacles and Uncle William raised the lid of the case.

Campion peered in with interest. A faintly musty aroma greeted them, and a moth flew out. Upon investigation there appeared a pair of knee boots, a khaki uniform, a pair of riding breeches, two pair of slacks, a Sam Browne belt and a "brass

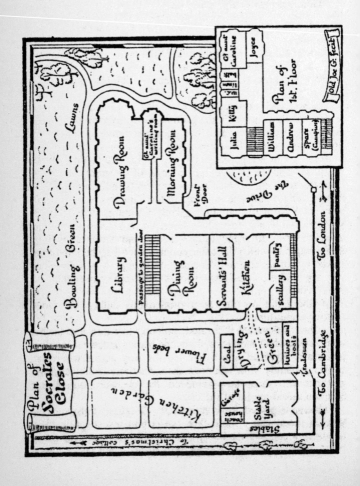

Plan of *Socrates Close*

Plan of 1st. Floor

Gt aunt Caroline

Joyce

Kitty

Julia

William

Andrew

Spare (Cousin)

Old Joe G: ?

Lawns

Bowling Green

Drawing Room

Morning Room

Gt aunt Caroline's writing room

Front Door

The Drive

To London

Library

passage to garden door

Dining Room

Servants' Hall

Kitchen

Pantry

scullery

Flower beds

Coal

Drying Green

Knives and boots

Glasshouse

To Cambridge

Kitchen Garden

Coach house

Harness

Stable Yard

Stables

To Christmas's cottage

hat." Uncle William took the garments out one by one and laid them on the floor.

"Ah," he said, as the bottom of the trunk appeared, "here it is."

Campion was before him. He picked up the holster and unfastened the stud. There were a couple of oily rags within, and that was all.

"God bless my soul!" said Uncle William.

11

And So To Bed

Back in the morning room Uncle William began to show signs of coherent thought again. The motley of veins on his face had multiplied and he appeared to be on the point of exhaustion.

"Not a sign of it, Campion," he said huskily. "There's some very dirty work going on here."

His companion tactfully refrained from observing that so much must have been obvious for some time, and the older man continued.

"There were some cartridges up there, too," he said. "I remember now. They were lying loose at the bottom of the trunk. I shall get into hot water, I suppose, when the police hear about this." He lowered his voice and peered at Campion, his little blue eyes watery with apprehension. "Do they know what sort of bullet killed Andrew?" he said. "Haven't you heard? This is terrible—terrible."

He sat down in his green leather chair and shot a hopeless glance at the whisky decanter. His worst fears were realised and he turned away again.

"I wish I knew where that blackguard was skulking," he bellowed suddenly. "I thought Scotland Yard could find anyone in a day?" He pulled himself up. "Still, I mustn't talk about George, I suppose. Just because I mentioned his name to that policeman I had half an hour's pi-jaw from the old lady. Makes me furious," he went on, his face suffusing with angry colour. "Why should I be put to all this worry and anxiety just to cover up the tracks of a blackmailing scoundrel who's never done an honest day's work in his life? He must have walked into the house, got the gun and laid in wait for Andrew. That is, of course, if Andrew was shot with my gun. That isn't proved yet, is it?"

"It doesn't follow," said Mr. Campion mildly. "Even if he was shot with an army bullet, there must be several hundred thousand army service revolvers kicking about the country."

Uncle William brightened. "Yes, that's true," he said. "Still, I bet it was George. Extraordinary way he came in to dinner that Saturday night. No one let him into the building, you know. He may have been skulking about the house for hours. That's the sort of ruffian the fellow is. Treats the place like his own when he's here, though I must say mother always gets rid of him. There's a touch of the Amazon about the old lady still, in spite of her age."

He paused for a moment, rumbling speculatively. Suddenly he went on again.

"It turned my stomach over when he came in just after the clock-weight fell. A silly transpontine appearance. Reminded me of the sort of melodramas I used to see as a boy. And now the old lady's trying to shield him, that's what annoys me."

Mr. Campion, who possessed the gift of self-effacement to an extraordinary degree, stood placidly leaning against the mantelpiece while the old man continued.

"She lives too much in the past," Uncle William insisted. "The scandals of the past matter more to her than any catastrophe that might happen now. I don't suppose this fellow George holds anything very important over her, but there's no way of telling. Look at the reason why she cut Andrew out of her will."

Mr. Campion appeared interested. "A storm in a teacup?" he enquired.

"I thought so," Uncle William confided. "After all, the governor, God bless him, can't be irritated now. Yet it was that book of Andrew's that did it. *Hypocrites, or the Mask of Learning*. A rotten title. I told him so."

"I've never heard of it," said Mr. Campion.

"You wouldn't," said Uncle William brutally. "I don't suppose it sold half a dozen copies. I told mother it wasn't worth worrying about, but she never takes any notice of me. It showed old Andrew's impudence, though," he added savagely, "and it served him right. Fancy a fellow living on his aunt's charity while he wrote a blackguardly attack on his dead uncle!"

"An attack on Doctor Faraday?" enquired his companion.

William nodded. "That's right. Old Andrew noticed that there was a great boom in memoirs—old wallahs retelling their club stories and getting their own back generally—and it occurred to him that he might make a fiver or two by having a smack at the governor. Anyway, he wrote the thing. Silliest piece of work I ever read, and I'm not a literary man."

"It was published?" asked Mr. Campion.

"Oh, yes. Some little tin-pot firm brought it out. Thought there might be a sale on the governor's name, I suppose. Andrew got six copies and nothing else, and yet I should think the publishers were out of pocket. Even then it wouldn't have mattered," he continued, with rising indignation, "but as soon as he got his six copies old Andrew wrote a flowery inscription on the fly-leaf of each and presented us all with a copy. There was one over for the spare room. Mother got Joyce to read the book to her. A nice little girl that, by the way," he remarked. "Only woman of any tact in the whole household. Yes, well, then the fat was in the fire. I haven't seen mother so angry since—oh, well, a long time ago. Of course, in the ordinary way we should have sued for defamation of family character, I suppose, but you can't get damages from a relative living on your own charity. Very awkward. Mother took the only weapon left to her. She sent for old Featherstone and altered her will. I was reading a book about an Italian fellow who sells beer in America at the time, I remember. I borrowed a phrase from it. I said to Andrew, I said: 'Laugh that off, won't you.' He sat in that chair over there. I can hear him swearing now."

"I'd like to see the book," said Mr. Campion.

"Would you?" Uncle William was eager to placate this young man, who, he realised, was the only person of influence liable to be even remotely friendly towards him.

"I've got a copy, as a matter of fact. The old lady destroyed all those she could get hold of, but I kept mine." He lowered his voice. "Between you and me, I believe it was half true. We Faradays aren't saints. The governor was human, like the rest of us." He rose to his feet. "I expect you'll turn in now?" he said.

"I'll get the book. You might keep it in your bag. It's got my name in it."

The two men went upstairs together and Campion stood in the doorway of Uncle William's room while the old man rummaged among the books which stood on the shelf beside his bed. Campion got the impression of a vast untidy room, as littered and rambling as its owner's mind. He had not much time for observation, however, for Uncle William returned to him almost immediately with a slim volume covered with brown paper.

"I labelled it 'Omar Khayyam' in case it was noticed on the shelf," he murmured. "Well, good night, and—er—ere, I say." He laid a heavy hand on the young man's shoulder, peered into his face and spoke with deadly earnestness. "I'm telling you as one man to another. I'm going to cut out the glass. Not another drink until this business is over." He nodded portentously and disappeared into his own room, shutting the door behind him.

In view of the empty decanter downstairs, Mr. Campion felt this statement somewhat unnecessary. However, he said nothing, but withdrew to his own room two doors down the passage.

It was now almost midnight, and for a reason which he was loath to admit, he did not feel like leaving the house until the morning. Anyhow, he reflected, Stanislaus could do nothing that night.

The guest room at Socrates Close was one of those large, comfortable apartments furnished with pieces that no one could possibly have bought for his own use. An ornate rosewood suite, a misshapen arm-chair, a remarkable wallpaper upon which the botanist had been at work again, and an assortment of pictures which took, Mr. Campion considered, his religious beliefs too much for granted, made up an apartment at once comfortable to the flesh and disturbing to the spirit.

Campion undressed, got into bed, and, switching on the reading lamp, examined Uncle Andrew's mess of pottage. The inscription on the fly-leaf was in highly questionable taste in view of the subject matter of the book.

"To my Cousin William Faraday, a true son of his father, and from a close study of whose disposition I have gained much of my insight into the complex character of the subject of this book. With the Author's thanks."

* * *

There was a frontispiece, an old-fashioned photograph of Doctor John Faraday. It was not a pleasant face; stern, and unrelieved by any sign of humour. Long, spoon-shaped side-whiskers increased the narrowness of the jaw and the mouth was drawn and puckered like the mouth of a string bag.

Mr. Campion began to read. Uncle Andrew's style was not distinguished, but it had the quality of vituperance. He wrote with an urge and a spitefulness which made him eminently readable. Campion found himself amazed that any firm should have risked the publication of such an attack, and reflected that Andrew had probably represented his influence with the family as something more than it actually was. Doctor Faraday, stripped of his academic honours, emerged as a narrow-minded, self-important man who hid his shortcomings beneath a hypocritical cloak of sanctity and his wife's charm. Several slightly discreditable stories of his youth had been unearthed or invented by the industrious Andrew, and the learned Doctor appeared as little more than a pompous Victorian humbug with unexpected twists of character for which the modern psychologists have long and unpleasant names. Andrew knew most of the names and used them freely.

By the time Mr. Campion had read the first three chapters and glanced at the end, he closed the book feeling a little sorry for the defunct dignitary, whatever his private character might have been.

He switched out the light and lay down to sleep, having decided to call upon the Inspector at the earliest possible moment on the morrow.

It was some time later when he woke up suddenly and sat up in bed, listening. The heavy curtains over the window shut out all light, so that the darkness was almost tangible, like black cotton wool filling the house. Campion was one of those people who are immediately in possession of all their thoughts and faculties the moment they open their eyes, and a feeling of apprehension seized him instantly. He caught a fleeting impression of the house as some sick, many-petticoated creature crouching frightened in the unrelenting darkness. There was now no sound at all to be heard, yet he knew that something had awakened him. He had a vague idea that it had been the gentle closing of a door.

For some time he remained where he was, his eyes closed, his ears strained to catch the least movement. At length, somewhere far off, he heard wood knocking gently against wood.

He sprang out of bed and crept towards the door, letting himself out without a sound.

The moonlight was streaming through the windows into the corridor and the ghostly light was comforting after the appalling blackness of his room. For an instant he stood rigid. Then something moved in the hall at the far end of the corridor, a furtive rustling.

He strode swiftly towards it, his feet making no sound on the thick carpet. Just for a moment it occurred to him that his behaviour was somewhat questionable for a guest on his first night in the house, but at the mouth of the corridor he stopped abruptly.

Standing in the centre of the small hall, the moonlight falling directly upon him, was the pyjama-clad figure of Uncle William. His eyes were bulging and there was a look of terror upon his face. His right arm was held stiffly away from him, and Campion, catching sight of it, was conscious of a sudden shock.

A stain, black in the moonlight, covered the hand and wrist and dripped terrifyingly from the finger-tips. At the instant that Campion himself caught sight of this apparition the door of Aunt Kitty's room directly across the hall burst open and a little tousled figure appeared upon the threshold. Her eyes lighted upon William, and a thin scream of terror echoed through the slumbering house.

The old man wheeled round, his hand thrust hastily behind him. He swore violently, entirely forgetting his erstwhile efforts to keep quiet. The house echoed with his voice. Doors began to open on the floor above, and Joyce appeared from her room on the other side of the hall. She was half asleep, and her hair fell over the shoulders of her dressing-gown.

"What is it? What's the matter? Aunt Kitty, what are you doing?"

The little figure in the fussy flannelette nightgown tottered out into the moonlight.

"His hand! His hand!" said Aunt Kitty breathlessly. "Look at his hand! Someone else has been murdered!" And again the high hysterical shriek broke from her lips.

It was at this moment that the door of Great-aunt Caroline's room opened and a figure, infinitesimally small shorn of its petticoats, stepped out towards them. Great-aunt Caroline's night attire was as dainty as were all her other clothes. She was swathed in filmy Shetland shawls, and her little dark face peered out from beneath an immense lace bonnet, which tied under her chin. Even at such a moment she dominated the entire proceedings.

"What is all this disturbance?"

The sound of her voice effectively silenced Aunt Kitty, who appeared to be on the verge of yet another hysterical outburst.

"William, what are you doing? Joyce, go back to your room."

Uncle William said nothing. He stood goggling, his mouth hanging open, his hand still thrust behind him, a grotesque absurd gesture in the circumstances.

"Answer me, sir." Great-aunt Faraday's voice was as commanding as ever.

Mr. Campion started forward, and William, hearing someone behind him, spun round, revealing his hand to the rest of the group. Campion heard Joyce's quick intake of breath, and old Mrs. Faraday came further out of her doorway. Campion caught Uncle William just as he slumped on to the floor.

"Switch on the light, someone," he said.

It was Joyce who obeyed him. The light shot up and Campion bent over the older man with a sigh of relief. There was nothing seriously wrong with Uncle William, and he was making a valiant effort to pull himself together.

"I'm all right," he said thickly. He raised his arm in his attempt to get up, and his hand came into view again. Instantly the horror was explained. There was a deep ragged wound from the knuckles to the wrist, but the terrifying stain which had dripped from the fingers was nothing but iodine, a whole bottle of which he seemed to have upset over himself.

It was at this moment that the second incident occurred.

"This I won't have! Madam, you'll catch your death of cold."

A strident voice from the top of the staircase made them all turn. A powerful figure in a long white calico gown was striding down upon them. Campion only just recognised in this commanding form the homely, pleasant-faced Alice, whom he had last seen bearing sustenance to Uncle William in the morning room. Her hair scraped back from her forehead, was plaited into a tight pigtail, and anger and concern had entirely altered her face. She turned on the group as if they had been so many lunatics.

"You'll kill her," she said fiercely. "That's what you'll do, dragging her out on to this cold landing with your screams and noise. Hasn't she enough to worry her without being disturbed in the middle of the night? She's the one I'm thinking of."

"Alice!" Great-aunt Caroline's voice, raised in protest, was lost in this cyclonic outburst.

Alice strode past Uncle William without glancing in his direction and now towered above her mistress.

"Will you get into your bed, ma'am?" she demanded.

Great-aunt Faraday did not speak, but neither did she move, and the other woman, who seemed to have become even larger and more elemental now that she stood amongst them, picked up her mistress as if she had been a child and carried her into the darkness of the bedroom beyond.

This move was done with such extraordinary ease that it struck Campion as being an amazing feat of strength. It was as though Alice had picked up a recalcitrant kitten in her progress.

As the door of Aunt Faraday's room shut firmly, the general interest returned to Uncle William. Campion helped him to his feet, where he stood shaking violently, his mouth still hanging open. The young man turned to Joyce.

"You get your aunt back to bed," he murmured. "I'll see to Mr. Faraday."

The girl nodded and moved over to Aunt Kitty, who was standing helplessly in the middle of the hall wringing her hands, tears streaming down her puckered old face.

Campion supported Uncle William back to his room, where he sat on the edge of his bed swaying backwards and forwards, mumbling unintelligibly. Had the old man been a woman, Mr. Campion would have diagnosed faintness as result of shock. As it was, he put the seizure down to some hitherto unsuspected cardiac trouble.

His eye lighted again on the wound and all his apprehension returned. It was no ordinary scratch, but a deep ragged cut like a knife-thrust that had gone astray. The iodine had added to its horrific appearance, whilst staunching the blood. The longer Mr. Campion looked at it the more the unpleasant thought was forced upon his mind that the end of the series of outrages at Socrates Close had not yet come.

"How did you do that?" he demanded, indicating the wound.

Uncle William thrust his hand behind him. An obstinate gleam shone in his watery blue eyes.

"Mind your own damned business," he said, speaking with a viciousness engendered by fright.

"I'm sorry," said Campion. "Well, I suppose you'll be all right now?"

As he turned towards the door, Uncle William thrust out his left hand appealingly.

"Don't go, for heaven's sake, old man," he said. "Must have a drink. I'll be myself again when I've had a drink. I've had a bit of a shock, between ourselves. Ask Joyce—yes, that's right, ask Joyce. She'll get me a brandy. The old lady trusts her with the keys."

Fortunately for Mr. Campion he encountered Joyce in the hall. She was white and frightened, but eminently practical.

"All right," she whispered, in response to his request. "You go back to him; I'll bring it along. Did he see who attacked him?"

This sudden question, which fitted in so well with his own hastily formed theories, startled the young man.

"He won't say anything," he whispered back.

She paused and seemed to be about to speak, but changed her mind and hurried down the stairs without saying another word. Campion went back to Uncle William.

He was still seated on the edge of his bed, his un-slippered feet resting on the thick woollen carpet. He looked ill and curiously frightened, but as he caught sight of Campion he stiffened and forced a smile.

"Made a bit of a fool of myself," he said with a hopeless attempt at lightness. "Always was a believer in iodine—army training, I suppose. If you hurt yourself, stick on a wad of iodine. It stings, but it's worth it. Saves no end of trouble afterwards. Unluckily my hand was a bit unsteady—being half asleep, don't you know—and I spilt the bottle over myself. I may be getting old—I don't know."

Campion looked at the wound again. "You ought to have a bandage on it," he remarked. "It's pretty deep. Is there such a thing in the house?"

"There's one in the first-aid box where I got the iodine." Uncle William was blinking at his wounded hand, from which the blood was beginning to ooze again. "It's in that oak corner cupboard in the hall. But don't go and get it and wake the house again, just as I did. There's a handkerchief in that top drawer; that'll do. Unlucky beggar I am! That girl's a long time with that drink. Just my luck if there isn't any. What's the use of living in a non-prohibition country if you don't keep anything in the house? When I get my money I shall go to America. It'll be a funny thing to have to go to America to get a drink."

Mr. Campion returned with the handkerchief and was still looking curiously at the wound, which seemed as though it might be the better for a few stitches, when Joyce came in, a glass in one hand and a decanter in the other. Uncle William rose immediately she appeared.

"That's a good girl," he said. "That's the only medicine that ever did me any good. Pour it out for me, will you, my dear? Can't trust this hand of mine."

As she gave him the glass the noticed the real extent of the damage for the first time, and an involuntary exclamation escaped her.

"Oh, how did it happen? Who did it?" she burst out.

Uncle William drained his glass and sat down again on the edge of the bed. The spirit made him cough, and a healthier colour returned to his face. As Joyce repeated her question he blinked at her.

"Yes," he echoed, "how did it happen? Most extraordinary thing. I've never liked cats. Filthy, dangerous animals. Great black beast got into my room. I went to put it out and it scratched me."

Having got over what he evidently considered to be the hump of his story, he continued with returning confidence.

"Must have got in from some place outside. I can't think how it managed it. But it's gone now."

He glanced about him as if to assure himself that this indeed was the case. The girl shot an incredulous glance at Campion, who showed no sign either of conviction or disbelief.

"I said to myself," Uncle William continued with terrific gusto, "cat scratches are poisonous. So I went along to the first-aid box in the hall, and the rest you know."

He seemed to consider that this was the end of the matter, but Joyce was frankly dissatisfied.

"A cat?" she demanded. "Are you sure?"

In spite of his unsteady hand, Uncle William was helping himself to another brandy.

"I said a cat, and I mean a cat," he said with an attempt at dignity.

"But, Uncle William, you can't ask us to believe you if you say things like that," Joyce protested. "How could there be a cat in here?"

"I don't know." The old man spoke with his back to her. "I'm only telling you what I saw. I had my window open at the bottom–there it is, you can see for yourself. I woke to hear the thing—to hear the thing—well, to hear the thing. And I hate the creatures. I'm like old Roberts on that respect. He couldn't bear 'em and I can't bear 'em. I picked the creature up and I pushed it through the window and it scratched me. There you are. Isn't that clear? I don't know what you're making such a fuss about."

The girl reddened. "All right," she said. "If you'll give me that handkerchief, Mr. Campion, I'll tie his hand up. You'll have to see the doctor in the morning, uncle."

"You leave me alone, my dear. I'll be all right. I've had plenty of cuts before now."

Uncle William was still on his dignity, but there was yet a furtive uneasiness in his eyes. The bandaging complete, a certain embarrassing argument followed as to whether the brandy should remain or no. A compromise having been reached, the young people left the old man in bed with a small tot at his side. In the corridor Joyce turned to Campion.

"What happened?" she whispered.

The young man seemed troubled. "Look here," he murmured, "don't go downstairs with that stuff. Take it into your room or leave it in the hall, or something. And when you shut your door behind you, turn the key."

Her eyes met his questioningly, but he said no more, and she went off, switching out the light in the hall as she passed into her room.

Campion stood where he was for some moments before he turned and went back to his bed. As he passed Uncle William's room he heard a faint sound from within and paused to listen. When he moved on again his face was very grave and his pale eyes were narrowed.

The sound he had heard was Uncle William quietly locking his door.

12

Committee Stage

Mr. Campion lit a cigarette and sank down in a protesting basket-chair before the fire in the small sitting-room at "The Three Keys," which Inspector Oates had engaged for himself to ensure a little privacy; a personal extravagance which he felt was justified in view of the sensation which the case was making in the town.

Like all guest-rooms furnished by unimaginative hosts, it presented an atmosphere of aloof, if not downright grudging, hospitality. Even the fire kept itself a trifle too much to itself behind the narrow bars of the little grate.

Campion glanced at the small clock with the loud voice on the mantelpiece. At any moment now Mr. Oates should return from the inquest on Andrew Seeley. It would be the most formal of formal affairs, probably little more than a mere notice of adjournment. It was the first time Campion had felt really alone since his arrival, and he permitted himself the leisure to reflect that active adventure, however strenuous, was apt to be less harrowing than taking part in this slow nemesis which was so obviously engulfing Socrates Close and its occupants.

He was glad to sit back and consider the matter coldly in these neutral surroundings, for he had felt the atmosphere of the house settling down upon him, robbing him of his impartiality, drawing him into itself, forcing him to see life confined within its own tiny boundaries.

Murder had been committed on two occasions. That seemed to be the only fact that emerged concrete and clear from the hotchpotch of unrelated incidents, tendencies and motives into which he had plunged. Uncle William, the obvious culprit, became less and less obvious the longer he knew him.

The incident of the night before returned to him vividly.

Quite plainly Uncle William had been the victim of an attack. He had also been ill. The fact that he had refused so obstinately to give any reasonable account of his assailant was out of character. William was not the sort of man to shield anyone, nor was he likely to manufacture any incident so dramatic or so subtle as a faked attack upon himself. Mr. Campion shuddered to think of the kind of ambuscade Uncle William might have arranged had he ever conceived the idea of such a method of shelving the suspicion against him. Certainly he would have emerged scatheless, without the wound in which Doctor Lavrock had put three stitches that morning.

With the elimination of Uncle William's guilt there remained his fear, his locked door and that furtive element in the old house which had made Campion advise Joyce to lock herself in her room and had caused him to leave his own door half open and to lie awake listening for soft footsteps in the corridor.

If Uncle William was out of it, whose was the mind behind these lunatic crimes? The same mind which had conceived the idea of binding a man hand and foot before shooting the top of his head off?

It was at this point in his meditations that the thought which he had been resisting subconsciously all the morning forced itself upon him. Alice: not the red-eyed, pleasant-faced woman who had opened the door to the police, but the herculean elemental creature in the white calico nightgown, the being whose fanatical love for her mistress had been so strikingly displayed during the scene on the landing the night before. Here was sufficient strength to account for Andrew. Here was the necessary intimate knowledge of the household, and here also, he felt unpleasantly sure, was the requisite courage. But, and it was at this point that his mind jibbed, here was not the madness, the intellectual cunning. For that he knew he must look to an accomplice, an instigator, rather.

In the sanctuary of the inspector's siting-room he considered Mrs. Caroline Faraday.

Here was a remarkable personality, a woman who at an advanced age retained her intellect, while possessing no longer any vestige of emotion.

From a purely altruistic point of view there were several reasons why the community at Socrates Close, the little world which she governed so completely, would be better off without Andrew Seeley. When he reflected upon certain phases of the dead man's character as it had emerged, Campion was seized by the uncomfortable impression that there were, almost certainly, many other reasons not quite so obvious. The motive for Julia's murder was as yet to be found. But she had not been a pleasant woman. She had been petty, bad-tempered, dogmatic; all important anti-social crimes in so small and so self-contained a community.

When one is so near death oneself life loses much of its importance. Mrs. Faraday had said as much only the day before. Was it possible that it was she who had done these things, using Alice's strength, courage and blind trust in her mistress as a means?

Campion rose to his feet and threw his cigarette into the fire. Now was not the time for speculation, he reflected. Conjecture profiteth man little, and it was with a species of relief that he swung round to face the doorway as the Inspector came in.

"Hullo, Campion." Mr. Oates's habitual gloom momentarily dispersed. He folded his raincoat neatly and placed it on the table with his hat on top of it. "Adjourned till Tuesday," he said. "That old fellow William Faraday gave evidence of identification. I saw he'd got his hand in a sling. Anything up?"

"In a way, yes, and in a way, no," said Mr. Campion. "Do take one of your own chairs. The wicker contraption is a snare and a delusion. Try the one with the brass studs."

The Inspector seated himself and took out his pipe. "I hope you're not going to be long unless you've got something important to say," he said. "I want to go down and have another look at that stream. I only gave it the once-over yesterday. It's quite evident to me, if we're going to make a case of this business, that we've got to get the gun. The first inquest on the woman is fixed for Monday. I don't see why these coroner fellows can't do two in a day. I don't suppose they'll adjourn that longer than Wednesday, unless we offer them a prospect of a trial and a conviction. I see the newspapers are comparatively quiet. I suppose they smell an unsatisfactory case."

"I told a man I know on the *Comet* in confidence that I didn't think it'd come to anything," said Campion.

Stanislaus looked at him sharply. "Have you found out anything!" he said.

"Fair do's," said Mr. Campion. "You know exactly how I stand in this business. I'm not the clever amateur helping the important policeman. I've just been asked down for the murder.

If it wasn't for Joyce and Marcus, and possibly Uncle William, I think I should go home."

Stanislaus put down his pipe. "Show us it," he said.

Mr. Campion put his hand in his pocket and drew out a small paper bag. From this he extracted a handkerchief, which he placed upon the table. Stanislaus rose and stood beside him and bent forward watching, while Campion unfolded the white cambric handkerchief and exposed the little wooden cylinder.

"I've opened it," he said, "but I used a handkerchief. Any finger-prints will still be intact, though I'm afraid even in this old-fashioned household they've all heard about using gloves. If you want to see what it's like and you don't want to touch it," he went on, "here is a replica. I went to the chemist whose name you will see on the label and bought myself a packet of Thyro-Tissue Reducer from the gentleman in charge, who seemed to think I was mad. I didn't make enquiries about previous purchasers, not wishing to poach, but I ascertained that in his opinion the stuff is principally an aperient with a large percentage of starch to give bulk."

As he spoke he produced a second cylinder from his pocket exactly like the first.

The Inspector opened it and drew out the zig-zag strip of pellets.

"Where did you find this?" he inquired, pointing to the package in the handkerchief.

With becoming modesty Mr. Campion related his adventure of the night before. The Inspector frowned when he found that Joyce had been a party to the discovery, but was quite frankly surprised and delighted when he heard of the hiding-place.

"No finger-prints on the knob?" he inquired. "No, I know there weren't. That place was kept as shiny as a new motor-car. We got all the prints there were yesterday. How did you hit on it, though? Did the girl put you up to it?"

Campion shook his head. "No, you're on the wrong track there. I found it out all by myself. It was the one place I could think of where you might not have looked."

Stanislaus regarded him with mild surprise. "Do you often hide things in bed knobs?" he said.

"Not since I was a child," said Mr. Campion, with dignity. "There were brass knobs on my crib. I remember the taste of them still."

The Inspector grunted. "My crib hadn't got knobs on," he

said. "You had all the advantages. Well, now we're getting somewhere. It struck me at once that someone must have tampered with some patent flimmery-flammery the old lady was taking. They say every woman of over forty takes something. That's why these fellows keep on advertising. You'd be surprised at the offers I get to say I derive my sparkle from pills and ointments and whatnot. This is much better," he repeated, brightening visibly. "I think I'll have a look at the exhibit all the same. The deceased's own finger-prints'll be all over it, of course."

Holding the cylinder carefully in one handkerchief and unscrewing the top, his hand protected by another, he peered into the box.

"About half gone," he announced. "And she didn't tear off the paper. That's a bit of luck. If morphine or conium was substituted for the one of these pellets there may be some traces of it left. We used to be rather down on the Home Office chemists at one time, I believe, but they're very hot fellows now. You'd be surprised. I'll take these, if you please."

He gathered the corners of the handkerchief which held the half-empty cylinder and replaced it carefully in the paper bag.

"Anything else?" he inquired, looking up.

Before speaking, Campion returned to his chair, where he sat blinking amicably behind his spectacles.

"A fair swop," he murmured. "What was the bullet like?"

"Point four five," said Stanislaus grudgingly. "And much good may that do you. The number of unregistered Army Webleys in the country must be colossal. When we find the actual gun we may be able to spot some slight irregularity in it which will have shown on the bullet—but what a hope! As soon as I heard of that coincidence on Thursday I knew I was in for trouble. If I get a conviction on this case," he added bitterly, "I'll eat my hat—the old brown one I wore when I arrested Summers."

Campion made no comment, and the Inspector returned to the case.

"What about old Faraday's hand?" he demanded. "How did that happen? I don't know if you know it, my lad, but that fellow has twenty-five minutes to account for, twenty-five mighty important minutes. Not all the statements about the exact time of that Sunday lunch tally."

Mr. Campion leant back in his chair and considered Uncle

William's position, and, incidentally, his own. At length he stated Uncle William's case simply, without exaggeration or elimination. When he had finished the Inspector sat staring at him.

"Not bad," he said. "Not at all. It's not enough to take to a jury, though."

"I should think not," said Mr. Campion in horror. "My dear fellow, consider the situation. There's Sir Gordon Woodthorpe's evidence. He's bound to remember the case of the man who gave him a false name. Bound to recognise him, too. Then there's the gun. You've got to find that, you know. Finally we come to the question of the rope. I suppose you'll have that window cord compared with the stuff taken off the body?"

"You bet I will." The Inspector spoke grimly. "It's a great idea having you in the house, Campion," he went on consideringly, "in spite of your funny position. However, to return to this chap William. I haven't examined this story of yours, but the impression with which it leaves me is not very favourable towards the man. Still, let's have it all. You know more about him than I do. And after all," he went on lugubriously, "if there was ever a case in the world that gave a fellow like myself a magnificent chance of making a fool of himself, this is it."

"Well, there's one thing," said Campion. He was speaking slowly now, choosing his words with care. "I told you I saw him putting the iodine on his hand. After that he practically fainted, or collapsed, anyhow. It struck me as being extraordinary. The seizure only lasted a minute and I took it for granted that his heart was not too good. But when I made tactful inquiries this morning from the doctor who came to stitch up the cut, I discovered Uncle William's heart was as sound as a bell. So the question remains—why the collapse?"

"It might have been anything," said the Inspector, clearly unimpressed by this line of reasoning. "If he had staged the whole thing it might have been part of his verisimilitude."

The younger man shook his head. "I haven't made myself clear," he said. "I know what I'm telling you is not evidence, but it's a strong impression and it might be useful. I believe the old boy was frightened last night, and I also believe that he was slightly—very slightly—poisoned."

After staring at him for some seconds in astonishment, Stanislaus laughed.

"Hand in the dark with poisoned dagger?" he said. "This is

police work, my lad, not the high-class feudal warfare you've been accustomed to."

Mr. Campion remained unruffled. "All right," he said. "Disregard the gipsy's warning if you like. But still, continuing my defence of Mr. Faraday—or Uncle William as I shall always think of him—I rather fancy that if you make enquiries at every public house on the direct route from Grantchester Meadows to Socrates Close you will find that on the Sunday in question Uncle William entered a place of refreshment, took a drink and departed, probably behaving a little queerly. They're bound to remember him. He's a local character."

The Inspector was unimpressed. "If there's a sound alibi for that twenty-five minutes, of course, any flimsy case we may have got against him falls flat," he said. "At the least hint of trouble, though, I suppose the family will brief a good man for the inquest. Do you know, Campion, in my opinion that's the one point where our judicial system goes to pieces. In a case like this where there's plenty of money, the least hint of trouble and you're up against a K.C. But if there's no money the law takes its course in its own sweet way with some young pup of a barrister defending at the trial, although there is always a good man for the Crown. I don't like this case. I wish I was in my own district. They're first-class fellows down here, but you can see that they don't like the scandal in the town any more than your young friend the lawyer does. What gives you the idea that William Faraday visited a pub, on his way home, even supposing this preposterous amnesia story is true?"

"On the first occasion that Uncle William experienced this distressing phenomenon," said Mr. Campion, deliberately ignoring the last part of the Inspector's remark, "he found himself standing outside the Roman Catholic Church with a glass in his hand. In other words, he had walked into a public house, ordered a drink and walked out with the glass in his hand. After all, amnesia is a remote form of paralysis, isn't it? The mind rejects memory, often because memory is unpleasant. Memory means restraint. Uncle William loses his memory and loses his restraints. He satisfies his natural desire. He has his drink."

"All very pretty," said the Inspector. "But you'll have a job reconciling that with the bath story."

Mr. Campion was silent for some seconds. "I should like to know how much the defunct Andrew had to do with that incident," he said. "I think we are both lucky in being spared Andrew's acquaintance, Stanislaus."

The Inspector grunted. "If you ask me, we're darned unlucky coming to this starchy place at all," he said. "I wish I was on a good straightforward burglary. Well, you've brought me a lot of interesting information and spoilt it by taking all the guts out of it. Wherever we look we're met by that cussed conjuror. Someone's doing devilish clever tricks."

Mr. Campion nodded. "There's something very queer inside that house," he said. "Something very, very queer."

"Madness," said the Inspector shortly. "Madness with an 'ism' of some sort. This is a job for a psychologist, I'm sure of that. That's the trouble. What a chemist says is evidence. What a psychologist says isn't. When they tried Palmer, chemical facts seem to have been largely a matter of opinion; that's where psychology stands to-day."

"Returning to the question of fair dealing," remarked Mr. Campion. "Have you found Cousin George?"

"That's another impossible job," the Inspector grumbled. "We've published a description and an appeal for him to come forward, but of course without result. Then he has no known address, no one seems to know much about him down here, he doesn't seem to have lodged in the town. All we know is that he was in London on Thursday. I say, no wonder he was off like a shot when he saw the girl. She behaved rather queerly about him, though. Personally, I think her behaviour has been rather queer all along. Oh, I've heard about the scandal," he went on hastily before Campion could speak, "and I realise that that may account for more in this case than it would in my family, for instance."

Both men were silent for some time. Then the Inspector relit his pipe.

"All this loose thinking is very irregular, you know," he said, grinning suddenly at Campion. "We shall concentrate on the gun. We've found a couple of witnesses who heard the shot, by the way. A man and his wife living in a cottage on the Grantchester Road say they heard a shot at about five minutes to one p.m. on the Sunday. The man says he went to the back door, but the meadows were all under a ground mist and he saw nothing. He says it was a 'thick day,' whatever that may mean. It seems to be a local term for spring weather. What a time for a murder, though, eh? Midday on a Sunday; everybody at home eating."

"Returning to the question of Cousin George," persisted Mr. Campion, "I take it that you don't consider him important?"

Stanislaus Oates growled. "Not very," he said. "Suppose we do find him? Suppose that by chance he walks into our arms, what then? We can't arrest him. We can only ask him where he was on Sunday at the time of the crime. Unless he's an absolute fool he'll have a satisfactory answer for that. Besides, why should he have anything to do with it at all? He wasn't known to have any grudge against Andrew. He was in the house for about an hour on the night before the first murder, but he hasn't been seen anywhere near it since. Just because he was in the habit of holding up his aunt for a pound or two from time to time it doesn't follow that he was a potential murderer. No, Campion, you can't get away from it. This was an inside job. There was nothing accidental about either killing. They were deliberately planned crimes. Someone had good reason to want both those people out of the way. I may be wrong, but I have a feeling that that person is still at work. You look out for yourself. The mind that is responsible for this little lot isn't going to have its plans upset by any nicely-spoken little gent in hornrimmed spectacles. There's your gipsy's warning."

Mr. Campion did not answer for some moments. The Inspector's words had driven him back in spite of himself to his theory of earlier that morning.

"I'll come down with you and see the scene of the crime, if you don't mind," he said at last, rising to his feet. "I never like to miss an opportunity of watching the old war-horse going into action."

But although they walked for some considerable distance alone together, Mr. Campion said nothing of the question that was weighing on his mind. Had Mrs. Faraday overestimated her autocracy in her own domain and ordered the execution of Andrew Seeley for crime or crimes as yet unknown?

13

Man Friday

    "It's very irregular you coming along like this," the Inspector grumbled. They had turned out of the new road, crossed a maze of narrow streets and now took the path across the meadows to the river. "Very irregular," he repeated gloomily. "I don't want to sound ungrateful, old man," he added hastily, "and by all means come along. I only mention it because there'll be Bowditch down there and one or two other fellows."

    Mr. Campion smiled. "That's all right," he said. "I'll efface myself as much as possible. You go right ahead. Pretend I'm not there. If you do it well enough the others will think they're seeing things and that always adds a little fun to the proceedings."

    There were several plain-clothes men on the banks of the Granta and a uniformed man by the bridge, to say nothing of the one or two hopeful spectators. The prospect was cold and gloomy and served to emphasise the melancholy futility of any further proceedings so far as the unfortunate Andrew Seeley was concerned.

    As they approached, one of the raincoated figures came hurrying towards them. This proved to be Detective-Sergeant Bowditch, the Inspector's colleague from the Yard. There was a legend in the Force that Bowditch had been born in a helmet, and he certainly suggested the policeman in mufti more successfully than any man Mr. Campion had ever seen. He was tall, squarely built, with a red face and a thick soft black moustache. His small eyes were surrounded by creases and his whole appearance conveyed a quite unwarrantable cheerfulness.

    "Hullo, sir," he said, and smiled, his face diffused with a delight for which there was no visible cause. He glanced inquiringly at Campion, but receiving no explanation for the young man's presence favoured him also with a welcoming beam. Stanislaus eyed him gloomily.

"Found anything?" he inquired.

"No," said Mr. Bowditch, adding still more cheerfully, "no. Come down to have a look?"

He did not seem to expect to receive a reply, and went on: "We've combed both banks from the willows to the road, and there's not a sign of anything. Of course, it's some time since it happened."

Stanislaus nodded sourly. "I know," he said. "Hullo, what's this?"

The three men glanced down the footpath to where a fourth man hurried towards them, something in his hand. The new-comer turned out to be a grey-faced sergeant of the local police, bearing a tattered green felt object.

"I found this under some dead leaves in that bit of copse up there," he said, pointing to the clump of trees just below the footpath bridge on the south side of the river. "I don't know if it's anything of importance, but it was under a pile of leaves and doesn't seem to have been there very long."

Stanislaus took the exhibit with interest. It was the battered relic of a green trilby hat. Headband and lining were gone and the braid with which the edge of the brim had been bound was frayed.

"Not the hat the deceased wore to church on the Sunday in question," said Mr. Bowditch jovially. "Apart from the fact that the deceased wore a bowler on that occasion, the condition of this hat precludes any such eventuality."

The Inspector's withering glance had the effect of silencing his subordinate without in any way diminishing his good temper.

"Anything else of interest?" Stanislaus inquired of the finder of the hat. "What's in that hut over there?" He pointed to a little shanty standing among the haze of budding leaves in the copse.

"There's nothing there, sir, save for a few bits of sacks, dead leaves and so on." The man was unenthusiastic. "Seems to have been used as a storage place for tools and a shelter for the workmen clearing the wood at some time or other. Shall I verify that, sir?"

"Oh, no; no need. I'll come and have a look later. Thank you very much, Davidson."

As the man went off, Stanislaus handed over the battered hat to Bowditch.

"You can take charge of that," he said. "I don't think it's anything to do with this business. I shall make a point of seeing where it was found, though. You say there's absolutely no sign from the road to the willows to show where the body was put into the water? Of course it might have floated down for miles, though the cottager says he heard the shot from his direction."

"That's so," said Mr. Bowditch happily. "But if you'll step along and have a look at this stream, sir, you'll see right away what occurred to me."

As they moved on down the footpath towards the little humpbacked stone bridge, he continued:

"You'll see," he said, "the current is slow at the sides but swift in the centre. It is also comparatively deep here. Well," he continued, still with his smile, "you see what I mean? In order to get a body to drift any way you'd have to place it in the swift part of the stream. In other words, if I was doing it myself I'd drop it over this here bridge. *If* I was doing it," he said, and broke into a roar of laughter, which he speedily suppressed at an aggrieved glance from Inspector Oates.

There was obviously a good deal of sense in Mr. Bowditch's observation. Mr. Campion, considering the scene, came to the same conclusion himself. He also recollected Mr. Cheetoo's dilations on the same subject. There was, as the observant student had noticed, a strong eddy just below the bridge which would have held any floating object for some considerable time if it had not succeeded in sweeping it into the bank. It was evident that the Inspector himself was inclined to take Mr. Bowditch's line of reasoning, for he devoted his attention for some time to the bridge.

This was of the stone humpbacked variety, high enough to permit a small boat to pass beneath it when the river was at its normal level. It was topped by a low stone parapet on either side, and the surface of this the Inspector scrutinised carefully. After some moments of earnest contemplation he turned away regretfully.

"There's nothing," he said. "Of course. What can you expect? I suppose this bridge is used fairly often. Children run along the parapet. There is no moss, and any traces of mud, blood or dust that might have been left will have gone long ago in the downpour we've had in the last ten days. Come on. We'll take a look at the hut."

The hut, which lay fifteen yards or so from the footpath and possibly thirty from the bank, turned out to be one of those temporary structures which clearance men occasionally leave behind them. It was composed mainly of faggots, and roofed with sticks covered with a sack or two. It was quite sound, however, and the ground inside was dry and hard. The Inspector paused at the entrance and peered in.

One or two matted sacks stiff with mud lay in a corner, but for the rest the place was empty. There was no sign that it had been disturbed since its constructors had abandoned it.

"No traces of any kind?" the Inspector inquired.

"No footprints," said Mr. Bowditch joyously. "But then there wouldn't be on this stuff. There's no reason to suppose that the deceased came up here, is there?"

The stiff wiry twitch outside the hut betrayed nothing. It did not even show any traces of their own passage over it, in spite of the dampness of the ground. The Inspector's gloom increased.

"That hat," he said, "where was that found? This is a waste of time, Bowditch."

"That's right," said the red-faced man. "Still, it's all got to be done. Never overlook anything, and you can't miss the thing you're looking for. That's the idea, isn't it? The beautiful hat which our colleague discovered was located at a point over here. It was buried by somebody, and I should say he knew best." He glanced happily at the ruin in his hand.

They returned to the footpath again and walked on for a dozen yards or so, pausing at last before a heap of newly-turned leaves, wet and pungent in the fine rain which had now begun to fall.

"There you are," he said. "I think Davidson is right, too. This hadn't been here very long. It was buried under the leaves, not covered fairy-tale fashion by robins and such. What does that tell you, sir?"

There was a twinkle in his eye as he spoke, but it was not in the least disrespectful.

"I don't see why anyone should bury a hat unless they wanted to hide it," said the Inspector. "But that doesn't signify. I've never been on the scene of any outdoor crime yet where there wasn't someone's old clothes lying about. Still, as you say, it's funny this thing being buried. It's not much of a hat, anyway."

"You're right." Mr. Bowditch seemed to consider this a moment for laughter. "Some lie-about's," he said. "That's what that is. The property of a vagrant, if I might use a contradiction in terms."

The Inspector silenced him with a look. "The gun," he said. "I must have that gun. If it's been thrown away it's got to be found. There's the hat, too. The one the deceased was wearing when he left church. That's not so important, but it's odd that it hasn't turned up. Size seven and three-quarters, new, Henry Heath label on the lining. I'm going down to Socrates Close now if anybody wants me, but if it's the newspaper fellows let 'em look for me. I don't want this hat bellowed all over the place as an important clue. Be mysterious if you like."

Mr. Bowditch winked shamelessly at Campion. "I'll keep the hat under me hat," he said. "Well, good afternoon, sir. If the gun's about, we'll get it. We've taken about a ton of mud out of that river already, and we'll take another ton if necessary. But it's an unsatisfactory job dragging a stream that's full of weeds."

"Do murderers throw away guns near the scene of the crime?" said Mr. Campion mildly, as he and the Inspector went on their way together.

Mr. Oates paused to knock out his pipe on his shoe before replying.

"Very often," he said. "That's the funny thing about murder. A man may carry the whole thing through with remarkable ingenuity and then give himself right away immediately afterwards, just as though he had lost interest in the crime. It's queer about guns, too. If a man doesn't carry a gun habitually, and I don't suppose there's one in a thousand in England who does, his tendency is to chuck it away as soon as he has used it. He realises that it is incriminating if found upon him, but forgets that it can nearly always be tracked back to him. I bet the gun we're after is in that river somewhere. But, as old Bowditch pointed out, it's a devil of a place to drag."

Mr. Campion appeared satisfied, on this point at least. "If I may be permitted to say so," he ventured, after a pause, "the hat trick excites my curiosity. You are looking for a bowler hat and you find a venerable green felt. To my innocent mind this would suggest a swop. But a murderer would hardly finish off his star turn by coming home in his victim's hat, unless he was reverting to a time-honoured custom in bringing back his enemy's head or the nearest thing to it. On the other hand, if, as seems more probable, some disinterested third party found Andrew Seeley's new hat, and considering it vastly preferable to his own—a point no one can deny—discarded the one for the other, why should he take the trouble to bury his old hat? My experience of lie-abouts, as your happy friend Mr. Bowditch so neatly describes them, has taught me that their passion for tidiness is not marked, in fact they are apt to leave any unwanted part of their wardrobe precisely where they discard it."

The Inspector grunted. "Tramps are a law unto themselves," he said. "You never know what they're going to do. But the hat is too slender a clue to worry about yet. It's got to be noted, of course, but we can't waste time thinking about it. It's the lucky fellows on the outside, like yourself, who can enjoy the luxuries of conjecture. It *would* be a bowler hat," he went on, disobeying his own axiom. "The only hat in the world, with the possible exception of a topper, which can look old in five seconds. A spot of dust and a kick made it look like nothing on earth. A good felt is always a good felt, whatever you do to it, but a tramp could have gone off in Andrew Seeley's hat without looking in the least extraordinary." He sighed. "That's the worst of this darned case. For every single thing that's happened there might be half a dozen explanations. I had a report on the angle of the bullet this morning. The experts were hampered, of course, by the fact that the head appears to have been under water for about ten days, but they're smart fellows and they've got me this much. Hastings is appearing at the inquest, so there's no reason why I shouldn't tell you. The bullet entered the head in the very centre of the forehead. It took a slightly upward course, practically lifting the back of the skull off with it. There were powder burns on the skin of the forehead and these were pretty bad or they wouldn't have survived. That means the gun was fired close to, and it also means that the firer of the shot was probably a little shorter than Seeley if the dead man was standing up when it happened. But as his feet were bound that doesn't seem likely, so we're no better off. The really tantalising point is that there must have been a lot of blood about directly after the crime. If the man was shot lying down there must have been a pool of it, and if he was standing up the murderer must have been covered with it the moment he started shifting the body. Yet there's no sign, no trace at all of any blood in the vicinity. If he was carried or dragged to the bridge as old Bowditch suggests, and it certainly seems feasible, there must have been a trail of blood. But of course we mustn't forget the rain, and in spite of the fact that this footpath is so near the town it doesn't seem to have been used much at the time of year. Still, there ought to have been traces. Someone ought to have seen something. I'm advertising for witnesses. Of course the body may have floated right down. We shall follow the river up as far as this Byron's Pool, if need be." He shook his head. "As I said, it's no good conjecturing. We've got to get on with the routine. We'll get out that little car I've hired and go up to the house."

"If it isn't rude to ask, in what direction is duty calling you now?" inquired Mr. Campion.

The Inspector seemed surprised at the question. "That fellow William and his hand, of course," he said. "All new developments must be carefully watched. I think that's about the first rule in the book. We must find out how he hurt himself. There is just a chance that he was attacked, you know, and if so he must be made to talk."

"Here, I say, no bullying Uncle William," said Campion in mild alarm.

"Bullying?" The Inspector's expression was bitter. "It's as much as we're allowed to do to speak to witnesses these days. But if he tells me a cock-and-bull story he can go into the witness-box and tell it to the coroner—and the press."

"Ho!" said Mr. Campion.

"Eh?"

"I said 'Ho!'" repeated the young man. "A vulgar expression meaning 'indeed.' Oh, well, I'm sorry about all this. I'll come with you. By the way, I swore Joyce to secrecy."

"Good," conceded the Inspector. "I'm sorry the girl was in it. Still, I quite see you couldn't go ferreting about the house on your own. I left the package for the analysts and the photographers. We shall have a report in twenty-four hours if we're lucky. Of course," he went on, "William is the straight line to follow. He was the only member of the household out of doors at the time of the first murder, with the exception of one of the servants. You can't get away from that."

"Which one of the servants?" said Campion, conscious of an unwonted feeling of apprehension.

"The big red-faced woman," said the Inspector. "I've got her name down. The housemaid. Been with 'em for thirty years, just like the story books. She had the day off to go over to her married sister, who lives at Waterbeach, a mile or two out. Half a moment—I've got it. Nuddington. Alice Nuddington. She left the house at nine in the morning and got back at ten at night. We can verify her statement easily. All these things have got to be attended to."

Mr. Campion did not speak for some moments. The rain was driving in his face and the wet streets, with their urban drabness even more pronounced by their comparative desertion, gave the tragedy an air of sordidness which it did not really possess. The thought of Uncle William, that bewildered and floundering old reprobate, stirred a sense of compassion within him, however, and he plodded along by the Inspector's side.

"I must see the clothes that William wore to church," the Inspector remarked, more to himself than to his friend. "A dull routine job, this tracking of criminals. Murderers are the most unsatisfactory of the lot. Nine times out of ten you've got no past record to go on. What's the good of your beautiful filing system then? What's the good of your organisation? This is going to be a darned bad inconclusive business, you mark my words."

The Inspector's gloom, which increased even when they climbed into the two-seater Rover, was in such direct opposition to Mr. Bowditch's homeric cheerfulness that Mr. Campion felt called upon to comment upon it.

"I like your friend Bowditch," he said. "A happy man, I deduced."

Mr. Oates snorted. "Bowditch!" he said. "A nice chap and a good man. But that smile of his gets on my nerves. I feel I'm wandering about with an advertisement for fruit salts. I told him this was a murder and not a music-hall show, and he laughed till he was nearly sick. You can't do anything with a fellow like that."

He relapsed into thought, and it was not until they were in sight of the house that he spoke again.

"There you are," he said, jerking his hand in the direction of the creeper-covered building, "that's where our solution lies. It's someone underneath that roof. They all know more than they've said, and William Faraday comes in for special mention. Here we are."

However, the stolid gloom of Socrates Close, which seemed to be about to settle upon them once more as they stepped out of the car, was shattered for once. They entered the porch, the Inspector pulled the bell, and as the hollow peal sounded within the depths of the domestic quarters a loud feminine shriek, followed by a burst of hysterical laughter, came out to them quite clearly from the breakfast-room.

The front door was thrown open to them almost immediately by Marcus Featherstone, considerably paler than usual, his reddish hair standing almost upright. Behind him, in the hall near the service corridor, a little group of excited servants clung together, while the distressing sounds from the breakfast-room continued.

Marcus seized upon them. "Come in," he said. "I've been trying to 'phone you."

Stanislaus Oates was slightly surprised for once in his life. He stepped heavily into the hall, Campion following.

"What's the matter?" he demanded.

Marcus shot a harassed glance around him. "That awful noise in there is Kitty," he murmured. "Joyce is with her, but I'm afraid she's rather bad. You go back to the kitchen, will you please, cook," he added, turning to the maids. "There's absolutely nothing to be afraid of—absolutely nothing. Look here, Inspector, would you mind coming into the library? You, too, Campion, of course. The fact is, the household has had a bit of a scare."

The servants trailed off down the corridor, and Campion and the Inspector, their curiosity thoroughly aroused, followed Marcus into the great book-lined room in which poor Uncle William had never seen his father at his best.

It was a gloomy but imposing apartment, furnished principally by the enormous carved oak desk set facing the door and a high-backed yellow brocade chair, which stood behind it. The holland blinds were drawn, and as they entered Marcus switched on the lights.

When he turned to them he seemed more himself, and, if anything, a trifle shamefaced. He laughed awkwardly.

"Now I come to show you what has scared the whole household and driven poor Kitty into screaming hysteria, I feel a bit of a fool," he said. "It just goes to show how jumpy everyone is in the house. I pulled the blinds down again because the maids kept coming in to stare at the thing. There doesn't seem to be any key to this room."

As he spoke he moved over to the long narrow window directly behind the yellow chair and twitched the spring blind, which immediately shot up to the lintel, revealing a view of the bowling green and the phenomenon which had come like a bombshell into the startled household.

In the centre of one of the large panes was a boldly drawn

sign in crimson, simple, entirely inexplicable and certainly presenting a somewhat startling appearance. It consisted of two small circles one above the other, followed by a stroke, with an outer circle round the whole thing, thus:

The Inspector stared at it. "When did this appear?" he demanded.

"I don't know," said Marcus. "But they say it wasn't here yesterday, and it was discovered about fifteen minutes ago by Kitty, who has taken over Julia's duty of dusting her father's room. The blinds in this room were not drawn until after you left last night, Inspector, and it was not entered this morning as far as anyone remembers. Kitty came here with the duster just now, not having had time before. She pulled up the blind and discovered it. The unexpected sight frightened her—she seems to have been on edge, anyhow. Her screams brought the household and myself. I came back from the inquest with William to lunch and—well, there you are. Everybody is very frightened. It's a queer thing to happen, and I am afraid they are all very jumpy."

The Inspector walked gingerly round the yellow chair and peered at the glass.

"Chalk on the outside," he announced. "The rain's coming the other way and hasn't touched it. What an extraordinary thing! Someone's playing the fool. Any marks under the window? I believe there's a flower-bed here."

He raised the sash and leaned out. They heard him grunt softly, and the next moment he was back again, an incredulous expression upon his face.

"Well, what do you make of this?" he said. "You look here."

Campion and Marcus accepted his invitation with alacrity. Between the path which bounded the bowling green and the wall of the house there was a narrow flower-bed, and in the centre of this, deep and distinct, as though it had been made in plaster, was the single imprint of an immense naked foot.

There was something ludicrous about it. It was a caricature of a footprint with great splayed-out toes, the whole thing of a size that impressed one at a glance.

Campion and Marcus looked at one another, the same thought uppermost in both their minds. Feet like these were not to be hidden. Campion grinned at the Inspector.

"Looks like one of your boys," he said. "Rather overdoing the plain clothes, I should say."

Inspector Stanislaus Oates did not return his smile.

14

The Cat in the Bag

"It's absurd having a place of this size without a 'phone," said the Inspector, walking up the drive after some cursory telephoning from a neighbouring house. "Of course that mark and footprint is a joke in very bad taste on somebody's part, or at least I hope so. These things usually take the form of anonymous letters. I don't like it when people start fooling round the premises. I shall have the print photographed and measured and I shall have a man out to search for others. That's routine, Mr. Featherstone, and probably a waste of valuable time."

"Suppose it wasn't a joke?" said Mr. Campion slowly, his long thin figure bent slightly forward. "Suppose it wasn't an evidence of bad taste? Have you ever seen a mark like that before, Stanislaus? Did it mean anything to you?"

The Inspector looked at him sharply. He had known the young man long enough to be sure that these casual remarks that Mr. Campion occasionally let drop were never quite as fatuous

as they sounded. He considered the question seriously, therefore.

"I can't say I have," he said. "On the face of it, it looks like
a tramp mark, but none I've ever seen. A regular tramp usually
carried two bits of chalk, one red and one white," he explained
to Marcus. "They make signs to warn each other about the
neighbourhood. It's a sort of freemasonry. Of course this thing
might be the figure eighteen, but that doesn't make sense either.
Does it convey anything to you, Campion? You are an encyclo-
pædia of odd information."

The young man hesitated. "I may be potty, of course," he
said, "but I have a hunch that it's the letter 'B.' I saw it before
once, drawn by a child. She copied the whole alphabet like that,
as though only the inside whites of the letters registered on her
mind. The 'A' was a triangle with a sort of square-cut croquet
hoop underneath it, like this." He took out an envelope and
pencilled the figure on the back of it, which he held up for them
to see.

Marcus was sceptical, but the Inspector, who was a doting
father himself, was interested immediately.

"Yes, it might be that," he said. "I've heard of that before,
now you come to mention it. But it's certainly not a kid in this
case. Did you ever see a footprint like that? I'll have a cast made
of it if it's only as a souvenir."

By common consent they walked round the side of the house
to take another look at the flower-bed. Stanislaus had previously
covered the footprint with several thicknesses of newspaper,
weighted by stones at the corners.

"A man," he said, looking at it. "And rather unusually
heavy, I should say, although, of course, he was putting all his
weight upon this foot to get at the window."

"It's so extraordinary it being bare," Marcus burst out almost angrily. Like many men of his calling, the illogical irritated rather than attracted him.

The Inspector squatted on the edge of the gravel and peered forward. Then for the first time that afternoon he grinned.

"He had a sock on," he said, "but it doesn't seem to have reached past his instep. A sort of mitten. There are some shreds of worsted in this mud, I believe. We'll cover it up again if you don't mind." He replaced the paper and straightened himself. "Looks like old Bowditch's lie-about," he said.

"Aha!" said Mr. Campion. "The owner of the green hat. 'Mysterious nomad signals to accomplice within House of Secrets.'"

The Inspector paused in the very act of rising as this new explanation, with all its possibilities, suddenly presented itself to his mind. For a moment his grey eyes met Campion's speculatively. Then he shook his head. "No," he said, "that's not worth powder and shot. It's not that kind of show. Don't worry," he added, turning to Marcus. "We shan't neglect any clues. We shall follow everything up. That's routine—and a very slow business it is. I shall leave the fancy work to you, Campion," he continued, grinning at him mischievously. "You think as much as you like, my boy. I called the fellows on guard off last night at about twelve o'clock, but I'll put them back. We can't have monkey tricks like this going on, and the last thing I want is to have this household alarmed unnecessarily. We're all kid-glove men now, you know."

They entered the house by the side door, which led to a small passage running parallel to the staircase.

"I came up originally to see Mr. William Faraday," observed the Inspector, watching the others remove their wet coats. "Is he about?"

A slightly embarrassed expression appeared in Marcus's eyes.

"Mr. Faraday isn't very well, as a matter of fact," he said. "He's upstairs in his room. Is it important?"

The Inspector smiled, but stood his ground. "I think I'd better see him if you don't mind," he said, and added deliberately, "I don't mind if you're both present at the interview. A man can always have his lawyer with him if he's questioned by us nowadays."

Campion glanced at Marcus. "As we agreed before the

inquest this morning," he said, "I gave the Inspector all the information which Mr. Faraday did not consider relevant at the first enquiry. I feel it would be in his interests to see the Inspector."

Marcus's worried expression did not vanish. "He's up in his room," he repeated. "I'll go and tell him. You'll take off your coat, won't you, Inspector? I see you're very wet."

He hurried upstairs, and as Campion helped the Inspector off with his raincoat the older man chuckled.

"You'll get yourself into hot water," he observed. "It looks a bit like running with the hare and hunting with the hounds, but I suppose you've got your reasons."

"The best in the world," said Campion. "Based on the time-honoured theory that when a man is innocent the more he talks the better. My good man, this old boy has gone through two campaigns, including the Great War, without killing so much as a rabbit. He's not likely to have begun now. I admit he may know something, but he's no more guilty than I am."

The Inspector grunted, but made no other comment, and presently Marcus reappeared.

"Mr. Faraday is in his room," he said, "sitting before the fire in his dressing-gown. He tells me that he still feels very seedy, and although I advised him to see you, and I told you were kind enough to say that Campion and I might be present at the interview, he still doesn't feel like coming down. I wondered if you would mind seeing him in his room?"

"Not at all," said the Inspector, relieved that the news was no worse. "I'll come up right away."

Uncle William sat before his bedroom fire in a gaily coloured dressing-gown. His white hair stood on end and his moustache drooped dejectedly. He glanced up as they entered, but did not attempt to rise. He looked older and more pathetic than usual, his toes in his carpet slippers turned inwards, one pudgy hand resting on his knee and the other hanging in a black silk sling. He certainly looked ill. His skin was patchy and his eyes were slightly bloodshot.

Mr. Campion caught the Inspector glancing furtively at the old man's feet and was unable to repress a grin of delight. Uncle William's little fat pads were quite incapable of being the origin of the colossal mark on the flower-bed.

The invalid smiled faintly at Campion and nodded brusquely to the Inspector.

"What's the trouble now?" he said. "I'm a sick man and I don't want to be worried any more than I can help. I don't know if you can find yourselves chairs? I don't resent this intrusion, you know, but I'd like to get it over as soon as possible."

They found themselves chairs, and the Inspector went over the points of Mr. Campion's revelations of the morning. On the whole Uncle William behaved remarkably well. He admitted to the amnesia and the visit to Sir Gordon Woodthorpe. He was a little more touchy on the subject of the gun, but the Inspector was patient, even sympathetic, and Uncle William, finding that he had a good audience, forgot his trepidation and began to speak freely.

The interview progressed most favourably, Marcus carrying his client with real skill over the embarrassing points of his story, and it was not until the Inspector cleared his throat and, prefacing his question with a word of apology, came to the matter of the incident on the night before that Uncle William's obstinacy began to show.

"That hand of yours, sir," the Inspector began innocently. "I understand that there was a little trouble here last night. I wonder if you would tell me in your own words how you came to have such a wound?"

For the first time a dangerous expression came into Uncle William's little bleared eyes.

"A most trivial business," he said petulantly. "But I suppose even the silliest incident becomes important when you people get to work. It was the most simple thing in the world. I told Campion here and I told my young niece." He cleared his throat and regarded the Inspector severely. "I sleep with my window open at the bottom, don't you know, and late last night I was awakened by a great hulking cat scratching about the place. I hate cats, so I hopped out of bed, caught the creature by the middle and pushed it through the window. In its resentment it scratched me. I went out to put some iodine on my hand, and unfortunately roused the house. That's all there is to say."

Marcus seemed worried and Campion regretful, but the Inspector showed no change of expression whatsoever. He jotted down some hieroglyphics in his private note-book and then glanced up.

"Can I see the hand, sir?" he said.

Uncle William blew out his cheeks. "That's rather irregular—er—officer, isn't it?" he demanded.

The Inspector ignored the gratuitous insult, and Campion experienced a return of the admiration he had always felt for this quiet, grave man with the penetrating grey eyes.

"I'd like to see it, sir." The Inspector's tone was at once respectful and commanding.

For one moment it looked as though Uncle William was about to refuse point-blank, but Marcus tactfully stepped forward.

"Perhaps I can help you with the bandage?"

The old man looked up balefully. "All right," he said. "Have it your own way. But if you get into trouble from old Lavrock don't blame me. He told me I was lucky not to have cut an artery, and I didn't know," he added, muttering the words under his breath, "that it was considered etiquette for a lawyer to assist the policy in jockeying his unfortunate client in the very midst of a bereavement."

"It's a lawyer's duty to do all he can to protect his client's interests, sir," said Marcus, with some asperity.

"Huh!" said Uncle William ungraciously.

By this time the outer bandages had been removed, and with consummate care Marcus lifted off the strip of oiled silk which lay beneath. When he came to the lint matters proved more difficult, and it was not until warm water had been procured and gently applied that the wound lay revealed.

Stanislaus rose to examine it, and a certain sternness became evident in his manner.

"Three stitches, I see," he said. "One single cut. Thank you, Mr. Faraday. That's all I want to see, Mr. Featherstone."

Uncle William, in spite of his indisposition, was quite sufficiently in possession of his wits to know that this display of his wound had not strengthened his story. He devoted himself ostentatiously to the business of rebandaging, and it was some considerable time before the wrappings were arranged to his satisfaction.

Meanwhile the Inspector waited, patient and polite. Finally, however, his moment came.

"Would you mind telling me once more, sir, how you got that cut?"

A high-pitched squawk of exasperation escaped Uncle William. "Am I to spend the rest of my life repeating the story of a perfectly ordinary incident?" he said bitterly. "Are you in the full possession of your senses, sir? I told you, a cat came into my room last night and it scratched me. I don't know what this country is coming to. Damned incompetence, wherever you go."

The Inspector remained unruffled. "Describe the cat," he said resignedly.

Uncle William blustered, but none of the three men looked at him, and finally he took the plunge.

"Quite a large cat," he said. "Darkish. I didn't go examining it, don't you know. It was my idea to get it out of the room—not to make a pet of it."

Still no one spoke, and he continued, floundering further and further into the morass.

"I've seen cats like it in South Africa. Very fierce and rather large."

"Known to you?" The Inspector's tone was impersonal.

Uncle William was crimson, but he stuck to his guns.

"How d'you mean—known to me?" he demanded belligerently. "I don't go about making the acquaintance of stray cats. No, I'd never seen it in my life before as far as I know. Does that satisfy you?"

"Was your light on or off when you picked the cat up?" said the Inspector, writing busily.

"Off," returned Uncle William triumphantly.

"How did you know it was a cat?" said the Inspector stolidly. Apart from the fact that he now omitted the word "sir," he gave no sign of his growing irritation.

Uncle William's blue eyes were glassy. "Eh?" he ejaculated.

"How did you know it was a cat?" the Inspector repeated.

Uncle William blew up. Much subterranean rumbling was followed by an explosion in a much higher key than he or anyone else had expected.

"Because it mewed at me!" he bellowed. "Said 'Meeow, meeow,' like that. I don't know what you think you're doing, coming here and asking these damfool questions. Featherstone, you're a rotten lawyer if you can't protect me from this sort of thing. I'm a sick man in no condition to be badgered by a pack of imbeciles."

Marcus cleared his throat. "Mr. Faraday," he began gently, "in my official capacity I must advise you to tell the Inspector all you know. In your own interests, it is imperative that the police should hear the whole truth."

This interruption had a quietening effect upon Uncle William without in any way lessening his obstinacy. He continued to grumble.

"I don't know why you can't take a plain statement," he said. "The whole thing is nothing to do with you, anyhow. I knew it was a cat because it mewed and because I felt its fur, I suppose. It may not have been a cat. It may have been a young tiger, for all I know." He laughed bitterly at his own joke.

"You're not sure if it was a cat," said the Inspector, with some satisfaction, and wrote again in his book. "Are you sure it was an animal?"

Uncle William, having once erupted, seemed to have spent most of his power.

"Whatever it was, I put it out of the window," he said shortly.

The Inspector rose, crossed to the window and looked out. It was a straight drop to the flower-bed beneath. He said nothing, but returned to his seat.

Uncle William began to mutter again. "You know, Inspector," he said, "I get the impression that you don't believe a word I say. That's my story, and I'll stick to it. Very insulting to be disbelieved in one's own house."

Mr. Oates chose to ignore this remark. "Can you give me the address of your doctor, sir?" he said.

"What the devil for?" said Uncle William, his little eyes opening wide. "He won't tell you much. Doctors don't blab, you know. Still, I'll tell you something to save you bullying him. He is as stupid about the cat as you are. Asked me if it was a one-clawed cat, silly fool. His name is Lavrock, if you must worm out the whole of my private affairs. That's all I've got to say."

The Inspector rose to his feet. "Very well, sir," he said. "I may as well warn you that you'll probably have to tell the coroner all this. He may feel that it has some bearing on the case."

Marcus also rose. "Inspector," he said, "you won't go for a moment or two, will you? I should like to have a word with my client before you're out of reach."

For the first time during the interview a smile appeared on Mr. Oates's face.

"I shall be about the house for some time, Mr. Featherstone," he said.

He and Campion left Marcus with his recalcitrant client, and when they reached the corridor the Inspector paused.

"I'd like to go up to that attic now," he said. "I shall want to see that cord and the gun holster."

"I'm sorry about Uncle William," murmured Mr. Campion. "You haven't seen him at his best."

The Inspector snorted. "Witnesses like that make me feel vicious," he said. "If I didn't feel that I might not be able to produce this evidence in court I'd have a damned good mind to run him in, telling me a pack of lies like that. That's a knife wound, probably a sharp pen-knife, by the look of it. He's shielding someone, of course, in which case he probably knows who did the whole thing."

Campion shook his head. "I don't think he knows," he said. "But there's always the chance he thinks he does."

"Take me to the attic," said the Inspector, with decision. "Routine; that's the only way to get anywhere. We all fall back on it in the end."

15

The Outside Job

It was almost three o'clock when the Inspector, who had made the library his headquarters, neared the end of his investigations at Socrates Close for the day. Mr. Bowditch and a police photographer had completed their work on the footprint, and now stood beside the Inspector contemplating an array of shoes on the ground before them. Stanislaus had procured a pair from every member of the household, including the two Christmasses, father and son, who lived in a small cottage on the edge of the estate.

At the moment matters were at a deadlock. The Inspector was depressed, the photographer puzzled and the irrepressible Bowditch quite unable to restrain his amusement.

"Well," he said, "we've got a metric photograph and we've

got a plaster cast. Here are the measurements. It doesn't look as though Cinderella is among this lot." He indicated the row of shoes before them. "There isn't one here that isn't nearly an inch out in both dimensions."

Stanislaus grumbled. "I suppose we ought to have a barefoot parade," he said, "and I would if the discrepancy was the other way about. But it's useless to pretend that anyone could have a foot like that without it being known."

Bowditch laughed noisily. "That's a fact," he said. "Even old Tubby Lane at Bow Street hasn't got trotters like that. It looks to me like something out of the Natural History Museum."

Stanislaus frowned. "I suppose there's no doubt at all about it being genuine?" he suggested.

But Bowditch was convinced upon this point. "Oh, no, that's real all right," he said. "You can see the nail marks quite clearly, and there's a thread or two of blue worsted in the heel of the cast. You'll find that's a real foot all right, whatever you might be led to believe. And what a foot! It's the first time I've come across anything so funny in the whole of my official life."

The Inspector scowled. He was still contemplating the shoes. "The nearest in size are these over here," he remarked. "They belong to young Christmas. You'd better go over and have a look at his feet, Bowditch. Take some measurements. Don't laugh; behave like a policeman."

The prospect of possibly seeing the original of the print in the flesh was too much for Mr. Bowditch. His face grew redder and his small blue eyes filled with unshed tears of laughter.

"I'm there already," he said. "You'd better come along, governor," he added, turning to the photographer. "We'll have them photographed, and framed."

"Consummate imbecile," said the Inspector to Campion as the door closed behind the hopeful Bowditch and his assistant. "I don't mind a man having a sense of humour, but that fellow carries on like a halfpenny comic."

Mr. Campion made no direct comment. "Do you still think it was a joke?" he ventured after a pause.

"I don't think," said the Inspector bitterly. "I gave that up when I discovered the mess it gets one into. As if we hadn't got enough trouble already without some flatfooted fool complicating things by scribbling on the window-pane! All these shoes can go back now. Come in!"

His last remark was occasioned by a gentle tapping on the

door. Marcus entered in response to his invitation. The young man looked weary and considerably aggrieved. He raised his eyebrows at the array of footwear, but did not remark upon it, a circumstance which endeared him to the Inspector.

"I'm tremendously sorry," he said, "but Mr. Faraday sticks to his story about the cat."

The Inspector grunted. "Did you point out to him that he would be on oath in the coroner's court?" he said.

"Yes," Marcus admitted. "But he seems to believe in the story. But, after all, this incident hardly comes into your province, does it?"

Oates did not answer immediately. The thrust had gone home.

"You haven't got to protect Mr. Faraday from me, Mr. Featherstone," he remarked presently. "If he needs to be protected from anyone it's himself."

It was Mr. Campion who took the news of Uncle William's obstinacy to heart.

"I see I shall have to go on a pub-crawl on Uncle William's behalf," he said, with a meaning glance towards the Inspector. "Marcus, there's a job for you and me. You've written to Sir Gordon Woodthorpe, of course?"

Marcus, who had answered this question once before, glanced at his friend in astonishment, but he caught sight of the interested expression on the Inspector's face and answered immediately.

"Of course," he said.

The Inspector's depression increased. "I shall leave that mark on the window for the time being," he said. "You can reassure the household. There'll be a couple of plain-clothes men in the garden to-night."

"Then you're inclined to think this thing's not a hoax, Inspector?" said Marcus, jumping at any straw which pointed away from the awkward subject of Uncle William.

In spite of the natural police dislike of lay questioning, Mr. Oates did not snub him. On the contrary, he answered civilly, albeit non-committally.

"I am quite satisfied that the foot that made the print on the bed outside could not have worn any of the shoes here," he said. "I can't say any more than that."

Mr. Campion, who had moved to the window and now stood

looking at the red chalk sign thoughtfully, spoke without turning round.

"Supposing for one moment that it's all perfectly genuine?" he said. "It's clearly a message of some sort to someone inside. Following this line of reasoning, where do we arrive? At two interesting conclusions. One, that the writer did not know the house, because this room, as you know, is hardly ever used, and two, that he is only friendly with one member of the household, since otherwise he would surely have come to call in the ordinary way."

He wheeled round and faced them, a slight inoffensive figure against the window-panes.

"A message like this must necessarily be very simple," he said, "and I suggest to you, Stanislaus, that it means one of three things—'Come and meet at the usual place,' or 'Something has been done,' or, more simply, 'I am on the scene again.'"

"No one in the household admits to ever having seen that mark before, and there's only one known prevaricator in the place," said the Inspector viciously.

Further conversation was interrupted by the return of Bowditch. He was slightly crestfallen.

"Not a hope," he said. "I measured his right foot. Length, twelve and three-quarters, width across the ball nearly five inches. Now this cast, you know, is thirteen and a quarter by six and a tenth." He mentioned the figures with pride. "Harrison's going over the garden looking for any other tracks," he added. "But it's all this short well-kept grass, and there was rain in the night, so it's not easy. It's only the house that protects the print we have got."

Mr. Oates nodded. "All right," he said resignedly. "Well, I must be getting back."

Campion escorted the Inspector and his jovial aide to their car, Marcus tactfully remaining in the library.

"Got all your bits and pieces?" Campion enquired as he helped the policeman into his raincoat. "Rope, and what not?"

"I have," said Stanislaus shortly. "And you're not as bright as you think you are, my lad. Here's a thing you ought to have found out." He took a key from his pocket and placed it in the young man's hand. "That belongs to your own door," he said. "But it also fits any lock on the first floor. All those locks are alike and the keys are interchangeable. I didn't notice it yesterday, but I ought to have guessed. Lots of houses are like that. Good-bye."

Mr. Campion pocketed the key, not in the least discomforted. "I shall come and see you to-morrow," he said, "to hear all the news, always supposing some great flat-footed monster hasn't devoured me, of course."

The Inspector snorted and switched on his engine. "You're all alike, you untrained youngsters," he said. "You all go for the picturesque. That's a hoax, you'll find, I bet."

"I'll take you," said Campion.

"All right. I'll go my limit—five bob."

"Done," said the younger man. He returned to the house and Marcus met him in the hall. He was worried and still aggrieved by the turn events had taken.

"That mark on the window, Campion," he said. "What exactly does it mean? Is there any explanation for it?"

They wandered back to the library. "Well, there's only one obvious inference, isn't there?" said Mr. Campion, pulling down the blinds. "And that is that there is someone else on the scene. The footmark means what it meant to Robinson Crusoe; there's a Man Friday about."

Marcus brightened. "If you ask me, that something to be thankful for," he said. "William's attitude alarms me. I don't know why he of all people should try to make things more difficult."

"Uncle William is a very attractive bad old hat," said Mr. Campion. "Stanislaus is only taking this attitude because it's the orthodox police attitude. They always take the most obvious line and follow it up. If it leads them nowhere they abandon it and take the next most obvious, and so on. That's why they're practically inescapable in the end."

"But you," Marcus persisted, "what do you think?"

Mr. Campion was silent. His own theorising had been partially forgotten in the excitement of the past two hours. Now, however, his face grew grave as the possibilities of the case returned to him. Marcus was still waiting for an answer, and he was only saved from an embarrassing situation by a knock on the door behind them.

"Mr. Campion, may I trouble you for your arm?"

It was Great-aunt Caroline, frail and vivid as ever, in a magnificent Maltese cap and fichu. She smiled at Marcus.

"You will find Joyce in the morning-room," she said. "I

wish you would go and talk to her. I am afraid she has had a very trying afternoon with poor Catherine."

These instructions were delivered with grace and something of regal condescension. The next moment Mr. Campion found himself escorting the old lady to her sitting-room. He had to stoop a little to allow her small hand to rest comfortably upon his forearm.

Great-aunt Caroline did not speak until she was safely seated in her high-backed walnut chair, with Campion standing on the hearth-rug before her. She sat regarding him approvingly, her little bright eyes resting on his face, a slightly amused smile on her mouth.

"Emily is quite right," she said. "You are a clever young man. I am very pleased with you. You are handling this disturbing business very well, especially poor William. Poor William is a very difficult man—a very silly man—yet some of my husband's brothers were quite as foolish as he. The police, of course, still suspect him." She glanced at the young man sharply and Mr. Campion met her gaze.

"I think they do," he said, and hesitated.

She smiled at him. "My dear young man," she said, "I shall say nothing, whatever you tell me."

Mr. Campion took off his spectacles and for the first time a little weariness was apparent in his face. He returned her smile.

"I shall remember that," he said, and added quietly, "my position here is invidious, as you know, and things are a little awkward. But this morning I obtained what I am perfectly certain will turn out to be positive proof of Mr. Faraday's innocence. I haven't told this to anyone yet, and I do not want to, since I thought it might work out best for all concerned if the police went on in their own way at the moment."

The old lady's expression was inscrutable. "That's very good news," she said. "I won't ask you any more than that. By the way, I am afraid I have been guilty of an indiscretion; concealing evidence."

Her smile deepened at the expression on his face, and she continued in her soft small voice.

"I have a letter here which came for Andrew some two or three days after his disappearance. I ought to have handed it over to the police, I know, but fortunately I took the precaution of reading it first, and as the writer has some little position in the world to keep up, and the letter did not seem to be very important, I thought it a pity that she should be dragged into this affair. So I kept the note, but it has been weighing on my conscience. Here it is."

She unlocked a tiny drawer in the bureau and drew out a thick white envelope addressed to "Andrew Seeley, Esq." in a precise feminine hand. Great-aunt Caroline unfolded the sheet it contained with little bony fingers almost as white as the paper itself.

"I don't know if you follow the scholastic world at all," she said, "but the writer of this letter is Miss Margaret Lisle-Chevreuse, Principal of the Templeton College for Women at York, one of the finest posts in the country. You will understand that hers is a position to which any sort of notoriety would be most injurious. She is a maiden lady, of course, and since I remember her here about twenty-five years ago she is now, I suppose, almost fifty. Perhaps you will read the letter. I think it speaks for itself. I had never any idea that she knew Andrew at all well."

Mr. Campion took the paper with a certain amount of embarrassment and began to read.

My dear Andy,—I was startled to see your handwriting among my letters this morning. My dear man, you have made a very handsome apology, although why you should think I needed one after fifteen years I cannot imagine. I am delighted to hear that you are coming up North and I do most sincerely look forward to seeing you again. You say I shall see a very great change in you: I dread to think of the change you will certainly see in me. No, I do not still wear my hair bound round my ears! My dear girls would think I had taken leave of my senses if I suddenly changed back to that style.

As for the rest of your letter, what can I possibly say? There was a time when I thought you had broken my heart, but as we grow older these things became mercifully fainter.

Wait until you see me.

I cannot tell you how happy I was to get your letter. I had not forgotten you.

I am sorry to hear that your life with your cousins is not a happy one. Relatives are always difficult.

However, as you say, there is a good deal of our lives

*left. Come to see me the moment you arrive, my dear
friend.*

Affectionately yours,
Margaret

As he finished reading, Mr. Campion folded the letter
thoughtfully between his fingers. Aunt Caroline came to his
rescue.

"She will have seen about his death in the papers, poor
soul," she said. "Poor unfortunate Andrew! He seems to have
been on the verge of behaving like a gentleman for once in his
life—unless he was thinking of his future. But we mustn't be
uncharitable. I hope you don't blame me for not turning this over
to the police, 'Mr. Campion.' What shall we do with it?"

The young man glanced meaningly at the dancing fire. The
old lady nodded.

"I think so, too," she said.

When the last remnants of the envelope and its contents had
been consumed by the flames, Mrs. Faraday sighed.

"As you grow older, young man," she said, "you will find
that not the least surprising thing in life is the fact that every
man, however unworthy, can engender an undying spark of
affection in the heart of some unlikely woman. Well, I have
nothing more to confess. I am very relieved by what you have to
tell me concerning poor William. You see, I happen to know,
beyond any doubt whatever, that he is not guilty."

The last words were spoken with such conviction that Mr.
Campion started. The little old lady sat looking up at him, her
black eyes smiling and very shrewd.

"Good-bye until dinner," she said. "Would you mind
sending Alice in to me? I am afraid this bell is out of order. I
don't know how I should get on without Alice."

16

Black Sunday

Aunt Caroline's indomitable spirit took her to church on the following morning in spite of the fact that she must have been well aware that her appearance would cause a certain amount of unwelcome interest from the gaping populace. Both Uncle William and Aunt Kitty kept to their beds to avoid the ordeal, but Campion and Joyce accompanied the old lady willy-nilly.

As Campion followed the dominant figure up the aisle to her pew he heard a faint stir among the congregation, the rustle of prayer-books, the swish of skirts. But Great-aunt Caroline progressed slowly and stiffly, no expression at all upon her face, her black stick scraping on the stones.

It was a nightmare service for Joyce, and she was grateful for Mr. Campion's presence. He acquitted himself perfectly, finding the places in Aunt Caroline's prayer-book as though to the manner born. This was all the more extraordinary, for he was hardly aware of the proceedings in that great impersonal church. His mind was occupied by a theory so startling and terrifying that he dared hardly consider it. Ever since that moment in the night when he had awakened with the idea ready made in his mind and had lain piecing together the jig-saw fragments of the problem, the theory had fascinated him. At the moment it was too nebulous to be spoken. He could see the expression of shocked incredulity on Stanislaus Oates's face were such an eventuality pointed out to him. And yet, if it were true, if this monstrous notion were something more than a night thought, then he shuddered at the realisation of the danger to all beneath the haunted roof of Socrates Close.

Marcus Featherstone was waiting for them at the house when they returned. Uncle William, also, had recovered sufficiently to put in an appearance. The two men were sitting in front of the fire in the morning-room when Joyce and Campion came in. It was evident that their conversation had not been pleasant. Uncle William was sulky, sitting hunched up in his chair sucking disconsolately at an empty pipe, while Marcus, on whom the strain of the past three days was beginning to tell, was still flushed with exasperation.

He rose eagerly as they came in and went over to the girl and kissed her, an involuntary caress which startled them both nearly as much as it shocked Uncle William. Joyce was delighted, and Campion made a mental note of the fact that the disaster, however terrible, was at least rousing Marcus from that superior lethargy which had been so apparent in his letter. Uncle William, sensing an advantage, made use of it.

"I suppose you must embarrass everybody?" he remarked. "Kissing before lunch is like drinking before breakfast, damned bad taste. The whole morale of this house seems to be in jeopardy. Once we old families start going downhill we go down pretty fast. Well, I suppose mother got all the notoriety she wanted in church this morning. I wasn't going to be a party to it. I stayed in bed to get out of it. Matter of fact, I've a good mind to go to bed and stay there until this whole thing's been cleared up."

Campion noticed that he had dispensed with his sling this morning, and, reducing the bandage to a minimum, kept his hand in his pocket as much as possible.

"This young fool," the old man went on, indicating Marcus with a jerk of his unrepentant head, "has been trying to chivvy me into telling some cock-and-bull story about being attacked. He says he's been to see Lavrock. Julia was poisoned. Goodness knows how much conium was found in the poor girl! If Lavrock had been a decent fellow I should have thought he might have kept that to himself."

"Mr. Faraday"—Marcus's face was crimson—"I told you that in confidence, in an earnest and I am afraid foolhardy attempt to convince you of the danger of your position. The information was given me in confidence, and I particularly asked you to respect mine."

"More fool you," said Uncle William unpardonably. "When a man's beset by suspicious fools he's a fool himself if he respects any man's confidence. The whole conduct of this case has been a scandal. You'll find yourself in a very bad position when it's all over, my boy. Your reputation will suffer."

Marcus opened his mouth to reply, but thought better of it and permitted Joyce to lead him out of the room.

Uncle William chuckled. "That's put him in his place," he said. "He's supposed to be our lawyer, not a prosecuting counsel. Well, Campion," he went on, his sudden bravado vanishing, "what's going to happen to me?"

Mr. Campion looked at him regretfully. "That cat story," he said. "That's bad, you know."

"Best I could think of, my boy, in the time," said Uncle William unexpectedly.

"Well, it's not too late," Campion observed.

Uncle William hesitated. Then he cocked an eye in the young man's direction.

"Fact of it is, I'm blessed if I know what it was," he said slowly. "I was a bit tight at the time. Something let out at me, I know that. On the whole, I think I'll stick to the cat. I'd tell you if I knew what it was," he added ingenuously, "but I don't. As I told you, there's something queer going on here. I've been made fool enough in this business already. And I've learnt one thing: if you make a statement, stick to it. There's going to be the devil to pay over that specialist fellow. No, if I said it was a cat, a cat it was. That's my last word. Oh, Lord, here's Kitty," he went on half under his breath, as the door opened. "I can't stand a snivelling woman." And with singular ungraciousness he got up and walked out, pushing past his faded little sister, who turned and looked after him, indignation in her pale eyes.

Mr. Campion remained on the hearth-rug and Aunt Kitty stood hesitating just inside the room, apparently trying to make up her mind whether to brave the devil she knew not, or to follow the one she did. She wore the same flat-breasted black frock in which Campion had first seen her. Her eyes were red-rimmed and watery and the thin curls round her face were dampish and dejected. At length she decided to come in.

She closed the door behind her and, keeping her eyes modestly groundward, advanced towards the fireplace and stooped to poke the blazing coals.

From where he stood Campion could see her face. She was mumbling her lips together as though forcing herself to speak. Quite suddenly she straightened and turned upon him with that air of drama which he had noticed in her before. She stood trembling, a curious little figure in her neat black, her crumpled cheeks flushed and the poker clasped firmly in her hand.

"Mr. Campion," she said, "Mr. Campion, you're not the police, are you?"

He did not smile. Behind his spectacles his eyes were watching every changing line in her face.

"No," he said gravely. "I am here on behalf of Mrs. Faraday. Is there anything I can do for you?"

Aunt Kitty's courage seemed to be about to fail her again, but she recovered herself.

"You mustn't believe a word William says," she went on breathlessly. "I ought not to talk like this. I know he's my brother, but he's not to be believed."

She paused and then fired another unexpected question at him.

"Do you believe in the supernatural, Mr. Campion? I mean," she went on, taking a step nearer and speaking with terrifying intensity, "do you believe in the power of Evil?"

"Yes," said Mr. Campion.

Aunt Kitty seemed satisfied, for she nodded reassuringly to herself.

"You ought to be afraid to stay here," she remarked. "I'm not afraid, not really, because I'm a religious woman, and I've got the armour of religion to protect and help me. But the others haven't, and there is no way of escape for the wicked. They shall perish, just as Andrew perished. But," she continued, the poker trembling in her hand, "Evil doesn't perish. The active spirit of Evil is abroad. It's in this house." She lowered her voice. "Did you see that mark on the window in the library? That's the beginning. When I saw it I recognised it. Andrew told me once that if he died first he would come back and haunt us. Well," she finished triumphantly, "he's doing it."

Mr. Campion, who had stood many ordeals in his life, wiped his forehead with his handkerchief, but Aunt Kitty's tongue was loosed.

"I couldn't go to church this morning," she said, "because I felt that as soon as I set foot in that sacred building the contamination which I have suffered here would show in black upon my face. This house is Evil. William says a cat attacked him. That was no cat, Mr. Campion. William was attacked in his sleep. In the darkness Lucifer stretched out his hand and made a mark upon him, warning him."

She was nearly exhausted now, but the prophetic fire still flickered.

"If William turned his heart and confessed that an Evil power struck him in the dark he might be saved yet," she said. "But he won't. He likes to think it was something tangible, something of this world. He likes to think it was an animal, a poor dumb thing. Andrew was a wicked man, Mr. Campion. I sometimes think," she added, her voice sinking again to a whisper, "that Andrew was possessed. No, it's not the police we need in this house. It's the clergy. This sinful building should be exorcised. When a man dies of fever they have the house fumigated. When the wrath of God overtakes Andrew we do nothing except call in the police to find out who His agent was. I'm a silly old woman, I know, but I'm warning you, young man. You keep away from here. Andrew brought Evil into the house and the black wing is over it still."

She stopped and suddenly became aware of the poker in her hand. Its presence seemed to embarrass her, and she dropped it noisily into the fireplace. The clatter it made brought her to earth.

"Oh," she said, with a guilty glance towards the door, "I ought not to have done that. Mother does so dislike a noise."

She took out her handkerchief and dabbed her eyes with it. The metamorphosis was complete. From a sibyl in prophetic ecstasy she had become once again the down-trodden poor relation.

Mr. Campion never quite forgave himself for his next remark.

"And your sister?" he murmured.

Aunt Kitty burst into tears. "Poor misguided Julia," she whispered, "she was only selfish." And added, with terrible inconsequentiality, "God is a jealous God."

The luncheon gong relieved the tension, and after an agonising meal Mr. Campion once more visited Great-aunt Caroline.

She received him in her little sitting-room, as usual, and listened to his request in amused silence.

"You want me to leave my house?" she said at last, when he had finished. "Certainly not. My dear young man, at my age physical danger, that is to say the danger of death, is ever present wherever I am. I ceased to worry about that long ago. In fact," she went on unexpectedly, "my position now is that of someone waiting on a platform for a train already overdue. No, I am afraid that whatever you tell me I shall remain where I am."

Campion took his defeat calmly. He looked very young, standing on the hearthrug before her. He had removed his spectacles and all trace of his lackadaisical and inconsequential manner had vanished.

"If I were only sure," he said, "it would be different. I should insist. But I am not sure. There is an explanation of this affair which frightens me. If it is the truth, no one in this house is safe. As it is, you will see that I can't possibly make any accusation, now, but I beg you to leave yourself."

Great-aunt Caroline sat back in her chair, her hands folded.

"No one in this house is safe," she repeated. "Almost my exact words to you, young man, if you remember. But I shall not stir, and you may do as you please about the others. Personally, until you are certain I should let them remain where they are. If Nemesis is to overtake them, you know, it will. However, I feel rather differently about Joyce. Does she come within the scope of your rather sweeping suggestion?"

"Certainly," said Campion emphatically.

"Then Joyce shall go," said the old lady with decision. "If you will send her to me I will see that she raises no objections. She will want to stay with Miss Held, I suppose: a charming girl, quite unusually intelligent. And you yourself, Mr. Campion— what a curious name that is; I wonder why you chose it?—what do you propose to do?"

Campion looked hurt. "I remain where I am, if I may," he said. "But I wish you would go yourself. I suppose it's no use my reopening the subject?"

Her small mouth set in a firm obstinate line. "None whatever," she said shortly.

Mr. Campion realised that he had heard the literal truth.

17

Open Verdict

The gaiety and warmth of Ann Held's unacademic study seemed only half-hearted when its owner and Mr. Campion sat one on either side of the fire at half-past five on Monday, waiting for Marcus and Joyce to return from the inquest on Aunt Julia. Ann, who had cheerfully shouldered half Joyce's troubles, smiled at the bespectacled young man opposite her.

"Of course I'm awfully glad to have you," she said, "but why didn't you stay for the verdict?"

Campion turned a mournful face towards her. "I couldn't bear Stanislaus's cold and slightly unchristian attitude any longer," he said. "He's an old friend of mine, and contrary to the best traditions of the amateur sleuth, I have put my foot in it rather badly with him. It's most unfair, too," he went on. "I gave him the broadest possible hint; in fact I told him that if he visited every public-house between the Grantchester meadows footpath and Socrates Close he would find Uncle William's alibi. But just because I didn't go further and mention that I had already interviewed the redoubtable Mrs. Finch, of 'The Red Bull,' who had assured me that she could state on her oath that Mr. William Faraday, dazed and a little queer, had entered her establishment at fifteen minutes to one and left it in an aimless fashion half an hour later, he is quite ridiculously annoyed with me. I consider myself down-trodden. Did you ever read a book called *Misunderstood?*"

Ann Held began to laugh. "I always thought that child deserved all he got," she remarked.

"He did," said Mr. Campion. "So do I. That's where the tragedy comes in. They're late," he went on. "The jury must have taken longer to make up their minds than I expected. That coroner is a first-class man. He knows what he is about, and he seems to be able to write faster than most of his tribe."

"I don't see what that has to do with it," said Miss Held.

He enlightened her. "Everything said in the court is taken down by the coroner in longhand. That's why witnesses are encouraged to be short and snappy. We are extremely lucky to get this inquest over in one day," he added, "although of course there was precious little evidence of any kind to be given."

Ann curled up in her chair. "This is a most remarkable business," she said, "and of course I'm an outsider, so I may easily make a fool of myself. But it seems to me that this is obviously a matter for—well, a medico-psychologist, or whatever you call them."

Mr. Campion stretched his long thin legs to the blaze and the firelight flickered on his spectacles.

"It is," he said. "But what's the good of that? The difficulty about psychology is that it hasn't any rules. I mean, if one person can imagine the state of mind in which another might perform certain acts, then those acts are sound psychology. In other words, given a person's batty enough, there is nothing he or she may not do. That's as far as anyone seems to have got at present."

"Batty," said Ann Held. "You've said it. I suppose they'll bring this in a verdict of murder."

"Oh, no," said Mr. Campion. "At least, I hope not. No one will be more surprised than my ex-friend Inspector Oates if they do. Of course they may do anything. There's a problem in psychology for you. Why does the collective mind of twelve men work more irrationally, more prejudicially than that of any of those same twelve men taken separately? Hullo, here they are."

He swung round in his chair and rose as Joyce and Marcus entered. Joyce looked exhausted, and she sank wearily into a chair. Campion looked enquiringly at Marcus.

"Open verdict?" he asked.

The young man nodded. "Yes. 'The deceased met her death by conium poisoning, but there is not sufficient evidence to show whether it was self-administered or not.' They were away for some time. I think there was a strong vote in favour of suicide. Ann, you're a heroine to put up with us like this."

"You sit down," said his hostess. "I'm making tea. Joyce, you look all in."

There was a welcome pause while the little brass kettle on the hob was persuaded to boil and the tea brewed. Joyce took off her hat and passed her hand over her hair.

"It's wonderful to be back here after that terrible room," she said. "I hadn't realised it was going to be so public, and I loathed the people who came to watch. What's it got to do with them, anyhow? They tell me I shan't be needed to-morrow. I'm so glad. Ann, I don't know what I should do without you."

Miss Held smiled at her across the teacups. "Mr. Campion was saying they are lucky to get it over so soon," she remarked.

"We are," said Marcus. "By the way, I thought the coroner was splendid. He's a first-class man." He paused, recalling the scene to his mind. "Uncle William came out unexpectedly well," he remarked. "I hope he has the same luck to-morrow when the inquest on Andrew is resumed."

"It is extraordinary," said Joyce slowly, "what a different person Uncle William is in public. It's just as though he's able to put over the impression one always feels he's trying to create at home."

Marcus smiled sourly. "He'll have Campion to thank if he doesn't make an extremely awkward impression to-morrow at the inquest on Andrew," he said. "But I think that alibi will save his bacon altogether. By the way, I had a line from Sir Gordon Woodthorpe this morning. He's going to be a very decent old boy over the business. Uncle William really has been a first-class lunatic. Still, it's the alibi which is really important. It's rather odd that the police, by concentrating on the time of Seeley's murder, have punctured what case they had against William completely. Why did you wait until to-day to tell the Inspector, Campion?"

"That's what Stanislaus says," said that young man regretfully. "In fact, he's very rude about it. Yet I gave him every hint I could. You see, I wanted him to concentrate on Uncle William, because," he added slowly, "I believe that Uncle William has the key of the whole problem in his hand if he could only realise it."

The three looked at him questioningly, but he offered no further explanation, and something in his manner prevented them from pressing him. Joyce shivered.

"When that expert gave evidence that there had been a trace of conium in Aunt Julia's cup, I was waiting for a verdict of murder," she said. "Then of course that long rigmarole about the patent medicine we found came out. That cleared Aunt Kitty.

But they didn't say they had found any trace of conium in the paper which held the medicine."

"No," said Marcus. "That's why there wasn't a murder verdict. There wasn't any trace. But it doesn't take much imagination to see that that was the way the stuff was administered. The drug must have been soaked into one of the pellets which was then recoated. It probably looked exactly like the others."

Joyce nodded. There was a far-away look in her brown eyes.

"Albert," she said, "we're all being indiscreet, and thank goodness it doesn't matter here. Did you ever find out about the rope?"

He nodded. "It was identical," he said. "This isn't to be broadcast, of course, although it'll all come out to-morrow. Yes, it was obviously the same stuff. That takes us straight back to the house again. We haven't accounted for the clock weight yet, either."

The girl leant back and closed her eyes. "I'm ashamed to say it," she said, "but when Aunt Faraday insisted that I should leave the house yesterday I was glad. I never thought I was a funk before, but I am. That ludicrous footmark, the attack on Uncle William, the dreadful atmosphere of something dark and awful going on right under one's nose, it got me down. Poor Aunt Kitty! Is she all right? She looked so little and helpless in the box."

"I think of all the people in that house," said Mr. Campion judicially, "Aunt Kitty's position is the safest. But I'm glad you're out of it."

Once again they looked at him enquiringly, and it was Ann Held who put the question.

"When?" she said. "When will you know?"

To their astonishment he rose to his feet and strode restlessly up and down the room. Neither Marcus nor Joyce had ever seen him so agitated before.

"I don't know," he said. "My theory is only a theory. I have no proof. I have only an idea that came in the night. Look here, my children, I must go back. I shall see you all to-morrow."

Marcus followed him to the doorway. "I say," he said anxiously, "it's not a thing I advise, of course, but if you need a revolver . . ."

Campion shook his head. "Thanks, old boy, I have one," he

said. "To tell you the truth, there's only one thing I could have to make me feel really safe."

"And that?" enquired Marcus eagerly.

"Suits of armour and solitary confinement for four," said Mr. Campion.

18

THIS IS THE REPORT OF THE DEPUTY CORONER (MR. W. T. THOMAS) SITTING IN THE TEMPORARY CAMBRIDGE CORONER'S COURT, DIRECTING THE JURY IN THE INQUEST ON THE BODY OF ANDREW SEELEY, OF SOCRATES CLOSE, TRUMPINGTON ROAD, CAMBRIDGE, AT THE CONCLUSION OF THE THIRD DAY OF THE HEARING, FRIDAY, THE 18TH OF APRIL

Ladies and Gentlemen of the Jury, we are here to inquire into the death of Andrew Seeley, 61 years of age, of Socrates Close, Trumpington Road, Cambridge, whose body was taken from the River Granta on April 10th last.

We have heard the evidence of various witnesses summoned to this court, and we must agree, I think, with Inspector Oates, of Scotland Yard, when he tells us that we have heard all the available evidence to help you to arrive at your decision.

We know that Andrew Seeley had been missing from his home since Sunday, March 29th, when he attended morning service in the company of his aunt, Mrs. Faraday, his niece by marriage, Miss Blount, and his three cousins, Mrs. Berry, Miss Julia Faraday, and Mr. William Faraday, all of the same address.

Now, the unfinished letter which has been read to you indicates quite clearly that the deceased had every intention and expectation of returning to finish it after the service. With reference to this letter, there is one point about it which may have appeared to some of you as extraordinary. The intended recipient has not been traced. But you must remember that Mr. Seeley does not seem to have been a man who talked much about his friends or his personal affairs, and it is quite conceivable that he should have correspondents of whom the rest of the household knew nothing. I must say here that I am surprised and a little shocked to hear that this person, who, unless she is abroad or otherwise prevented from reading the newspapers, must have recognised herself as the one addressed in this letter, which has been widely published, should not have come forward in spite of police appeals. However, this is a small point, and we must not let it confuse us as to the main issue.

We have heard evidence to show that Andrew Seeley did not drive home with his three cousins as had apparently been his intention before entering the church. You have heard the deposition of John Christmas, stating that the deceased instructed him to drive the two ladies, Mrs. Berry and Miss Julia Faraday, home in the car, as the deceased and his cousin, William Faraday, had decided to walk. He has gone on to say that these instructions astonished him, as they were contrary to custom. You will remember that you have heard that the habit was not for the car to proceed directly home, but to take a roundabout route in order to arrive at the same time as the slower horse carriage, in which Mrs. Caroline Faraday chose to drive with her great-niece companion, Miss Joyce Blount. So you will see that should the two men have decided to walk straight home, they would have arrived not much later than the rest of the party.

We now come to the evidence of William Faraday, cousin of the deceased, and I ask you to consider this very carefully.

We know that the service concluded at half-past twelve. William Faraday has told us that he accompanied his cousin as far as Coe Fen Lane, leading to Sheep's Meadows. Here, he tells us, there was a thick ground mist, a fact which has been borne out by other witnesses. He has also said that he suggested to his cousin that they should return, pointing out that the route they were taking was an extremely roundabout one. This, he says, his cousin refused to admit, and they quarrelled.

Mr. Faraday then went on to tell us that he turned back alone and remembers coming out on to the road by the Leys School. There, he states, he was seized by an attack of amnesia, a complaint from which he has suffered intermittently for some time. You have heard expert evidence in support of this statement, although no one has come forward who has actually seen Mr. Faraday under the influence of the malady before the date in question. However, that does not of itself make his statement untrue. Indeed, we know that he visited a very famous doctor as far back as June of last year and described his case.

Continuing William Faraday's evidence we come to some very important points. I must ask you to make particular note of the times mentioned. Mr. Faraday says he remembered no more after the attack seized him until he found himself walking into the gates of his home in Trumpington Road at a time which the evidence of the rest of the family shows to have been 1:35 P.M.

There I want to leave Mr. Faraday's evidence for a moment.

The next part of this tragic story which we have to consider is the discovery of the body of Andrew Seeley by two students whose evidence you have heard. You have had medical evidence which shows that the deceased met his death as the result of a bullet wound in the head. You have also heard experts who have told you that in their opinion the shot was fired at close range. The bullet taken from the body has been proved to be one discharged from a .45 revolver, the type of weapon which was used in the army during the late war, and of which there are, no doubt, many examples still unregistered in this country.

The medical evidence has also shown that the body had probably remained in the water for some considerable time. Doctor Hastings, of the Home Office, has told us that in his opinion death took place before the body was put into the water, and that as nearly as can be ascertained, it had remained immersed for a period not less than eleven days and not more than fourteen. Now Andrew Seeley was last seen on Sunday, March 30th. This, you will see, is twelve days before the discovery of his injured body in the river.

We now come to the evidence of Stanley Waybridge, of Ladysmith Cottages, Grantchester Road, who has told us that on Sunday, 30th of March last, he was just about to sit down to the midday meal which his wife had set upon the table, remarking that she was five minutes early and thus providentially fixing the time in his mind as 12:55, when he heard a shot from the direction of the river. Being naturally interested and surprised to hear such a noise on a Sunday, he went to his back door to see if he could catch a glimpse of the firer of the shot. But, he has told us, and his statement coincides with that of William Faraday, there was a thick ground mist rising to a height of five or six feet in the valley and over the river, and he saw no one. His wife called to him that his meal was becoming cold, and he returned to it, not unnaturally forgetting the entire incident until nearly a fortnight later, when the body was discovered.

Now, I must warn you that there is no proof that the shot

which Stanley Waybridge and his wife heard was the same shot which killed Andrew Seeley, but you must also remember that although the police have made unremitting enquiries no one has been found who heard any other shot in that vicinity on the Sunday in question, or indeed on any of the three subsequent days. Doctor Hastings has said that the condition of the body is consistent with death having taken place at this time. I think it is safe, therefore, for us to agree that at least the probability is that this was the fatal shot which Stanley Waybridge heard at five minutes to one o'clock.

This brings us to the conclusion that if our surmise is correct, Andrew Seeley met his death somewhere in the near vicinity of the river within ten minutes of his arrival there, presuming he walked straight to that place after leaving the church. Mr. Faraday has told you that in his opinion it was about ten or twelve minutes after they left church that he parted from his cousin. Witnesses have come forward to show that these two men, William Faraday and the deceased, were seen turning into Coe Lane together at the time stated, but no one seems to have encountered either of them on the lonely footpath between the lane and the river. Nor will you, as residents of Cambridge, find anything remarkable in this. The town is empty at this time of year, and most people who had been abroad in the morning would be hurrying to their homes for luncheon and not walking in the meadows, more especially as the weather was damp and misty.

Yet there can be no doubt that Andrew Seeley encountered somebody, for here we come to what is, perhaps, the most remarkable feature of this strange and terrible history. When Andrew Seeley's body was found, it was not only wounded in the head, Ladies and Gentlemen, but it was bound. Police witnesses have shown you exactly how. It is this binding which precludes any suggestion that Mr. Seeley had taken his own life, even had the half-finished letter he left behind him not been sufficient to cast a grave doubt in our minds on the likelihood of this eventuality.

Whoever accompanied or met Andrew Seeley on that Sunday afternoon bound him and afterwards brutally shot him. Now this is no sudden emotional crime. Whoever killed Andrew Seeley must have premeditated the act. The rope which bound the body has been exhibited to you, together with a portion of skylight cord brought by the police from an attic in the deceased's home, easily accessible to anyone in the household. We have heard the evidence of experts upon this subject, and we have compared the two pieces of cord ourselves. I think it is reasonable to admit that there is no difference in the texture, or the gauge, of these two pieces, when we make due allowance for the time that the one has been immersed in water.

In this long and difficult inquiry we have been confronted again and again by evidence which has pointed in one direction. But we must not blind ourselves to the fact that this evidence has in every case been purely circumstantial, and when we come to examine direct and proven fact we are faced with a wide gulf between those facts and the explanation which the circumstantial evidence would seem to bring most naturally into our minds.

To continue with the evidence which Mr. Featherstone, solicitor acting for the Faraday family, has felt it right to produce.

Mrs. Finch, proprietress of "The Red Bull" hotel in Knox Street, has come forward and has told you positively and upon oath that William Faraday entered her establishment, betraying every symptom of the malady from which he says he suffers, at—and this is important, Ladies and Gentlemen—fifteen minutes to one on the Sunday in question, and remained there until fifteen minutes past, behaving in a way which she has described to us as absent-minded. I have questioned this witness carefully before you, and I think we must agree that she has said nothing, nor has she behaved in any way which could lead us to believe that her evidence is not reliable. Alfred Robins, the potboy employed by Mrs. Finch at "The Red Bull" hotel, is a witness whose story corroborates his employer's in every detail. And we also have to consider the evidence of Frederick Shepherd, builder's clerk, of Grey Street, who has told us that he entered the saloon bar of "The Red Bull" hotel at ten minutes to one on the Sunday, to find a man at the bar whom he took to be tipsy, and with whom he had a drink. When asked if he could identify this man in the court, you will remember that he unhesitatingly picked out William Faraday.

Now I feel it is only just to interpolate here an inference, which has occurred to me, and which may also have occurred to you. The process of tying up a man, even if he has been previously stunned, or perhaps shot, and of lifting that body, is an arduous undertaking and would leave, one may legitimately suppose, signs upon the clothing and hands of anyone who had performed such an act. Moreover, the wound which the deceased sustained was of a very grievous nature, and there would be a considerable amount of blood in the vicinity of his body after it had been made. I feel that we must ask ourselves, could any man have lifted or moved such a body without becoming stained? Each of the three witnesses produced by Mr. Featherstone has told you upon oath that at five minutes to one on the Sunday Mr. Faraday was immaculately dressed, and that he looked, as Mrs. Finch described him, as though he came straight from church.

We now come to the question of the weapon. Mr. Faraday reported to the police through his solicitor that he had at one time been the possessor of a revolver of the same calibre as that from which the fatal shot was fired. William Faraday's revolver was stored, with his old army uniform, in an unlocked trunk in the same attic from which the police have procured the window cord. The police have searched for this revolver and found it to be missing. I should like to dwell upon the point that Mr. Faraday made the statement voluntarily. The trunk was kept unlocked. It was within reach of all in the household, and yet the person who removed it might have been reasonably assured that the loss would not be discovered for months, and possibly for years.

No weapon has been found. Inspector Oates has told you of the lengths to which the police, in their zeal, have gone to discover it, without success. Neither of these two revolvers, then—for it has not been shown that they are identical—has been produced.

Ladies and Gentlemen, you have now to consider your verdict. But before you retire I should like to remind you of one thing: this is not a police court. We are here only to decide in what manner this unfortunate man met his death. That is, the cause of death alone is our concern. If you find upon the evidence that he was murdered, you must say so. If you consider that you have not heard enough evidence to show either in what manner, or by whose hand, he died, then you must bring in a verdict coinciding with that view. But if you are agreed that the evidence has clearly indicated the man or woman who is responsible for this cruel and, as far as we know, motiveless crime, then it is your solemn duty to point him out. Ladies and Gentlemen of the Jury, you may retire to consider your verdict.

After a deliberation of only twenty minutes the jury brought in a verdict of "Wilful Murder by Person or Persons Unknown."

19

Under the Black Wing

The coroner had departed and the jury has shuffled out after him, having delivered their verdict. Stolid officials shepherded the spectators out of the court by the public entrance, but the principal actors remained in the centre of the slightly stuffy room, waiting to make their exit from a side door where Mr. Campion's car was awaiting them. The Faraday automobile was drawn up at the public entrance, so that the idle crowd which always collects on such occasions might be misled and wait in vain for the victims of their insatiable curiosity.

It was while Uncle William, pink and slightly triumphant, was still surrounded by congratulatory acquaintances, that Joyce and Mr. Campion, who were standing talking to Marcus, noticed simultaneously the florid and unexpected face of Cousin George peering at them over the heads of the other spectators in the slowly moving group at the back of the court. Moreover, it was at the very moment that Mr. Fred Shepherd, builder's clerk, of Grey Street, was shaking Uncle William vigorously by the hand, and the old man was trying to appear grateful without being unduly friendly, that he also caught sight of his cousin. His little blue eyes dilated, he blew out his cheeks, and he left the startled Mr. Shepherd very suddenly indeed, pushing his way over to Marcus.

The unexpected length and severity of the ordeal which the inquest had proved, had told upon them all, more especially upon Uncle William, who had certainly borne the brunt of the coroner's careful questioning. Now that it was over, although the mystery seemed no nearer solution, they all felt that at least there was some respite from the tension of the past week, and, a moment before George's appearance, thankfulness has almost reached the point of rejoicing in the little group. Even the Inspector seemed relieved. He had made his peace with Mr. Campion on the second day of the hearing, and now strolled over to join him. As he did so he caught a glimpse of the startled expression upon Joyce's face, and followed the direction of her glance across the hall, until he too saw the heavy red face and little dark eyes of George Makepeace Faraday.

The man met his gaze for an instant, and then turned abruptly and disappeared among the out-going crowd.

The Inspector darted after him, but the chairs and benches which lay in his path impeded his progress, and by the time he came out into the evening sunshine the man had vanished, just as he had vanished before, after his precipitate flight from Tomb Yard. Hampered by the mob, the Inspector gave up any idea of a chase and returned to join the others.

When he found the family again they were standing in a group in the side entrance, waiting to enter Campion's venerable Bentley. Campion detached himself from the others to speak to the Inspector.

"I say," he said, coming up, "did you see that fellow?"

"I did," said the Inspector bitterly. "But he was too sharp for me again. I'd like to have a word with that customer—and I shall. If he's back in the town we ought to find him easily enough."

Campion nodded, but he did not speak, and the Inspector went on regretfully.

"This inquest hasn't got us anywhere, you know," he said. "This'll be another case for the Black List against the police if we don't look out. It's too bad."

He was speaking softly, although there was not much danger of being overheard. He looked gloomy and dejected, and if Mr. Campion had not had sufficient troubles of his own he would have been sorry for him.

"What are they going to do now?" the Inspector demanded, jerking his head towards the three others.

"Mrs. Faraday has ordered us all to return to dinner," said Campion. "Miss Blount is returning to the house to-night, very much against my advice. How about you; are you leaving the town?"

"Are you?" said Stanislaus.

The young man shook his head wearily. "No," he said. "Not

for a little while. To tell you the truth, I daren't. I have a feeling that the really important part of this affair is going to begin at any moment now." He paused and glanced at the other man enquiringly from behind his big spectacles.

Somewhat grudgingly the Inspector gave him the information he desired.

"I shan't go up to-night," he said. "And if you get a line on anything, for heaven's sake let me know. No more monkey tricks behind my back—hints or no hints."

"Right," said Campion. "And you come across if you have any conversation with Cousin George."

Oates scowled. "He's no use to us really," he said. He sighed. "What a rotten unsatisfactory case this is! I knew it would be the moment I spotted that coincidence at the beginning. I'm not a superstitious man, but you can't help noticing queer things when they happen over and over again. If I had my way about this case I'd write 'Act of God' across the docket and shut it up in a drawer." He stopped abruptly, alarmed at the expression which passed across his friend's face. "What's up!" he demanded.

"That's one of my own pet superstitions," said Mr. Campion. "Look here, when shall I see you again? To-morrow, I hope?"

"I shall be here," said the Inspector. "I wish you'd come across with this airy-fairy theory of yours. What's rattling you?"

Mr. Campion's reply was entirely unexpected. "I say, Stanislaus," he said, "what's the penalty for arson?"

The Inspector did not reply, and Campion turned away. He seemed fagged out and worried. The Inspector drew him back again.

"What's on your mind?" he insisted.

Campion sighed. "I don't know that I shall ever be able to convince you of it," he said, "but I tell you I would rather take that carload of people to East Lane on Saturday night than back to that house. I've waited five days, but I've a feeling that if it's coming, it's coming to-night."

"I don't follow you," said the Inspector grumpily. "But if you're expecting another attack from the same source you're on the wrong track. Whoever is responsible for this lot will wait for another six months or so now, you mark my words."

"We're up against something you never dreamed of," said

Mr. Campion. "See you to-morrow." And he strode out to the car, where the others awaited him impatiently.

Marcus and Uncle William sat in the back. They were both weary, both a little apprehensive. Joyce, a bright spot of colour burning in her cheeks, sat in front next to Campion. They drove slowly through the town. The 'Varsity had officially returned the day before, and the place had sprung to life. Young men in amazing motorcars filled the streets, bicycles had become a menace, and battered "squares" and ragged gowns were every-where. As they emerged into the long broad sweep of Trump-ington Road, Joyce sighed with relief and spoke.

"Oh, I'm glad it's all over," she said. "Did you—did you see Cousin George? I'm afraid he'll be at home when we get there. It's just like him to turn up and worry Aunt Caroline for money at a time like this. He's bound to come, don't you think?"

Mr. Campion looked at her dubiously. "I say," he said, "do you think it's wise, quite apart from Cousin George, to have come back to the house so soon? Why not make up your mind to stay with Ann for another day or so?"

The girl shook her head. "No, I'm all right now," she said. "I don't want to burden Ann any more than I can help. She's been so very sporting, bearing with me all this week. Besides, I've sent my things back. I shall stay at Socrates to-night."

She could see he was disappointed, and hastened to vindicate herself.

"I've been away five days," she said. "I went as soon as you insisted, but nothing happened, did it? Besides, if Cousin George does come I shall be a great help to Great-aunt Caroline, and she needs someone, poor darling."

Mr. Campion made no reply, and they continued down the road and turned into the gate in silence.

Alice admitted them. She was smiling, and her red face shone above her severe black afternoon frock and stiff white apron. It was evident that the news of the verdict which Mr. Featherstone, senior, had just brought to the house, had already percolated to the domestic quarters.

"Mrs. Faraday is in the drawing-room," said Alice, "Mr. Featherstone and Mrs. Kitty are with her. She said for you all to go in."

The great drawing-room, which caught the last rays of the evening sun, was much brighter than Campion had expected. Great-aunt Faraday sat bolt upright in her chair by the fireplace, a frail but luxurious creature in her magnificent laces. Aunt Kitty sat beside her, an insignificant pathetic little body. The strain of giving evidence had told upon her, and her webby eyelids fluttered nervously.

Featherstone, senior, who looked older than both of them, his natural air of monumental ruin even more pronounced than usual, sat opposite and at a distance at which they must have appeared a mere blur to him. He rose unsteadily to his feet as Joyce entered, the others following her.

Aunt Kitty, who could be relied upon to do the embarrassing thing, bounced up with a squeal of excitement, tripped across the room, threw her arms around the uneasy bulk of Uncle William's shoulders and burst out hysterically: "Dear, dear Willie! Safe at last! Safe!"

Uncle William, who was very much on edge already, drew back from her.

"Don't be a fool, Kitty," he muttered testily. "I've been made a scapegoat in this affair, I know that, but I'm not going to be treated to it for the rest of my life, thank you." He stalked past her and sat down.

Aunt Kitty looked hurt and a little frightened now that she found herself alone in the middle of the room. She stood fluttering until Joyce put an arm round her and led her to a settee on the opposite side of the fireplace to Great-aunt Caroline.

Old Featherstone cleared his throat. "Well," he began in his deep and something too musical voice, "as I have been telling Mrs. Faraday, I think we are all to be congratulated. We have, of course, to be very grateful to the woman Finch and her employee. We were lucky to get hold of them, more especially as we received no help in that direction from you, Mr. Faraday."

Uncle William scowled at him. "I was ill, I tell you," he said. "Nobody seems to realise that. I was very ill. I still am very ill. This affair might have been the death of me. Not one of you seems to have grasped that."

"Oh, but we have, Willie. That's what has been frightening us." Aunt Kitty had spoken before Joyce could stop her, and it was, unfortunately, only too obvious what she meant.

Uncle William exploded. "I like that!" he said. "Twelve perfect strangers have told the world quite plainly that I'm as innocent as a new-born babe and yet the moment I come back into this house I'm accused by my own sister. Not one of you here has any sympathy except Campion. And I don't know why you're congratulating yourself, Featherstone. It was Campion who found you all your witnesses. Remarkable! He deduced where I'd been when I didn't know myself."

"William." Great-aunt Caroline, who had sat very still during this interlude, her sharp black eyes taking in the varying expressions of the little group, now stirred herself. "William," she repeated, "now is not the time for ingratitude. If you are not thankful for your deliverance, I am. Come and sit here by me, if you please."

Uncle William went. He muttered to himself a little and the words "scapegoat" and "disgusting exhibition" were distinctly audible, but finally he sat down.

Great-aunt Caroline smiled at old Featherstone. "I am very grateful to you," she said. "You have been a very true old friend. Now, I want you all to sit down, for I have something to say before we go in to dinner."

Marcus glanced sharply at Campion. The same thought was in both their minds. Surely Great-aunt Caroline should be acquainted with Cousin George's presence in the town? However, the opportunity passed, for the old lady was already speaking again.

"I am very glad that this inquest has ended as it has," she began, "and I am very grateful to all of you who have helped us. But there is a point of which I feel we must not lose sight. It is this: this terrible affair is not yet at an end, and the odium which has fallen upon this house is still as strong as though some one of us had been arrested."

"Oh, mama, how can you?—how can you?" Aunt Kitty burst into tears.

Great-aunt Caroline turned to her regretfully. "Don't be foolish, Catherine," she said. "Sensibility is very charming, but at this time it is out of place. These are facts, and we must face them. A verdict of murder against someone unknown has been passed upon Andrew's body. Therefore until that murderer is found and brought to justice, this house, and everyone in it, will remain under a cloud. I have already told this to Mr. Featherstone, and he quite agrees with me. Dinner will be served informally this evening, rather earlier than usual. If anyone wishes to talk to me I shall be in my writing-room. Mr. Featherstone, will you give me your arm?"

The old man rose ponderously to his feet and, very conscious that he made a picture of distinguished old fashioned gallantry which needed only Mrs. Faraday to complete it, offered her his arm.

They had advanced perhaps three paces when the blow fell. There was a shrill burst of protest from the hall outside, followed by a man's strident tones. The next moment the white door of the sacred drawing-room at Socrates Close was shattered open, and Cousin George, followed by a flustered and dishevelled Alice, precipitated himself into the room.

Old Featherstone, who could not see the intruder's features, was perhaps the only member of the company who did not receive a distinct physical shock.

Cousin George, not quite sure of himself in Tomb Yard, had not presented an attractive personality: but Cousin George with the whip hand, Cousin George truculent and with a drunken gleam in his small eyes, was a revolting specimen. Even Great-aunt Caroline stopped in her tracks, silent and trembling. Aunt Kitty screamed. Cousin George waved to her. Then he strode into the room, slamming the door in Alice's face.

"Hallo, Kitty, here's the devil again," he said, revealing an unexpectedly deep voice and educated accent. He glanced round the room at the company. No one spoke or moved. The man was exultant, and he made a peculiarly unpleasant figure in his grease-spotted blue suit, with his coarse red face, sagging mouth and general air of leering satisfaction.

"Sit down, everybody," he said thickly. "Bring out the fatted calf. The Prodigal returns."

Aunt Caroline stiffened herself for the effort. "George," she said, "you will come to my writing-room and speak to me there, if you please."

Cousin George laughed loudly and unpleasantly. "Sorry, aunt," he said as he lounged against the closed door with considerable theatrical effect, "sorry, but this is where the formula begins to differ. No hustling me into a back room. George has returned in force. George is going to be made a great fuss of. In fact, George is going to stay."

There was a snort and a rustle from the back of the room as Uncle William, who, to do him justice, was not a complete coward, sailed into battle. He planted himself squarely in front of the intruder, who appeared to be enjoying himself immensely, and thrust his pink face close to the other man's.

"You infernal blackguard!" he said, his voice leaping out of control. "We've had enough of you. You get out of this house.

And to save the police trouble, call at the station on your way out of the town. They're looking for you, I don't mind telling you."

Cousin George's amusement increased. He put his head back until it rested on the wood and, still smiling insolently into the old man's face, he opened his mouth and used a single epithet the like of which had never before defiled the stately precincts of Socrates Close, and then, while the frozen silence was still tingling, he raised his arm and caught the pink face so near his own a flip with the back of his hand, so that Uncle William tottered back livid with astonishment and the sudden pain.

Campion and Marcus leapt forward simultaneously, and Cousin George was pinioned before he realised what had happened. The man was as strong as an ox, but his captors were young, and, Mr. Campion at least, by no means unpractised. Realising himself helpless, the intruder began to laugh.

"All right," he said. "Chuck me out. You'll regret it to the day of your death."

Old Featherstone, who had only just grasped who the newcomer was, and being fearful for his dignity if not for his balance, peered round him helplessly. Finally he cleared his throat.

"Marcus, my boy," he said, "move away from that door, will you? Mrs. Faraday and I were just going out."

Uncle William, who was rumbling ferociously, hovered in the centre of the room, uncertain whether to attack verbally or physically, when Cousin George spoke again.

"You'll be sorry if you don't let me speak," he said. "I've got you by the short hairs. You send your lawyer away, Aunt, and listen to me."

To the complete astonishment of most of her hearers, Aunt Caroline seemed to give way.

"Mr. Campion, Marcus," she said, "you will oblige me by coming over here. George, sit down. What have you to say?"

The man's triumph was insufferable, and although the young men obeyed the old lady, it was evident that they did so grudgingly. Freed, Cousin George shook himself.

"Thank you," he drawled. "Now, sit down, all of you. Keep old Foxy here if you like, aunt, but remember you have yourself to blame if you don't like him hearing what I say."

Aunt Caroline's attitude surprised everyone. She returned to her chair by the fire almost meekly. Old Featherstone stepped after her and stood gracefully by her side. Although he could see very little of the proceedings, at least he could hear, and he had the satisfaction of knowing that he looked magnificent.

Cousin George threw himself into the most comfortable chair in the room and began to speak with spirituous and theatrical arrogance.

"This is funny," he said. "You don't know how funny you all are. *I'm* going to laugh now. This is where I step in and sit pretty for the rest of my life. No more fobbing me off with a few pounds, Aunt. I'm back to stay this time. You're all going to sit up and dance while I call the tune. And you," he added, wagging a none-too-clean forefinger at Uncle William, "you pompous old humbug, you're going to run round me like a spaniel if I want you to."

He took a cigarette out of his pocket and lit it, quite conscious of the sensation he was causing, and enjoying it to the full. Both Uncle William and Aunt Kitty, who knew the smell of tobacco had never before permeated the drawing-room, were aghast at this desecration, and they turned to their mother appealingly.

Great-aunt Caroline sat quite still, no muscle of her face moving; only her black eyes, which never left her nephew's face, seemed alive.

Cousin George spat a shred of chewed tobacco on to the Chinese carpet and ground his muddy heel into the soft pile with flagrant delight.

"I've looked forward to this," he said. "Now it's come. I've got you just where I want you. Are you going to keep the lawyers here, Aunt?"

"Yes." Aunt Caroline's voice was perfectly composed, but her icy tone could not quell Cousin George, who was more than a little drunk, both with liquor and his own elation. He sniffed.

"Right; here goes. The police have been looking for me, haven't they? I should have been down before if I'd known that, but I didn't. And why? Because I was 'inside.' I got out this morning and read about the inquest. I read about Julia, too. She's gone, has she? Well, that's a stroke of luck I didn't expect. Who's that man?" He pointed to Campion. "I've seen him before. If he's something to do with the police, all the worse for you, Aunt. Shall I go on?"

"Yes," said Great-aunt Caroline again.

Cousin George shrugged his shoulders. "Well, here I am, here I stay—*j'y suis, j'y reste*. Not one of you is going to raise a finger to turn me out of this house. Because if you do," he added, lowering his voice, "I shall tell all I know, and you'll have a murder trial in the family before you know where you are. You've come in for a bit of publicity already, but that's nothing to the stink I'll raise. You see, I happened to follow Andrew from church on Sunday, the thirteenth of March. It won't be circumstantial evidence; it'll be an eye-witness account."

He paused and looked about him. There was deadly silence in the room. His words had electrified the company. Great-aunt Caroline alone appeared to be perfectly unmoved.

"You will explain, George," she said.

Cousin George shook his head. "You don't catch me like that. You know and I know that I've got you all just like that." He thrust out his hand, the fingers extended, and slowly clenched it. "As long as I'm comfortable I shall say nothing," he went on. "I know what suits me. You see," he added, a tremor of satisfaction in his voice, "it's one of you. You all know that. And I know which one it is. Now let's hear your airs and graces. William, ring that bell over there and tell the maid to get me some whisky."

All eyes were turned upon Uncle William, and he shot an imploring glance towards his mother, but Great-aunt Caroline nodded, and humbly Uncle William rose and pulled the bell.

It was capitulation.

Cousin George laughed noisily. "That's it," he said, "I'm going to make you do that often."

When the startled Alice appeared it was he who gave the order.

"Whisky and soda," he said before anyone else could speak, "and make it snappy."

The woman shot a scandalised glance at her mistress, but receiving Great-aunt Caroline's nod, she hurried out.

Cousin George leant back. "Murder trials arouse public interest in oneself, don't they, Aunt?" he drawled. "I think I could place a short intimate biography of myself with several great newspapers should I be compelled to tell all I know about old Andrew. Don't you think so?"

The immediate result of this comparatively innocent remark was extraordinary. Great-aunt Caroline stiffened.

"Mr. Featherstone," she said, "you would oblige me by excusing yourself from my table to-night. Since you are such an old friend, I know I may ask you this."

Old Featherstone bent forward, and although he lowered his voice, its rumblings echoed quite clearly through the room.

"Dear lady," he said, "this is blackmail, you know. There's a very severe penalty for blackmail."

"Yes," said Cousin George casually from the depths of his chair. "But so few people prosecute, do they, old Foxy? This family won't prosecute me, don't you worry. You run along and do what you're told."

The old man would have spoken again, but Great-aunt Caroline laid a hand on his arm, so that he thought better of it, and, with a bow to his client and her household and a stony near-sighted stare for Cousin George, he strode out of the door. Alice, returning with a tray, stood aside for him to pass.

Cousin George's comment was cut short, no doubt, by the appearance of this refreshment, which he insisted upon having on the floor by his chair. When the woman had gone out he sat with his glass in his hand, his legs straddled out before him.

"Do the tame puppies remain?" he said, pointing to Campion and Marcus.

Marcus was livid and the muscles of his jaw throbbed visibly. Mr. Campion, on the other hand, appeared almost imbecile, a mask of affable stupidity covering his personality completely.

"If you prefer it, no," said Great-aunt Caroline.

Cousin George surveyed the two young men with an insolent stare.

"I don't care who hears what I've got to say," he said. "I know what I know, and I've got a witness to prove it. I've got the whip hand. I've got to be bribed not to tell all I know to the police. I should have been here before, only, as I say, I got a bit drunk and beat up a policeman last Thursday, so they put me in for seven days. One of the Faradays of Socrates Close drunk and disorderly—that's a paragraph for the local paper! Perhaps you'd like to write it out for me, William. Or perhaps you'd like to save your energy. I'm going to keep you busy in future. Yes, Aunt, I think you can turn these two lounge lizards out to grass. The family and I must get better acquainted. A little heart-to-heart talk will show us all where we stand. Oh, and by the way, neither of you need trouble to send for the police. I saw them as soon as I arrived in Cambridge this afternoon. They were quite satisfied as to my movements. If everything isn't arranged satisfactorily here I shall pay them another visit. I said I held the ace; I do."

He poured himself out another drink and raised his glass provocatively to William.

"They drew out all the evidence against you at the inquest, and you got off," he said. "But that doesn't mean that everyone's satisfied. Why, it's obvious to the whole world that one of you did it, and I'm in the happy position of knowing which one. However, since you are my own flesh and blood, rather than turn you over to the police, I'll keep you in order myself."

Great-aunt Caroline, whose composure was almost trance-like, turned to Campion and Marcus.

"I should like you both," she said, "to take Joyce into the breakfast-room and wait there for a little while. Joyce, dear, please tell Alice to lay another place at the dinner-table. She will have seen that Mr. Featherstone has gone and may not be aware that Cousin George is staying."

"Tell her to prepare a room for me," said Cousin George. "I'll have old Andrew's. I bet he knew how to make himself comfortable. I'll want a fire in it and a bottle of whisky on the mantelpiece. These are the only things I insist upon. Now then, clear out. I have something to say to my dear relations."

But Aunt Kitty, whose frail nerves had stood up against this ordeal so valiantly, now gave way completely. She darted into the centre of the room like a small terrified rabbit.

"The spirit of Evil!" she shouted hysterically. "The spirit of Evil is abroad! Another fiend has been sent to torment us. Oh! Oh! Oh!"

Each of the three final exclamations was uttered in a tone higher and more piercing than the last. She swayed uncertainly for some seconds, and finally collapsed upon the floor, sobbing and kicking like a maniac. The sight was distressing and a little terrifying.

For the first time since his arrival Cousin George was discomforted. He drew his feet away from the abject figure, and picking up his glass put the siphon under his arm. Then, with a decanter in his free hand, he turned towards the door.

"I can't stand this," he said. "I shall be in the library until you've pulled yourself together sufficiently to listen to me intelligently. I'll have my food served to me pronto on old Uncle John's desk. And from henceforward, remember that room is my room. I'm master of this house now."

Mr. Campion opened the door, and as Cousin George stared at him he bent forward and spoke softly.

"Pull up the blinds when you go into the library," he murmured. "You'll see there's a message for you on one of the window-panes."

The man stared at him, but Campion said no more, and finally Cousin George stumbled out into the passage.

20

The Devil in the House

"If it wasn't for old Harrison Gregory, damn me! I'd go up and sleep at the club," said Uncle William.

He was striding up and down the morning-room, his plump hands clasped behind his back, his short white hair standing on end and his moustache bristling.

The other two occupants of the room were also on their feet. Mr. Campion leant against the mantelpiece so vague and ineffectual that he appeared to be hardly alive. Marcus stood by the window farthest away from the fire, his chin sunk upon his breast, his hands thrust deep into his pockets. The unshaded bulbs in the brass water-lily calyx shed an unfriendly glare, and the whole house breathed an atmosphere of tension that was well-nigh unbearable. The door was closed, but even its thick wooden panels could not keep out the sounds which emanated from the library where Cousin George sat in the late Master of Ignatius's chair spilling spirit and soda water over the sacred desk and bellowing commands from time to time.

He had insisted that the door of the library should remain open, and his insulting comments leapt after every flying figure which flitted past his blurred line of vision on the way to the stairs or the front door.

The quiet old house was seething. Fifty-year-old customs

had been swept ruthlessly aside, habits of a life-time were shattered, and it seemed as though the very furniture protested against this desecration of its calm.

Uncle William, who had received one of the most violent shocks of his career at the end of a long period of stress, was beside himself. He had reached the stage when he could not bear to remain still. A major revolution in the country would probably have had much the same effect upon him.

Dinner had been a fiasco. Aunt Kitty had not appeared and had remained in her room, where even now Joyce was attempting to get her off to sleep. Cousin George, also, had mercifully decided to stay in the library, where he criticised loudly the food that was brought to him. Great-aunt Caroline had not been present either, and this perhaps had shaken the morale of the household more than anything else could have done. Except in times of illness, Mrs. Faraday had taken the head of her table since the day of her husband's funeral in 1896.

Uncle William burst out again. "I can't understand Mother," he said. "If she won't let us chuck him out, why won't she let us send for the police? The fellow comes here with a cock-and-bull story and she takes it seriously. Really, you would almost think she believed in it."

Marcus shrugged his shoulders. "Somehow the bounder put up a very convincing story," he remarked.

Uncle William stopped in his tracks, and his little blue eyes seemed to be on the verge of popping out of his head.

"Do you mean to say . . . ?" he began, and his voice trailed into silence. He turned to Campion. "Do *you* think George knows anything?" he demanded. "Good Heavens, do you mean to tell me that you think someone in this house—one of us—put old Andrew out of the way, and Julia? I mean, after all that's come out at the inquest?" He sat down suddenly on one of the small chairs by the table. "God bless my soul!"

Marcus straightened himself and lounged restlessly down the length of the room.

"I think it's a great pity Mrs. Faraday won't send for the police," he said. "A great pity, and rather extraordinary."

"Mother's old," said Uncle William, jumping to his feet. "I think I shall go out and call the police myself. That'll be heaping coals of fire upon their heads after the disgusting way they treated me. I tell you, George is appalling," he went on, his voice rising unexpectedly. "Coming here, behaving like a—like a drunken anarchist in a house of sorrow. Assaulting people," he added, rubbing his cheek angrily. "If it hadn't been for Mother I'd have taken a dog-whip to the fellow, old as I am. Yes, I shall go for the police. I'd like to see that fellow taken out of here in handcuffs, Faraday or no Faraday," he added vindictively. "Yes, well, I've made up my mind. I'm going."

"No," murmured Mr. Campion.

Uncle William turned a baleful eye upon him. "What's that, sir?"

"No," said Mr. Campion again. "Don't do that. There's all this mystery to be solved. You let him stay here."

Uncle William threw himself down in his chair again. "Oh, well," he said resignedly, "badger me. Everybody badgers me. Hullo, what's that?"

His last remark was occasioned by an extra loud remark from the library. Marcus strode to the door and threw it open just as Joyce, the colour flaming in her cheeks, came hurrying in. Across the hall Cousin George's voice, thick and inexpressibly vulgar, came clearly to them.

"Don't be a little stiff. Come and let me have a look at you. Sorry I can't get up. You're the only thing worth looking at in this——household."

Marcus, whose carefully cultured languor and sophistication had undergone such a ruthless battering during the last few days, received his final blow. His shoulders stiffened and his head went down. Joyce, who saw his face, threw up an arm, checking for an instant his precipitate rush, an instant that gave Campion time to get across the room and haul his friend back.

"Not yet," he pleaded, "not yet."

Joyce shut the door and put her back against it. Marcus, like all men who are very seldom angry, was pig-headed in his wrath. His face had become a dusky red and his eyes were blinded slits.

"I'm sorry," he said huskily. "I can't stand that chap. I shall break his neck. Get out of my way."

Joyce began to cry. Apparently she did not realise it, for the tears rolled down her cheeks, and she made no attempt to hide them.

"Don't," she said. "Don't make any more trouble. Don't! Don't!"

Uncle William, who had observed this incident with interest, his mind seizing upon it as a relief from his own mental chaos, now rose to a height of which no one had suspected him capable.

He produced an immense stiff white handkerchief, and pushing past the two young men, dabbed the girl's face with it.

"There, there, my dear," he said. "Come along, come along. We'll soon have the bounder under lock and key—and probably hanged. There, there."

This intervention saved the situation. Uncle William's persistent belief that the arrest of Cousin George would solve all their difficulties had a humorous element in it which even at this most trying stage of the proceedings appealed to them irresistibly. Marcus put an arm round the girl's shoulders and led her across the room to the fireplace.

Mr. Campion and Uncle William remained near the door. "Poor little thing," said Uncle William huskily. "Damned shame. If the fellow hadn't got our name I'd see him hanged with pleasure."

Mr. Campion made no comment, for at this moment the door again opened and Alice entered. She shut the door firmly behind her, and, taking a deep breath, burst out with her complaint.

" 'Tisn't right, sir. You've got to stop it. She's in there," she said.

They stared at her, uncomprehending, and Joyce hurried forward.

"Who's in where, Alice? What's the matter?"

"The mistress, Miss." The woman was nearly in tears. "She's gone in to that—that person alone, and he's not in a fit state, Miss. You can see that for yourselves. Why, he might kill her." She opened the door and pointed across the hall. "There. You can see, she's gone in and shut the door."

Uncle William took advantage of her invitation. He peered across the hall. The library door was visible from the breakfast-room threshold, and he could see that it was indeed shut. He returned to the room.

"It's a fact," he said. "What ought we to do about it? I suppose she knows what she's doing, and if she does, she won't thank us for interfering. But I don't know . . ."

"I've listened," said Alice shamelessly. "I've listened at the door. You can hear her talking to him quietly. I heard him swear, too. I'm sure it was that, although I couldn't catch the word. I'd go in myself, only you know how wilful the mistress is." She paused questioningly.

Instinctively they turned towards Campion. "Wait," he said.

"It's all we can do. This, I fancy, is Mrs. Faraday's idea. After all, if she cannot manage Cousin George, no one can."

"By Jove, you're right there," said Uncle William, brightening up. "Leave him to Mother. You mark my words, he'll come skulking out of that room with his tail between his legs like the cur he is."

Alice appeared unsatisfied, but receiving no assistance from the others, she relinquished her idea of interrupting the interview. She planted herself in the doorway.

"If you'll excuse me, Miss," she murmured, "I'll wait here. Then if she calls or anything I can go straight in. And if she comes out I can dodge back without her seeing me."

Fifteen terrible minutes had passed. Conversation had ceased and the morning-room was cold and silent. Uncle William sat hunched up in one green arm-chair, Joyce curled up in the other, with Marcus perched on the arm. Mr. Campion lounged by the bookcase and Alice stood half in and half out of the open door.

After what seemed an eternity Uncle William stirred. "About time that yob came skulking out," he said, "isn't it? Another five minutes and I shall send for the police. What do we pay rates for if a fellow can walk into your house and behave like an animal?"

Alice moved silently back from the doorway. "Someone's coming," she murmured.

They all listened intently. From across the hall had come the metallic click of the library latch. The question in all their minds would be answered in a moment now: Who would come out of the library, who would remain in possession? Who had triumphed?

And then, shattering all their hopes, Cousin George's voice, thicker and more indistinct than before, was heard shouting: "I've got you! You can't shift me, whichever way you turn." And then, coming towards them over the tiles, they heard the sharp click-clack of Great-aunt Faraday's cane.

With great presence of mind Alice picked up a flower bowl from the sideboard and stood back to allow her mistress to enter. Then she moved silently out of the room, closing the door behind her.

Great-aunt Faraday paused just inside the door and stood looking at them as they rose. She was still wonderfully composed, although the hand which held her cane trembled a little. She had changed her frock; her stiff black gown was the one which she usually wore in the evenings and her cap and fichu were of fine needle-point. She tapped the ground with her stick.

"I will have a chair here, Marcus," she said. "Just here. I am tired of standing."

When she was safely seated in her somewhat peculiar position a yard or so inside the doorway, she surveyed her audience and nodded to them to sit down.

"William," she said, "would you be so good as to go into my writing-room and wait there for me. I shall like a word with you before I go to bed."

Uncle William rose with a good grace, all things considered, and went off, reserving his muttered protest until he was outside the room. When he had gone the old lady cleared her throat.

"George will remain here to-night," she said. "However, as I feel I owe you all a little explanation, I thought I would have a word with you before retiring. George, as you have heard, has come here with an extraordinary story. I allowed him to remain because I know him well enough to realise that, odious as he is, he is not a complete fool, and I feared that he would not take such a dangerous line as this unless he had some information to lend weight to his threats. I have just been talking to him," she continued. "I waited until this moment to do so because it occurred to me that the more drunk he became the more likely he would be to betray himself. Unfortunately, I think he has a stronger will than I gave him credit for. He is also very drunk indeed, and apart from getting anything out of him, I am afraid the interview has only served to convince me that the creature knows a great deal."

Joyce sprang up. "You don't mean that you think he really did see who killed Uncle Andrew?" she demanded.

Great-aunt Caroline nodded. "Yes, my dear," she said simply, "I do."

The effect of this gentle statement was startling in the extreme.

"Well, let's get the police," said Marcus. "They'll make him talk, if he really does know anything."

The old lady shook her head. "My dear boy," she said, her small voice surprisingly calm after the excitement in his own, "not yet. The police cannot detain George, and I feel that we owe it to ourselves to hear what he knows before the officials get hold of him."

"Then you think . . . ?" Joyce's voice trailed away.

The old lady shot her a swift bird-like glance.

"George remains in this house to-night, my dear," she said. "To-morrow, when he is sober, I shall talk to him again. Until then I do not want the police even to know that he is here. For," she went on deliberately, "should the unthinkable occur and we find ourselves involved in a murder trial, I see no way of preventing him from making all the capital he can out of any scandal he may be able to lay his hands upon, and that, I am afraid, is well within his power."

"But, Mrs. Faraday"—Marcus's tone was scandalised—"nothing is worse than murder, surely?"

A grim expression spread over old Mrs. Faraday's face. "That is a matter of opinion, Marcus," she said. "Now, there are several things I want you to do for me. In the first place, I should consider it a great favour if you would consent to stay in this house to-night."

Marcus was astonished. "Why, certainly, if you wish it, Mrs. Faraday," he said.

Great-aunt Caroline nodded to him. She appeared satisfied.

"Joyce, my dear," she said, "I want you to sleep in my room. The bed in the alcove has been made up. Marcus, you will have Joyce's room. No doubt William can lend you everything you require. And then," she went on solemnly, "if you and Mr. Campion would take George up to his room—that is, Andrew's old room—I should be very grateful. I shall go to bed now. Joyce, will you come with me? First of all, run along and tell William I'll see him in the morning instead of to-night, and then ask Alice to prepare your room for Marcus."

As Joyce went out the old lady turned once again to the young men.

"Even in the midst of tribulation such as this, a thought of general philosophy may occur to one," she said unexpectedly. "If either of you should be forced to listen to one of those misguided enthusiasts who decry the niceties of our conventional system—remember George. There are no doubt many other people in the world quite as wicked as he is, but a modicum of manners prevents them from making such a deplorable display. Now, I am afraid I have given you a most unpleasant task, but I feel that, unhampered by William, the two of you may be able to get George to his room, by whatever method you may think fit, which is more than I or anyone else in the house could possibly do. I shall go to my room now, and perhaps in fifteen minutes' time you will be good enough to make your first attempt. Good night."

Mr. Campion held the door open for her, and was rewarded. Mrs. Faraday stopped and smiled at him.

"Don't worry," she said. "This is the only shock from which you could not have protected me. I am very grateful for your presence here."

"My hat," said Marcus as Campion closed the door, "I'm itching to get my hands on that chap. I suppose we couldn't accidentally tip him over the banisters? He doesn't know anything, do you think so?"

Mr. Campion took off his spectacles. "It's the best thing that ever happened if he does," he said. "We shan't be able to do much with him to-night, but we'll have a shot in the morning. I'm afraid old Stanislaus is going to be angry with me again. I'm glad you're going to stay the night. I have a feeling that something is going to happen."

"Something else?" said Marcus.

Campion nodded, but did not speak, for at this moment the door opened again and Uncle William returned. If Great-aunt Caroline had hoped that he would take himself directly to bed, she had under-estimated him. He had come back prepared for war.

"Now that Mother's gone to bed, let's have a go at that fellow," he said, bounding into the room, his pink face glistening. "I don't know what the old lady thinks she's doing trying to get me out of the way. I'm not as young as I used to be, but I'm not the man I was in the Mess at Jo'burg if I can't put that blackguard under the table! *In vino veritas*, you know. We'll have the truth out of him."

Marcus looked at Campion, and the expression upon his face was so comic that the other nearly laughed. Uncle William went on.

"I've been thinking it over," he said. "At last we're up against something we can deal with, something tangible, instead of all this poking about in the dark. Suppose I go in and have it out with him?"

Mr. Campion hastily changed the subject. "I say, I have only one pair of pyjamas with me," he remarked. "Can you lend Marcus a pair? He's staying the night."

Faced with an even more simple problem than the eviction of Cousin George, Uncle William was at home.

"Certainly, my boy," he said. "Come up and I'll get you all you want."

"You go and look him out some things," suggested Campion. "He's having Joyce's room. She's sleeping with Mrs. Faraday."

"I'll find you everything," said Uncle William. "Pyjamas, dressing-gown, shaving tackle. Be delighted."

The moment his rotund form had disappeared up the staircase Campion turned to Marcus.

"Come on," he said. "Now or never." And together they bore down upon Cousin George.

It was as well, Mr. Campion considered as they entered the study of the late Dr. Faraday of Ignatius for the purpose of putting Cousin George to bed, that the dead do not turn in their graves.

Cousin George, his collar and tie unloosed, his swollen face purple and sagging, wallowed across the desk which now had a surface like a four-ale bar on a Saturday night. He barely raised an eyelid as they entered, but as they advanced upon him he threw out his hand in an unwieldy gesture which wiped a soda-water siphon on to the ground.

"What's the matter?" he demanded.

"Bed," said Campion clearly in his ear, and nodding to Marcus, he suddenly gripped the man beneath the arm and jerked him to his feet.

Cousin George struggled, and the strength of the man surprised his captors. They were both determined, however, and in a few moments he found himself borne precipitately towards the door. He began to swear, revealing a vocabulary which indicated that he had travelled extensively.

"Shut up," said Marcus, suddenly taking the initiative. With a viciousness for which Mr. Campion had not given him credit, he caught the two ends of Cousin George's tie, and, jerking them round to the back of the man's neck, wound the silk about his wrist until he had a strangle-hold. Cousin George's voice grew fainter and he began to cough and gasp painfully.

"Don't kill him," protested Campion.

"He's all right," said Marcus. "Come on."

The stairs were negotiated with comparatively little difficulty, and at length the struggling group came to a stop outside Andrew's room. Marcus released his hold on the man's neck and threw the door open.

"Now then," he said, "in he goes."

Cousin George was shot unceremoniously into the room, Campion switched on the light, and they closed the door upon him. The key, left by the thoughtful Alice, confronted them, projecting from the outside lock. Marcus turned it and thrust it into his pocket just as a furious onslaught from within echoed throughout the house.

Uncle William, with a pair of unexpectedly vituperant pyjamas over his arm, put his head out of his door.

"Oh, I missed it," he said. "Never mind. There's to-morrow."

Mr. Campion straightened himself. "I expect he'll make a din for half an hour or so," he said, raising his voice against the pandemonium. "We had better get to bed. We can't do much till the morning."

Uncle William nodded. "By far the most sensible thing to do," he agreed. "Come along, Marcus. I'll show you your room."

It was at this moment that it occurred to Cousin George to sing the more obscene verses of a well-known chanty at the top of his voice.

21

The Owner of the Green Hat

Mr. Campion sat on the end of his bed watching the moonlight streaming into his room through the wide-open window. The house was at last in silence and darkness. Cousin George had made the night hideous for a good hour after he had been locked safely in his room, and a shaken household had lain awake quaking in its beds while unexpurgated versions of various nautical and military ballads, punctuated by violent crashes of furniture and crockery, resounded through the house.

Gradually Cousin George had wearied of singing and had taken to shouting profanities and libels on his relatives at the top of his voice. Finally these also had ceased, and after much trampling a last stupendous crash had jarred the stately precincts of Socrates Close and silence had fallen, profound and soothing. Slowly the house had dropped off to sleep. Mr. Campion alone sat watching.

The plain-clothes men had been removed from the garden two or three days before. Mr. Oates's belief in his friend's intuition had not been sufficiently strong to warrant so expensive a guard.

Mr. Campion sat silent in the moonlight. He had taken off his spectacles and also his coat and waistcoat. He wore a pullover tucked into his trousers, which were suspended by a belt. His sleeves were rolled up, and he had removed his watch and his signet ring. Arrayed thus, he had been sitting motionless on the end of his bed for perhaps two hours. Through the open window he could hear the chimes from the Roman Catholic church quite clearly.

He had just heard the clock strike a quarter to three, and the moonlight was waning, when he heard the sound which made him slip off his bed and creep stealthily to the window. Keeping close to the curtain, he waited, listening. The sound came again, a husky breathy whisper.

It was nearer now, and suddenly he made out the words, simple ludicrous words, but in the night strangely terrifying.

"Old Bee. . . . Old Bee. . . . Old Bee. . . . "

Campion stretched out a hand and gripped the sill, and then, exerting a slow and even force, he drew himself silently out into the opening of the window and peered down.

The garden was still faintly lit by the waning moonlight, and the strip of grass beneath his window was clear. He noticed that there was still a light in George's room, but no sound issued therefrom. As he waited, his ears strained, he heard the whisper again, this time much closer.

"Old Bee. . . . Old Bee. . . ."

Then, even as he watched, a dark shape detached itself from the shadows beneath George's window, and the young man caught a glimpse of an uncouth stooping figure, doubly grotesque in the deceptive light. It might have been human, it might have been a gorilla fantastically clothed, but Campion saw it

with a welcome quickening of his pulse. He leapt up on to the
sill and stood for a moment poised above the apparition.

The figure on the ground twisted round and raised a white
blur of a face to the window. In a moment he was off, streaking
through the garden, a fantastic figure bounding along like a great
black balloon on the end of a string.

Campion dropped to the ground, falling on his hands and
knees upon the wet turf. He was on his feet again chasing after
the fugitive, who led him unerringly towards the little gate into
the lane at the far end of the kitchen garden. For so large a
creature the quarry developed an extraordinary turn of speed, but
Campion, his blood whipped by the cold air and his nerves
strained by the hours of waiting, gained upon him, and on the
stretch of rough grass before the gate he overtook the flying
figure, and, hurling himself upon it, brought it heavily to the
ground.

The stranger grunted, and the next moment Campion was
seized in a steel grip and dragged ignominiously over his
opponent's head. The mysterious visitor, whoever he was, was
not a negligible adversary. However, Mr. Campion seemed to
have achieved some of Marcus's viciousness, and he felt his
pent-up wrath concentrating upon this tangible enemy. He
scrambled to his feet and caught the stranger round the legs in a
Rugger tackle just as he was about to make his escape, and it was
at this point that Campion made the interesting discovery that the
other's feet were bare.

The figure slumped to the ground again, Campion on top of
him, and two immense hands came up out of the darkness and
gripped the young man by the throat. In this moment of partial
suffocation Campion realised with thankfulness that his opponent was unarmed. He struck out savagely, his knuckles coming
into contact with a hard and stubbly chin. The stranger grunted
and swore softly. Until now he had been terrifyingly silent.

Although he was lying upon his back his grip on Campion's
throat did not relax, and he was revealing an almost simian
strength. The grip was becoming a strangle-hold when Campion
lurched forward, driving his knee into the other man's wind. The
hold on his throat relaxed and the man doubled up, gasping.

He was by no means beaten, however. He rained unscientific
blows with his huge flails of arms, battering the young man's
lean sides and unprotected head. Campion straddled himself
across the great body, and exerting every ounce of his strength,

drove punch after punch into the man's face. He was fighting like a maniac, and the other, although he certainly possessed the greater strength, was evidently out of training. Gradually the rain of flail blows slackened, and Campion, driving his knee steadily into the other's wind, had him gasping and writhing like a fish out of water. Without relinquishing his position, Campion bent forward.

"Had enough?" he whispered.

"Yus," said the voice huskily, and relapsed into breathless grunting.

"You're old Bee, aren't you?" said Mr. Campion, risking yet another shot in the dark.

"I'm no one," said the man suddenly, and exerting an unexpected reserve of strength, pitched his captor on to the turf again, at the same time catching him a blow on the side of the head which made the bones of his skull crunch together.

It did not knock him out, however. Through a maze of eddying blackness Campion lurched back and caught the panting creature just as he rose again to the attack. This time luck rather than judgment favoured him. He stumbled, cannoning into the other and catching him in the pit of the stomach with his head. His opponent let out a roar and doubled up. Campion wriggled from beneath the choking mass, which threatened to suffocate him, and staggered to his feet at the precise moment that a third figure loomed up out of the half darkness and turned a torch full upon his face.

"Hullo, sir, what's up?"

It was young Christmas, whose cottage faced on to the lane at the corner of the garden, not twenty yards distant. Campion pulled himself together with an effort. He was still dizzy, but his purpose remained clear in his mind.

"Bring that torch over here," he said breathlessly. "Let's see what we've got."

Young Christmas, a large, raw-boned young man of thirty or so, advanced cautiously towards the writhing object on the ground and turned his torch full upon it. Mr. Campion's antagonist lay revealed.

He made an extraordinary spectacle lying spreadeagled upon the ground, gasping as though his last hour had come. He was a shortish man, powerfully built, with immense arms. His face was surrounded by creases of fat and almost covered with a short, stubbly beard of indeterminate hue, while his long matted hair was plentifully flecked with grey. For the rest, he was indescribably dirty, and blackened lips and broken nose did not add to the charm of his appearance. He was dressed in ragged green-black garments, none of which made any pretence of fitting him. But it was at his feet, sticking out from beneath his ragged trouser legs, that young Christmas was staring.

"Lumme!" he said. "Look at 'em. It's him!"

One glance at the monstrous extremities half covered by the remnants of odd socks was sufficient. Here, without doubt, was the origin of the print upon the flower-bed.

The sight of these feet seemed to restore Mr. Campion's mental balance.

"Here, I say," he said, "can you let me bring this fellow into your place? I fancy he's going to have a good deal to say."

"Why, yes, sir, I'll get a light." Young Mr. Christmas was a little startled, but eminently obliging. "I 'eard a bit of a noise, sir," he said, "so I come out to see what was up. What about this chap 'ere?"

"I'll bring him in," said Mr. Campion grimly.

Seated in a chair by the side of Mr. Christmas's table, and seen by the light of a swinging oil lamp, the intruder looked even less prepossessing than he had done in the garden. His small, grey-green eyes shifted furtively from side to side, and he stirred uncomfortably, half rubbing half scratching the injured portions of his unpleasant self somewhere within the rag-bag drapery which was his costume.

"I wasn't doing anything," he began, revealing the familiar mendicant whine. "You didn't ought to 'ave touched me. I can get you into trouble for this."

"Shut up," said Mr. Campion from the sink where he had been putting his head under the pump, and from which he now emerged rubbing himself vigorously with a towel. "Is your father about, Christmas?" he murmured. "I don't want to wake him if we can help it."

"Oh, no, sir, that's all right. It'll take more than this to disturb the old 'un." Young Christmas seemed convinced on this point, and Mr. Campion was satisfied.

Their visitor, who was growing momentarily more and more disturbed, began to whine again.

"I can 'ave the police on yer if yer touch me again," he said.

"I am the police," said Mr. Campion fiercely. "Ever heard of a plain-clothes man? Well, here is one. You're under arrest, and if you don't talk I'll see that you're strung up. You're wanted. We've been waiting for you."

A crafty light appeared in the stranger's face. "You can't tell me," he said. "I know a 'busy' when I see one. I 'aven't been on the road for thirty years without gettin' inside once or twice. You're no policeman. Besides," he added triumphantly, "I know every 'busy' from 'ere to York."

"I am Chief Detective Inspector Campion of Scotland Yard," said the young man brusquely. "I am down here to investigate the murder of Andrew Seeley on a footbridge over the Granta on Sunday, March 30th. I have reason to believe that you are the man I want. But I am going to give you a chance, although your confederate has already been arrested. He has told his story, and unless yours tallies with it in every detail, you'll find yourself in the dock before you know where you are."

The man who had listened to this harangue in silence and had clearly only understood about half of it, sucked in his breath noisily.

"You 'aven't cautioned me yet," he said suspiciously.

"Cautioned you?" said Mr. Campion, with consummate contempt. "We Scotland Yard men don't behave like lock-up sergeants. You're coming across with all you know and you're coming across immediately. Ever heard of the third degree?"

"I got a friend," the other answered sullenly. "A proper gentleman 'oo knows about these things. And 'e says the third degree ain't allowed any longer. I can 'ave my lawyer if I like."

"Your friend George Faraday is under lock and key," said Mr. Campion truthfully. "That's where his erroneous information had taken him. Look here, my man, do you want another fight?"

The young man's threatening attitude, together with his uncanny knowledge of his visitor's acquaintance, had their effect. The disreputable old bundle fidgeted uneasily.

"Do you want another thrashing?" the young man repeated, entirely disregarding the other's anthropoid physique.

"No," said the stranger. "And I'm not sayin' nothin', see?"

Mr. Campion consulted young Christmas's washing book, which he had taken from a shelf by the sink.

"Let me see, we have your name," he said. "Address, none. Alias, Old Bee."

"That's not an alias," said the bundle, falling into the trap. "That's a sort of nickname—you know, among friends. I'm

Thomas Beveridge, and I'm registered at Warley Workhouse in Kent, and there's nothin' known against me."

"We know all about that," said Mr. Campion, having apparently appointed Mr. Christmas, junior, as a member of His Majesty's Police Force. "Now then, before I take you down to the station I'll have your statement here. You are charged, together with George Makepeace Faraday, whose statement we already have, with wilfully murdering Andrew Seeley by shooting him, afterwards binding his body and hurling it into the River Granta. Now what have you got to say?"

It was Mr. Campion's manner, together with the terrifying and unfounded charge brought so suddenly against him, which undermined Mr. Beveridge's morale.

"I never!" he said indignantly. " 'Ere, you got this all wrong. George never told you that."

"The police draw their own conclusions," said Mr. Campion loftily. "Are you coming clean or have I got to beat it out of you?"

"I'd like a cup o' coffee," said Mr. Beveridge unexpectedly. "I've been man-'andled—that's wot. And I'd like my boots, too. I took 'em orf by the gate—wishin' not to disturb anyone. Can't say fairer than that, can I?"

"Fetch me that bit of bike tyre," said Campion to young Mr. Christmas.

" 'Ere!" protested Mr. Beveridge hastily, "wait a minute. Wait a minute. I 'aven't said I won't say nothin'."

Mr. Campion raised his hand with a magnificently conceding gesture, and young Christmas, who was proving himself a resourceful assistant, stopped in his tracks and returned to the table.

Mr. Beveridge spread out his immense and dirty hands. "I don't know anything, and I want my boots," he said. "Matter of fact, I was at Norwich that Sunday."

"What?" said Mr. Campion, with scorn. "Don't waste my time, my man." He leant across the table and his hard, grey eyes fixed his victim's. "You dare to put forward a statement like that when you came into this garden to-night wearing the hat of the murdered man?"

This unparalleled piece of bluff was Mr. Beveridge's last straw. He crumpled.

"I didn't kill 'im," he said. "George and I didn't touch the gun till afterwards, that's a fact."

Mr. Campion heaved a sigh of relief and consulted the washing book again.

"I suppose you realise," he said coldly, "that you've said either too much or not quite enough?"

The great form in the little wooden chair shivered and his dirty eyelids drooped.

"All right," he said. "I'll tell you. But it wasn't me—so 'elp me Gawd, it wasn't George nor me."

22

In the Morning

After Alice had placed the can of hot water on the washstand and carefully covered it with a towel, she crossed the room, pulled up the blind and paused at the end of Marcus Featherstone's bed. Having allowed him sufficient time to awaken and recall his unhappy thoughts, she made her announcement.

"Mr. Campion isn't in his room, sir. His bed hasn't been slept in. I thought perhaps I'd better tell you instead of Mr. William. And old Mr. Christmas, the mistress's coachman, came into the kitchen just before I came upstairs, to say that his son must have got up and dressed in the night, for there's no sign of him."

Marcus sat up in bed in Uncle William's voluminous and exotic pyjamas and reviewed the situation.

"Campion gone?" he said. "Half a minute and I'll put on a dressing-gown and come along."

He slipped on the multi-coloured bath-robe, another evidence of Uncle William's hospitality, and followed the woman across the hall and down the corridor to Mr. Campion's room. No one else seemed to be stirring. George and William's rooms were silent, and apart from the cheerful domestic clatter below the stairs the house was still sleeping.

Alice led the way into Campion's room. It was neat.

Campion's portmanteau lay on the luggage-rack, his dressing-gown hung over the monstrous arm-chair, and apart from the fact that the window was wide open at the bottom and the bed was unslept in, there was nothing out of the ordinary to be seen.

Marcus looked round sleepily. "What an extraordinary thing," he said. "Oh, well, Alice, I suppose he knows what he's doing. How about Mr. George Faraday? Have you been in to him yet?"

"No, sir. The door was locked. I've knocked, but I can't make him hear. I expect he's sleeping heavy after—well, after last night, sir."

"Very likely," agreed Marcus grimly. "Wait a minute. I put the key in my pocket, I think. Mr. Campion and I locked him in last night. Look here, you go and mix him up a stiff Worcester sauce and I'll get the key."

"Oh, don't you trouble, sir. All the keys on this floor fit. I'll mix Mr. George the same as Mr. Andrew used to have."

"I'll wait for you here," said Marcus. "I think I had better take it in."

As the woman went off down the corridor to the service stairs he strolled over to Campion's window and stood looking out. He was a man who hated mysteries, and he felt unduly resentful at what he could only feel was an unnecessary piece of theatre. After all, there was no reason why Campion shouldn't have said he was going out. In one way, Marcus was glad. It would give him an opportunity to wake the nauseous George himself. No man is at his best on the morning after such an indulgence, and Marcus was young enough to enjoy the prospect of seeing Cousin George a little sorry for himself, and perhaps, even, of using a little unnecessary force in waking him.

When Alice returned with a tray, on which stood a glass containing an unappetising brown concoction, he took it from her, and detaching the key from Campion's room, fitted it in the lock of George's door. He knocked and listened. There was no response from within, and he knocked again. Receiving no reply, it was with some satisfaction that he turned the key, and, throwing open the door, went in, Alice at his elbow.

He was confronted by the yellow gleam of electric light, and his irritation increased. He thrust out his hand and switched off the current as a smothered scream from Alice made him spin round to find her staring horror-stricken at the sight before them.

The room was in chaos. Books, garments, bed-clothes were

strewn recklessly over the floor. In the midst of them, lying face downwards, his body contorted in the most horrible and unnatural position, was Cousin George.

There was no doubt that he was dead. His body seemed to have been petrified in the midst of some terrible convulsion.

Marcus, dazed and a little sick, stepped forward unsteadily, and as he bent over the body there came to him the strong unmistakable smell of bitter almonds. He drew back and turned to Alice, who, white-faced and grim, had closed the door behind her with commendable presence of mind. She laid her fingers to her lips.

"Hush, sir," she whispered. "Don't frighten the house. What is it?"

"He's dead," said Marcus stupidly.

"I can see that," said Alice. "How did he come by it?"

"Poison, I think," he said huskily. "I don't know. We must get the police, Alice. Good God! Another murder!"

The realisation of it came to him in a sudden chaotic vision. The whole ghastly procession of the law presented itself to his mind: the police in the house again, the endless questioning, the inquest, the Press campaign, Kitty in the witness-box, William in the witness-box, Joyce and Campion, all of them questioned, cross-questioned, perhaps even suspected.

Alice's voice cut into his jumble of thoughts. "You mustn't frighten the mistress. What shall we do, sir?"

"Telephone to the police station," said Marcus. "Inspector Oates is still in the town, I believe. Yes, that's right, Alice, telephone."

"We haven't got the machine in the house, sir. Shall I go down to Mrs. Palfrey's? We've been borrowing hers lately."

This trivial difficulty sobered the young man more quickly, perhaps, than anything else would have done. He began to think clearly.

"Look here," he said, "we'll relock this door and I'll go and dress. You go down to Mrs. Palfrey's and ring up the police. Inspector Redgrave is in charge, I expect, at this time. Ask him if Inspector Oates is still in the town, and if so tell him from me that I should be very much obliged if he would come down here, as something most unexpected has occurred. If you are sure that no one of the Palfrey household is within earshot, tell him what has happened. Anyway, get him to see that he must come at once. Can you do that?"

She nodded, and he felt suddenly grateful for her wonderful stolidity. She turned on the electric light.

"What are you doing that for?"

"We'll leave it just as it was if you don't mind, sir. Come along."

He followed her out of the room, relocked the door, and returned the key to Campion's room.

"I'll go and dress now, then," he said, and stopped abruptly. Alice had already gone.

As he struggled into his clothes he experienced that sudden clarity of mind which so often comes just before the nerves reach their breaking-point. Another murder had been committed. Therefore a murderer was at large. In the business of the inquest he had rather lost sight of this all-important point, but the question remained. If Uncle William had no stain upon his character, who had? George had come to the house with a story which no one but Mrs. Caroline Faraday appeared to have believed. George had made an accusation. He had stated that he knew who had murdered Andrew. Now he was dead. Was it possible that Julia's hitherto motiveless murder could be explained by the fact that she knew something? The ranks were getting thin.

He found himself reviewing Kitty's position, and then old Mrs. Faraday's. The older woman alone had credited George's story, yet she had been driving home in her four-wheeler with Joyce at the time when Andrew was presumed to have met his death. The same excuse applied to Kitty. Even though Julia was dead, there was still young Christmas to prove that she had not left the car from the time she had come out of church to the moment when he set her down at Socrates Close.

Marcus's mind returned to William. Mrs. Finch, of "The Red Bull," had proved to everyone's satisfaction where William had been at the time of Uncle Andrew's death, if Andrew had died from the shot which the cottager on the Granchester Road had heard. But supposing Andrew had not died at that time? Then the whole exasperating problem began all over again.

And now there was another murder. It never occurred to Marcus to put any other construction upon the fate of the terrible twisted thing in the wrecked room. He felt dizzy. His orderly mind revolted at the inexplicable. His father's words returned to him with startling force: "I wondered when the bad blood in that family was going to tell." What bad blood? Whose bad blood?

It was as though the old house was cracking up under his eyes.

This, then, was what Campion had been afraid of. Yes, and where was he? It was not like Campion to disappear, to go off without any word of explanation. He struggled into his coat and went downstairs.

As he entered the hall he ran into Alice. She seemed relieved to see him.

"Oh, sir," she said breathlessly, "I was just coming up. I've been on the 'phone. Inspector Redgrave is coming down right away, and so is Inspector Oates. And, oh, sir, I spoke to Mr. Campion."

"Campion? Where?" said Marcus in astonishment.

"On the 'phone, sir. He was at the police station. Mrs. Palfrey's maid was in the hall, so I didn't like to say what had happened, but when the Inspector realised I was hesitating, he said, 'Wait a minute,' and then I heard Mr. Campion's voice. And oh, sir"—she looked at Marcus with genuine mystification in her brown eyes—"Mr. Campion seemed to expect something, for he said, 'Quick, Alice, who is it?' And so I just said, 'Mr. George, sir.' "

"Yes," said Marcus eagerly. "What did Campion say?"

"He said, 'Thank God,' sir," said Alice.

23

A Legacy

Marcus was still in the hall when Inspector Oates's red two-seater, followed by the official police car, drew up outside the front door, and Campion, backed by Oates, Inspector Redgrave and the police doctor, came hurrying in. In spite of his apprehension and the cold feeling of doom which had taken possession of him, Marcus was a little shocked by Mr. Campion's appearance. He wore a raincoat much too large for him, smacking strongly of the police, which was buttoned up to his throat, and he was the possessor also of a remarkably fine black eye. For the rest, he was hatless and his fair hair was dishevelled.

There was something in his manner, however, which suggested triumph rather than despair. He took Marcus's arm.

"Who knows yet?" he said.

"No one except Alice and I," said Marcus.

"That's splendid. Where did it happen. In his room?"

Marcus nodded. He was bewildered. As Alice had said, it was rather as though Mr. Campion had expected this appalling development.

Inspector Oates, he noticed, did not share Mr. Campion's air of suppressed satisfaction. He came forward now and spoke quietly.

"If you'll go first, Mr. Featherstone, we'll go straight up to the room. The household will have to be told immediately, but I don't want to alarm anyone."

As they mounted the stairs Marcus turned to Campion. "Where have you been?" he whispered.

"Brawling," said Mr. Campion. "I don't want to raise your hopes, but I think we know now. I'll tell you about it later."

He stumbled on the top stair, and Marcus, suddenly catching sight of his face by the light of the upper hall, realised that he was almost dropping with fatigue."

As the procession came to a full stop outside George's room, Uncle William's door opened, and a pink and military figure in a dragon-infested dressing-gown appeared upon the threshold. For some seconds he stared in astonishment, but as he caught sight of the Inspector fitting a key into George's door an expression of satisfaction spread over his face.

"So you've seen the wisdom of my suggestion at last and sent for the police," he said. "It's high time that fellow was under lock and key, the drunken scoundrel. God bless my soul, Campion. What have you done to your face? Had a scrap with the bounder?"

With his hand on the door the Inspector paused irresolute. He had no liking for William, and now, he felt, was no time for explanations.

"I shall have to ask you to remain in your room, sir, for a few minutes at any rate," he said, adopting his most official tone, "and I should like to have a few words with you later."

Uncle William stared at him, his pink face growing slowly puce with indignation.

"D'you realise you're ordering me about in my own house?" he said. "I didn't know the police could bully a man in his own house at eight o'clock in the morning. You attend to your duty, my man. There's your quarry, in there."

He retreated into his room, slamming the door behind him.

The inspector sighed, and turned the key in the lock of George's room. The little procession followed him. He paused just inside the door and the others edged in behind him. Not until the door was closed did he speak.

"Is this exactly how you found him?"

"Exactly," said Marcus. "I didn't go much nearer than this. You see—well, can't you smell anything?"

"Cyanide," said the little doctor, who stood on the Inspector's right. "It's very strong. Tell it a mile off. Precious little I can do for you, Inspector. Can I make my examination right away, or do you want to take photographs?"

Stanislaus Oates turned to Campion. "Here's your chance, my lad," he said. "If you're right, prove it now."

Campion stepped forward cautiously, avoiding the débris with which the floor was littered.

A sudden frenzied knocking on the door checked him as Aunt Kitty's voice, shrill and imperative, came to them through the panelling.

"What is it? What's happened! I demand to know."

Campion turned to Marcus. "Go and quieten her, there's a good chap," he said. "And don't let her get in, for God's sake."

Marcus had no choice but to obey, and he went unwillingly from the room. Inspector Redgrave edged the door open for him and held it firm, so that any sudden rush from the distracted woman without might be withstood.

As Marcus came out into the corridor Aunt Kitty fell into his arms. Her blue woollen dressing-gown was fastened up to her throat, and it seemed that she had been alarmed in the midst of her hairdressing, for although the front curls were released from their papers and neatly arranged, the back was in disarray.

"Marcus," she said, "what's happened? What are they doing to George?"

Gently, but exerting a certain amount of force nevertheless, Marcus led the old lady back towards her room, doing his best to calm her piteous outburst. As they passed William's door his choleric face appeared again. Seeing no more formidable person than Marcus and his sister, he emerged and joined them.

"If that scoundrel is putting up any opposition," he began, "I'd be glad to do anything I could. What's happened, my boy? Won't the ruffian stir?"

Marcus was debating what would be the best way to break the news, which after all must come out sooner or later, when Great-aunt Caroline's door opened and Joyce came hurrying out.

"What's the matter?" she demanded. "What's happened? Great-aunt wants to know."

They were standing in the upper hall now, and Aunt Kitty would be denied no longer.

"I must know," she said. "Some other horror is upon us. I can feel it. I warned that young man. . . ." She began to cry again.

"Oh, Aunt Kitty, darling!" There was a hint of exasperation in Joyce's voice, but she put an arm round the older woman soothingly. "Now then, Marcus," she said, "what is it?"

"Cousin George is dead," said Marcus baldly, forgetting his intention to break the news gently.

"Dead?" said Uncle William, his jaw dropping open. "Good God!" It took him some seconds to assimilate this information, but when the first shock was over he suddenly smiled. "Fell down in a drunken fit, I'll be bound," he said. "And serve him right. Damned good job. Save us no end of trouble."

Aunt Kitty, who held the belief of her generation that death immediately sanctified the most unredeemed of rogues, began to sob afresh. Joyce caught Marcus's arm just as he was turning away.

"Is that true?" she demanded. "Did he die naturally, or . . . ?"

"Poisoned, I think," said Marcus, whose finesse had left him entirely. "Don't be frightened."

The girl drew back from him, her face working. "Another," she said huskily. "Where's it going to end?"

"Eh?" said Uncle William, whose slower wits had only just grasped the inference of Marcus's last remark. "Poisoned? You don't mean to say that someone gave the fellow a dose of something? Not another mystery? This is too much. It's damnable. Someone'll get into a lot of trouble for this." He stopped abruptly, his mouth hanging open. "Good God!" he said again.

Aunt Kitty emitted a sound which indicated that she would have screamed had she had sufficient strength to do so. But chronic hysteria is exhausting and, having dwelt in that state for well-nigh a fortnight, her nerves were numbed, and she hung limply on Joyce's arm crying weakly, strands of thin grey hair straggling over her blue dressing-gown.

A heavy step behind them in the corridor made them turn to find Inspector Redgrave approaching them, his good-tempered, square-cut face alight with friendly interest.

"Mr. William Faraday and Mr. Marcus Featherstone," he said, "we should be very much obliged if you would step along to the bedroom down here, gentlemen. Inspector Oates has a question to ask."

Marcus shot an enquiring glance at Joyce, and she nodded. "We'll be all right," she said.

The atmosphere of the late Uncle Andrew's bedroom was singular for a chamber of death. Inspector Oates, his grey face flushed, stood in the centre of the room looking down at something which the doctor held in a white handkerchief. Cousin George's body lay upon the bed covered with a sheet. But the atmosphere was not the one of constraint and terror which Marcus expected. The faint air of triumph, of finality, which had been noticeable in Campion's demeanour earlier that morning was here intensified. It had spread to the others. Nor was Cousin George the object of interest which one might have expected in the circumstances.

As Marcus and William entered, the Inspector was speaking, and they caught his last words.

"Well, we know now," he was saying. "There's just this last point. Ah, Mr. Faraday, here you are."

Uncle William, who was bearing up wonderfully considering the shock he had just received, stumbled into the room, his gaze resting fascinated upon the shapeless mass on the bed.

Campion, who had been seated listlessly in a chair on the far side of the room, now rose. At a sign from the Inspector he spoke.

"Uncle William," he said, forgetting in his eagerness the more ceremonious form of address, "we are on the last lap of this mystery, and we appeal to you, all of us, for your assistance and co-operation."

This was hardly the way Inspector Oates would have put it, but he was forced to admit that it probably saved a lot of time. Uncle William rose like a salmon to a fly.

"My boy," he said warmly, "you can count on me. This is a bad business—a very bad business. George was a bounder.

Ought to have been hanged. But I don't like to see him lying dead under my own roof, poor fellow."

"That cat," said Mr. Campion wearily. "You were in here, in your Cousin Andrew's room, weren't you, when it scratched you?"

Uncle William's little round eyes flickered as his mind fluttered round the possible ramifications contained in this direct question. However, as he said himself, when beaten Uncle William was a sportsman.

"Yes," he said. "Not to put too fine a point upon it, I was."

"When you came in here that night, letting yourself in with the key from your own door, you did not turn on the light, did you?" the tired voice continued.

"No," said Uncle William cautiously.

"Exactly what happened, then?" said Mr. Campion.

Uncle William hesitated and glanced about him, and Inspector Oates made haste to reassure him.

"No word of what you tell us will ever go beyond this room, I give you my word, sir," he said.

It was unfortunately typical of Uncle William that he ʌould accept this extraordinarily handsome concession as th gh he were conferring the favour and not the policeman.

"Very proper," he said. "Well, to tell you the truth, Campion, my boy, I was a bit rattled that night, if you remember, and when a man's rattled he needs a drink. I believe I said something to you about it just before I went to bed?"

"You did," said Mr. Campion, tactfully refraining from reminding him of the exact nature of his remark.

"Good," said Uncle William, and paused, considering how best to get over the more delicate parts of his story. "After I had undressed," he began at last, "I felt I must have a night-cap. I knew that the decanter downstairs was empty, and I didn't want to go stumbling about waking the household, don't you know. Then I suddenly remembered that old Andrew, my cousin, who was a bit of a toper, between ourselves, had a parcel of trick books among this lot over here." He waved his hand to the bookcase opposite them. "They were brought from America and were made to conceal cigarettes and flasks and other odds and ends."

He paused, gratified. The others were listening to him with breathless attention.

"In one of these copies," he continued, "that big brown book over there, I think, Andrew used to keep a spot of brandy. There's a sort of box inside the book, if you understood me. Well, it just occurred to me that old Andrew might possibly have left something in that flask, and realising that he wouldn't need it any more, poor fellow, I thought I'd come in and get it. The key of my door fits this door, so I let myself in quietly. I didn't switch the light on because I didn't want to alarm the policemen who I understood were posted in the garden. The curtains were drawn, but you never know when a chink's going to show."

He glanced at them belligerently, on guard for any sign of a smile, but they were all much too interested in his story.

"You came in here in the dark, then," said Campion. "Did you go over to the bookcase?"

"Yes," admitted Uncle William. "I thought I could find it in the dark. I knew where it was, you see. I came quietly across the room, like this."

He imitated his progress, advancing gingerly towards the bookcase. When he was within a couple of feet of it he stopped and turned to them.

"Of course I don't know what happened," he said. "That's the trouble. For the life of me I can't imagine what happened, as I told Campion. I thought the room was empty, but as I put out my hand something caught me. Most uncanny experience, all alone in here in the dark. I confess I retreated. I remember shutting the door and locking it behind me, thinking that I'd catch the fellow prisoner, don't you know. Then there was that business with the iodine. And the next morning I looked in here and found this room empty. So I took it for granted it was a cat in here," he finished lamely, adding brusquely, "I don't believe in the supernatural."

"Did you have another look for the whisky, sir?" said Inspector Oates.

"No," said Uncle William. "My experience put me off it don't you know. It was brandy, as a matter of fact. Still here, I expect."

He bent down to take a huge volume labelled. "De Quincey's Essays" from the extreme end of the lowest shelf. The author's name was just visible below the fringe of scalloped leather. His plump fingers were within an inch of the volume when Mr. Campion's lean arm shot forward and caught the older man under the wrist, knocking it into the air.

"Here you are, Stanislaus," he said.

Uncle William, speechless with annoyance and astonishment, was astounded to see the two Inspectors hurry forward and bend down eagerly as Campion caught hold of the leather frill and ripped it sideways. The substance was old and tore easily, and as it fell away a murmur of astonishment escaped the little audience. Campion showed his discovery with justifiable pride.

"Simple, isn't it?" he said. "Almost childish. And, as it happens, very effective."

Projecting point downwards from the under side of the upper shelf and driven firmly into the wood was the small blade of a pen-knife, razor sharp and hitherto hidden behind the frill. The trap was so arranged that anyone stretching out a hand to take the book must run the back of his wrist on to the knife.

"Look out," said Campion sharply, as the doctor bent down to touch it with his hand. "If you take that to your laboratory, sir," he went on, "I think you'll find traces of an alkaline poison on it. Mr. Faraday was intended to come back for the contents of this book a little earlier than he actually did, in which case the air would not have had so long to weaken the potency of the bacillus, or whatever it is."

"Eh?" said Uncle William. "Someone set a trap for me? Good Lord, might have killed me!"

"No doubt that was the idea, sir," said Inspector Redgrave soberly.

Marcus, who had been watching the whole incident like a man in a nightmare, now experienced all the sensations of waking up. He felt his eyes slowly peeling open. Then he said huskily: "The murderer is dead?"

"George!" said Uncle William triumphantly.

Mr. Campion looked at him queerly. "No," he said. "Andrew. Andrew died and left us all a legacy."

24

Audience

Great-aunt Faraday, seated among the pillows in her enormous Louis XV bed, might easily have been its original owner, in her fine Brussels night bonnet and rose-coloured quilted silk jacket. She sat bolt upright, as usual, her hands folded on the linen.

Mr. Campion stood before her at the foot of the bed. He had done his best to repair his appearance, but he still looked deadly tried, and there was, of course, no disguising the black eye.

"Andrew," said Mrs. Faraday. "How very remarkable. And yet, how extremely likely. Sit down, young man, and tell me all about it."

Campion brought a little gilt chair from the other side of the room and set it so that he sat looking at the old lady over an expanse of embroidered counterpane. Mrs. Faraday beckoned him closer.

"On my left side, if you please," she said. "Although I never confess it, I am slightly deaf in my right ear."

Campion did as he was told, and when he had settled himself to her satisfaction she spoke again.

"I can understand it perhaps even better than you can," she said. "Andrew was a very extraordinary man. He was insane, of course, in a very strange and terrible way. I do not care for he modern psychologists, so I cannot tell you the new names for the old disorders, but you have only to look at Andrew's bedroom to see that he was not normal, and that he would go to any length, at whatever discomfort to himself, to inflict a little pain upon others. But it is not for me to tell you. Let me hear the whole story from the time that this explanation first occurred to you."

Campion, who was nearly exhausted but still valiant, composed his thoughts, and putting them into the shortest possible words, did exactly as she told him.

"You put me on to it," he said, "when you gave me that letter from Miss Lisle-Chevreuse to read. Until then I was floundering. I knew that there was some great obvious explanation right under my nose, but I couldn't see it. The Inspector, with his straightforward methodical procedure, made me feel ashamed. He was getting somewhere, however slowly; while I was fluttering round in circles.

"Then I read that letter, and it seemed to me to be a piquant piece of irony that the lady should have written to Andrew practically accepting what must have been an offer of marriage at the very time that he was lying dead in the River Granta. She had answered immediately, therefore he must have written to her on the day of his death. Then there was the bookmaker's cheque and Andrew's unusually heavy plunge. Frankly, I suspected them."

Mrs. Faraday nodded. "I understand," she said. "Go on."

"It then occurred to me," said the young man slowly, "that all the evidence which pointed so strongly to Andrew's death being by murder was of this dramatic and sensational kind—the half-finished letter, the body bound with the window-cord which was so easily identifiable. It was as though fate had suddenly become theatrically minded."

"Quite," agreed Mrs. Faraday.

Campion continued. "Once having arrived at that point," he said, "it was natural, of course, to suspect that fate of being human, and since the only person who could have manufactured the evidence was Andrew I began to suspect him." He paused and looked at the old lady gravely. "I could not at first imagine the mind of a man who, having decided to kill himself, would yet go to the time and trouble of preparing death traps for those he left behind. But neither could I imagine the mind of a man who could write a whole book for the purpose of annoying those with whom he lived. I felt he might get the idea, but the writing of a book is a long and tedious business, and the man who carried such a thing through was obviously no ordinary person."

At the mention of Andrew's book a chilly light had come into Mrs. Faraday's eyes.

"Andrew was an odious creature," she said. "More odious even, I think, than George. But Andrew, having more brains, was a better dissembler and less of an animal."

"Then there was Julia," said Mr. Campion diffidently. "You convinced me that she was not a suicide. Then Joyce and I discovered the patent medicine, and it was obvious how murder could have been done. The arrangement of the capsules in the zigzag paper made it possible for the murderer to ensure that the attempt upon his victim would take place upon any future fate he cared to choose. Since Julia only took one capsule a day, he had only to count the days and replace one of the capsules with his poisonous compound.

"Joyce had previously told me that Andrew was a man who enjoyed prying into other people's affairs, and it dawned upon me that this idiosyncrasy of Julia's would be just the sort of secret he might light upon. He probably knew already that Kitty took the tea in every morning, and it would be obvious to him that this idea gave him an excellent chance of destroying Julia, whom he loathed, and of casting a most unwarrantable suspicion upon the unfortunate Kitty." He paused to take breath. "When I reached this point in my calculations I was helpless. I felt you ought to leave the house, and I am afraid the police will insist upon that now, for a time at least. You see, I thought that if I was right there was no telling where these death-traps would end. Naturally I could make no accusation until I was sure, and at that point I had no proof of any sort.

"Then there was this question of William's hand. You have heard how that happened. But William was under the impression that someone or something had stabbed at him. That threw my conjectures out altogether. It was not until George arrived yesterday and said that he had actually seen Andrew die that I realised that there was a chance of ever proving my theory at all."

Great-aunt Caroline's little black eyes were fixed on the young man's face, and he marvelled at the calmness with which she accepted the extraordinary story he was unravelling.

"George mentioned a second witness," Campion went on slowly, "and that gave me my strongest hope. As soon as that sign appeared on the library window I guessed that someone from outside, probably a tramp, was trying to communicate with someone he believed to be inside the house. William had said that he saw George in the company of a tramp on the day of Andrew's death. I didn't pay much attention to it at the time because . . ."

A grim smile spread over the old lady's face. "Because poor William is apt to describe any ill-dressed person as a tramp," she said. "Yes, I quite see that. Go on."

"Well," said Mr. Campion, "last night it was obvious that this mysterious person was not in communication with George because George had been in retirement for the past few days. It was also obvious that the tramp was in the vicinity of this house, so I pinned my hope on the supposition that the tramp was watching this house, had seen George arrive and would attempt to get into touch with him during the night. It was a wild chance, but I sat up waiting for him, and he came. Then I interviewed him."

"So I see," said the old lady, glancing sharply at Mr. Campion's injured eye. "I am really very grateful to you."

"I considered it a privilege," said Campion gallantly.

The black eyes flickered and a faint smile spread over the little ivory face.

"You have many more brains that is usual in your family," said Mrs. Faraday. "And yet you have a great deal of their charm. It is hardly fair. You had a lot of trouble with this person?"

"Not so much as he had with me," said Mr. Campion modestly. "By a series of vulgar methods, which I won't describe, I persuaded him to tell me the more pertinent of his experiences—a most extraordinary yarn. It seems that this man—his name is Beveridge, and example of workhouse humour, he tells me—entered Cambridge with George on the Saturday before Andrew's death. Beveridge had known George for some time, and seems to have had an immense admiration for him."

"There was a flashy quality about George," said Mrs. Faraday unexpectedly. "I can understand him being a triton among minnows. Go on."

"On Sunday morning," Campion continued, "these two were seen by the members of the household who went to church by car reeling down the Trumpington Road. This, according to Beveridge, was intentional upon George's part, and was calculated to annoy William and Andrew—William especially, for whom George seems to have had an extraordinary dislike. Later, however, at about eleven o'clock when the hostelries opened, George and Beveridge became genuinely merry, but not actually drunk. Anyhow, according to Beveridge, and its sounds credible, they saw William and Andrew walking down Trumpington Road and were going to cross the road to accost them when the cousins turned off down the new road. Beveridge and George followed at a discreet distance, and when the others stopped to argue and William turned back alone they actually spoke to him. But William, who must have been in the throes of his attack, stared at them vacantly and wandered on. George was startled by this, according to Beveridge, and they continued their pursuit of Andrew, very probably with the idea of getting money out of him.

"When they reached the meadows and were about fifty yards behind him in the mist, Andrew began to behave very peculiarly, and George, guessing that something was afoot, began to go carefully, shadowing him instead of attempting to overtake him. Beveridge's explanation is not very lucid, but apparently what happened was that Andrew suddenly disappeared once he had crossed the foot-bridge. They could not see very well, naturally, and they were hurrying on to find him when he suddenly reappeared, bearing a coil of rope in one hand and something they could not see in the other. They had only just time to take refuge behind a large clump of osiers, practically on the riverbank, and Beveridge swears that neither he nor George had any idea of what was happening until Andrew's bowler hat came skimming through the mist, landing almost at their feet.

"The next thing they made out was Andrew's shadowy figure standing on the bridge parapet over the stream. He was stooping down. Beveridge says he thought he was tying up his shoes, although he knows now that he was tying his feet together. He then took a gun from his side pocket and, according to Beveridge's story, before they fully realised that they were seeing a fellow-man committing suicide, there was an explosion, and he pitched forward into the stream, throwing up a shower of water which actually splashed them."

Mrs. Faraday, who had been listening to this recital with her eyes downcast, now looked up.

"But I understood that Andrew's hands were bound," she said.

Campion nodded. "That's where he was so clever. They were bound. That is to say, there was a piece of rope tied round each wrist. If only the body had been found sooner we might have wondered at the fact that they were still not tied together, but after being so long in the water it seemed only natural to suppose just what Andrew wanted us to suppose—that the cord had broken some considerable time after death."

"Very ingenious," said the old lady. "And typical of a

certain kind of insanity. I think Andrew was an ingenious man without being clever. All though his life he ruined his chances by mistaking this gift of ingenuity for intelligence. He lost his money in a scheme which looked ingenious, and yet would never have deceived a really intelligent investor." She nodded to herself. "He was always an odd, bitter creature," she said, "and the older he grew the more of a misogynist he became. Finally, he was attracted by the more specious of the modern psychologists, whose explanations appealed to him. About a year ago I disinherited him for an offence which was quite unforgivable, and I fear that this may have driven him to think of suicide, for now I come to consider it he had certainly very little to live for. His violent anti-social mania, coupled with this diabolical ingenuity, probably drove him to consider these appalling crimes which he had not the courage to commit if he remained alive."

"But," said Campion, unable to restrain the question which had worried him from the beginning, "where is the satisfaction in a crime like this? He left these traps, we know, but if he were dead, what fun could he get out of their success?"

Mrs. Faraday pursed up her lips. "It is an illustration," she said, "of a certain type of mentality which you, as a healthy-minded being, may find it difficult to grasp. However, you must take it from me; Andrew had one extraordinary defect. He was so mentally short-sighted that he was not capable of foreseeing the most ordinary consequences of his actions other than the immediate effect at which he was aiming. I think his insanity lay largely in the possession of this peculiar blind spot."

"But he planned these murders so cleverly," protested Mr. Campion.

"Yes," said Mrs. Faraday. "But if you come to consider his plan as a whole, it was extraordinarily ragged and inconclusive. He set out to devise a colossal scheme that would bring death and disaster to this whole household, and to a certain extent he was successful. Yet consider it coldly, as I am afraid I do. His own death was designed to throw suspicion on William, Julia's death upon Kitty. How ridiculous! Why should William and Kitty decide upon independent murders within a few days of one another? Each of these diabolical ingenuities of Andrew's might have succeeded alone, but taken together they weaken each other. Then this elementary death-trap for William in the bookcase. Andrew does not seem to have made up his mind whether he wished William hanged or poisoned. His whole mind was taken up with the ingenuities of his crime; that is why he was only successful in the primary stages which are unfortunately ineradicable. Moreover," she continued, speaking slowly and gently as though Campion were a child, "and this, I think, is a very significant point, while Andrew was planning his crime he had the sensation of knowing that the house and everyone in it was in his power. Once the crimes were committed he would be in danger of being hoist with his own petard."

She paused and regarded him shrewdly.

"Yes, I understand," he said. "And yet, how nearly the whole thing failed at the beginning. His most important ingenuity miscarried, you see, the ingenuity of the gun."

"Of course," said Mrs. Faraday, "I interrupted in the middle of your story. You were telling me that Andrew's body had just fallen into the water."

"Yes," said Mr. Campion, jerking his mind back with an effort to the more concrete facts of the history, a feat which presented no difficulty to the remarkable old lady sitting propped up among the pillows. "Beveridge says that he and George rushed forward on to the bridge. They peered over the parapet and just made out Andrew's body slipping slowly down the river. They were debating what they should do, thinking that it was just an ordinary case of suicide, when George noticed something caught under the parapet on the opposite side of the narrow bridge. He picked it up and found to his astonishment that it was a heavy Service revolver, through the stock-ring of which a piece of fine cord had been knotted. He pulled in about twelve feet of this cord from the river and discovered tied on the other end of a long cylindrical weight from a grandfather clock."

"The opposite side of the bridge?" enquired Great-aunt Caroline.

"Yes," said Campion. "Directly across the footway from the parapet on which Andrew had stood. He had hung the weight over the bridge, you see, so that after he had fired and the muscles of his hand had relaxed the gun would be jerked out of his hand and across the bridge into the river on the other side, thus preventing any chance of the gun being found with the body and giving the show away."

"And yet the revolver caught," observed the old lady. "How?"

"Beveridge says the cord became imprisoned between two stones," Campion explained. "George seems to have taken in the situation at a glance. Beveridge says he thought there were money-making possibilities in the knowledge of such a secret. Of course, he dared not risk carrying the gun away, but if it remained where it was Andrew's death would be no secret. George was a little drunk at the time, and recklessness seems to have been his strong point. He picked up the gun and the weight and, winding the cord round them, like a child's skipping rope, remarked—so Beveridge says—'Always make it more difficult!' Then he whirled the bundle round his head and pitched it as far as he could up into the trees on the other side of the river. The missile was naturally extremely heavy, so that it did not go very far, but the cord became unwound in mid-air and the whole thing caught in the branches of an elm, about half a dozen yards from the bank. The weight, being the heavier, pulled the gun up into a crotched branch where it stuck, as black as the wood itself, while the weight hung down on the cord in the thick ivy which covers the trunk. Your chauffeur, Beveridge and I found it at five o'clock this morning when we went down to look for it. No wonder the police didn't spot it. It took us about half an hour when we knew where it was."

"Very clever," said Great-aunt Caroline. "Of Andrew, I mean. That clock weight fell down in the middle of dinner on the Saturday before he disappeared. He must have taken it immediately. I remember he went out late that night." She was silent for some moments, staring in front of her, her eyes narrowed, her hands folded peacefully on the coverlet. "I suppose you wonder why I kept Andrew in the house after disinheriting him?" she remarked suddenly. "But I think I was justified. I had one distressing relative who was liable to blackmail me for small sums at any moment in George. I did not wish to create another in Andrew. Although he had no hold of any kind over me, you understand," she remarked. "I wished to be spared the possibility of unpleasant scenes. Besides," she added, fixing Campion sternly, "you may have noticed that I have a certain amount of authority over everyone under my roof. I was wrong about Andrew. I should have realised he was mad."

She stirred restlessly among her embroidered pillows.

"Tell me," she murmured pathetically, "is it really necessary for me to leave this house while the place is ransacked by inquisitive policemen? Poor Hugh Featherstone will do me the honour of inviting me to his home, I know that, but I am old and do not want to leave my beautiful bedroom, which gives me a sense of well-being every time I look at it."

Campion glanced round the magnificent period apartment. It was a wonderful room.

"I am sorry," he said regretfully. "But a thorough search must be made. You never know in a case like this; consider the unfortunate George. That was a sheer accident."

"Yes," said Great-aunt Caroline, suddenly grave, "he was poisoned with cyanide, wasn't he? That must have been just wanton wickedness on Andrew's part."

"That was ingenious too," said Mr. Campion. "We were amazed at first, because, you know, cyanide has such a very distinctive smell. In the ordinary way you would think no man in his senses would get as far as putting it into his mouth by mistake. Cyanide, or prussic acid, is one of the most deadly poisons. People have died from the fumes of it, I believe. Fortunately, however, in George's case, the explanation was quite obvious. There was a pipe rack on Andrew's dressing-table. I noticed it myself when Joyce and I were examining the room. It contained five extremely filthy blackened pipes and one very good new one, a temptation to any man. I don't know if you have noticed," he added, "the way a man picks up a pipe and sucks it vigorously to make sure the stem is clear? It's a sort of involuntary movement."

"I have," said Great-aunt Faraday. "A very disgusting habit. I dislike tobacco in any form and in a pipe particularly."

"Well," said Mr. Campion apologetically, "a pipe is practically the only thing a man puts straight into his mouth. This new pipe in Andrew's rack had a vulcanite mouthpiece which unscrewed. The wooden part of the stem of the pipe was practically filled with finely powdered cyanide. The Inspector thinks there was probably some piece of easily removable fluff or wool sticking out of the actual mouthpiece, which a man would naturally flick out with his fingers. The obstruction was sufficient to keep the smell of the cyanide in the pipe. A few charred fragments of tobacco in the bowl served the same purpose. After removing the wool, or whatever it was, and knocking out the ash, the natural impulse would be to put the pipe in the mouth and suck vigorously. George must have fallen straight into the trap. I don't know who Andrew intended it for, but I fancy he thought of the idea—another ingenuity—and could not resist trying it. He does not seem to have liked anyone, although it is certainly to his credit that, as far as we know, he made no attempt upon you or Joyce."

"How could he hurt us more than by leaving us with this chaos?" Great-aunt Caroline said acidly. "Andrew was not clever, but he had intuitions. If Marcus had been of my generation—delightful boy though he is—he might have thought twice about marrying a girl who had been involved in such a public scandal, however innocently. But times are changing rapidly. I don't think Andrew realised that."

She was silent for some moments, and Mr. Campion began to wonder if his audience was at an end, but presently he became aware that she was looking at him speculatively.

"Mr. Campion," she said, "——I have grown used to that name, I quite like it——I have said that George blackmailed me. I think enough of you not to want you to believe that I have anything in my family of which I am ashamed. I shall tell you about George."

There was something in her tone which told Mr. Campion that he was being greatly honoured.

"George," said Great-aunt Caroline, "was the son of my husband's brother Joseph." The little black eyes grew hard. "A despicable character, and a disgrace to his family. This person was shipped off to the colonies many years ago. He returned with a certain amount of money and a wife. They lived in Newmarket, quite near us, you see. She was a peculiar-looking woman and of a very definite type, which we in those days chose to ignore. They had a child, a girl, and when that child was born the rumours that had been rife about the mother, were proved beyond a doubt. By some horrible machination of heredity the stain in the woman's blood had come out." She lowered her voice. "The child was a blackamoor."

Mr. Campion had a vision of the painful stir in a Society of sixty years before.

Great-aunt Caroline stiffened. "They left, of course, and the disgraceful business was hushed up. But to my own and to my husband's horror, although the first child died, these criminal people had a second. That child was George. You may consider," she went on after a pause, "that I am foolish in remembering, in feeling it so strongly, but George bears our name and he is always threatening to reveal his half-caste blood, of which he is not in the least ashamed. I admit there is no stain in our side of the family, but people are malicious and notoriously careless in working out relationships, and—a touch of the tarbrush! It is unthinkable."

As she sat up stiffly, her high lace bonnet adding to her dignity, Mr. Campion understood what it was that she considered worse than murder. He said nothing. He felt very honoured by her confidence.

Presently she went on. "That is why I am afraid poor Joyce may have given a strange impression by her attitude towards George. You see, she knows this story. Considering her to be by far the most intelligent person of my household, I explained the matter to her in case, in event of my death, the story should come as a shock to her. There, young man, you have the whole explanation."

Campion hesitated. There was still one point which was bothering him.

"Mrs. Faraday," he said, "you told me a week ago that you were sure that William was innocent. But you couldn't have known about Mrs. Finch at the time. Forgive me, but how were you sure?"

He feared for one terrible moment that she might be offended, but she looked up at him, a half-humorous smile playing about her mouth.

"Since you have done so much deduction yourself, young man," she said, "my reasoning should appeal to you, simple as it is. You may have noticed hanging in the hall downstairs an old panama hat with a turned-up brim. That hat belonged to Andrew. Since you know William, it will not strike you as absurd that this hat was a bone of contention between him and Andrew. Little things may please little minds; they also annoy them. I have known Andrew sulk for a whole day because he had seen William pottering in the garden in that old hat, and William insisted upon wearing it whenever he could get hold of it simply because he liked to be contrary. Andrew did not like the panama worn in the garden, so William always put it on to go out there. Now, when Andrew disappeared, and during the ten days in which he was still missing, William wore this hat in the garden every day. I could see him from my window pottering among the flowerbeds, where he does a great deal of damage, they tell me. But after Andrew's body was discovered, although I have seen William several times in the garden, he has never worn the old panama, but has appeared in his own grey trilby, a thing I have never seen him wear in the garden before in my life. I understood the repugnance he felt for the panama. There is a primitive strain in us all, which makes us a little afraid of the clothes of the dead. So you see, I knew that Andrew's death had come as a surprise to William."

Campion looked at her admiringly. "I think you're the cleverest woman I've ever met," he said.

The old lady gave him her hand. "You are a very good boy," she said. "I don't want you to desert me for a little while yet. I shall be very much out of my element in Hugh Featherstone's great barn of a house. You never knew his wife, did you? Such an unyielding, academic soul. I always felt her beds might be hard. Then there'll be the reporters again. There'll have to be an inquest on George."

Her appeal was gracious and ineffably feminine.

"I shall stay," he said. "You can leave it all to me." She leant back among her pillows and sighed faintly. Campion, assuming that the interview was at an end, rose and made for the door. Great-aunt Caroline's fine clear voice came to him from the depths of the great pink and gold bed.

"Heredity is a very extraordinary thing," it said. "I have always thought that I was a much more intelligent person than your grandmother, dear Emily."

25

The Token

It was six o'clock in the evening, over a fortnight later, when the family had been reinstated in a thoroughly over-hauled Socrates Close, when Mr. Campion approached his Bentley to set out once again for London. He was giving the Inspector a lift, and had arranged to go down to the town to fetch him. Stanislaus Oates had revisited Cambridge for a couple of days at the finish of the affair.

Campion was alone. His adieux had been made. Great-aunt Caroline had given him his last audience. Ann had been visited, and he had received a benison from Joyce and Marcus. Young Christmas had brought the Bentley round to the front door, treating the old car with awe, as well he might, since it was a good six years younger than the Faraday Daimler.

Campion was just about to enter his chariot when a bright pink face, surmounted by a short fringe of stubbly white hair, peered out of the darkness of the porch and Uncle William trotted down the steps towards him.

"My boy, my boy!" he said. "I thought I'd missed you. Just wanted to have a word with you, you know. I'd like to tell you how grateful I am, for one thing. We Faradays aren't very grateful as a rule, but I am. You got us out of a devil of a mess and I don't mind admitting it. I can't say more than that."

"Not at all," said Mr. Campion, rather embarrassed by this entirely unexpected tribute.

Uncle William shook his head. "You can't fool me," he said. "Things looked bad at one time. Why, I might have been murdered! A fellow can't overlook a thing like that." A faint smile spread over his face. "I was right all along, as a matter of fact. I thought I'd like to remind you. D'you remember what I said to you the first time I saw you, when we were sitting in Marcus's study? What a damned uncomfortable house that is, by the way. I said, 'There's Andrew lying in the mortuary making all this fuss'—and he was. I was plumb right. Well, good-bye, my boy. I'm grateful. Any time you want a quiet weekend, don't forget us."

Mr. Campion checked a wild impulse to laugh with commendable fortitude.

"Thank you," he said gravely. "Good-bye, sir."

Uncle William shook hands vigorously. "No need to 'sir' me, my boy. You called me 'Uncle William' once and I liked it. Glad to have you in the family." He hesitated. There was plainly something on his mind. At last it came. "I'd like to make you a little present," he said awkwardly. "It isn't much—haven't got much. But I've heard Marcus say that you've got a wonderful collection of curios. I've got a little thing here that I brought back from my travels many years ago. If you'll accept it I shall be very proud."

Campion, who had some experience of grateful clients and their gifts, was conscious of a strong feeling of apprehension, but he had formed an affection for Uncle William and adopted therefore a suitable expression of modest eagerness. Uncle William was watching him anxiously.

"Got it just in here," he said. "Come and have a look."

His excitement was pathetic, and Campion climbed out of the car, devoutly hoping that the Inspector would grant him a few minutes' grace. He followed Uncle William up the steps to the porch.

There, on the wooden seat, was a large glass case, and in it, reposing on an uncomfortable bed of conchs and dried seaweed, was one of the familiar "mermaid skeletons" which unscrupulous fishermen compose from monkeys, skulls and torsos and the bones of tropical fish. This ancient fraud was now indicated by Uncle William with pride.

"Bought it off a fellow in Port Said," he said. "Struck me as being remarkable then. Does still. Will you take it? I've had it for thirty years. Haven't got anything else of interest."

Mr. Campion seemed overcome. "It's awfully good of you," he began nervously.

"Then you take it, my boy." Uncle William's delight was childlike. "I put all my things out on my bed," he went on confidentially. "Looked at 'em. Chose that. Couldn't give you anything I'd like better myself."

Mr. Campion accepted the gift in the spirit in which it was made, and together he and Uncle William hoisted the unwieldy trophy into the back of the Bentley. They then shook hands again.

Mr. Campion had just started the engine when Uncle William recollected his other mission.

"Here, wait a minute," he said. "I nearly forgot. Mother told me to give you this. You're not to open it until you get home. I think she thinks you're a child. Still, we must humour the old lady. Here you are."

He slipped a packet into the young man's hand and stepped back from the car.

"I shall see you when you come down for the young people's wedding," he shouted. "That'll be coming along in the summer. Hope to be able to read you the first chapters of my memoirs by then. I'm writing 'em, you know. That newspaper fellow put the idea into my head, only he wanted me to write 'em for his newspaper—right in the middle of all this business. I didn't thank the fellow for his impertinence at the time, but afterwards it occurred to me that a decently-bound book would bring credit to us all. It'll give me something to do. Shan't have many people to talk to while Kitty's in that nursing home. Still, perhaps it's as well. I've got to look after myself. I'm still under the doctor, you know." His little blue eyes flickered. "I shall stick to my nightcap whatever he says. Good-bye, my boy. If there's ever anything I can do for you let me know."

"Good-bye," said Mr. Campion. He let in the clutch and drove slowly out of the gates of the quiet old house, lying peaceful and innocent in the evening light. Uncle William stood on the steps and waved his handkerchief.

Stanislaus Oates was inclined to be truculent at the delay, but the sight of the "mermaid" restored his good humour to such an extent that Mr. Campion felt it had justified itself already.

"What's the penalty for speeding with a Chief Detective-Inspector in the front seat?" he enquired as they struck the open road to Bishop's Stortford and the City.

"Death," said the Inspector solemnly. "Same as with any other passenger. Take it easy. I want to lean back and feel at peace with the world once more."

"I don't know what you've got to grumble about," said Campion. "You've come out of this very well. My godson will be able to read all about his father in the enthusiastic Press. The Press had a good innings, by the way. I say, did it ever occur to you, Stanislaus, that your coincidence hunch was quite justified? If you and I hadn't both chosen Tomb Yard for a rendezvous on that particular Thursday you would have had a conversation with Cousin George. He would have tried to sell you the first rights in his little mystery story. You would have got it all out of him without paying, and the riddle of Andrew's death would have been solved on the day that his body was found."

Stanislaus considered this remark gravely. "Very likely," he admitted at last. "Of course, you can't put too much faith in that old blackguard Beveridge's story, although it went down so well at the inquest. That fellow George had a nerve, if a half of what Beveridge says is true. Fancy hiding the gun and then singling me out—probably because I'd just got promotion—to come and tell his rotten story to. He thought we might strike a deal, I suppose. I got the kudos, he got the cash."

"Ingenuity seems to run in the family," remarked Mr. Campion. "Beveridge is an interesting character, too. I think, perhaps his intense admiration for George was the most extraordinary thing about him."

"Oh, I don't know," said the Inspector. "That flashy type does appeal to a simple imagination. What does strike me as extraordinary is that the old devil should have had the nerve to pinch the dead man's hat. I know he tore out the lining—I know he battered it. But fancy seeing a man commit suicide, watching your friend destroy the evidence to make it look as much like murder as possible, and then rolling jauntily off in the corpse's bowler, only pausing to bury your old hat under a heap of leaves a few hundred yards down the path!"

"I can understand Beveridge doing it," said Campion, "but not George standing for it. I suppose he was pretty well oiled."

"Must have been," grumbled the Inspector, "to chuck that gun where he did. I thought old Bowditch would have a fit when he heard where it was all the time. That stopped him laughing," he added viciously. "By the way, you were quite right about that footprint. I owe you five shillings. And that makes me about four and ninepence out of pocket, I don't mind telling you. Even you've come off better. You've got a mermaid."

"Modest though I am, I should like to point out that I was right about the 'B' too," said Mr. Campion. "Extraordinary what a long time it took the jury to see that," he continued. "Even when Beveridge explained it himself. Oh, and by the way, Stanislaus, to reopen an old and a sore subject, why didn't you follow up Uncle William's alibi at the very beginning? When I hinted it so plainly?"

"Because I was dead sure it didn't exist," said Stanislaus after a pause. "This is a very exceptional case. You wouldn't have come out of it so well if it wasn't. I didn't follow up William's alibi because I was more than certain he hadn't got one."

"You thought he'd done it?" said Mr. Campion in astonishment.

"I *knew* he'd done it," said the Inspector. "If this had been an ordinary case he would have done it. You don't have clever lunatics providing false evidence, or half-false evidence, which is worse, in every case you come across, or where would you be? You might as well go bughouse yourself and leave it at that. I'm sorry I was wild with you at the time, Campion, but when you came out with that pub keeper I felt I was getting past my job. Of course, you know," he went on eagerly, "even at the finish I didn't quite believe it, although that last cyanide murder was pretty convincing. It had got the right mixture of cleverness and lunacy—an elaborate, ingenious scheme to kill any old person who happened to be about. But, of course, afterwards, when we went into it and followed up Seeley's movements, found he'd been a medical student, discovered the retort and a couple of saucepans in the potting shed, and finally got the chemist who sold him the cyanide, it was different."

"He distilled the conium himself, I suppose?" said Campion. "Simply boiled a lot of hemlock down? We shall never be able to prove that. Still, I don't suppose was difficult."

"It wasn't," said the Inspector. "You heard old Hastings at the inquest. He said it wasn't. It probably gave Andrew something to do. Must be a terrible life idling about in a house like that."

Mr. Campion nodded. "Typical of him to pick on conium," he observed. "State poison of Athens. They killed Socrates with it, didn't they?"

"I don't know about Socrates," said the Inspector. "It made a mess of Socrates Close. It was so simple; that's what scared me. So was the cyanide. Anyone can get hold of cyanide in England by talking about wasps' nest and signing their name in a book. No, the only thing Seeley seems to have made a hash of in the poison line was the stuff on the knife. Hastings told me he thought it was some sort of a snake poison, probably scraped off one of those poison arrows people bring back with them from the Gold Coast. He couldn't locate it. It was very slight. But he said there was something there."

"What a blessing he didn't put an extra dose of his home-distilled conium in the brandy flask and leave it at that," said Mr. Campion, appalled at the sudden thought.

"Not ingenious enough," said the Inspector. "These little extra stunts of his were all after-thoughts—little clever ideas he didn't want to waste. I say, look out, Campion. No blinding! It's a beautiful evening. Let's take our time."

The young man slowed down obligingly. "One more point and my mind will be at rest," he said. "Surely Uncle Andrew didn't go to church with a coil of rope, a revolver and a clock weight concealed upon him? Where did he hide them until he was ready for them? I understand how he got rid of his cousin. Uncle William is the kind of man who could be relied upon to jib at walking a couple of miles out of his way, and I should think

Andrew was a past master at picking a quarrel with him. But where exactly did he put his paraphernalia?"

"In the shed by the river," said the Inspector. "I haven't dwelt on this point much, because I felt we ought to have noticed something, even if the scent was ten days' old. But I tell you in confidence we took a brick out of the river, and not one that belonged to the bridge, and I think that brick was the original weight intended for the revolver. But then the clock weight fell down in the middle of dinner and called attention to itself, so to speak. Obviously it occurred to him as being an improvement on the brick. Oh, well, it's all cleared up now, but it's been a harassing month. I'm on quite a nice little job in Stepney at the moment. Clean case of coining. Seems like a breath of fresh air."

Mr. Campion did not answer, and presently, as they approached the outskirts of the City, the Inspector spoke again.

"You never would have thought it, would you?" he remarked. "They seemed such nice people."

But Mr. Campion was lost in his own thoughts.

It was not until he was back in his own flat in Bottle Street, with Lugg hovering round him like an excited hen with a lost chick, that he remembered the package which Uncle William had thrust into his hand as he left Socrates Close. He took it out of his pocket now and began to unwrap it slowly. Lugg watched with interest.

"Another souvenir?" he said dubiously. "You'll have a job to beat that lot in the hall. You ought to have took me with you."

"That's where you're wrong," said his master feelingly. "Be quiet a minute."

"Touchy, ain't yer?" the big man protested.

Campion ignored him. He had removed the wrappings and there now lay revealed a small wooden box of Tunbridge Wells ware. He picked it up admiringly and lifted the lid. As he caught sight of the contents an exclamation escaped him, and Lugg, who was peering under his arm, was silent with respectful astonishment.

On a nest of quilted pink silk lay a heart-shaped miniature. It was a delicately lovely piece of work, the frame set with small rubies and brilliants.

On the ivory was a portrait of a girl.

Her sleek black hair was parted in the centre and arranged in small curls on either side of her face. Her dark eyes were grave and large, her small nose straight, her lips smiled. She was very beautiful.

It took Mr. Campion some time to realise that he held an early portrait of Mrs. Caroline Faraday.

F. J. Goodman

Margery Allingham was the eldest child in a family 'who regarded writing as the only reasonable way of passing the time, let alone earning a living'.

She wasted no time in carrying on the family tradition and produced her first novel at the age of seventeen. Ever since then, for more years than she considers it delicate to remind her, she has been producing suspense novels of a quality which have earned her an international following.

In America she was recently voted one of 'the world's ten best mystery writers' and her latest books are her greatest successes.

Miss Allingham, who is married to P. Youngman Carter, divides her time between a home in Essex and a flat in Bloomsbury, once the studio of the Victorian illustrator and novelist George du Maurier.

Special Offer
Buy a Bantam Book
for only 50¢.

Now you can have Bantam's catalog filled with hundreds of titles plus take advantage of our unique and exciting bonus book offer. A special offer which gives you the opportunity to purchase a Bantam book for only 50¢. Here's how!

By ordering any five books at the regular price per order, you can also choose any other single book listed (up to a $5.95 value) for just 50¢. Some restrictions do apply, but for further details why not send for Bantam's catalog of titles today!

Just send us your name and address and we will send you a catalog!

BANTAM BOOKS, INC.
P.O. Box 1006, South Holland, Ill. 60473

Mr./Mrs./Ms. _____
                    (please print)

Address _____

City _____ State _____ Zip _____

FC(A)-11/89

Please allow four to six weeks for delivery.